JENA'S SON

JERI HAWKINS

Jena's Son by Jeri Hawkins
RockHawk Publishing, LLC

This is a work of fiction.

Cover by Haider A.
Editor: Sarah Kortright

ISBN: 979-8-218-78817-9

Dedicated to

My amazing husband and my wonderful kids and grandkids who are most definitely something to be proud of.

Special Thanks

Coach Nathaniel Goolsby who provided invaluable information on the South, barbershops, baseball, and life.

Many thanks & lots of love

PROLOGUE

She tucked her long brown hair behind her ear and rubbed her swollen belly as it tightened and squeezed. She took a deep breath in through her nose and exhaled through her mouth. It didn't hurt but it forced her to be still. The tightening eased, her body relaxed, and she felt the baby give a kick. With her finger she traced the spot on her belly where the little foot protruded. "Soon," she said smiling, "I'll see you soon." She leaned back into the pile of pillows stacked on her bed and wondered if it would be a boy or a girl. What color hair and eyes would the baby have? She prayed for a healthy baby and an easy delivery. A long labor scared her because she wasn't sure how she'd be able to do it. In her own mind she'd always been weak and timid. Other people made decisions for her and mostly she was okay with that. She didn't fuss or argue about the direction her life would take. There were no big plans or lofty goals, she figured God would ordain her steps and for all the rest she'd do like her Daddy taught her and play the hand she was dealt.

Submitting to others wasn't hard for her. In fact, she preferred it. She did as she was told without complaint. She knew that in the sight of others she was viewed in much the same way she saw herself: quiet, dainty, fragile, timid, and often scared. The thought of child birth was terrifying.

Her smile deepened while she watched her belly move with the little life inside. The baby was active. The pair played together. A little foot would poke up and mama would push back on her belly. "I love you little one. I'm going to do my best to take care of you." She started to sing as they played. "Twinkle, twinkle, little star, how I wonder what you are…"

PART ONE

CHAPTER 1

Olympia, Mississippi
1955

The aged whitewashed screen door bounced against the frame as Steven banged loud enough for the whole neighborhood to hear. He'd been seeking the barber, Ezekiel, for months with no success. The famed barbershop over on State Street closed years before, now a mere shadow of itself stood just a few blocks away. It didn't take a reporter to notice Ezekiel's front porch was in need of repair. Rusted nails stood upright above the sagging wood planks. The four-side red brick was faded with years of weather, the paint on the awnings and trim peeled back in white ribbons. Flower beds scarcely defined the landscaping, with more weeds than flowers and only patches of wispy grass grew around the yard. The windows revealed nothing through their dusty panes as they stared lifelessly at the lopsided old Ford in the driveway, sitting on its rim.

A raspy voice called out, "Come on in. Take a seat." Steven guessed it was Ezekiel and let himself in. Before sitting on the dusty lime-green sofa, he dug for his camera in the satchel slung across his shoulder. "Document, document, document," he said to himself under his breath, snapping a picture of the wall that was covered in photos. He could hear someone in the kitchen but his mind was in research mode, he had to document as much as he could. The room was hot and sweat trickled down his back. The Mississippi humidity had to be eighty percent. He brushed his stringy blond hair out of his face and snapped another picture. He glanced around the small living room in awe. Every ounce of wall space was covered with images of baseball legends, most from the Negro leagues like Satchel Paige, Cool Papa Bell, and Smoky Joe, but there were others there as well, like Lou Gehrig, DiMaggio, and Jimmie Foxx. He recognized ball fields in Cuba where Americans, black and white, played ball with Cubans as island breezes bent the tall palms. Most of the photos were of baseball greats, but hanging in a place of honor was a picture of the Brown Bomber, Joe Louis, one of the greatest boxers of all time standing in what he assumed was an early version of Ezekiel's barbershop. Gooseflesh rippled across his arm and his hair stood on end as he gazed into history, observing legends.

With camera in hand, Steven wiped his brow and moved closer to the wall to get a better view of the memorabilia. He stood before black and white photographs never seen in magazines or newspapers, faces of greats unaltered by the intrusion of professional photographers. Raw, sometimes blurred or grainy, images of greatness. Nearly half of the shots were in the barbershop: wide-mouthed shots of men laughing or an occasional photo filled with men wearing serious looks, broad-shouldered suits, and full of strong conversation. Other photos were on the ball field, during games, at practice, and playing around. Mouth agape, he couldn't help but notice the individual he came to research wasn't anywhere on the wall. No autographed photo, bat, nor ball held his name.

Steven heard the soft click of dress shoes on hardwood. Ezekiel came from the kitchen with two glasses of ice and two colas that he set down on the coffee table and motioned for Steven to sit. Obediently, he went to the lime-green sofa and plunked himself down, feeling like a star-struck child. Despite his age, Ezekiel's weathered brown face held few wrinkles, but etched in it, carved over ninety years, were the smiles, joys, tears, and heartaches of a man who held a thousand stories. Ezekiel was agile, and he looked good for his age. His hands showed the most wear: his knuckles were wide and his hands gnarled, his fingers arched to the side instead of laying straight. His arms however looked tone and defined as if he still worked out. Word was, Ezekiel was hard-nosed and unfriendly but Steven was ready to weather the storm to get the story. And there was only one story he cared about.

"So what is it you want?" Ezekiel asked, rubbing his bald head from back to front.

Steven stuttered with his answer. He knew Ezekiel had never granted an interview before and he was unsure why he'd said yes now. He didn't want to mess up this opportunity.

"Well boy, cat got your tongue?" Ezekiel snapped.

Steven shook his head, his blond hair wisping back and forth, and replied, "No, sir."

"Then have a drink of that cola right there and maybe it'll loosen you up a bit."

Steven reached for the glass and drizzled his drink over the ice while glancing at Ezekiel every few seconds. Ezekiel's dark skin and large glaring eyes were intimidating, his furrowed brow certainly caused Steven to reconsider. Once he had poured the entire bottle of cola and taken a sip he seemed to find the courage to speak. "Mr. Johnson, I've come to interview you about a baseball player."

Ezekiel stared and waited. He watched the young man take nervous sips of his drink before Steven added, "Randall Wilson. That's who I want to ask you questions about."

Ezekiel leaned back in his seat, folded his hands and peered at the boy, letting him fidget. "What do you know about Randall Wilson?"

The young boy's tongue seemed to loosen even more and he started to ramble. "Not as much as I'd like to. He was my favorite player as a kid.

He played right field, but I've seen him play first base, short stop, and catcher. He had a .463 batting average, could steal bases like nobody's business, and he wasn't even in his prime. He woulda been the second negro to follow Jackie, and I'd say he was ten times better than Jackie. He'da been the first mulatto to be offered a position in the majors." Steven abruptly stopped talking and sat like a stone wondering if the look on Ezekiel's face was a scowl or contemplation.

"Sounds like you already know all there is," Ezekiel said.

Steven glanced around hoping for more. "Well, there isn't much out there. I want to know everything. I'm writing a book."

"Well, you're mixed up on your facts. Randall wasn't better than Jackie who went to college, served his country, fought in a war, and played other sports. Baseball wasn't even his best. No comparison."

The finality of Ezekiel's statement felt like a punch in the gut. Steven stuttered, looking for the right words. "Well, sir, I only meant that Randall was better at baseball. I mean, he was faster than Cool Papa Bell."

Ezekiel's tone rose slightly. "Wrong again, young man. Are you sure you're a reporter? You done any research? What kind of book is this gonna be? Fiction?" Ezekiel scowled, rocked his drink back and forth clinking his ice against the glass and let Steven squirm.

"Well, I...uh..." Steven said.

"Well, what? I know it's a fact. Cool Papa Bell could round those bases on a muddy infield in thirteen seconds, twelve on a clear day. What's Randall ever been clocked at? Fifteen? Fourteen, maybe?"

Steven sat with his hands on his knees, his mouth wide open, unsure of what to say next.

Sipping his cola, Ezekiel leaned back in his chair remembering things he thought he'd long forgotten. Things he'd tucked away deep down in his heart the day he'd closed the door, turned the key.

Steven managed to find his courage and a few words to make his point. "Sir, I don't mean to be rude, but when I was a kid my dad did a lot of business in Cuba. I saw Randall both years he was there. My dad was busy and I spent almost all my time at the ball field. I saw every game in person and I know without a stopwatch that Randall was faster and better than all the players by far, and he was the youngest. I kept a notebook of all his stats and lots of famous white ball players used to come down there, too. They'd play against each other all the time. I know Randall is the best."

A smile broke out on Ezekiel's face. So the white boy did know a little something. He was right: Randall was fast. Cool Papa would come into town and visit some family he had in the area. He always came into the barbershop for a fresh cut and would go to the ball field for some fun. Ezekiel'd known Cool Papa since he was a young fella. He also knew that Cool Papa and Randall raced one another many times. Ezekiel remembered the day Randall got the best of ole' Papa. On a sunny afternoon in July - Randall could have only been about sixteen - on a straight away, Randall inched Papa out. Everyone had good fun with it and Randall gained some bragging rights, but he'd never been clocked faster than Cool Papa 'round the bags.

Ezekiel closed his eyes. The memories could almost conjure up the waxy aroma of shoe polish, the sounds of chatter in the barber shop, and the sweet smell of fresh-cut grass before a game. He could hear the crack of the bat and the hush of the crowd. And quick as lightnin' he could see Randall on an infield double, rounding the bases, his eyes set on home.

Ezekiel leaned back in his chair and sipped on his soda pop. Steven noticed the nostalgic look resting on Ezekiel's face. There were several seconds before he spoke in almost a whisper. "I remember the first time I saw him..."

CHAPTER 2

Olympia, Mississippi
April 20, 1934

Five empty chairs faced mirrors that spanned the length of the wall, combs sat in jars and clippers rested silently on the countertop. Ezekiel left the front door unlocked and headed to the back to grab towels. The sun peeked over the horizon while the nip of cold hung in the air. He was sweeping the front sidewalk when he saw her coming. Her milky white hand towed the small golden-colored boy next to her. The sight of them surprised him. He felt like he knew them. He'd heard about them for years, lent a hand when it was needed, and felt a kinship toward them, but this was the first time he'd seen them in person. It seemed impossible that he had never laid eyes on them. He stepped back inside before they saw him.

Folks had stopped talking about her and she'd gradually become a tall tale, a ghostly figure around town. The white lady and her little boy were an anomaly. Everyone knew about her, but nobody really knew her.

From the back of the barbershop, he could see her. She released the boy's hand and looked down at him, her lips moving, seeming to give instruction. The boy crammed his hands in his pockets as he looked up at his mother and shrugged, accepting whatever she said. Ezekiel moved back out of view. He didn't want to scare her. Hattie said she was skittish, quiet and soft-spoken around strangers. He saw her hand push on the door and heard the bell jingle. He waited a few seconds before answering, "Be right out."

Jena stood frozen just inside the doorway, unable to move forward or flee. The door swung closed behind her. To his knowledge, this was her first time in a business on the Negro side of town. He knew she traded with the Bait Man because people had seen her leaving him vegetables and him giving her fish and crawdads. He knew she got wood from Drew, but that was usually once a year. The Goolsbys delivered milk and cheese to people around town and he'd heard that she received a delivery once a week. He also heard that she didn't come out and speak when the Goolsby's delivered so nobody actually saw her up close, just at a distance walking with her boy.

The odd pair were seen by townsfolk down at the creek fishing and gathering wild mushrooms and berries, but aside from the meager contact she and her boy had with people, they stayed almost entirely to themselves. He wondered when the last time she saw her family was. He thought about his own son and how the years had passed on by without having seen or heard from him.

"Good mornin'," the older man cheerfully greeted them.

Standing face to face, Jena looked into the barber's eyes but was unable to speak. She bowed her head and averted her eyes to the floor. She laced her fingers together and circled her thumbs one over the other. Ezekiel assumed it was nerves. Maybe it was that she hadn't talked to any adults in a long time or it could have been that she'd never really talked to a black man before. If nothing else, he was confident she'd never been in a barbershop on the black side of town. Generally, white folks didn't come to the black side of town, nonetheless, the smile on the barber's face was welcoming. Still, all she could do was stand there, frozen, paralyzed like a deer who'd been startled.

"Hello, sir," the little boy replied, his eyes wide and bright. There was no mistaking his eager curiosity.

The barber sat the towels down on the counter and eyed a mess he'd never seen in all his years of barbering. He walked slowly toward the boy, while his mom, wide-eyed, stumbled back. As if palming a basketball the barber grabbed the boy's head turning it this way and that. After close examination Ezekiel asked, "Boy, what happened to you?"

The boy shrugged. "I dunno."

"Well…are ya here to get a haircut?"

With his hands still in his pockets he looked up at his mother, she was still clearly within terror's grip, and she said nothing. The little boy looked back to the barber, "Yes, sir."

"Well son, come here, lemme see what we can do. Have a seat right here." He pointed to the chair closest to the back of the shop. The boy obediently went and plopped himself down in the big leather chair. Ezekiel pumped the chair higher and grabbed a comb, even though it wouldn't do any good.

Watching from the mirror, Ezekiel tried to decide if he recognized any features in the little brown face. His hair was mostly dark brown with a few strands of blond in it. He had his mama's almond-shaped eyes with long lashes girls wished for and hazel eyes folks got dreamy about. His skin was golden brown and even with the tangled tumbleweed mess upon his head he was still handsome. A good-lookin' kid, a little skinny, but no worse for the wear. Ezekiel wiped away all the questions swirling in his mind. What did it matter? What would it change?

"So son, what's your name?"

"Randall."

"That's a pretty good name."

"Thanks."

"I'm Mr. Johnson, but you can call me Ezekiel or just Zeke."

The boy nodded. Ezekiel tried to run his fingers through the tangled curls. The ringlets were dry and stuck out every which way, growing wildly like brambles alongside an old country highway. Lint was not only embedded deep, but hung off the ends of hair like ornaments on a scraggly Christmas tree. The little afro was flat on one side from where the boy slept on it.

Ezekiel ran his hands over the tangled mess one last time, looked up into the mirror, and caught sight of the boy's mother, pale and trembling like a jackrabbit. Ezekiel asked, "How about we give you something to be proud of?"

The boy's head bobbed up and down enthusiastically while a barely audible "yes" escaped his mother's constricted vocal cords.

"Now ma'am, you just take a seat right over there." Ezekiel pointed with the comb. "…and we'll be done right here in a jiffy."

Obediently she moved to the row of benches that sat along the back wall. Ezekiel steadied the boy's head, still debating where to start. He popped a clean white towel and draped it around the boy's neck, fastening a black cape over that. He walked over and turned the radio on to some orchestra music, went back, and began cutting large chunks of hair, trying to clear a path for the clippers.

"You missin' a sock? I think I just found one," Ezekiel teased, dropping another clump of tangles to the floor. Randall giggled.

"So where do you go to school?"

"Don't go. Mom hasn't found one for me yet."

Ezekiel nodded in understanding. He can't go with the white folks and she don't know the black ones, Ezekiel thought as he snipped chunks of hair. A bulk of the tangles now lay in clumps on the floor. Ezekiel reached for the clippers and clicked them on. A quick jolt of the blades sent them humming.

"Randall, you ever have your hair cut before?"

"No, sir."

"If I catch a snag this might hurt."

"I'll be okay. My mom used to try and comb my hair. She pulled so hard it made me cry. But I don't cry no more." His little hand came up and patted his own head to assure Ezekiel he'd be okay.

"Alright then. Here we go."

Ezekiel's steady hand glided over the boy's patchy cut. More hair fell until one-eighth of an inch of stubble rested evenly all around. The clippers continued to hum while Ezekiel edged him up, making a neat hairline.

After Ezekiel finished cutting, with a long soft-bristled brush, he dusted the hair from the boy's face and neck. Randall reached up to touch his nearly bald head, delighting in the new sensation.

"Thanks!"

Ezekiel rubbed the boy's head affectionately. "Now you can't let that turn into a nappy mess again. You come in here every couple weeks, ya hear?"

Randall nodded agreeably. "Yes, sir!"

"Before you go, lemme show you how to use this." Ezekiel handed him a tin of hair grease. "Put your hand out."

Randall obeyed as Ezekiel stuck a finger into the thick grease. He wiped a nickle-sized wad into the boy's hand. "Now put some hot breath on there," he instructed the boy, breathing warm air into his own hand as an example. He rubbed his own hands together to warm the gooey grease making it pliable. The boy diligently copied each step.

"Now take your hands and rub them all over your head. Make sure you get the grease everywhere."

Randall rubbed furiously.

"Nice and even, you don't want a big ole glob of grease in the middle of your head."

Randall giggled while his little hands rubbed awkwardly back and forth on his freshly cut hair. "Oww – it's stabbing me."

Ezekiel chuckled while he unwrapped a new tight-bristled brush. "Take this," he said.

He took the small caramel-colored hand into his own, placed the brush in the boy's palm, and guided the brush to the top of his head.

"Here's how you do it."

He began stroking forward, brushing the stubble into small waves. Ezekiel glanced back up to the mirror. The white lady had relaxed some. At least she had loosened the death grip on her pocketbook. Ezekiel released the boy's hand and Randall kept brushing. "I've never brushed my hair before," he said with a toothless grin, admiring himself from each side in the mirror.

"Now you be sure to brush ten times each night before bed, and when you wake up in the mornin' you'll have that hair trained in no time."

"Oh yes, sir. I will. I will."

Ezekiel removed the black cape and the white towel protecting the boy's neck. As if on cue the white lady rose and timidly approached. Some coins jingled in her hand and her voice shook. "How much do we owe you, sir?"

Ezekiel glanced at the coins, then at the woman's patched, but pressed skirt. He guessed these may be her last, considering her gaunt face and rail-thin frame. Ezekiel spun the barber chair so that Randall faced him. "Well, let's see now, a young man like yourself should be able to pay for his own haircut. Lemme see your muscles."

Randall bent his arm and squeezed.

"Oh! Now those are some big muscles young man. Mighty big! I bet you could pay off your haircut and new hairbrush in a couple of weeks if you come over in the afternoon and help me out for a few hours."

Randall's entire face lit up before his mother cut in. "Sir, we don't want to trouble you."

"It's no trouble. Call me Zeke," he said, extending his hand. Cautiously she extended her own. "I'm Jena."

"Nice to meet you." He gave her a firm handshake.

He turned to Randall. "Now that you're my new assistant, I want you to come by tomorrow afternoon."

"Sir," her voice low, nearly a whisper. She wasn't sure why she was going to confide in a total stranger, "I have a job down at the meat-packing plant and I have to leave early. It's too far for him to walk alone. I don't get back until late."

Zeke put his hand up, "Just bring him by before you leave. He can stay the whole day till you come an' get him."

Jena's eyes glistened and she shook her head. "I couldn't trouble you like that."

"It's no trouble. No trouble at all. If you need a reference I think you know Hattie who works over at the hospital."

Jena nodded and kept her eyes averted to the floor. "I do know her. She mentioned you before. That's why we came. Than-k..." her voice broke.

He tried to console her and placed a hand on her shoulder. "Just remember, you've got something to be proud of."

For a moment she looked confused. He wondered if she understood, he wondered if she remembered. He was sure she did. Gingerly, he ushered her to the door. "I'll be in the back makin' breakfast. Door'll be open." Jena nodded moving quickly into the street before he could witness the dam completely break. With Randall's new brush crammed in his pocket and his little golden hand tucked within hers, she pulled him down the street as he looked back shouting and waving.

"See you tomorrow Mr. Zeke!"

"See you tomorrow little man."

Jena and Randall hustled down the street toward their tiny place near the railroad tracks, but at the fork in the road she turned left instead of right. Randall was talking and asking question after question, but Jena didn't hear him; her mind was racing, she was overwhelmed and not quite sure what to do. She wanted to scream and shout and laugh all at the same time. A little tornado swirled about inside her, picking up all the emotions she'd neatly tucked away the past five years and mixed them together into a blustery mess.

Going to the barbershop had been more powerful than she could have imagined. Something about his presence and his kindness reminded her of the safety she'd known as a child. There was a peace about him that she longed for. A spring of joy fluttered in her heart. Nostalgia gave her courage; she hadn't felt hopeful in a long time. She looked at her wristwatch and decided there was still time. Her mama always went to the store about this time. Maybe she'd catch her out and say hello. Maybe her mama could see what a handsome boy Randall had become.

Jena hadn't been in town since Randall was a baby, she tried to keep him from the stares and the comments. She didn't want her boy hearing their wicked talk. Today might be more of the same, but the hope of a chance to see her mama was growing greater than her fear of the townsfolk or her daddy. The pair walked briskly down the street past the bakery where she delighted in the smell of warm, fresh bread drifting on the air. The butcher shop was filled with ladies getting their Sunday roasts and pork chops. Jena glanced at the group of women, but knew her mama wasn't there, she would be in the grocery. Jena picked up her pace.

Just like she imagined, her mama was standing by the canned goods, her hair wrapped up in a bun. Jena watched as Mama picked up Daddy's favorite can of beans and placed them in her basket. For a second Mama turned and saw them, but not before the store manager shouted at Jena to take her nigger boy out of the store. In the comotion, Mama spun and hid her face, she turned her back to them as if she hadn't seen them. A firm hand gripped Jena's arm, yanked her around and shoved the two of them toward the door. "Go on girl! Git!" The force of his shove sent them both tumbling into the street. A horn blared and a man shouted, "Get out of the road!" A crowd gathered. Before she could grab Randall, Jena saw her mother dart from the store. The world started to spin and her heart thudded wildly in her chest as she scrambled for her crying son. The hushed tones of sinful gossip had started, she could hear them, hateful and full of venom. A foot swung from the horde and connected with Randall's side knocking him over. He gasped, desperate to suck in air. She tucked him beneath her, tears clouding her vision, as the crowd became like a murder of crows pecking at her. Someone shouted, "Your daddy should have taken care of that little bastard years ago!" Under her breath she cried out, "Please deliver us, Lord! Help us! Please!"

She was reminded of the nursery rhyme, "Sticks and stones may break your bones but words will never hurt you." What a lie, she thought. Though she tried to shut them out, their words were worming their way into deep, dark crevices of her mind and heart, to haunt her if she let them. The crowd increased in number and volume. How could she be so naive to bring Randall here? "If not for me, Lord, please spare Randall!" Jena begged.

Time stood still. She covered her boy with her body the best she could trying to protect him. Rocks stung their skin and she begged the crowd to stop. She prayed that they wouldn't die in the street. Dust began to choke them. "Mama, you're hurting me," Randall cried out, but she didn't move because she knew whatever he was enduring was better than what they'd face if she got up. It wasn't until she heard the whistle and a voice repeatedly shouting, "Break it up!" that she thought they might survive.

A police officer broke through the crowd shouting, "What's going on here?" He yanked Jena to her feet and saw the boy tucked beneath her. He remembered her. The first time he'd seen her he'd felt compassion, but now he was repulsed. "I should take you in for creating a public disturbance." He reached down and jerked Randall up by the arm, his face muddy and tear streaked.

A lady shouted at the policeman, "She has some nerve to bring that little colored boy over here as if he's one of us!" He shouted back, "Don't you worry about this here, I'm gonna take care of it!" Jena panicked, what did he mean? Just seconds before she was terrified the crowd was going to kill them, now she was horrified they would be going to jail. What would happen to Randall? "Lord, please," she begged under her breath.

"There's nothing to see here. Y'all go on about your day," the policeman shouted, but they could still be heard cursing at her as the policeman drug them to his car. He opened the back door. "Get in." Jena grabbed Randall and obeyed, sobs rattling her as she kissed his head, his own little shoulders heaving.

Jena didn't look up to see where they were headed until the town turned into tall trees and a single-lane winding road. "Where are you taking us?" she asked, a tremor edging her voice. He didn't answer. He kept driving. Eventually, Jena recognized where they were. He'd taken a long road out past the railroad tracks, looped around, and came back up in front of their shack. He stopped. "Get out." Jena nodded and started to say thanks, but he cut her off. "Don't come back to town. I won't help you next time. Your folks are good people and they don't deserve what you did to them." Jena felt her face get hot. She wanted to lash out, to pound her fists, to scream but the fury was trapped within her. What did he mean? What she did to her family? What about what they did to her! Like buckshot tearing up flesh, old wounds were ripped open and fresh ones made, while the emotional bloodshed drained her. She felt faint. "Help me, Lord. Please help me," she whispered. All she could think was to get into the house. The officer opened the door and grabbed her by the arm. She pulled away. "I can do it," she said with Randall in her arms clinging to the front of her. An unexpected peace washed over her and the words the barber said were a reminder to her, "You have something to be proud of." She gave Randall a quick squeeze and set him down so he could walk, she grabbed his hand and held her head a little higher as they took a step down the lane to their home. No matter who forsook her, she knew the Lord hadn't. And He wouldn't.

CHAPTER 3

Olympia, Mississippi
Ezekiel, 1928

Rays of light shot across the early morning sky and a crisp, fierce wind brushed the sleeping street clean. Ezekiel stepped out of the barbershop, broom in hand, part of his morning routine. He enjoyed tidying up before customers started coming, but today it seemed the Lord had taken care of it for him. The straw bristles rustled on the cobblestone as he glanced up and down the tree-lined street, enjoying the relative silence. Nothin' stirrin' yet. Soon the barbershop would fill with folks getting spiffed up for the weekend. Old-timers would play checkers with soda pop tops chattin' it up, while youngsters would drop in for a trim and share a bit of news, talk baseball, and brag of the swingin' clubs they were headed to that night.

Inside the barbershop, the hardwood floors shined with fresh wax, metal finishes gleamed with polish. The pendulum from the clock was the only sound in the room. Ezekiel's dress shoes clicked on the hardwood as he came to the front with the crisp white towels.

Ezekiel thought of his son, Jimmie, trying to remember the last time he'd seen him. When his son was little they had enjoyed opening the shop together. Up early, they would fry bacon and scramble eggs in a bit of the bacon drippin's and roll out a couple of biscuits. He could picture Jimmie's lopsided grin and how his cheek pulled farther up one side than the other, exposing his chipped tooth. It was a distant memory for Jimmie never smiled anymore. Somewhere along the way Jimmie lost his innocence and joy, exchanging them for hot anger which was strong and steady, burning up his soul until there was nothing left but ash. Ezekiel argued with his son that unforgiveness had robbed him of life. Jimmie argued that there could be no life without justice.

The kind of justice Jimmie longed for never came, and as the embers of anger burned he turned to drinking and pleasure trying to quench the hurt and frustration he felt. Vengeance had become Jimmie's justice and his life. He used his scorching fury to administer his judgments and he had joined company with like-minded men. Rumor had it Jimmie and seven others were administering vigilante justice on the other side of town. Ezekiel didn't like it, but Jimmie was twenty-two and had to make his own decisions and suffer his own consequences. Regardless, it could only add up to trouble. Ezekiel gave the broom a swish and headed back inside. The shop was in perfect order. Clippers rested on the mahogany countertop waiting patiently to do their job while razors sharpened on the leather strap were ready to swipe stubby faces clean. Swivel chairs faced the mirror that ran the length of the wall. The oak floors shined with a fresh coat of wax and a picture of Jack Johnson hung on the wall. Ezekiel pulled on his white smock and buttoned it up. He wound the old Seth Thomas clock, giving its pendulum a swing so that it could tick away the hours. Ready for the day, he headed to the back to fold and stack the last batch of bleached white towels. He wondered which of his regulars would be the first to arrive.

Time flew as the barbershop buzzed like a hive with a steady rotation of customers coming through. Ezekiel and his two brothers worked non-stop while the shop hummed with the sound of clippers and the steady rhythm of conversation. Throughout the day laughter burst forth and a familiar shout, "Oh you know that's right, tell it brother!" Ezekiel soaked up the conversation, offered advice when asked, and knew more about the goin's on in Olympia, Mississippi and three other counties than just about anybody. Talk at the barbershop was more reliable than the Olympia Examiner, the local paper.

Ezekiel was to meet his daughter Hattie soon but he decided to take one more customer, a smooth young brother who came in bragging. Ezekiel knew the type. As the young man took a seat in his chair, Ezekiel popped a clean towel and wrapped it around the young man's neck while he chattered faster than a jay bird. Patient, allowing the young man's story to unfold, Ezekiel listened without seeming overly interested. He stirred warm water into a clay mug half full of shaving cream and swirled until a velvety lather was on the short, thick brush. He lathered the chin full of stubble, picked up a sharpened blade, and began to shave while the brother talked. "Yeah, man. Some dudes went over last night and took care of that situation. Retribution, man. It was real sweet. Got a white girl and she didn't even know what hit her. Can't identify anybody. Knocked out." After he said it, the young man clapped his hands together and gave a little jump. Ezekiel almost cut him. "Hey!" he said, placing a hand on the young man's shoulder, "Stay still in the chair. I almost slit your throat."

"Oh yeah. For sure. For sure, man."

Ezekiel went back to shaving and prompted the young man. "So why'd they do it?"

"You know man, come on, for the colored girl that got raped by them white boys. Retribution, man. Retribution. They hit us, we hit them," he said as he punched his fist into his palm. This time Ezekiel was ready and pulled the blade away. "Hey! Sit still."

A rock of dread sank in Ezekiel's belly. Slowly, as if the conversation had drained the life from him, he finished up the young man's face, wiping him with a warm washcloth, pondering the last few minutes. His head hung low and he begged the Lord with an inaudible whisper, "Please, Lord, no. Not my boy." The young man bounced up from the chair as lively as he'd come in, said thanks, handed Ezekiel some coins for his shave and went on his way. Ezekiel moved toward the back, even though the barbershop was still full. He needed to get out, take a walk, get something to eat. Deep in his belly he knew. Nobody had to tell him this was the group Jimmie was hanging with—trouble. This mess wouldn't just affect Jimmie and his friends, but the whole town. These young brothers didn't realize, when the cops found out it was some coloreds they would be like bloodhounds ravenous for prey, hunting until the perpetrator was found. They'd scour the area until one turned up and anyone, guilty or not, would do.

After tidying up his area, Ezekiel went to the back and prayed. "Good Lord, please watch over my son wherever he is. Please don't let him have anything to do with this. Thank you, Lord." He took off his white coat and hung it on the brass hook. His hands clung to the coat as if to steady himself. The knot in his stomach told him his prayers were too late. Breathing became difficult. He looked at the tile and tried to fill his lungs. Convincing himself he just needed some fresh air he prayed again, this time for himself, trying to still his racing heart. He left by the back door and walked down the street to Millie's diner. Hattie would be waiting.

Hattie could pass for white, her long blonde curls hung in loose ringlets and her blue eyes and straight nose fooled most people of her heritage. When she took a hot comb to her hair to straighten it, it would lay like wispy corn silk against her creamy skin and she passed as white. Ezekiel's wife had been light skinned, but Hattie wasn't his, not biologically anyway. When his wife gave birth, he fell in love and raised Hattie as his own. He thought it might be hard, but it hadn't been. Not for him.

"Hey, Daddy!"

"Hey, sweetie pie. How was the hospital today?"

"Same as usual," she answered grinning, as if she had a secret.

He leaned over to give her a kiss before sitting down. Townsfolk knew she wasn't white but strangers didn't have a clue. She stuck out in the room full of colored folks, but none turned to pay her any mind. They'd seen her since she was born and colored folk always knew their own people.

"Daddy! Did you hear? Did you hear what them boys did? It's all over town." She lowered her voice to a whisper. "You think Jimmie was part of it?"

Ezekiel sighed and rubbed his face. "I hope not."

The waitress interrupted, her voice loud and booming, "Hey Zeke, Hattie, what can I get ya'll?"

Without looking up Ezekiel rattled off his order. "Coffee, fried chicken, mashed potatoes, greens." He came by so often he knew the menu by heart.

"Ummm...." Hattie started, "How about a fried bologna sandwich with a pickle on the side."

"Anythin' else?" the waitress asked.

"Sweet tea," Hattie added.

The waitress looked back at Ezekiel. "No apple pie? It's fresh."

Ezekiel put up a hand. "That's all for me. Thank you, though."

She smiled and closed her notepad. "Be right back with the coffee and tea," the waitress said, her skirt swinging behind her as she left.

Alone again, Hattie pressed, "Daddy. Do ya think? I mean, Jimmie wouldn't after what happened to Mama."

Ezekiel sighed and twisted his dark, weathered hands together. "I hope he wouldn't, but what happened to Mama might be why he would."

"But it was so long ago."

"Some wounds are hard to heal. Your brother was broken up seein' his mama near death."

"I'm sorry, Daddy. I didn't mean to bring up old, hurtful stuff."

Ezekiel reached across the table to reassure his daughter, "It's alright, sweetie. It's alright." He patted her hand. "Now let's talk about something else. Any miracles at the hospital today?"

Hattie giggled before answering, "No, Daddy. Why you always want a miracle at the hospital? You know them people are sick."

"That's why I hope for a miracle."

"But if you keep hopin' for a miracle and all the people get well, then I won't have a job."

The waitress delivered the sweet tea and coffee. Ezekiel drank his black.

He chuckled. "Good. Then I'll have you home more."

"You just want me to cook you dinner."

"Girl, you know that's right. You and your mama were the best cooks in the whole state!"

"Daddy, quit," Hattie teased.

Ezekiel sipped his coffee and looked over the rim at his daughter. He wouldn't trade her for the world, but the horror that came to her being, Ezekiel never wished on anybody.

CHAPTER 4

Olympia, Mississippi
March 15, 1929

The labor and delivery ward had a different flow to it compared to the rest of the hospital. A particular energy circulated through the ward that welcomed life rather than watched it go. Grandparents and family members crowded into waiting rooms while others waited outside nervously smoking until someone came to tell them the baby had been born. Elation radiated at the sound of a newborn cry. Joy washed over folks at the sight of little babies making their appearance. It was cause for merriment and rejoicing, which was the case for the majority of people. Most times folks left as if floating on a cloud, proud to announce a new addition to the family. New dads passed out cigars to loved ones and sometimes to complete strangers as they proudly shared, "It's a boy!" or "It's a girl!" The arduous journey from their mama's belly into the world was over and life was ready to begin with great celebration.

Today was no exception, the ward was overrun with soon-to-be mothers. Nurses shouted orders while others were running to and fro collecting equipment and rolling patients down the hall to delivery rooms. With so many babies expected to be delivered the level of excitement was elevated. On the opposite end of the spectrum, tucked in a solitary room at the end of the hall, there was a bit of anxious anticipation, a sense of forbearance that hung like a thick fog.

Hattie usually worked with the older terminal patients but today she'd been sent to labor and delivery. She'd worked there before and liked it, but the scheduling nurse usually put her on the fourth floor. She said Hattie had a way with helping people peacefully pass on, especially the cancer patients.

Tonight there were more babies being born than doctors and nurses available. She was assigned to Jena Wilson, the young girl who had been beaten and assaulted almost a year before. Hattie recognized her from the paper, but even if she hadn't recognized her, the hospital grapevine was bandying about like some cackling hens.

Nobody wanted to help her or be associated with her, she was like a plague worse than leprosy, even the doctors were wary. With strong resolve, Hattie purposed that no matter what, she'd treat this young woman with the dignity she'd offer to anybody else. She understood what it was like to be the subject of malicious talk. She was annoyed the gossip mill was running at full speed about this young woman who'd already suffered so much.

It was about mid-day when she'd come in. To avoid a scene, the nurses decided to put her in a room away from the other mothers-to-be. It was more to appease the others than for Jena's comfort, but it worked out fine because Jena didn't mind being alone. When Hattie came in and introduced herself, Jena was mid contraction. Hattie watched as Jena arched her back in pain trying to silently endure her contraction. She let out a deep groan. Hattie walked over with a wet cloth and wiped Jena's sweaty brow. "Don't forget to breathe," Hattie encouraged. "Exhale. Nice and slow. You can cry out if you need to." Jena looked into Hattie's crystal blue eyes, nodded and smiled. Jena was only five or six years younger than Hattie, but she accepted the advice as if Hattie had been birthin' babies all her life. For several hours the pair worked together in relative silence, a trust developing like deep waters. As Jena's time grew near, in between contractions, Hattie gathered tools and clean sheets, but when Jena's face began to grimace Hattie stopped and went to Jena's bedside. Jena squeezed Hattie's hand, her whole body tensing as she labored. Jena was almost ready to push.

Hustling to get freshly laundered gowns for the doctor, Hattie knew there wasn't much time before the baby would come. "Sweetie," Hattie said, "I'm gonna check you, I think it's almost time for you to push." Jena nodded and Hattie made a quick check. "We're not all the way there, but I'm going to get the doctor. I can feel the baby's head." Contractions came strong and steady. But doctors were slow to come.

"Ms. Wilson, can I get you a warm blanket or anything?" Hattie asked.

Another wave of pain rolled across Jena's abdomen, unable to speak she shook her head. Once the pain eased, Hattie asked Jena if she wanted to turn on her side. "Ma'am, sometimes laborin' is easier that way." Jena nodded and allowed Hattie to help her turn on her side before the next contraction. It did ease the pain in her back and she was thankful. Beads of sweat rolled down her face and Hattie was quick with a cool damp towel. "I gotta push," Jena said between contractions. Hattie nodded and rushed to the door and hollered, "I need a doctor. Now!"

A doctor and two nurses came rushing in. In just a few strong pushes, Jena delivered. It was a smooth delivery. Hattie knew they hadn't needed the doctor, she'd delivered plenty of babies on her own as a midwife to people who couldn't come to the hospital and she knew everything with Jena's delivery was near perfect, until they saw the baby. A hush that was more defining than a high pitched scream permeated the room. One might have thought the baby was stillborn or disfigured. To the people in the room it was sufficiently worse. The baby was colored. Hattie noticed first, after a long push, his head crowned with dark curly hair. When he was fully delivered, his brown skin was unmistakable. Hattie thought the doctor might faint and rushed to his side. He held the baby low where Jena couldn't see him even though she asked multiple times if the baby was okay. The doctor didn't respond as he continued to work. "Well, is it a boy or a girl?" Jena asked. It was Hattie who answered, "It's a boy, ma'am." Jena smiled and leaned back on the bed, "A boy," she said softly. The doctor tied off and clipped the cord, handed the baby to Hattie and whispered for her to get rid of it. The doctor washed up, patted Jena and said, I'm going to have a talk with your folks." He left without another word.

The other two nurses left the room, snickering and tale-bearing even before they were out of earshot. Normally, Hattie would have given the baby to his mama, but in this case she wasn't sure what to do. Standing at the counter Hattie took warm water and wiped the baby down before she bundled him. Hattie felt a swell of anger rise up and felt the flood of crimson turning her cheeks red with fury. She wiped the baby's face with a warm washcloth and smiled at him trying to stay focused for Jena and the baby in her arms. "What a handsome fella," she said, trying to clear her mind and override the nurse's rude comments. She was incensed and offended by their talk, thoughts raced through her head and she wondered, Why wouldn't somebody want him? In that moment, she was sure she despised white folks. They were so hateful for no good reason. What's this little baby done to anybody? She picked up the little bundle and wondered what she was going to do. She couldn't just get rid of him like the doctor said. What did he expect her to do? Go out back and toss the baby into the dumpster like a sack of garbage? A soft low voice broke her reprieve. "Let me see him."

The front door slammed and Ezekiel heard Hattie come through fussin'. She'd worked a double and Ezekiel figured she was tired and hungry making all that racket like she was. He walked toward the front of the house to greet her. She dropped her bag and jacket on the couch as she came in. Ezekiel reached out to touch her. "Hey honey, what's got you so worked up?"

"Daddy, some days I just can't stand them white folks!"

He gave her a tight hug and motioned for her to take a seat on the couch. "Why don't you tell me about it and get it off your chest."

Hattie stood back up and paced around the room. "Daddy! Ohhh, they just make me so mad."

"Well, quit stallin' and tell me what happened."

She rubbed her face and pulled the hair pins that kept her bonnet in place. "You know who my patient was tonight?" Ezekiel shook his head. "No idea. Who was it?." His mind was on the cancer patients she usually helped, not on labor and delivery. He was a bit shocked when she said it was the girl from the papers nearly a year before. He remembered her face from the newspaper. She'd been beaten pretty badly.

Hattie paced and tossed her bonnet and pins on the coffee table before she unleashed her fury. "Daddy! It was a nightmare. Those white folks just went into shock seeing a little brown baby birthed from a white lady." Ezekiel put his hand to his mouth and leaned back hearing the news. Hattie didn't notice and continued on. "I think they lost their ever lovin' minds! It was so quiet in the room, didn't nobody make a peep. Not even the baby. But after a second he gave a holler." Hattie paced the room a bit more, biting her nails before she went on. "Daddy! They even told me to dispose of the baby. They said to get rid of him! What'd they want me to do? Put him in the dumpster? How cruel! Daddy! Can you believe it?" Ezekiel shook his head, he really didn't want to think they'd expect his daughter to just toss a baby, live or deceased, in the dumpster.

"Daddy, I wasn't gonna do it. I mean I wasn't sure what I was gonna do, so I just wrapped the baby in a blanket preparing to leave the room and you know what happened?"

Ezekiel shook his head, the conversation was going too fast, he was still trying to process everything." I can't imagine honey, what happened?"

"Daddy, it was like God was there in the room showing me what to do. I knew the doctor would be back soon and I knew he'd be real mad if I hadn't done what he asked. Out of nowhere I heard the white lady, Jena is her name, she called softly to me and she said, 'Let me see him.'"

"So I took him over so she could see him. Then she said, 'Give him to me.' So I gave him to her." Hattie stopped pacing and kneeled before her daddy, taking his hand in hers." Daddy, it was so sweet. That little mouth was ready to nurse and his head was turning toward his mama." Hattie smiled thinking on it. "And you know what, Daddy? That white lady nursed her little brown baby. Daddy, he's so beautiful, you'd just love him if you saw him."

Ezekiel smiled and nodded. A tear snuck down the side of his cheek. When his wife gave birth it hadn't been difficult for her either. She was always in love with Hattie and never rejected her, not even for a second. His wife had given birth at home, her sisters had come to help and Ezekiel remembered the overwhelming joy and excitement of new life that filled the house. In her first few minutes she'd grabbed hold of his finger as he caressed her cheek and he'd fallen in love. He remembered naming her after his mother.

She got back up and paced the living room as she went on with the story. "Daddy, you should have heard the hollerin' goin' on. Everybody knew the minute the doctor told Mr. Wilson, Jena's daddy, because you could hear him hollerin' all the way down the hall. And let me tell you he was puttin' up a fuss. He said, 'My daughter ain't keepin' no nigger baby.' But when I left, she still had her baby. She said she was keepin' him. I didn't take her for the bold type, but she sure was strong as an ox, like a mama bear with her cub, in the face of all them doctors and her daddy, who was all red in the face from all that hollerin' he was doin'. She didn't let them take her baby. She held him real tight and told them doctors time and again she was keepin' him. I think the angel of the Lord was in the room because nobody dared to touch her either."

Exhausted, Hattie flopped onto the couch and sighed from telling the story. "I don't know what she's gonna do. Her daddy told her she wasn't comin' home with that baby. He told her to pick between her baby and her family. She said she wasn't giving up her baby and I hope she don't. But I guess we'll see. She's got a few days at the hospital and then she goes home. I guess they might convince her to give him up, but I hope she don't. I sure hope she don't."

Nodding, Ezekiel wondered what would happen in the next few days. It wasn't likely her daddy would change his mind or his heart and let her keep the baby. Nobody in the community would fault him for trying to put this behind his family by getting rid of the baby. Ezekiel guessed that Mr. Wilson probably felt anger toward a baby conceived the way he was and the baby was negro. Ezkeiel could understand Mr. Wilson rejecting the child, in fact he thought it might be the more natural thing. It would take God's love to change a man's heart.

Not to be foolish, Ezekiel also knew people sometimes just dumped babies and left them to die, or took 'em like a sack of puppies and threw 'em in the river. He hoped she wouldn't, he prayed she wouldn't, but the pressure on her from family and the community would be unbearable. Ezekiel bowed his head. "Lord, help her," he said.

"Daddy? Daddy?" Hattie shook him. "What are you thinking?"

"I was just prayin' for the white lady and her baby."

She nodded, understanding. "Daddy, her name is Jena. I told her that her baby sure is handsome. She done real good, Daddy." Hattie said with a smile as she leaned over to rest her head on her Daddy's shoulder. He wrapped his arm around her and gave her a hug. "Daddy, I told her he's something to be proud of." Ezekiel nodded and hugged her tighter. Those were the same words he'd said to Hattie's mama about her.

March 23, 1929

Dear Diary,

I suppose I should start by writing Dear Lord, because I know I'm not writing to my diary. That would be silly, crazy even – writing to a piece of paper. But some days, I do feel a bit crazy, out of sorts, like I'm living in a different universe, an alien on an unknown planet. A little over a year ago, I lay on a picnic blanket under a big oak near the lake daydreaming about my future. I remember that day so clear—like it was yesterday, I was just nineteen. It was about eighty-five degrees, warm enough to go to the water hole, but not so hot you'd wish you could die. There were four of us, Mary, Ashley, Irene and me. We giggled in the breezy afternoon while bees hummed along grassy patches looking for pollen that was so abundant it colored the air yellow. We sipped sarsaparillas from glass bottles and we talked about boys we'd liked in school.

We had plans to go off to secretarial school and we imagined husbands and families with a bunch of kids. Mary and Ashley both had beaus they were hoping would propose, but I wanted something a little different. Don't go gettin' me wrong, I wanted to get married and have some babies, kiss my husband with lipstick on when he comes through the front door, and have supper ready for him after a long day at work. I imagined I'd hang laundry on the line and watch it pop in the wind under a cool blue sky. I wanted to cook good dinners where the aroma fills your senses before you get to the door. I wanted to bless my family with a tidy house and all the things a girl dreams of when she's young, but deep inside I thought different things, too. I don't know where I thought I'd be in a year or so, but I am one hundred percent sure I never thought I'd be here.

I'm a girl with no husband, a brand new baby, kicked out of my house, away from my family and everything I know, no source of income, living in a shack and scared out of my wits. I've never been on my own before. I've never taken care of a baby. I don't know what to do. I always imagined when I had my first baby my mama would be there with me, right by my side, guiding me, but she's not. It's just me and my baby, and You, Lord.

It's not freezing but my fingers are numb out from under the blankets writing and the wind is whistling through the loose boards. My baby and I are cuddled up together under the blankets tryin' to keep warm. He's sleeping real peaceful right now, but I don't know about later. I don't have any more wood for the stove. I think I saw the beady eyes of a rat poke out from a hole in the wall. I don't have a husband, who's going to kill it? Oh Lord, how am I ever going to make it? My poor baby, he doesn't deserve this.

CHAPTER 5

Olympia, Mississippi
March 1929

The front page of the newspaper didn't have her picture plastered on it, but it might as well have. Both sides of town had tongues waggin' full of gossip, that the assaulted white girl had given birth to a colored baby. Tensions were high. There were talks of lynchin'. You could feel the pressure of a storm comin'. Folks were nervous. The news stirred gossip across neighboring counties. Black women birthed babies of different shades from light to dark and nobody paid much mind, but a white woman birthing a brown baby was practically unheard of. It was expected that the local Klan would have gone out hunting the culprit, but months had passed since the incident and the shock of it seemed to paralyze the city. However, it didn't stop the busybodies who spent their day talking about it. The police had no fresh leads and none had come from the previous year. Rumor had it, it was some boys from Chicago. Ezekiel suspected different.

Night Men rode, subtlety stirring up trouble, but lacked their usual vigor. Jena's father refused his Klan meetings and sat in his rocker instead of accompanying the Night Riders. He wanted it all to go away like a bad nightmare. Mr. Wilson was infuriated that his daughter was adding fuel to the fire by not getting rid of it. Nonetheless, townsfolk gossip had grown into wild stories so far from truth that they lacked basic facts. Some were downright unrecognizable.

Anytime customers came into the barbershop talking about her, Ezekiel tried to change the direction of the conversation, he'd rather talk about anything other than the white girl and her brown baby especially since the talk tended to be malicious. He admired her courage. She stayed to herself and didn't start trouble. She kept her head down and tried to make ends meet. Mostly people left her alone. They might ride by and shout some hateful things, or throw some eggs, but mostly they didn't try to hurt her.

He knew the things people did because he'd hear the talk. He couldn't go to the ballfield, the market, or Millie's diner without hearing somebody gossiping. The talk was fierce and cruel, he was thankful Jena didn't hear it. Hattie did though, the hospital was full of it, but every now and again, she'd have good news because she'd go and visit Jena and her baby. He was real happy when Hattie told him that she'd dropped off a crate with some baby items and a few things for Jena. Sometimes Hattie would drop the crate anonymously, she didn't want to shame Jena or anything, and sometimes if it felt right she'd stop in and say hello, hold the baby, and be on her way.

It would be seven more months before the gossip shifted. October 29, 1929, Black Friday, the stock market crashed and the stories of bodies falling from tall city buildings captivated and horrified the country, overtaking interest in the small town white lady and her disgrace. By then, people practically forgot about her and her little brown baby.

March 31, 1929

Dear Lord,

Help us. Please help us. My baby's cryin' and I don't know what to do. I can't go to my mama and I don't know what to do. I tried to feed him, but he won't nurse. I tried to change him and keep him warm. Lord, please don't let him die. I've been through too much and I'm sure You got a plan for him. I know that's why You wanted me to keep him. You have a plan for him.

I went to the doctor I've known my whole life to get some help. I went and stood on Dr. Hertsfield's front porch, I banged on the screen door and made a fuss calling for him till he answered. He and his family live in a farmhouse just outside of town and mostly he's real friendly. Every year in the fall he'd host a get-together and just about everyone in town would be invited. They'd have ponies for the kids to ride, sack races, and egg tosses. Boys would chase girls and pull their pigtails while the women chatted and the men smoked cigars that Dr. Hertsfiled got special from Savannah.

My mother and I would come a day or so early and help Mrs. Hertsfield cook and set up. I was often in charge of ironing the tablecloths that would cover the lines of tables set up in the front yard. I usually got to squeeze the lemons for gallons and gallons of lemonade. The secret was to use a wooden spoon to squish the lemons with the skin on to get the oil and juice. And instead of just dumping in scoops of sugar Mrs. Hertsfield warmed the water and made a sugar syrup to mix with the water and lemons. She won best lemonade at the State Fair. On a special day she'd throw in some mint sprigs or strawberries for a little twist. It was Mrs. Hertsfield's famous recipe and I had to promise to keep it a secret. When my parents would visit to play cards, my brother and I would sit in the big rocking chairs on the front porch and play checkers, listening to the crickets as the sun went down and the mosquitos came out.

Lord, today was different. Did you see what happened? My visit today wasn't like my childhood at all, it was like a nightmare., I stood on the porch like an unwelcome stranger at a house I'd once considered a second home. As I walked down the half mile gravel driveway, my baby still crying, I looked back up the hill at the two-story farmhouse with its yellow siding and white trim and a strange sense came over me. I knew I'd never again be welcome at the once friendly place with a green tin roof that sounded so pretty when it rained. "I'm sorry," were his last words before he turned and closed the door in my face. I have to admit I was a bit stunned. I looked over at the chairs I'd sat in more times than I could count and I wished I could be a girl again, playing checkers with my older brother Joseph—but I can't.

"He won't help us," ran through my head over and over the whole walk back across town and through the woods to our shack, just a little before the train tracks. I think I probably knew that before I went, but when you've known someone your whole life, you just don't believe they'll turn you away. His eyes were moist when he said that he couldn't help me. I thought he might shed a tear because I was beggin' so much and my baby was cryin' so loud. He just swallowed hard and shook his head. I asked him, What about the doctor's oath to help people? Didn't he take that oath? And didn't it mean anything? But he didn't answer, he just picked at a piece of the screen that was coming loose from the frame. I heard his wife call to him and ask him who was at the door. That was when he said he was sorry and shut the door.

Lord, help me. Please. I don't have anybody. I don't know what to do. My baby is hot, too hot, I'm sure. I barely know my beautiful little baby, but I love him so much. He settled down to sleep but he hasn't eaten. Don't let him die. He's depending on me and I'm depending on You. The bible says You're a healer. Heal him, Lord. Please.

CHAPTER 6

Olympia, Mississippi
April 2, 1929

Hattie drove down the long country road that led to the old mercantile storehouse. As she turned onto the wide gravel road originally designed for deliveries she could see that Jena had been hard at work making the storage shed into a home. A grin pulled at her cheeks, she just never expected Jena to have such grit and determination. She appeared so mousy and quiet with her long straight brown hair that hid half of her face and the tiny freckles that speckled her nose and cheeks. Hattie figured Jena had been like that her whole life; shy, gentle, timid maybe. Originally, Hattie had concerns that Jena wasn't likely to make it on her own. She smiled at herself for being wrong. Jena, somewhere in her, had a deep well of strength. The other thing Hattie was sure of was that there was only one kind of strength like that.

The gravel road was lined with low-hanging trees hiding the shack from the road, but toward the end it opened up to a small clearing. In the front, near the door, was fresh turned soil where wild daisies had been transplanted. It was early spring and the plants might not take, likely there would be one more good frost before the weather warmed for good, but Hattie applauded the effort. Off to the right side of their sparse dwelling in the clearing where they'd get the most sun, were short neat rows of rich dark naked soil which hosted a few tiny green sprouts. Hattie guessed they were radishes or cucumbers. Bean poles were already staked and ready with twine. Without being too nosy, Hattie was pretty confident she saw a miniature chicken coop and a few hens toward the back as she pulled up and parked. Jena surprised her at every turn.

Soft humming could be heard as Hattie approached the door. She had some cloth diapers and a few extra pins stuck through a bar of soap and one pair of rubber pants. She gave three quick knocks. "Yes?" She could hear Jena's soft drawl. "It's Hattie. I wanted to come by and check on you and the baby."

Jena swung the door open with a glow of sheer delight illuminating her face. Her voice was soft and sincere, "Hi Hattie, I'm so glad to see you! Please come in." Hattie passed through the door, hugged Jena and handed her the gifts. "Oh, thank you," she said, surprised. "You didn't have to."

"I know, but I wanted to, and who can't use more diapers?"

"That's so true. I feel like all I do is nurse, change diapers, and wash, wash, wash."

"Well, hopefully now you can wash a little less often."

Jena blushed before asking Hattie if she'd like to have a seat. "Can I make us some tea?"

"I'd love that," Hattie said, taking a seat in the only chair in the room. The Mahogany rocker had a generous seat and the motion was balanced and effortless, Hattie only had to give a gentle push to keep herself in motion. She recognized the quality, it was comfy with an afghan folded neatly across the back swaying as she rocked. Hattie wondered where it'd come from. Nice rockers like these weren't easy to come by and she couldn't imagine Jena had money to spare.

The small space was cozy, Jena decorated it with a few simple things. Next to the door were some shelves she imagined were originally for storage and Jena had covered them with a curtain she'd made from a white sheet embroidered with ivy and bold purple, yellow, and orange colored flowers. There were only two windows and each had café rods with a gingham yellow curtain on each one. The bigger of the two brought light in the front side of the shack and the smaller one sat right between the cupboard and the black pot-bellied stove that filled the space with the smell of slow-burning oak, offering its own few slivers of light to the dim room. Hung against the back wall was a washtub and a washboard that Hattie imagined was for bathing and laundry. The bed was tucked into the back right corner neatly made with crisp corners about two feet from the stove, just enough room to walk and plenty close enough to keep warm on cold nights. On the nightstand next to the bed was a kerosene lamp half full of amber liquid and a black leather bound bible. A piece of ribbon marked a page hanging out where Hattie suspected were the Psalms.

All her life Hattie'd seen houses like this, some even with dirt floors, but she'd never seen a white woman in one. Most of the poor white folks around town had running water and bathrooms, some even had electricity. Jena had to pump water from the well and use an outhouse. But more strength to her, she was making it work without complaint.

Jena pulled a tin of tea from the shelf along with two cups and a mason jar filled with sugar. She set the kettle on the stove and added another piece of kindling. Jena wiped her hands on her skirt and went over to where Randall was laying on the bed trying to pull his foot up to his mouth. She picked him up and looked over at Hattie. "Would you like to hold him?" Startled by the question Hattie paused then answered. "You wouldn't mind?" Jena shook her head. "It'd be real nice. Not too many people come by."

Hattie reached her hands out ready to accept the little fella. Jena placed him in Hattie's arms. She leaned back holding him upright and began to rock. He balled up his chunky fist and rubbed his face, tossing his head back and forth as if he could rub the sleep away. He yawned but fought to stay awake and reached for a golden lock of hair. Hattie glanced at Jena who was beaming with pride.

Finally catching a blonde curl in his chubby little hand, he gave a tug and squinted realizing he did not recognize the new face with fair skin and blue eyes. A cry lingered on his lips. He couldn't decide if he should holler. She smiled, he decided he liked her and smiled back. Her thick lips colored with a soft pink rouge might be the only give away that she was like him, mulatto. She touched his cheek with a single finger and tickled him under the chin. Caught up in watching his expressions, she spoke without looking up. "He's so handsome, Jena."

Blushing again, Jena turned toward the kettle that had begun to whistle. She poured hot water over the tea leaves and let them steep, choosing to watch the steam rise from the cups instead of turning back to face Hattie who was making cooing noises with the baby. Filled with doubt, questions plagued her. Why? Why was she here? Why did she come? Jena pushed them away as quickly as they materialized. She was happy that a grown person was here, holding her baby, calling him handsome, bringing gifts. It was a bit like normal. She closed her eyes to feel the essence of another person in the house. They'd been so desperate and starved for affection she exhaled long and slow, praying under her breath, thanking God for the visit, no matter why, no matter how, no matter the reason, she was thankful.

"I don't have any cream, but would you like some sugar?"

"Oh yes, please, just one lump will do."

Jena stirred in a spoonful of sugar, placed the cup next to Hattie and seated herself on the edge of the bed. "Thank you," Hattie said, reaching for the cup with her free hand. Soft like a lullaby she blew the steaming brew before taking a sip and setting it back down. "How's the baby been for ya? Is he nursing well? He looks like a rollie-pollie." Jena nodded. "Yeah, he does real good. I was scared one day. He had a high fever and I couldn't get him to nurse, I asked God to heal him." Hattie nodded, her eyes still locked on Randall making faces at him. "Did he nurse after you prayed?" Jena twisted her hands in her skirt. "Oh yes! Just a short while later, he did and his fever came down too."

"Praise the Lord!" Hattie shouted startling the baby.

Jena smiled. "Yes, praise the Lord! I was so relieved." She changed subjects. "How are things for you at the hospital?"

"They're tough some days. I mostly work in the cancer ward. Those folks don't fare so well and some days are just sad."

"I see, that would be difficult. How was it you came to work with me when Randall was born?"

Hattie looked up and smiled. "Oh, I think it was a special appointment from the Lord that brought me to your room that night. I hadn't worked in labor and delivery for quite some time."

Jena's cheeks reddened again. "I sure am thankful for ya."

"I was happy to be there. God knew what he was doing! I'm sure about that! And look at this little fella, just as big and handsome as ever."

The deep waters shared between them seemed to do their own talking with an understanding that didn't need words. Hattie sat rocking till the baby fell asleep. Jena delighted in her quiet company. When the last sips of tea were cold, and dusk started to settle, Hattie passed the baby back to Jena and got up to leave.

"Thank you, Hattie, for coming."

Hattie leaned over and hugged her. "If you need anything, I mean anything, you know where to find me at the hospital." Jena nodded. "I know where to find you." Hattie paused at the door. "If for any reason you can't get me and you need help, go to the barbershop on the black side. There's a barber named Ezekiel, you can trust him. He'll help you."

Jena nodded, knowing she'd never try to go to the negro side of town. She imagined they'd run her out on a rail. Her whole life she knew she wasn't allowed on the black side of town. Her daddy said it just a few times, but it was the way he said it that struck the fear in her. She wasn't even sure what the fear was. She just knew she wasn't supposed to go, she wasn't allowed to go, so she didn't. If she needed Hattie, she didn't know what she'd do, because surely she'd never break Daddy's rule and go to the negro side of town.

April 13, 1929

Dear Lord,

It's storming. Air, sharp as glass, is squeezing through the cracks I thought I filled. The newspaper says it's a cold snap. Says it's unusual for this time of year. I don't really care what the paper says. I just want it to hurry up and pass. The wind is whipping real good and it sounds like a thousand little demons pounding on the sides of the shack about to rip it right off the foundation. Fists full of rain are pounding on the tin roof. It's like the whole place is going to blow away with us right along with it. I'm so scared I want to tear my hair out, cover my ears, and wail long and loud like a banshee but I don't want to scare Randall. Help me be strong for him.

The dark clouds have stolen the daylight, but through the blur of my tears I can see the ink on my page running like tiny rivers. There's something else bothering me. I can't seem to move past it. I need to tell You, Lord. My body doesn't remember the pain as much as the terror that comes in my sleep. I can't see their faces. I only feel their hands seizing me, their hot breath on the back of my neck. A large firm hand closes over my mouth and silences my screams. I can't breathe. My arms are pinned, I can't do anything.

When I close my eyes I can smell the damp earth, I imagine my grave. I'm lying at the bottom of it. There's no casket. My body is in the mud and the water is rising. My left arm lays at an awkward angle while my right hand holds a bundle of sweet white Alyssum. I love those tiny white flowers I used to pick from Mama's garden. I can still feel my girl parts hurting.

The first shovel full of wet earth smashes my flowers. The rain is cold. I can't stop the shaking. Another shovel-full covers my face. Can You see me, Lord? Lying there? Are You crying for me?

I can't do it.

I can't keep going.

Can You take me home, Lord? Please.

The baby is crying. He needs me.

The beating of the rain has stopped. Now it's just a slow tink, tink, tink of raindrops on the rooftop. The walls are still. For now, the demons are gone. Bright rays of light slice through the darkness. Is that You, Lord?

CHAPTER 7

Olympia, Mississippi
April 1929

Ezekiel set the supper table waiting on Hattie to get home from the hospital. He'd had a slow day at the barbershop and left early to make dinner. Meat loaf, green beans and mashed potatoes with whipped butter were Hattie's favorites and he left them sitting on the warm stove. He even put the biscuits left from breakfast in the oven. He sat at the table with his arms crossed and foot tapping. He was itchin' to know if there was any news about the white lady, Jena, and her baby. The stir at the barbershop was that her family had put her out. It was Hattie who had told him about the miracle with Mr. Redding, a kindly older Jewish man, who let Jena and the baby rent the old shack that stood near the railroad. The small building was originally used as a storage shed for the mercantile and café back when they served train passengers. After the train station moved a few miles down the tracks the mercantile and café were shut down. Years later they caught fire, some thought it was kids playing, but nobody really knew what happened. The mercantile and café were gone but the storage shed, the outhouse, and the well were all still in good working order. During his career with the railroad, Mr. Redding worked with white folks, black folks, Chinese, and all kinds in the railroad industry and he didn't have a bias in regards to Jena and her mulatto baby. He simply heard that there was a need and he could help. He put in an old wood stove and a cooler box before the mama and baby moved in. She'd have to pump water outside and bring it in, it would be a hassle, but rumor was the rent was more than fair to compensate. Sometimes Ezekiel wondered how people came up with all the information they did, but plenty of people worked in the homes of white folks and had the opportunity to hear lots of things they probably shouldn't.

Ezekiel heard Hattie bumbling like an ox through the front door. She was bumping into everything. "What are you doin' in there?" Ezekiel called out as he went to investigate. "Jimmie," Ezekiel said under his breath as he reached to catch his son as he stumbled forward. Jimmie's face was bloodied. He smelled like rancid liquor and stale smoke. His top lip was swollen and split wide open, teeth and gums exposed, Jimmie was grinning like a mad man. His head lulled back and forth as if disconnected from his body. Ezekiel eased his son down. Bloody slobber drooled from his lips and pooled on the hardwood floor. Ezekiel went to the back of the house and got a few towels. As Ezekiel lifted Jimmie's head, he took a wild swing at his dad. Ezekiel hollered at him. "Jimmie! Stop!" Jimmie's eyes were wild and he whipped his head around trying to figure out where he was. He was cursing and yelling that he was gonna git them and they'd regret it. Ezekiel wondered what his son was talking about and tried to get him on his feet and at least into the kitchen where he could put some pressure on that lip and stop the bleeding.

At the table, with a cool damp rag, Ezekiel applied pressure while Jimmie struggled against the help. His dad fussed at him and the two argued. A high pitched scream rang out, "Daddy!" They could hear her hurried footsteps as she followed the trail of blood smeared from the living room to the kitchen.

Taken aback by the sight of her brother Hattie's voice grew low, nearly a whisper laced with sisterly concern. "Jimmie, what happened?" She reached for his chin to lift up his head and look at his face, but he slapped her hand away, still cursing. Her eyes were wide as tears pooled.

"He's drunk. Just leave him be."

Jimmie cursed more and spat bloody drool in their direction, lunging only once before crashing to the floor in a stupor, likely leaving another knot on his head. Hattie clung to her dad and cried. "Daddy, what's wrong with him?"

Ezekiel shook his head. "I don't know honey." He led her to a chair. "Why don't you sit down and try to eat."

"Daddy, I can't. We can't just leave him like that."

Ezekiel looked down at his son who had finally passed out. Had he been home alone he'd have left his wayward son right where he fell, but out of compassion for his daughter he got his hands under Jimmie's armpits and drug him back to the living room. With a hefty heave Ezekiel got him up onto the couch. "See now Hattie, he's gonna bleed all over your Mama's couch."

"Oh Daddy, stop fussin'. I'll stitch him up."

"Alright, sweetie. What do you need?"

After Hattie gave simple directions Ezekiel gathered a few clean towels and some alcohol while Hattie burned a needle over an open flame on the stove. She threaded the needle with some fine string Ezekiel used to make fishing lures and started stitching. After an hour the bleeding stopped and eight tiny stitches closed the gap. Ezekiel guessed Jimmie must have been in a knife fight to get a deep gash like that. Maybe a broken bottle, it didn't really matter, he just didn't want no trouble and Jimmie was full of trouble.

Dinner was cold, the biscuits were burnt and the pair ate in silence each wondering what ripple of unrest was about to follow Jimmie into their home. Hattie used her fork to push the food around on her plate. "Daddy, why does he have to be like this? I can't stand it and it scares me."

Ezekiel wiped his face with a napkin before responding. "He scares me too, honey. I can't tell him nothin' and he don't listen. I do know that he's hurtin' and angry. He thinks all this trouble is gonna give him some peace."

A tear slipped down Hattie's cheek. "I just can't take it, Daddy. I just can't."

Ezekiel placed a hand on his daughter's shoulder and tried to reassure her, but he knew until Jimmie decided to forgive and let go of his hurt, nothing was going to change.

April 29, 1929

Dear Lord,

I walked to my parents house today. The trees had lime green shoots and the sky was like a blue topaz with just a few cotton puff clouds. Birds were singing and I was sure something good was going to happen. I tied Randall to my front with his chubby little legs dangling. He was heavy but the sun felt good on my pale skin. I think I got a little burnt.

My daddy answered. I didn't even see my mama. He just started shouting and cursing. I'm tryin' to understand but I don't. My daddy hates me, he hates my baby, he says he disowns me, as if he never knew me. How could he say such a thing? After all the years of holding me in his lap and teaching me things, buying me presents and building me doll houses. How could he? How could he stop loving me? I'm his flesh and blood. Can you just turn off your heart and the love that flows from there? Can you, Lord? I'm holding my baby and I just can't imagine, how could anybody want or expect me to give him up? I just don't know what to do,

Lord. Can't my daddy understand that little Randall grew in my body for nearly a year? We're bonded, me and him. We're blood.

I'm trying to see his side of things. I know I come about this baby out of wedlock, I can see that it's embarrassing for my family, maybe for You, too, Lord. I know I'm shamed. I know I'm never gonna be married. I know the whole town's talking about me. I see them folks riding by—looking. I see the broken eggs on my front door and I hear their ugly words. I know some of 'em are real mean and I don't know why. I've never done nothing to them. And, none of it was my fault. I didn't ask for this to happen to me, but my whole life I heard Daddy say, "Life ain't always fair; you just gotta play the hand you're dealt."

Lord, why can't my daddy see I'm doing exactly like he said; I'm playin' the hand I was dealt. I'm standing on my convictions. I won't deny it, I love my baby. I'll give my life for him.

You know, I'm not sure if I'm angry or I'm thankful that I don't remember what happened or who done it. But, one thing is for sure. I didn't ask for that to happen to me. I remember the hospital. I remember my girl parts hurting real bad. I remember my body with black and blue marks. I remember the stitches that held the back of my head together. I remember my arm set in a cast, broke in two places. I remember my eye swoll shut. Who would have chosen that?

Who would have said yes to the shame? I'll never forget the humiliation I felt seeing my picture on the front page of the newspaper. There I was, lying in the street with a crowd around me. The second photo was from my hospital bed, my hair all tangled, mascara smeared down my cheek and a big bold headline that read; Local Girl Assaulted, Left for Dead. It didn't give all the details, but it gave enough. I could barely look anybody in the eye. I thought my life was over.

I thought things couldn't get worse, then I missed two of my monthlies. Mama took me for a test, but I think she already knew. She gave me a look one morning when the smell of eggs sent me running for the toilet. I didn't know what it was, but the look on her face said that she did. Later, after the test confirmed what Mama already suspected, she and Daddy said I had to get rid of it. It wasn't legal and they'd have to find somebody who would help us. They made all the arrangements, but when it came time, I couldn't do it. Lord, You understand—right? I mean, my heart just couldn't. Well, I think it was You, Your Holy Spirit helping me, giving me boldness I've never had in my life. I'd never defied my parents until that day.

The morning of the appointment, we got up to leave, it was still dark. We had to drive to Alabama and the car was all packed with blankets and pillows so I'd be comfortable on the ride back. Mama made ham sandwiches and some pickled eggs, she even packed sweet tea in Mason jars as if everything were normal and we were going on a picnic, but it didn't feel right. The air was crisp and pricked at my skin like hundreds of tiny needles. The leaves were starting to fall and I could see the silhouette of the trees as the full moon glared through the empty patches. The memory of that night is clear in my mind. Everyone tried to act normal, but nothing was normal. Mama was trying hard to make it easy for me.

When my Daddy told me to get in the car I said, "No." Just as simple as that. My Daddy started hollering and putting up such a fuss Mama was afraid he'd wake the neighbors. He said things a girl shouldn't hear her Daddy say, but I did hear and I'm not sure I'll ever forget, but I forgave him. I wanted him to understand I couldn't kill my baby. My baby was innocent, he didn't do anything wrong and as his mama, it's my job to protect him. Isn't that right, Lord? I mean look at him, he's so handsome.

Today was much the same. When I saw my Daddy he practically threw us off the front porch. He grabbed me by the arm real hard and dragged me across the yard and slung me toward the street. Thankfully, I didn't fall or hurt Randall. I stood in the street with tears staining my cheeks. I couldn't hear what he said, but I could see the rage in his eyes and the fury all over his crimson face. His fists were clenched and I wondered if he would hit me. If he was going to, I wouldn't have been able to move. Miraculously, Randall slept. I don't know how, but he did. The neighbors started coming out and looking from the safety of their porches. Joseph had come out, he was watching, too.

I don't know what compelled me, but it was as if two hands rested on my shoulders and turned me round, toward the railroad tracks and our little shack. When we crossed over the railroad tracks and I closed the door behind us, a weight hit me and my heart hurt real bad, because I finally realized. We may never be welcomed back home.

CHAPTER 8

Olympia, Mississippi
April 1929

The barbershop bustled with excitement as people crowded around the new radio. Ezekiel, and his two brothers Claude, and Joe each pitched in twenty-five bucks to get a tall standing Marconi console. It took all three of them to carry it in and push it against the back wall. The smooth, wavy grains in the wood were stained the color of sun tea and polished to a gleam on the four-foot console. The white porcelain knob, in the middle of the radio, twisted back and forth to tune the round black-faced dial that brought the speaker to life. Sound crackled from the fabric below and the shop squealed with delight. Most folks didn't have radios at home and hearing songs and voices on the talking box was akin to a miracle. Many of the sharecroppers didn't have electricity, most still used candles and kerosene to light their homes. Other folks had electricity but a radio was an expense most families just couldn't afford.

"Hey, Zeke," Fred shouted over the chatter, "We gonna get the Negro League World Series on this here contraption?"

Ezekiel wondered. "I don't know. I guess it depends on how far the broadcast goes. You know they play up there in Chicago. We'll probably get some local games."

Fred couldn't help but complain, "Well, you know, we was the last ones down here in Mississippi with a radio station."

Claude shot back at Fred. "Who cares. That was seven years ago, we got four now and three national ones for ya to listen to. Why you worried about it anyway? You ain't payin' for it. Listen to the news and the weather and quit fussin', we'll get some baseball games, too."

"You don't tell me what to do Claude! I'll worry about what I feel like worryin' about!"

"Y'all quit fussin' like some women," Ezekiel butted in before changing the subject. . "Y'all hear about that airfield over in Jackson? It should be opening up soon."

Claude was aggravated and snapped at his brother, "Well, why would we care? We ain't gonna be in them planes."

"I'm just tryin' to change the conversation so y'all will quit arguin'," Ezekiel said. "We just spent some big money, can y'all just enjoy it?"

Claude nodded. "Yeah, sure Zeke. I'm sure the Davis Airfield is gonna be real nice." He turned to the gentleman in his chair. "What can I do ya for today?" "Gimmie a full groomin'." "You got it," Claude answered, draping him with a cover.

The rest of the barbershop settled into a casual chatter and fuss over the new radio. Fred turned back to his game of checkers, while Ezekiel played with the dials, tuning in a local station. He wondered what his son, Jimmie, might be up to. He imagined how much Jimmie would like the new radio. They'd dreamed about getting one, and now that they had one, Jimmie wasn't around to enjoy it. As Ezekiel tuned the radio he prayed and asked the Lord to watch over his boy and keep him safe.

The next few months brought new business due to a piqued interest in the talking box. Folks would come in to get a trimmin' just to hear radio shows. Silence would hush over the room when the comedy show was on and stir right back up when the show went off and the orchestra music or a band started to play. The barbershop had always been a hub of activity, but the radio transformed it into the most popular place in town. Joe half-joked they should charge a nickel for everybody coming in just to listen to the radio. Baseball games were the favorite time of day to come in and have a listen, and the room would be packed. Music and comedies were popular and folks popped in at the top of the hour for news. No matter how long the wait for a cut got, nobody seemed to mind.

May 1, 1929

Dear Lord,

I don't know what to do. The pantry is bare and my pocketbook is empty. I've got enough flour for a biscuit. The water pump is frozen. I don't have enough wood for the fire tonight. I don't have anything to cut a tree, and it's getting dark. I've gathered all the scraps I could find the last few days. I even burned some chicken poop and feathers and whatnot, but I need the chickens to stay alive so I don't want to burn their bedding. I don't know why it's still so cold. Lord, please don't let us freeze to death.

The weather was warmin' up real nice, but winter wanted one last blast to freeze us out. I got a few things planted in the little patch on the side of the house. I covered them, I hope they make it through this cold spell so that we'll have something to put up this summer. It was hard work, but Randall's coming up on a month and a half. I can tie him in a little bundle to the front of me and work for a good while before he starts fussing. Usually, if I just stroke his little curls and sing softly he'll wait a little while longer and I can get a few more things done. I've lost a lot of weight but little Randall is a chunker. I've never seen a baby who smiles so much. I wish my mama could see him.

I wrote to her.

She hasn't responded.

Maybe it hasn't been enough time.

I imagined she would come on her own and I daydreamed I'd see her walking down the lane. After all, it was my daddy who put me out. The day I came home from the hospital Mama was crying just as much as I was when Daddy drug me down the hallway screaming. I guess he thought I'd change my mind and I guess I thought he'd change his. Neither happened, and if it weren't for that sweet nurse Hattie I probably wouldn't have a place now. I don't know what I would have done. I don't know where I would have gone. She knows the man that owns this shack and I gave him most of what I'd saved to live here for a year. It was a mighty nice offer and he fixed up the place for us.

Daddy's never been here. He threw my stuff out into the yard; my clothes, my dolls, my old school books, bed sheets, just about everything I ever owned. I don't know how some of my things found their way here. I think it was my brother Joseph that gathered it all up and brought it here. Mama must have packed a few of the wood crates because tucked inside some of the folded clothes were jars of her strawberry jam, some of last season's peaches and there was a cast iron skillet, a clay mixing bowl with a big wooden spoon, and a table setting with a mug to drink from. It wasn't a lot, but I was thankful. I took it as a sign that at least maybe Mama still loves me. I know Joseph does, but he won't disobey Daddy. Well, at least not most of the time.

Mama only saw Randall for a few minutes at the hospital. She didn't hold him. Her eyes were moist when she looked at me and a tear trickled down her cheek. She said he looked like me.

Mama left the hospital and didn't come back. I think she was embarrassed about her daughter, her grandbaby, and if that wasn't enough, Daddy was making such a horrible fuss. I think he was the most disconcerting part, hollering through the whole hospital. I figured Mama didn't come back because Daddy wouldn't let her. He told me at the hospital that I couldn't bring my baby home, and if I didn't get rid of that little negro baby then he would have no choice but to disown me.

I don't think I believed him, because when my friend Irene dropped me off at home, I had my baby with me. Irene had come to the hospital when no one else did. Her daddy is Irish. She and her daddy have the same wild reddish-orange hair that sticks out every which way and seems untamable. Irene said her dad understood what it was like to have everyone hate you because of how you looked. He said in the old country it was like that. He meant Ireland. He told her they fought a lot there with the British. Said they just wanted to be left alone and to live and take care of their families. That's why he told Irene that it was good to stand by me as her friend. I'm sure glad he did.

I believe Irene came because she's my friend and she wouldn't abandon me, but sometimes I wonder if she came because she felt bad—guilty maybe. I don't like to think that and I push those thoughts away, but the truth is, the night I was attacked was that same night we were all at the lake, except my friends went to the picture show and I walked home alone. That's when it happened, right after sunset when the shadows reach long to cover the earth and the light disappears.

All my friends came to see me during my pregnancy even though they couldn't understand why I'd want to keep the baby. We all talked about my options and our futures like we had that day at the lake, but things had changed. Conversation was awkward, everyone was careful around me. They couldn't be natural anymore. I think they pitied me. Eventually they stopped coming, except for Irene.

When I was pregnant I stayed home almost the whole time. Daddy didn't like me to go out, he hated the gossip. Irene understood and came by to bring me new magazines and sweets. She even knit a baby blanket and booties for me. She said it was real Christian of me and real forgiving of me to keep my baby, but that's not why I did it. I did it because I love my baby. He's a part of me. Killing him would be like killing a part of me. Folks said that a part of him would be evil for the way he came into being, but I don't believe that. The bible says that the heart is deceitful and desperately wicked, it doesn't say a person's heart is wicked by the way they came into being. I just don't believe what those people say about my baby and I wish they'd quit saying it. It doesn't help and he's just a baby. What does he know about grown folks' business?

Before I gave birth, my family was somewhat supportive. They weren't outright hateful. Mama knit a little sweater and sewed a few sleepers. Joseph made a cradle, he's good with his hands. When he had free time he made rockers and sold them. He'd made the cradle with long rails to rock the baby to sleep. If Randall was white, maybe we'd still be home, but once Daddy found out my baby was negro, Daddy smashed the cradle. His rage exploded like nothing I'd ever seen. The violence of it scared me. That's the hard part for me. Why does his color matter?

I tried to understand it from Daddy's perspective. I tried to imagine the dreams that he had for me, like walking me down the aisle in a white dress on my wedding day. In an instant, his dreams were shattered like glass into a million little shards, never to be whole again.

I love my mama and daddy, my brother, all my friends, but little Randall needs me and he'd have nobody if I left him. I wish they could understand that. I just want Daddy to see it from my perspective. I knew the little life inside of me was innocent and I love this little part of me. I need Daddy to understand, I can't do anything different. I just can't. My heart won't let me.

CHAPTER 9

Arcata, California
June 12, 1945

The Great War left huge gaps in the Negro Leagues and gave Randall an opportunity to travel and play when he was only sixteen. His height and broad shoulders made him look older. Working at the barbershop and playing baseball with grown men practically his whole childhood gave him an edge of maturity. Besides, he knew a couple of fellas that had doctored their birth certificates to say they were older so they could play too.

The bus pulled a wide turn into the parking lot of the Arcata ballfield. The players were grouchy and smelly after the long ride up the California coast. They'd played several stops along the way. The San Diego Tigers, and the Los Angeles White Sox were a double-header after their trip to Mexico. They'd won one and lost one. Across the border, teams were tough, but the Mississippi Blues managed to win three of the four games.

The weather was balmy which Randall appreciated since nothing else was pleasant on their summer road trip. They played seven games in five days. They were all business, there was no sightseeing or siestas. A few of the fellas found pleasure with the local girls and some tequila. Randall refrained from extra partying. Ezekiel had warned him to stay away from trouble multiple times, but besides that, the managers kept them on the go. Many nights they slept on the bus on their way to the next games. This week would be no different. Events were scheduled without enough travel time between and they hoped they'd make it on time. If they won, they got sixty percent of the ticket sales, but if they lost they only got forty percent and they'd get an earful from the manager all the way to the next game.

At the next stop they'd be facing some of the best of the Negro Leagues. A sign hung above the entrance to the stadium: "The Greatest Show in Diamond History." Crowds would be big. Names of greats cluttered the banner; Ray Campanella, Don Newcompe, and Larry Doby to name a few. All names Randall recognized and admired. One day, his name would be amongst those on the opening banner. He was young and relatively unknown. His pride soared and he was confident. After this season, they'd know.

Randall got off the bus last. He tucked his pen and paper back in his duffle bag. He'd been writing to folks back home. His mom was at the top of the list. He felt like his letters kept her going. They at least made him feel better about being gone so much.

He pulled at his sweat-stained shirt and took a sniff. "Ugh." The team was three days without bathing and not a shower in sight. They were expected to eat, go to bed, and be at the ball field early; it was another triple header. They'd play the San Francisco Sea Lions, the Oakland Larks, and the Portland Rosebuds before moving on and heading back East.

The barren California scenery was unimpressive. The orange groves stood in neat rows, but Randall didn't care for the tall slim palm trees or the brown rugged look of the West. He was bothered that he got ashy in the dry arid climate and needed more lotion. The food made his stomach hurt, and he often just wanted to go home. The one thing that gave him pause and made him stand in awe was the great Pacific Ocean. He especially liked to watch the sun take a dip into the cool water, painting the sky orange before it all went dark and the stars lit up the night. When he watched, he thought of Nina. One day he'd bring her here. They'd get ice cream and walk along the shore and he'd wrap his arm around her shoulders to keep her warm. He missed her. He wrote back home about the ocean more than once, because he knew nobody back home had ever seen anything like it. He was sure he never did it justice. The expanse of it, its majesty were beyond words. Giant ships looked tiny like ants resting on its surface. The rivers back home flowed one way, the lakes were still, easily traversed because they didn't go anywhere, but the great Pacific was alive. It seemed to inhale and exhale with each swell rising and crashing on the earth. He always watched from a distance, usually atop the cliffs, never venturing to the edge of the water. The cool after spray of a crashing wave was as close as he got. The saltiness flavored the air and assailed his senses. Even at a distance he could feel its power. It thrilled and terrified him.

As the in-house barber he made a little money on the side cutting hair. Everybody wanted to look fresh before their games, but tonight he didn't want to do anything. His legs were cramped from being on the bus all day. He hadn't done much on the long ride up here. It was hot and stuffy and he had a headache. He played a couple of hands of cards, joked with the fellas, and watched the coastline as they passed town after town. Now he longed for a cool shower to get refreshed and some food to fill his belly.

Randall dropped his bag on the bed and a few large roaches scattered from beneath. He'd seen plenty of roaches in his life but these were scary. He hated to hear them scratching around on the wood floor. Rumor was, sometimes they flew. He wasn't sure if the guys were pulling his leg about that, but he didn't want to find out. He stomped on the culprits and knew he'd sleep better knowing they would have no chance to come visit him in his sleep. He pulled the sheets back and checked for bed bugs, he didn't want to deal with any of those either. Two stops ago the team had learned their lesson after spending most of the game itching the small red spots they'd acquired during the night.

There was a lot of good advice Ezekiel shared before Randall left for the road, but there was some stuff he either left out or didn't know. Now Randall had his own bit of wisdom he'd gained from experience. He looked at the clock on the nightstand. It was late. He leaned back on the bed and closed his eyes, he'd get up in a minute and find the showers and get some food.

"Boy, get up!" the manager shouted. "You're late!" Randall rubbed his eyes. "What time is it?" The manager popped him on the head. "You're supposed to be dressed and on the field warming up." Randall rubbed the spot where he'd been hit. The manager dropped a cold greasy ham and egg sandwich in his lap. "You got two minutes to be outside." Randall nodded. He could smell himself but there was no time to fix that. He knew the greasy sandwich was going to bother his stomach, but there wouldn't be time to eat anything else. He peeled back the wax paper and took a bite. He wished for something else as grease dripped down his arm. He tried to imagine breakfast back home. Nobody in the West seemed to serve biscuits and gravy or grits with cream. Nobody made fried catfish or crawdads, no sweet potatoes or okra, none of the things Randall loved. There were citrus trees everywhere and there were these hard green things that were the same shape as a pear but had a skin like a gator. He refused to try them. They just did things different out here. He couldn't wait to get home.

They'd lost the first game but not before scoring five runs in the seventh inning. They'd pulled ahead with one run only to lose in the bottom of the ninth; a ball that dropped into left field with a high bounce right over the left fielder's head, allowing two runs to cross the plate. The team complained about how they hated the field. It was covered in dirt and rocks. If a ball hit the ground it was going to bounce and gain momentum and your cleats didn't help because they couldn't pierce the compacted crusty dirt. Slips and falls were common. He missed the lush green, freshly-cut fields, tucked away in a thicket of trees back home.

Randall punched his glove twice and squatted down in center field waiting for the next hitter. He wiped his brow, the sun was directly overhead. His mouth felt full of cotton and his arms felt like logs. He was soaked in sweat and for the first time in his life he hoped they wouldn't hit it to him. His head spun and he felt woozy. A runner eased off second. Strike one, came the first pitch. Randall wiped his head again. Second pitch, wide and outside. "Ball," the umpire shouted. A foul ball made the count two strikes, one ball. "Come on," Randall said under his breath, "Strike him out." Randall watched the wind up, he could tell a fastball was coming. He watched the batter tighten his grip, he was going to swing for the fences. Right as the ball made it to the plate he could hear the pop of wood making contact. The ball was headed to centerfield. Randall sprinted toward the fence, but lost the ball in the sun. A rock seemed to jump up and grab his foot and he went tumbling forward with his glove open, he crashed into the ground face first. He landed with a thud and looked up as the ball dropped just inside the outfield fence. He scrambled to his feet, wobbly, his head spinning. He charged ahead, grabbed the ball and turned to throw, double vision impaired his sight. He threw to where he thought the second baseman was. The throw was off and the runner rounded second and headed for third.

The infield stopped the play, but not before a runner had crossed the plate. He could see the team manager with his hat of screaming obscenities at him. He touched his face, blood dripped from his gravel scraped face. He wiped at it with the back of his arm. Two batters up, two strikeouts, but the inning ended with two runs crossing the plate. Randall jogged in, with dirt crusted on his scraped up face and blood smeared down the front of his shirt he was a sorry sight. "What the hell?" the manager shouted. "Sit down, Wilson!" He nodded at the doc to take a look at him. "Might need stitches," the doc announced. "Well then, stitch him up! I need him back out there!" the manager shouted.

Randall flinched when the doc poured alcohol on his face and started wiping away ground in pebbles, dirt, and dried blood. Likewise he wasn't prepared for the four stitches across his cheek the doc hastily put in. The doc pressed hard on the cut to suppress the swelling. Randall doubled his fists, he struggled not to pull away. "Harold, go pinch-hit for Wilson." Randall punched the bench he was sitting on. Never in his life had anyone pinch-hit for him nor had he ever played so poorly. The road was getting to him, he could feel it sapping his energy like a blood sucking leech.

The team left Mississippi in early May and played as many games as managers could book. After the doc patched him up, Randall hung his head. His only relief was that no one from back home was here to witness this. He could just imagine the jokes Claude and Joe would be making, especially him diving face first into the ground. He could just imagine their faces now.

The game ended in a loss. Before making his way to the bus Randall stopped at the bathroom, they were pulling an overnighter, which meant sleeping on the bus. He wanted to get cleaned up, at least wipe off some of the stink. Not that it would help that much, the whole bus was going to be ripe with funk. The mirror reflected someone he didn't recognize. Half of his face was scratched and bruised. His light skin was changing colors. He took off his shirt, soaked the washcloth with cool water and squeezed it down his neck and across his chest. He was parched. He stuck his face under the faucet and gulped water. After he felt full he wiped his chest and his pits. He didn't want to smell himself the rest of the ride; it would be bad enough to have to smell everyone else. He just wanted to go home. He missed his mama, Ezekiel, Hattie, the fellas at the barbershop. He wasn't sure he could keep going like this, but everyone had worked so hard to get him here.

The triple-header at their next stop was a bust. The Mississippi Blues lost every game.

CHAPTER 10

Olympia, Mississippi
May 1, 1929

The morning was frosty, close to forty degrees. It was Hattie's day off and she regularly liked to sleep in, but today sleep was evasive. The weight of the blankets trapping the warmth between the covers was like sitting in Mama's lap bundled up in her arms. The memory made it difficult to climb from beneath the covers and into the biting cold. A strong voice in her gut compelled her to swing her feet from beneath the covers. She frowned at her thin socks as shards of cold stabbed at her feet. She pulled a wool shawl round her shoulders before slipping into her house slippers.

Spring was taking its sweet time arriving. The night frost hadn't passed and the lingering cold summoned an unusual foreboding. Like the uncomfortable lump forming in Hattie's stomach. She couldn't pinpoint the source of dread; she simply knew it was about Jena. She was sure Jena didn't have any more split wood and the branches she'd collected wouldn't stand a fighting chance against the steady barrage of dropping temperatures. Hattie wasn't confident Jena had food either.

Shuffling to the kitchen Hattie put the kettle on for coffee. Today she needed it strong and black. She thought about eggs but she needed to take action. She poured a cup of coffee, sat at the table, and focused. She opened her bible and read. "Speak to me, Lord." She prayed looking for more answers. After an hour at the table, Hattie rose, having the assurance she needed. She knew what she needed to do.

Ezekiel was surprised to see Hattie in the barbershop. So were Claude and Joe. She didn't come by much and everybody there was real glad to see her. She hugged each of her Uncles and a few regulars. "Daddy, can I talk to you in the back?" He nodded. "Yeah. Let me finish up."

Hattie paced next to the small table while she waited. Ezekiel came back and poured a cup of stale coffee. He took a seat at the table before Hattie got started. "Daddy, it's Jena."

"What happened?" he said between sips.

"I woke up and I just knew she needed help."

Zeke nodded, warming his fingers against the hot cup. To be honest, he had his own concerns for Jena. "Well, you got a plan?" Hattie nodded and told him everything.

After Hattie left, Ezekiel excused himself, pulled on his jacket, went out the back and headed down the street with purpose. On his walk home he stopped by Henry's farm and borrowed a wagon and a mule. They chatted for a bit and then Ezekiel headed over to the mercantile to load up on a few groceries. He grabbed staples mostly; flour, sugar, grits, potatoes, canned goods and some meat. He had two crates full of food with some fresh milk he suspected wouldn't last long. He got some laundry powder and a bar of lye just in case. He wanted her to have enough for the month. That would help buy some time to figure out how she could get some work.

He snapped the reins with a quick pop. A steady clop of hooves kept them moving along the old country road to a spot he knew always had good dry split wood. Drew had a big grove where he kept rows and rows of wood dryin' for the next winter. He worked trees, he trimmed 'em, climbed 'em, cleared 'em, and sometimes even healed 'em. He and his boys did a little carving and carpentry but not too much. Their main thing was trees. Drew was smart about business, he knew what his clients needed and he delivered. He understood poor folks usually needed the trimmed or felled tree for their own households. He'd cut a discount and let 'em pay just for the trimming. For the rich folks who didn't want a single leaf or pine needle left in their yard, he charged a fee for cleaning up and hauling off the wood which he split, dried, and sold the next year. Ezekiel admired Drew's business savvy. Drew got paid for clearin' and he got paid for selling. That was good sense any way you sliced it and was why Ezekiel offered a trade. For a cord of wood he bartered a couple of haircuts, full groomin' with shoe shines for Drew and his boys, Drew extended his hand and shook on it, real pleased. Drew liked the deal so much he helped Ezekiel fill the back of the wagon and even sent a couple of his boys to help unload.

Back in town Hattie sat at the counter of Millie's Diner waiting on her order while her stomach gave an angry growl. The whole place smelled deliciously like frying bacon and warm maple syrup. Mabel gave her a hot buttered biscuit and a cup of coffee. "Thank ya, Mabel," Hattie said as she smiled down at the biscuit and took a bite. The diner wasn't too busy so Hattie chatted with Mable, who her Uncle Joe was soft on. They flirted every time he came in. She could see why he liked her. She was real friendly, always smiling and making people's day better because she was fun and cute, kinda tall with long legs and wide hips that made her skirt swish when she walked.

As soon as everything was ready, Hattie headed out of town over to the shack near the old railroad station. Jena wasn't expecting her and Hattie wasn't sure what she'd find. Pleasantly she found Jena up and dressed, hanging clothes to dry. Diapers hung in neat rows like white bunting. She smiled when she recognized the car and put a friendly hand up in welcome. Randall was bundled securely to her front.

"Hey, Jena," Hattie called from the car window, "You free? I thought you two might join me for a picnic." Jena's face lit up, she reached for her hair tucking a strand behind her ear revealing the fullness of her face. She stuttered, "Why…well…y-y-yes…we'd love to."

Hattie cut off the car and stepped out. "I thought we could go for a ride and sit by the lake."

Jena sucked in a breath and put both hands to her face. "Oh yes! That would be so delightful. Will you give me a few minutes? I just want to bundle up the baby."

"Of course, I'll wait for you right here."

Jena hurried to the house and Hattie busied herself hanging the rest of the clothes in the basket. She looked around and noticed no smoke drifted from the black pipe on the roof, nor was there any wood to be seen outside. This mornin', on the ride over, every smoke stack on every house had a steady plume coming from it.

Only a few minutes passed before Jena reappeared with a wool shawl wrapped around her and the baby. A knapsack was filled with a couple of diapers. Hattie opened the passenger door and helped Jena and the baby in. The car rattled and sputtered as Hattie cranked the key. They made a turn onto an old back road which opened up to a spot by the lake. "Sure smells good in here." Jena said as her stomach rumbled. "I picked us up some lunch. I hope you like beef stew?" "I sure do," Jena said, smiling wide. "Good, cuz Millie's makes some of the best. You want a biscuit? There's a few in the bag right there." "I can wait," Jena said, even though her stomach said otherwise.

The rocking motion, as they ambled down the old country road, was soothing and Randall slept while Jena watched the trees as they passed. Budding lime green leaves dotted the trees despite the cold. Silence filled the space between them. Jena hadn't been in a car since she'd left her parents. Many Sundays after church, when the family would take a long drive to the lake, Mama would pack a picnic basket and they'd have lunch in the shade of a wide oak or a high reaching maple. They'd eat, and then Daddy and Joseph might go fishing while she and Mama would keep their hands busy knitting. Sometimes Mama would bring a book of poetry and read out loud while the men were away. Jena reminisced of her wildflower bouquets decorating the house after a Sunday ride.

A piercing wail broke the silence and no bouncing or sweet talk was going to help. Randall rooted around. Jena was sure he could smell the stew. She untied the sling and let him nurse as they drove. She took a deep breath, leaned back, and smiled. She watched Randall and caressed his cheek. She hadn't felt this alive in quite some time. The past few months proved difficult, well beyond anything she could have imagined, but at the moment, the drive reminded of her childhood, when she wasn't responsible for anything or anyone.

Hattie's presence brought peace, the smell of her skin like honeysuckle and her light and joyful presence like the comfort of a big sister. In the distance, storm clouds were forming. She looked away. She didn't even want to worry about what would happen a few hours from now or even later tonight. She pushed troublesome thoughts away and allowed herself to be lost in the moment. Besides, she thought, didn't the Lord say, don't worry about tomorrow for today's troubles are enough? She exhaled and decided to take the good Lord's advice and worry about tomorrow, tomorrow.

Rays of sunshine welcomed them as they unpacked. Jena wiped drool from her sleeping baby, tightened the wrap that held him and reached up toward the sky for a long cat-like stretch. Sequestered for her pregnancy, nowhere to go after her delivery, unwelcome just about everywhere, joy bubbled up as her body delighted in the indulgence." Thank You, Lord," she said under her breath. Hattie spread the blanket and brought the sack of food over and invited Jena to sit.

Hattie passed Jena a wide mouth pint jar and a spoon. "Thank you, Hattie. This is real special." The grumblings of Jena's stomach hurried Hattie's prayer. "Let's eat!" she said and held up her food in a toast to Jena with a clink of their glasses the feasting began. Hattie watched Jena's face as she savored the rich gravy and eagerly spooned another bite with a piece of carrot and beef. "This is so good," Jena said, "Thank you."

"It's my pleasure. Here," Hattie said, handing Jena a biscuit. "Thank you, Hattie. This is too much. I don't know what to say."

Hattie smiled. "You don't have to say anything. Just enjoy."

Jena tucked a strand of hair behind her ear and showed her face. A school-girlish grin spread across her face. "Okay, I will," Jena said before dipping her biscuit. The tightness in her belly eased and her body relaxed. They sat on the blanket in the same comfortable silence they shared in the hospital and watched the ducks come and go. More came than went. Randall stirred and took up bird watching. Jena untied him and let him down on the blanket he flailed his arms, kicked his feet, and squealed gladdened with his new found freedom.

Focused on the birds as they took to flight, their webbed toes tip-toeing across the surface of the water, Jena wondered where she would go if she could fly. More ducks drifted down from the sky, crash-landing on the surface of the water, forming ripples that fanned out around them, overlapping one another. Their honking enchanted the lake and Randall joined in with a sharp shriek of delight and a furious waving of his little arms. Both women glanced at him and giggled at his outburst. He noticed the attention and continued squawking along with the ducks.

"May I?" Hattie asked, and put her hands out hoping Jena would pass her the baby. Jena handed over the little fella. He smiled and reached for her face, patting it with his cubby paw-like hands. "If this little guy's grip is any indication of what kind of man he's going to be, he'll definitely be a giant."

Jena laughed. "He is a lot stronger than I expected him to be. He's fast, too. If I'm not careful he can swat a spoon right out of my hand."

"I can believe it," Hattie said, turning her attention to Randall. "Would you do that? Would you swat a spoon out of your mama's hand?" He giggled and reached for her face again.

Light filtered through the thinly covered maple growing by the bank of the lake and blanketed Jena with warmth despite the wind. She tucked her knees up to her chest, wrapped her arms around them, and rocked. Hattie continued to play with Randall while Jena stared at the water. Her mind elsewhere, in another time, another place. She wondered what was going on beneath the water. Were the fish anxious the ducks had come or were they immune to their presence? Was today ordinary? Or was today special because the seasons were changing and their lives were changing too? Death was always near, even if it wasn't ducks. The lake could freeze or fishermen could come. There were even bigger fish to be afraid of. Danger was part of the ebb and flow of life. Her eyes welled and she tucked her head between her knees. Hattie asked, "You okay?" Jena nodded and wiped her cheeks on her sleeve. "I'll take him for a short walk if you want to nap." Jena looked up, her eyes red and damp. "That'd be real nice." Hattie passed Jena a handkerchief. "Thank you," Jena whispered, ducking her head and covering her face. Her body shook in small waves, but she didn't make any sound. Hattie thought to give Jena a moment to collect herself. Hattie stood up with the baby and patted Jena on the shoulder. "Enjoy a few minutes of peace and quiet." Jena watched the pair head south along the water's edge. Jena eased herself onto her side, wrapped her shawl tightly across her shoulders, and with a full belly she drifted into a deep restful sleep under the midday sun.

Over an hour later Jena rubbed her eyes and pulled herself up. It was much cooler. Dark clouds covered the sun but it was Randall's little wail to be fed that woke her. Jena smiled and reached out for him. Hattie passed him back to his Mama. She grabbed him by the middle and lifted him above her head. He let out a wild giggle. She brought him back down, tucked him under her blouse, and rocked back and forth as she nursed him. Hattie looked on, treasuring the precious moment.

"Jena,"

"Hm?"

"Can I ask you a question?"

"Sure."

"What made you keep him? I mean, I was in the room when everyone was telling you to get rid of him."

Jena smiled and looked down at her baby, his hand kneading as he nursed. "I couldn't do anything else. He's a part of me."

Hattie smiled back. "That's what I thought. I was so proud of you when you stood your ground and kept him."

"I remember what you said; he's something to be proud of."

"It's true. My mama said the same thing about me when I was born."

"Why?" Jena asked.

"Most white people don't know, but I'm black, too. My mother was very light skinned, she was half black and my father white. They say he had crystal blue eyes like mine."

Jena asked, "Were they in love?" Hattie shook her head and Jena already knew. "He forced her?" Hattie nodded her head as a tear slipped down her cheek. Jena did not seem surprised but just nodded as if the admission answered a million questions and explained the deep waters that bound their spirits together.

Hitched to the wagon, the mule ambled along, clopping, one hoof after the other, down the dirt road and the rickety old wagon swayed under the weight of its load. Drew's boys had come along to help and stacked the wood while Ezekiel took the crates of food in and put them on the shelf. He opened the pot-bellied stove and found the embers completely dead. He guessed Jena and the baby had been without heat at least a day. He cleaned out the ashes and started a fresh fire. The outside temperature was decent now, but tonight was expected to drop back down to freezing. He peeked his head out the front door. "Hey boys, can you pump me some water? I need enough for this wash bucket." The boys did as they were asked and filled the bucket to overflowin' sloshing it everywhere as they carried it in.

He put the sack of flour and cornmeal on a shelf where Jena wouldn't have to lift it. The small tins of spam and canned ham he placed a bit higher. He filled the rest of the shelves with canned goods, a sack of dried beans, and a bag of salt. He even had to put a few items on the floor next to the laundry powder and kerosene. He put milk and salt pork in the cooler box. Hattie had been right, so far he hadn't found even a jar of sauerkraut or pickles. The only things on the shelves were empty canning jars and less than a spoonful of sugar in a quart jar. He wondered what Jena planned on eating that day. There was no cornbread on the stove and no bread set to rise. He set the wash tub filled with water next to the stove. She could use it for cookin' or bathin' but she'd have it and it wouldn't freeze. He prayed over the house and closed the door. The sky was overcast, rain was comin', and he was glad the room was warm when he left.

The wind that had been whirling about all morning delivered thunderclouds that darkened the sky. The car slowed and turned onto Jena's lane. A boom of thunder rattled the windows and Jena jumped. "I better grab the laundry before it starts pouring. Will you watch Randall for a sec?" Jena asked. "Of course," Hattie said, shifting the car into neutral and setting the brake. Jena handed Randall off and bolted out of the car. She snatched the laundry off the line without pulling the pins.

Hattie turned off the car and offered her finger for Randall to grab. He got a grip and tried to stuff it in his mouth before she scooped him up. Reaching into the backseat she grabbed the leftovers and headed inside. Just beyond the doorway, Jena was on her knees face down, her forehead touching the floor. The room was warm and the shelves were full. Hattie could hear Jena's sobs and got down on the floor with her. Hattie placed a hand on Jena's back. "Thank You, Jesus. Thank You, Jesus. Thank You, Jesus," Jena repeated over and over. They knelt on the floor, their tears pooling together. Wind whipped rain through the shack and Hattie got up and put Randall on the bed. She closed the door before the downpour soaked the house. She helped Jena up to the rocking chair, grabbed a kitchen towel and dabbed at Jena's face. There was a long silence as Jena stared at the pantry full of food. She rose from the rocking chair and stood next to the stove, closing her eyes and warming her hands." Jena, I have to be going. Are you going to be okay?" Jena wiped her nose. "Yes. We'll be more than okay." She embraced Hattie and clung to her. "Thank you, Hattie." "You're welcome. Stay warm and take care of that baby," Hattie said, giving Jena one last tight squeeze. "I'll come when I can." Jena held on tight. "We'll see you soon."

May 2, 1929

Thank You, Lord! I can't say it enough.

The thunder that was booming in my heart and causing me to tremble is quiet. It is as if You stepped into my storm and said, "Peace, be still." Oh Lord, I thank You. Thank You for answering my prayers. We have kerosine and candles. I can write at night!

Lord, You are truly amazing. I am overwhelmed by Your provision and love. This morning, as the storm clouds gathered, I anticipated a difficult day. I never imagined what You had planned for me. As You know, I didn't want to get out of the bed and if those diapers hadn't been so horribly smelly I wouldn't have. Who knew stinky diapers can motivate people?!

You saw the cloud of fear and heard the crying of my heart and You answered my prayers. The evening came and the rain eased to a drizzle, there was a knock at the door, even though the roads were muddy and uneven. I thought it might be Hattie coming back to tell me who brought all the groceries and the wood, but it wasn't. It was Irene. I could see her wild red curls through a crack in the door, and my heart leapt. If I hadn't cried so much earlier I might have cried again.

She said she had to come, she said she was compelled, she said the Lord told her to come. She found work for me!

I've always been good with my stitches and even sold some pieces at local fairs. Irene knows a lady in the next town with a boutique that sells hand-embroidered dresses and scarves. She needs help with orders and pieces for her boutique. Irene said she'd drop the work for me and pick it up when I'm ready for more. I'll get paid whenever I turn in work and the lady said she'll pay me for as much as I can handle.

Lord, this is all so very overwhelming. The blessings of the Lord really can be more than we can contain!

Oh Lord, my baby and I can make it. Thank You, Lord. You are so good to us!

CHAPTER 11

Olympia, Mississippi
June 18, 1929

Before the sun rose from its slumber and began to give light, Jena had watered the garden and fed the chickens. She had six hens and one rooster. One of them was sitting on a clutch. Maybe they'd have a few chicks this summer. She put an extra tray of water for them to cool off. The heat was already creeping up. Thankfully the water from the well was cool and refreshing. She drank deeply and then gave the handle an extra pump and splashed water onto her face and down her arms. She had enough cucumbers to pickle later in the afternoon, but first she wanted to take Randall to the creek before too many people came. She didn't like being seen. She picked him up from the blanket and checked his diaper. He hadn't soiled it yet.

Gathering her knapsack and a skinned branch with a net on one end, she tied Randall to the front of her and headed to the creek. Her muscles were more defined and her skin had a peachy color to it and the brown speckles spattered across the bridge of her nose were more pronounced. She walked down the lane and to the main road, her long hair loose, catching snatches of the breeze as she walked. She followed the road to the fork and turned left toward the bait shack. Even though she wasn't fishing, it had the easiest trail to the creek and Randall was getting increasingly heavy. She climbed down the moss-covered rocks, being sure to get a good foothold before taking the next step.

She had an idea to catch a few crawfish to cook with a potato and a ripe squash she had back at the house. She'd seen her brother do it plenty of times and she'd tried without success the past few times she'd come to the creek. Folks said catching crawfish was easier than regular fishing. She hoped with her net she could get four or five, at least enough for dinner.

She came to a sandbar, dropped her load and decided to let Randall play before she tried her hand at catching. The man down at the bait shop called them mud bugs. His drawl was so thick and fast she couldn't understand him sometimes. His instructions on catching crawdads had thankfully come with a visual display, grunting, and big hand motions. How hard could it be?

Jena unfurled a blanket, set Randall down, and took off her shoes. Digging her toes into the gritty sand she sat peacefully watching animals approach for a drink. A fat raccoon wobbled toward the water until he spotted her. He froze, eyeballed her and hissed, then he continued on his way to the water. Wading in and appearing to wash his hands and face. Jena realized he had the same idea as her when he stuck his face in the water and popped back up with a crawfish. His little paws ripped the body from the tail and he began to gnaw on the flesh. A deer with her fawn sipped water with a watchful eye. As long as she and Randall were quiet, the animals seemed content to share the creek. Randall spotted a bird as it hopped toward them, twisting its head back and forth, examining them. As soon as Randall let out a sharp squeal of delight, the little brown sparrow took flight. Randall flailed his arms and blew spit bubbles while Jena played with his soft curls. She took off his diaper and took him to the water and put his toes in. The sensation of cool water on his feet caused him to giggle and pee. Jena was glad she had him facing the water or she'd have been sprayed. She waded into the water up to her calves and sat down, letting her skirt get completely wet. Holding his torso, she set Randall on her lap and let him splash. He giggled and made more spit bubbles. Randall doubled up his fists and rubbed his eyes. "We better hurry," she said knowing naptime was nearing. She tied the baby to her front and went to work.

She slung her knapsack across her shoulder and grabbed her net. Still barefoot, she waded into the water and propped her net up and reached into a murky area to pull on a rock. It barely budged, instantly she felt something sharp prick her finger and she screamed falling back into the water as a huge catfish swished past her. Her heart was racing and her chest heaving. Randall wailed, his face red with fury. Startled, she jumped up, getting back to her feet and fighting the urge to run. Forget the crawfish. She just wanted to get home. She grabbed her pole and raced from the water. She gathered her shoes and headed back up the rocks following the trail to the road. Before she crossed, back to her side she saw the bait man. He waved to her. He was naked except for his cut off jeans which hung loosely from his hips. She felt lewd looking at his sun-baked naked body, but his wide toothless grin was clearly inviting and she didn't want to be rude. His hair was coarse and black, full of tight curls and stood on end poking out every which way. He was unshaved but only a few scraggly patches of facial hair grew. She waved back, completely soaked, heart still racing. Randall was still screaming when she said, "Hello."

"Hello, Ms. Lady." He held up his hand with one long bony finger pointed up. "One minute. One minute."

She pointed toward home. "I need to go. The baby is upset."

He smiled and nodded. "Okay. Okay. For you." He pulled a small net bag from behind him filled with crawfish. "Too many. You have some. You gived me squash."

"Yes, I did." She smiled and looked into his milky brown eyes. "Thank you." She accepted the bag gently touching his hands. "I don't know your name."

"Bait Man. Thas what e'rbody calls me. Bait Man."

Jena nodded. "Thank you, Bait Man."

He shooed her on. "Baby hungry. Go."

"Thank you again," she said as he left them at a trot toward the bait shack. She held the bag toward the heavens and thanked the Lord while Randall continued to holler. She hurried home and put the crawfish in the wash bucket with some fresh water and a lid so they couldn't escape.

Mid-day the cicada chirred nearly as loud as the train when it passed and stickiness clung to just about everything. Mississippi summers brought steamy hot temperatures that caused folks to move slow and rest on the porch with damp towels draped over their head or around their neck, fanning themselves for dear life. Others went down to the creek for a dip.

At the barbershop metal fans spun at full speed churning hot air through the room. The heat spared no one. Every shirt was stained and men wiped beads of sweat being sucked from every pore. Games of checkers took hours as if to preserve the last bits of energy that hadn't been sapped by the weighty air. Claude and Joe sat in their chairs sipping warm pop, unwilling to cut hair until the temperature dropped. Ezekiel was still cutting but wished he wasn't. Tiny pieces of cut hair were stuck to his damp skin. As he finished with a straight razor he thought about going to Millie's to get some lemonade and a fried egg sandwich with some potato salad. He'd invite Jimmie. He'd been working on the white side of town helping build new housing. For some reason, he'd come back early today. Ezekiel hoped it was due to the heat, but that wasn't likely. Jimmie probably got let go.

Ezekiel got a cool rag and wiped the man's neck instead. "A buck-fifty," Zeke said. The customer grumbled, "I should get a discount because it's so damn hot in here." "Man, don't even start with me. It's too hot. I shouldn't even be workin' because it's too hot. Now pay up and go on." The man gave him three fifty cent pieces and left, still grumbling. Zeke dropped the coins in his pocket and went to the back. Jimmie had a half empty pint of whiskey. "Son. What are you up to?" "Don't start," Jimmie said, his voice a deep growl. Ezekiel put his hands up in surrender. "Okay. I was just coming back here to see if you want to go with me to Millie's to get some lunch." "I ain't got no money." Ezekiel wanted to remind his son that if he hadn't spent it on illegal booze he'd have money, but he didn't, it would be a pointless argument. "My treat," he said instead. The past few months with Jimmie home had been trying, but it was good to see his son and he didn't want to make things ugly even though Jimmie didn't seem to share the sentiment.

Jimmie took another swig and nodded. "Yeah, sure. Let's go get some lunch." He covered his mouth with his hand and wiped the alcohol that had spilled down his beard. Ezekiel stepped toward the back door and Jimmie yelled, "What? We can't go out the front? You embarrassed?" Ezekiel held his son's gaze. "I always go out the back so nobody asks me for a cut on the way out, but if you want to go that way we can." Jimmie wiped his mouth again. "Naw, we can go out the back." Ezekiel pushed the screen open and stepped down into the grass. He followed the path in the alley to Millie's. He asked for a booth hoping that was the last outburst from his son.

It was twice as hot in the diner but Ezekiel was glad to be sitting. He asked for a cup of water and a sweet tea. "Sorry, Zeke. We're out of tea."

"How about lemonade?"

"Out of that, too."

"Okay, let me have water."

Jimmie was staring at the waitress like a ravenous wolf. "Hey pretty lady, what's your name?" She looked at him and rolled her eyes. "I'm here to take your order. That's it." He glared at her and grabbed her wrist. "You don't need to talk to me like that. I just wanted you to tell me your name." Ezekiel reached across. "Let her go," he commanded. Jimmie tipped his head to the side, smiled a sloppy smile and put his hands up, which was meant to appease all wrongs. Only Ezekiel knew it meant things were just getting riled up.

"Mabel, can we get two waters? I want an egg salad sandwich and some potato salad." She looked at the ground. "Sorry, Zeke, no egg salad. Hens ain't layin' in this heat." "Damn girl," Jimmie shouted, "Y'all ain't got shit here. How'd you call this a diner?" Mabel turned toward him and put one hand on her hip. "What?" he shouted. She scowled at him. Ezekiel cut in. "Can we just get some ham sandwiches and potato salad to go?" Her face softened as she turned to Ezekiel. "Sure, Zeke. Anything for you." Jimmie just couldn't be quiet, especially once he'd started drinking. "Well damn, I was for sure you were gonna say y'all didn't have bread or something. Y'all ain't got nothing else."

Ezekiel shook his head, put a couple coins in Mabel's hand and asked if she could rush their order. As she turned to leave Jimmie reached out and tugged at the hem of her skirt. "Stop!" she shouted. Leon was in the back and looked up to see what the commotion was about. "What y'all doin out there? Don't give my waitress a hard time or I'mma have to come out there." His booming voice was enough of a threat for Jimmie to simmer down, and if his voice wasn't enough, his six-foot- six-inch frame carrying two hundred and ninety-five pounds definitely was. Leon wasn't a trained boxer but he'd knocked plenty of folks out.

Mabel came back with two glasses of water and didn't say anything as she set them on the table. Ezekiel and Jimmie didn't say anything either. It was a few minutes before she came back with two greasy brown bags.

"We didn't have no potato salad because there wasn't no eggs. Leon gave y'all fried potatoes instead. There's extra in there." She set the bags on the table. Ezekiel rubbed his face, chugged the last of his water and took the bags. "Come on," he said to Jimmie, "and don't say nothin'." Jimmie shoved the table and sent the water cups tumbling. Mabel put her hand up. "I got it, just go." Jimmie opened his mouth to say something but thought better of it when he saw Leon moving toward them.

Once outside, Ezekiel handed Jimmie his bag of fried potatoes and his sandwich. Jimmie opened the bag and began to cram chunks of potato in his mouth. In the short walk back Jimmie'd nearly finished his food. Ezekiel pulled out a chair and sat down at the table. Jimmie pulled the chair out too, turned it backward, and sat down glaring at his father. He pulled the whiskey back out of his pocket and took another swig. "You want some?" he asked, and laughed. "Of course you don't. Good ole Ezekiel. Don't drink, don't smoke, don't cuss or gamble. Don't even fight for his wife when she's been assaulted." Jimmie took another swig.

Watching his son, Ezekiel lost his appetite, his anger building. "Why you back from work early, Jimmie?" His son shot up out of his seat, the chair clattering to the floor, and pointed accusingly at his dad. "You always think the worst. You always think I'm up to trouble." Jimmie took another swig and shouted, "You wanna see trouble. I'll show you trouble."

Hearing the commotion, Claude and Joe came from the front of the shop. "Hey, what's goin' on back here?" Jimmie sneered at them. "Y'all all think you're better than me."

Ezekiel shook his head. He didn't want to go through this again. Claude and Joe had seen it before. "Jimmie," Joe said, "you know that ain't true. Why don't you dump the rest of that drink out and we can talk." "NO!" Jimmie shouted. "And don't you worry about me. I got me a job. I'm gonna make more money than all of you." He waved his arms wildly toward them. Claude took a step toward him. "Why don't you just come on and sit down. We'll make you some coffee." "I don't want coffee. Y'all stay away from me." Jimmie shouted before he turned and bolted out the back door.

"Sorry, Zeke." Claude offered.

Ezekiel exhaled and shook his head.

Joe patted his brother on the back. "Don't worry brother. He'll be back."

Ezekiel rubbed his face. "I almost wish he wouldn't."

"Awe man, you don't mean that," Joe said.

"I kinda do," Zeke said. "Fellas, I know it's early but I'm going home." He looked at his food strewn across the floor, he shook his head, swept it up and dumped it in the wastebasket.

"Yeah, it's not gonna get busy in this heat. Go take a load off."

"Appreciate it fellas," Ezekiel said, clapping his brothers on the back. "I'll see you tomorrow."

June 20,1929

Dear Lord,

Oooh, look at Randall, I love to run my fingers through his soft curly hair and stare into his little brown eyes. Other than those eyes, I don't think he looks much like me. He's several shades darker than me and his mouth is wide while mine is tiny. His eyes smile and his lips stay set in a grin which usually turns into a giggle. His eyes follow me as I work. I sing to him, the same hymns Mama sang to me. He claps when we sing. He might have a musical gift the way he keeps up.

I think my brother Joseph must have snuck by again because there was a wood crate with some groceries and a few dollars tucked in it on the porch. There was some yarn and a crochet needle, too. I started a blanket but it won't be enough. I'll have to see if Irene will bring more yarn.

I sure am lonely. I stopped counting the months I haven't seen people. Randall smiles and coos, but I just wish for some company, grown folk company, every now and again. Irene comes but she doesn't stay. She's busy.

Mr. Redding, who rented me this place, gave me his wife's canning jars and her big stock pot so I could put up some food. There's a blackberry patch out back and I bet I could get some good jam if I can get enough sugar. I'll be able to put up corn and green beans. Maybe even some pickled eggs. We're going to be alright.

CHAPTER 12

Ezekiel
June 1929

Ezekiel tossed in his sleep. The argument he'd had the day before with his son still vexed him. The room was muggy and he could smell the familiar mold that liked to bloom in the hot, damp summers. Something wasn't right, Ezekiel reached over and turned on a light. He grabbed his trousers from the end of the bed and slipped his feet into his house shoes. A trickle of light filled the sky but a strong sweltry wind blasted through the house, the front door stood ajar. Jimmie was gone. Ezekiel rubbed his head. Hattie was going to be broken-hearted to find her brother gone without a goodbye. He went to the kitchen to start some coffee.

The percolator stopped bubbling and Ezekiel pulled it from the stove. Early the day before, he'd gone to the lake to think. He'd taken a cane pole and his straw hat to keep the sun off. He set himself up on the edge of the bank next to some reeds where the fish liked to hide. He didn't expect to bring anything home, especially since townsfolk said the fish weren't biting. Despite negative reports, he managed to bring home two good-sized catfish. He wanted to make amends and he aimed to start by cooking dinner. He wanted to sit with his grown children and have a nice meal. He breaded the catfish and fried it with a few sliced tomatoes on the side. He heard the door slam right as he was taking cornbread out of the oven. Jimmie had come home drunk. Hattie came in only minutes after.

Food was on the table, grace was said, and after a few bites the arguing started when Jimmie announced he was going to be a bootlegger. "Can't we have a nice dinner, Jimmie?" Ezekiel said, wishing his son would quit with the antics. Hattie kept her head down, poking at the food on her plate as the room grew tense. Jimmie ate like a hog cramming a chunk of catfish in his mouth spilling half of it on the floor before pulling a long rib bone from his lips. He delivered a devilish smile. "I'm gonna be a driver," he said, picking at his teeth with the fish bone. "Gonna work my way up." Ezekiel shook his head. "Jimmie, I already told you. I don't want to hear it." Jimmie slammed his fist on the table. "I don't give a damn if you want to hear it! You're gonna know this, I ain't never working for no white folks again! Ever!" Ezekiel set his knife and fork down, leaned back in his chair, and gave his son his full attention. Jimmie grinned. "I already got me a few clients. I deliver to 'em real regular." Ezekiel watched as Hattie wiped a tear from her cheek.

"I already told you, I don't want to hear anymore of this nonsense, but Jimmie..." Ezekiel said glaring at his son, "...if you do this, I don't want you coming back here. I don't want none of that mess here nor around your sister." Jimmie laughed like a wildman and crammed more food into his mouth. He chewed it and swallowed it with a gulp of water."It's always about Hattie. Poor little Hattie," Jimmie said, sneering and poking at his sister. She jerked away from his touch. "Leave her alone, Jimmie," Ezekiel warned. "Leave her alone. Leave her alone. Why? You gonna cry, Hattie?" Jimmie sneered. "Okay, I'll leave her alone. I'll leave you all alone." Jimmie went to his room and slammed the door. Ezekiel stood up and set his plate in the sink. The tension eased but as Hattie exhaled a floodgate of tears spilled over and Zeke couldn't even turn to look at her. He walked down the hall and knocked on Jimmie's door.

"Leave me alone," Jimmie shouted from behind the door. "I want you out of here in the morning," Ezekiel responded.

Sleep hadn't come. Ezekiel spent the night tossing and turning. He sat on the edge of his bed thumbing through the pages of his well-worn bible and turned to Psalm 91. He knew the psalm by heart, but wanted to see the words on the page, maybe just to reassure himself of God's protection. As he read out loud, his hand followed the words on the worn pages. "He that dwelleth in the secret place of the most High, shall abide under the shadow of the Almighty." He recited the psalm while he walked through the house as if it were building a fortification around them. He finished the prayer in Hattie's room before he brushed the curls from her face and kissed her forehead. The thought of something happening to her tore at his heart; Jimmie's decision would have consequences for everyone. He tried to push those thoughts from his head and got ready to leave for work.

November 14, 1929

Dear Lord,

The country is going crazy. Those poor folks lost all their money and they're jumping from buildings. I just don't understand. There's still plenty to live for. Help them, Lord. Help them understand all isn't lost. My heart just hurts looking at the newspaper. Irene came by to pick up my embroidery and bring me my pay. She brought a few newspapers and it's so hard to believe. What's happening?

Irene stayed for a bit today. She brought lunch, a warm shepherd's pie and a bottle of fresh milk. Randall was all bundled up because of the cold, but he kept trying to break out. He's so wiggly now and trying to get around. He's trying to scoot and crawl and he rolled right off the bed.

Irene held Randall and rocked him and kept saying how handsome he is. I think so, too!

Irene said my brother asked about me. She told him to come see me for himself. My heart longs to see him, but truth be told, I can't handle any more rejection.

We're going into our second winter here and I am so much more confident. Maybe I've grown thicker skin. The cold is biting, but not bothersome. I'm not as scared, but I still can't bring myself to kill the rat with his beady eyes.

Randall is asleep. I need to get to bed, too. It's warm under the blankets. We read the bible every night. Tonight I read how Mary was in the manger with baby Jesus. I feel a kindred spirit toward her, especially sleeping on our hay-filled mattress. She's a mama and people didn't like her baby either. She had to leave town and go to a place she didn't know. She had to wash diapers and scrub mud out of clothes. She probably had to sew new outfits every time Jesus hit a growth spurt. I bet she got spit up on her clean dress and I'm sure that late in the night she sat next to her baby watching him as he slept all tuckered out from playing all day. I think she smiled as she watched him and tousled his hair under the soft flickering glow of an oil lamp just like me. The day she gave him up on the cross must have brought unbearable pain. Is there any greater love than that of a parent and child? How'd you do it Lord? How'd you give your son for us?

CHAPTER 13

Olympia, Mississippi
November 1929

Drew sat in Ezekiel's chair with a pinstripe cape draped over him. He was getting a cut and a shave which he never usually did. His boys sat along the wall, their eyes glued to the face of the radio. Their mule stood just beyond the broad glass window waiting patiently. The boys listened to the comedy show and laughed while they waited. Ezekiel popped a towel and wrapped it around Drew's neck. "So how'd she seem?"

Drew shrugged and replied, "Better than most."

"She paid what you asked?"

"Yep, and didn't even haggle. But then again most white folks don't. They either pay or send you on."

Ezekiel nodded as he picked out Drew's hair before he sent the clippers humming. "She look like she's eating?"

"Well, she's pretty slim but none worse for the wear. She was splitting wood and got her garden all ready for winter. House looks good. I think she plugged up them gaps in the boards. Looks like some new pieces of siding are up."

Ezekiel kept trimming while Drew talked. Every time somebody came through the door a burst of bitter air rushed in and you could see folks tense up against the chill. A heaviness suffocated the room and it was unusually quiet.

"Baby is fat and happy. Giggled at the sight of us. She let the boys hold him while she got us a jar of strawberry jam. Said she made it herself. Real nice lady. Why do you care so much anyway?"

"I don't know," Ezekiel answered. He prayed more than once for Jena and her baby. He'd find peace then worry would sneak right back in a day or so later. Drew was still talking but he wasn't listening. He wasn't sure why he was so concerned. Maybe he felt some obligation. He hated thinking the worst of his son. It was hard to believe Jimmie could have been a part of what happened to that girl, but Ezekiel didn't want to be naive. People changed. Jimmie had changed. Just a few weeks earlier a customer sat in his chair with a story about a fight in a club on the east side. Ezekiel knew by the description that it was Jimmie. Nobody could say what started the fight. Ezekiel imagined his son started it, just like he had in the diner. Jimmie was arguing and the man he was squabbling with doubled up his fist and knocked Jimmie to the ground.

The kid telling the story said some bootleggers came in and drug Jimmie out to a waiting truck and left. Ezekiel rubbed his head with the back of his hand and worried he'd never see his son again. He knew men didn't play when it came to their money. Jimmie was playing a dangerous game.

Where had he gone wrong? Ezekiel wondered while he worked. He looked over at Drew's boys and realized he just wanted what every parent wanted for their kids; hard working, honest, and responsible. Kids who would surpass their parents achievements and live productive lives. He'd given Jimmie everything he could and now he had no means to help his son other than to pray. Jimmie was grown and had to make his own decisions, even if they were down a dark road. Jimmie grew up in a loving house and never knew a day of hunger or hardship, but he could never let go of what happened to his mama. Then her long painful death from the cancer sent Jimmie over the edge. It had only been a few years since her passing. It was still raw and painful. He pushed the thoughts away, refocused, and set to work on Drew's hairline. He added a side part in the short afro. Drew looked in the mirror. "Man, Zeke. I'm feelin' pretty fly right now. This is fancy," he said, patting his hair. "I like it."

"Wait till we get you shaved, you're really going to dig that." He went over to the strap and wet it with a bit of water and began sharpening the blade. The boys caught sight of him and asked if they could try. "Sure, come on," Ezekiel said and waved them over. He let them dip their fingers in a cup of water and wet the strap. He helped the elder boy first, placing the blade in his hand and showed him how to draw the blade down the strap just right. He fingered the blade and said, "Good job."

"Zeke!" they said, excited by their brilliant idea. "Can we shave our dad?"

"Why not?" Zeke answered smiling and looking at Drew who had a look on his face that said, "Don't even play like that." The boys begged for a yes, but Ezekiel said, "Not this time boys." Their shoulders slumped and they went back to the radio until it was their turn in the chair.

Drew's boys were funny and Ezekiel enjoyed their banter while they were in the shop. "Zeke," they asked, "You hear about them white folks jumpin' out of them tall buildings up North?"

"I sure have. Who hasn't seen them pictures?"

"We was just thinkin' how dumb they was. I mean they ain't lost everything. They's still white."

Ezekiel laughed. "Well, you got that right. They ain't lost that."

Drew looked at himself one good time in the mirror. "Whoooee, Zeke." He fingered his smooth chin. "I am looking good." He turned his face sideways in the mirror to get a better view. It seemed like he wasn't paying attention to the conversation until he said," Ya'll know them white folks is crazy. Lose all their money and just quit. Shoot! If black folks did that every time they didn't have no money, wouldn't be no more black folks." The room erupted with laughter. "You right, Drew," Joe shouted from across the room.

Drew went on. "You see, black folks are survivors. We been through plenty and we don't quit," he said tapping on his chest. A round of "Amens" went around the room. "Damn straight," Joe added.

Fred piped up to get his two cents in. He pushed his glasses up on his face and folded his arms across his chest and said, "The papers don't got good news. They say everybody's going broke. No work, no food, no money. People losing their houses."

Eli looked up from his game of checkers. "They say it's gonna affect the whole country. People's scared."

Drew's voice rose, strong and prophetic. "It ain't coming down here and I'll guarantee black folks will be just fine. We know how to live poor. We know how to make it, but them white folks and the people in the city are in for a shock."

"Yeah," Joe agreed, "We know that's right."

"I don't know about that," Fred said.

Drew added more. "You just make sure you plant your garden in the spring. Pickle your eggs for winter, stock up your cupboards and you'll make it just fine. Mark my words. Mississippi's still gonna have fishin' and huntin'. When the city folk run out of food we're gonna be alright. You ain't gonna catch me standin' in no line beggin' nobody. I wouldn't be one of those folks heading North. Ain't gonna be no jobs for whites or blacks. There's goin' be trouble, black folks are goin' to be the last one hired and the first ones fired."

The room nodded in agreement. Everything Drew said made good sense. With the crash, everyone expected to tighten their belts, but like Drew said, black folks done made it through worse.

Claude finally chimed in, "Yeah, down here we can go huntin' and fishin'. What they gonna do?"

Joe looked at his brother sideways. "Man, shut up. When's the last time you went huntin' or fishin' big boy?"

"Awe, you shut up. I could if I had to. All you can do is run your mouth."

"You two, don't even get started," Ezekiel said, and changed the subject. "Drew, you better watch out, the barbershop ain't going out of business anytime soon, these boys are gonna need a shave here pretty soon. I see a couple of whiskers."

The focus shifted to Drew's boys and their voices that were growing deep and new patchy whiskers that were poking out. The fear that shadowed the room when they first started drifted away. Drew's strong words rang true and people were encouraged that despite bad news across the country, they could make it.

Winter passed and Ezekiel nor Hattie had seen or heard from Jimmie. Life in Olympia moved forward strong and steady despite the effects of the market crash that hit northern cities hard. Folks in Olympia felt the grip of depression that plagued the country, but pressed on with steadfast knowing how to live when times were tough.

Work remained steady for Hattie at the hospital and the barbershop kept their regulars. Jena sewed, embroidered, and knit over the winter months and spent most of her extra earnings on kerosene so she could embroider even after the light of the sun dwindled. Her work was recognized in multiple boutiques and she had a steady client base, which brought a little relief as images in the paper grew steadily worse.

November 20, 1929

Dear Lord,

Thanksgiving is coming, but I'm not feeling thankful. In fact, I'm in a mood. I realize I'm starting to become scared of other people, being alone so long has made me wary. I don't want to go anywhere and I feel out of sorts, fearful. I know that I dwell on the wrong things. Most often, I dwell on things I cannot change, yet I desperately want to change. I want my family back. I miss them dearly. I long for the love I felt as a child and I try to give it to Randall, but I know what I have to offer him is not the same as what I received as a girl. I feel guilty. I was surrounded by family and love, warmth, gentleness, safety, and financial security; we never knew a day of lack. These are the things I know I can't pass on to my son and it pains me.

I hate that I'm so desperate for them. I carry an emptiness like an old deserted well echoing its loneliness. I don't want this to consume me, I want to cling to hope but it evades me.

My parents would love Randall if they met him.

I Thank You, Lord, for never leaving us.

CHAPTER 14

Olympia, MS
December 1929

Irene came a few days before Christmas to have a slice of Jena's pecan pie and a cup of tea. She brought Jena's wages which were substantial. Christmas shoppers had been generous. There would be enough to pay another year of rent and a little extra for savings.

Irene rocked back and forth updating Jena on the town news and of their old friends. She didn't have news of her family, but she brought small gifts for Jena and Randall. The toddler was curled up on the bed sawing logs, his mouth hanging open and a stream of drool pooling on the pillow. Jena stroked his curls before she bent down and pulled a slim box tied with twine from beneath the bed and handed it to Irene. "I made it for you." Irene fingered the box and began to tug at the string. "Jena, you didn't have to." Jena blushed and stared at the planks that made up her floor. "I know," she said as she tucked her hair behind her ear, "but you've been such a good friend to me and I don't know what I'd do without you." Irene sighed as if she regretted what was to come. She opened the box, unfolded the tissue and pulled out the scarf embroidered with a Peruvian Lily. "Jena, this is so beautiful. Thank you." She got up out of the rocker and wrapped her arms around Jena's neck. Jena whispered in her ear. "You've been an answer to my prayers." Irene pulled away and looked in Jena's eyes. "You're the best friend I ever had." They wrapped one another in a tight embrace. "I love you, Jena." "I love you too, Irene."

The well of loneliness grew deeper as Jena waved goodbye to her girlhood friend. Jena bundled herself with a shawl to ward off the cold as Irene drove down the long lane to the road and turned out of sight. She had a strong feeling it would be a long while before she saw Irene again.

March 15, 1930

Dear Lord,

It's spring and the new buds are sprouting. The trees have bright green on the tips of their branches and flowers are breaking through the frosty ground.

Can you believe my baby turned one today?! He's so big and walking all on his own. He stands on the porch and chucks rocks into the yard. After each throw he looks back to see if I'm watching, and when he does, I clap and he giggles. I love to hear his little laugh. I don't know if he'll be a southpaw or a righty, he throws with both. I just have to smile when the wind whips past us and blows his feathery curls all over. I just love him.

My pages have run out in my journal. I'll have to make a new one. I've got some pieces of fabric I'll make a cover with those. Writing helps me. I still have nightmares, not as many as I used to.

In my dreams, people are chasing me, and I'm trying to get away, but I can't. I want it to stop but it doesn't. It plays over and over. My life changed, crushing me into the darkness, burying me under its weight. It makes me cringe. In my dream I try to scream from that deep, dark place. My mouth is bound and I can't get the words out. J-J-Jes-Jesus.

Someday I'll be free from them.

PART TWO

CHAPTER 15

Olympia, Mississippi
1955

Sitting on the lime green sofa, Steven leaned back and fidgeted. Ezekiel had been in the back room for over fifteen minutes. He knew Ezekiel hadn't fallen asleep or something like that because he could hear him rumbling around. Steven called out, "Ezekiel, is everything okay?" "Yeah, be out in a minute."

After ten more minutes Ezekiel came to the front and placed four books on the coffee table before Steven. The first was a black leather-bound bible. Steven looked up at Ezekiel. "May I?" Ezekiel nodded. "Go ahead." The pages were worn and on the inside jacket cover were births and deaths. There were Randall's grandparents; Mr. Isaiah Randall Wilson and Ms. Audry Amanda Fender and their wedding date. Below their names were Joseph Randall Wilson and Jena Maryanne Wilson alongside their birthdates. Underneath Jena's name, in tiny neat cursive, was Randall Isaiah Wilson born March 15, 1929. There was no father listed.

Most of the pages had notes and cross references marked neatly in pencil. Dates were marked in the margins; he imagined the dates were days someone read those pages. There were drawings on a few pages next to appropriate scriptures. The bible was worn thin and barely holding the soft pages together. Steven set the bible down and looked at the other three books. He could tell they were journals. The first was leather bound with two long straps of leather to tie the journal closed. The second had a delicately quilted cover and upon opening, had the same tiny neat cursive as the bible. The last journal was hand-bound with a paper mache cover decorated with dried flowers and pressed leaves. It, too, had the same writing, but a little less neat, somewhat unsteady.

Steven looked at Ezekiel. "Whose are these?"

"Randall's mama. She wrote those journals."

Steven thumbed through the books. One had a loose paper with a fading print of a baby's hand. There was a photograph of a youngster. He held it up and asked, "Randall?" There was a catch in Ezekiel's answer. "Yeah."

He picked the bible back up. It felt warm and alive. The words, the markings, the notes had life as they leapt off the page at him. A pressed rose lay in the center. Steven wondered if it were from a special event. He imagined it bright, crimson, and full of life. "Her brother's casket. Died on the beaches of Normandy," Ezekiel said. Steven fingered it and put it back.

Ezekiel sipped his pop, leaned back and started talking. "Randall came out of nowhere. He was like a tornado dropping down out of the sky on a clear blue day. He was tearin' teams up, frustrating pitchers, stealing bases like nobody's business. He could drop a ball in a gap and make it to first with time to spare. He pitched for a while, but he was mostly in the outfield because he was fast. He'd play anywhere if it would help his team get on a winning streak." Ezekiel closed his eyes and immersed himself in the memory. "I used to love to watch him. He had real passion for the game."

Ezekiel sat up and leaned forward. His eyes lit up, a youthful vigor washed over him. "That boy used to try and wallop that ball out of the park every single day. He wasn't no Josh Gibson, but it didn't stop him from tryin' and he was so fast chasing down balls he'd rob hitters of a four bagger. He made it look effortless."

Steven nodded. He'd seen Randall outrun a ball. It looked so graceful and easy, folks in the stands complained he wasn't even trying hard. "Did you ever see him in Cuba?" Steven asked.

"No. I never did make it. One of my regrets. I hear that was some of his best ball."

"I thought so," Steven agreed.

"I've seen a few pictures of him there." Ezekiel choked up. "He was young and strong. He was smart about the game, studied players, knew their tendencies." Ezekiel smiled remembering the little guy who used to edge off the bag and strategize over how he was going to steal the next base. "Even in those photos you could tell how much he loved the game. They really captured his spirit."

"I remember a photographer that Randall seemed to know well. He took some incredible pictures that helped launch Randall's career."

Ezekiel nodded and rubbed his head. "Yeah, I suspect he did. Good fella. He's a real good fella, that photographer."

The pair sat in silence for a short while until Ezekiel dozed off. Steven took the next few hours and read through the journals. He read the last page, closed the journal, and set the diary on the coffee table. The words were a legacy poured from a heart and onto these worn pages. They were honest and real, some were heavy, some were light and touched with joy, while others cut with pain. He ran his hand through his hair and sighed. "Wow, I had no idea."

Ezekiel roused from his sleep. He rubbed his face, said nothing but got up and took the empty glasses to the kitchen. He was dismissive.

"Come back next week. I'll have a little something for you." Steven nodded in acceptance, placed his hands on his knees, got up from the couch, and let himself out the front door.

CHAPTER 16

Havana, Cuba
Winter 1946

Rich horns wailed a lonely tune as strings on the guitar plucked the same woeful song. Pup-pup-pa-pa-paaa… Tonight the horn wasn't fast and loud like Satchmo's Dinah. No, tonight the trumpets matched his longing for home. He sat at a table, took the last bite of the rich red stew with rice. The Ropa Vieja was his favorite. Savory and sweet. Instead of a side of beer he'd have coconut milk. He fell in love with the food and the people, genuine and hospitable. Even his teammates were generous, sharing their homes and families. His Spanish was getting to where he could have small conversations. The women were some of the most beautiful he'd ever seen in their brightly colored dresses at wild parties. Tourists loved Havana. This time of year there was no better place to be.

Dancers spun in tiered dresses while toes tapped the rumba. Randall smiled knowing he had finally mastered the footwork during his year-long stay. Playing in Cuba was better than barnstorming across the U.S. and the living conditions were better, too. He had his own room with a sink and a shared bathroom down the hall which was better than sleeping in a field next to the baseball diamond. He'd done that more times than he wanted to count.

A young lady reached her hand out to him. He thought to refuse, but decided against it. Her red dress was enticing like a flag firing up a bull. He caught the rhythm saturating his bones. His shoulders moved to the drums while his feet made small quick steps.

His linen shirt dripped with perspiration. Her hand lingered on his chest. The song ended and with two quick kisses, one on each cheek, he returned to his table to wait on his teammates.

Randall heard Alvarez before he saw him. "Hey, my man!" Randall stood to give his buddy a quick hug. "What's up? Where is everybody?" Randall asked. "They'll be here. You know they're always late."

The music pulsed through the room. "You played well today my friend. Maybe some of your best yet. You're hitting is going to get you noticed. There were scouts out there!" Randall sipped his drink. "That's the plan," He grinned.

"I don't think I've ever seen anybody score off a walk by stealing bases. How you do that?"

Randall laughed. "You just gotta be fast."

"I guess you do. You took second and third on a steal. And then you take home on a sacrifice fly."

"You gotta do what you gotta do." Randall felt puffed up. The team entered the room. The pitcher, Jose, bought drinks. "Randall! That was the best show I've seen from a young dude in a long time. Too bad you're headed back to the States. We'd keep you with us down here year round."

The pair clapped hands and hugged. "I love being down here. If I didn't miss home so much, I'd stay."

"Find a girl. She'll help you forget all about home my man." Randall laughed. "But seriously bro, you're gonna make it in the bigs. Keep showing those American white boys what you can do. Open the door for the rest of us."

Randall swallowed hard. "I will."

Jose turned to the crowd, "Oye, everybody. Tonight Randall here is the hero of the night. Drinks are on me!" He lifted a glass and the room cheered. People came by to show their respect. Randall felt like a celebrity.

Trumpets blared, pup-pup-pa-pa-paaa. Tambourines tapped against palms, light flickered and drinks were poured. The Fuegos ball club celebrated their 1-0 win over the Reds - an all white team from the States. Tomorrow night they'd play for the Championship, but for now, they'd celebrate. After the midnight toll of the bells, Randall excused himself and headed back down the flower-lined boulevard.

Visitors swayed in the streets just outside cantinas, imbibed, dancing to the rattle of the maracas still shaking in the night. Randall rubbed his face trying to stay awake for the short walk to the house. Havana had taught him many things in his few years of winter ball. It was nothing like home, but then it was. There were good folks who had embraced him as one of their own and there were bad ones that might try and do you harm.

Here, he'd seen Major Leaguers play with fellas from the Negro Leagues, Mexico and parts of South America were represented and the Cubans hosted them all. The one thing he didn't miss in the States was the constant focus on race. He just wanted to play ball. He rarely mentioned home or his people, but they were at the forefront of his mind, tugging at his heart.

There was a rustling behind him. He hoped it was nothing. Late at night people got robbed. He hoped the group behind him were just vagabond vacationers. He could hear their slurred English. Without looking back he tucked his hands in his pockets and kept going.

"Randall, stop! Wait up!" a voice shouted. "Randall! Hey, I know you!"

Randall didn't want to turn around, didn't want to be bothered. He wanted sleep. He ignored the person hoping they'd give up and go back to whatever they were doing. "Randall, come on man, it's me!" Randall picked up his pace. It was a thump to the back of the head that finally stopped him. He turned. "Did you just hit me with a rock?"

"Yeah. I hit you with a rock. What are you gonna do about it?"

Randall moved cautiously, squinting in the darkness, trying to identify the person. They were American, that much he was sure of. "Randall, you don't recognize me? Boy, I'd recognize you anywhere!"

April 20, 1934

Dear Lord,

As far back as I can remember I used to stay with my granny. We'd bake and eat sweet cakes and there'd be a few leftovers for me to take home. I felt safe curled up in her lap. I spent my days with Granny and she'd let me help her press the sheets after they hung on the line. Then she'd let me help her fold them. I remember running my hand across the warm cotton right at the edge of the fold, I'd lean over and sniff the sweet smell of lavender she put in the wash water. I learned a lot of things from my granny.

Why can't my son know his granny and his granddaddy? No daddy, no relatives. Why Lord? Why can't he have a granddaddy and a granny to love on him, to shower him with kisses and tell him he's handsome?

I saw my mama today. She ducked and hid when she saw us. She acted like she didn't know us and that hurt me real bad. Even so, I wish they'd want to see Randall, play with him, love on him. I wish my daddy would teach him how to play checkers and push him on a rope swing till he giggles so hard he thinks he'll fall off. And maybe, he would lose his grip and fall, getting a little scrape, but then his granddaddy would pick him up and dust him off, tell him he's alright, give him a pat on the bottom, and do it all over again.

He's got a bit of them in him. He's his own person, but he does things that remind me of them. When he laughs, he squints his eyes and grabs his belly just like Daddy. He pats me on the shoulder when he hugs me just like Mama. It makes me miss 'em every time. Lord, do You think they will ever forgive me? Do You think they'll ever welcome us?

My feelings got all stirred up when I went to the barbershop today. Hattie said it would be okay, and it was. The barber, Ezekiel, was so nice. He offered to keep Randall while I go to work. He's gonna let him work off his haircut. It's strange, I don't know if I feel guilty or sad. I know it's wrong leaving Randall with someone I don't even know, but what choices do I have?

I can keep leaving Randall by himself, but he's only five. I can't imagine my mama leaving me that young. I feel real guilty because I'm gone before the sun rises and back long after it sets. I think it's better if he's with someone.

Even if I don't have a husband and Randall doesn't have a daddy, I know You've been here with us. I know it with everything in me. I know when we had nobody, we had You. You never left us and I thank You Lord. I sure do. I don't know what we would do without You.

I better go to sleep and not burn all this candle. Good night, Lord. Tomorrow is going to be an early day. Help me through it. I sure am tired. Please help Randall be helpful at the barbershop.

CHAPTER 17

Olympia, MS
April 21, 1934

Skipping down the sidewalk with his hand tucked securely in his mother's, Randall whistled "happy birthday to me" even though his birthday wasn't anywhere close. It was rare for him and his mother to have company and completely unheard of for her to let him stay with anybody. In fact, he'd never stayed with anybody, not that anyone had ever invited him to stay, either. He was unsure why his mother said yes, but it didn't matter, he liked Zeke the moment he saw him. His dark skin and bald head appealed to him and he liked the way his shoes clicked on the tiles, making a nice rhythm. He liked it so much so, he tried to make his own shoes click as he skipped. He was sure he could do it if only his mom would let go of his arm and stop jerking him back every few steps.

The morning was cool but the day would warm up quick. He reached under his jacket and reattached the strap to his overalls that kept falling down. Mama said she'd fix them, but the one strap just always popped off. Randall rubbed his head to make sure his stubble was in place like Zeke had shown him. When Randall had gone home, before bed, he'd brushed and brushed and brushed it until his mama told him to stop. Even this morning he'd crammed his brush in his pocket. His overalls were pressed and neat, but maybe a bit too small. The hem was above his ankles, but below his knees. His boots were laced up and brushed clean, the best he could do. Mama always made him brush them and keep them real clean, 'specially since they were his only pair.

Before he knew it they were standing in front of the barbershop. He felt an excitement rare to his five-year-old body. His mother had never left him in someone else's care. Recently she'd left him when she went to her new job and he'd stayed home by himself. She'd given him strict instructions to not leave the house, not even to go in the garden. He wasn't scared then and he wasn't scared now.

He was busting at the seams knowing he'd get to stay with Zeke and work to pay off his brush and tin of hair grease. The hope of today had been churning over and over in his head since Zeke mentioned it the day before.

His mom stopped at the front door and before she grabbed the handle she bowed her head and prayed. He could hear her ask God to guide her, to stop her if this wasn't His provision. After Randall heard her say Amen, he cut in. "Mom, hurry. Can we go inside?"

"Hush, son. Give me a minute." She bowed her head again. "Help me, Lord. Help me, Jesus." She lifted her head with renewed confidence, grabbed the door handle and pulled. The bell over the door jingled. The smell of bacon drifted through the barber shop causing Jena's stomach to growl. Zeke called from the back, "Come on in. I'm back here." Randall tugged at his mom's hand, pulling her toward the back. Her hand trembled and fear rose up. She wasn't sure why. As the pair turned the corner she saw Zeke standing in front of a stove stirring a pot of grits and frying bacon. Randall broke free and ran toward Zeke. "Hi Zeke!" he shouted, "Are you glad to see us?"

Zeke reached out to give Randall a hug. "I sure am. You ready to work, little man?"

"Yeah!"

Jena stood in the doorway of the small washroom. She glanced around and saw that it was outfitted with a small stove and an icebox. Four chairs sat at a small round table that was set for three. Ezekiel saw her looking and asked, "Can you stay?" She shook her head looking at the floor. "Awe, come on, Mom." Randall pulled at her hand. "Honey, I can't. I have to get going. I can't be late."

Ezekiel walked to the icebox. "Don't leave just yet. I got a little something for you." He pulled out a ham sandwich wrapped in newspaper, an apple, and a jar of milk. Jena put her hands up and shook her head rejecting the food. "I couldn't," she said even as her stomach growled again. Ezekiel ignored her refusal and grabbed a knapsack hanging on a peg. He tucked the food in it along with a napkin and a thick slice of fried bacon. He placed the bag in her hand and gently he turned her toward the door. "Don't worry, everything will be alright." She nodded and before she got to the front door she managed to say, "Thank you." Ezekiel patted her shoulder. "You're welcome, sweetie. Take care at work today." She wiped her eyes and passed through the doorway. Randall hollered after his mama, "Don't worry, Mama, I'll work hard like ya taught me!" She blew kisses to him before she turned and hurried down the street.

June 1, 1934

Dear Lord,

I ran my hand through my hair and it's falling out in clumps. Lord, what's wrong with me? Is it all the worryin' I'm doing?

I don't know the barber, but Hattie said I can trust him and I know I can trust her. She's been so good since the day Randall was born. These folks have been kinder than family. Thank You for sending me good people.

It's been a long time since we've seen Hattie. She always says, "Everybody needs somebody." I hope all is well with her and she isn't in need. I don't know where to find her other than the hospital, but I'd never go there to look for her. I'd be scared I might get her in trouble.

Hattie used to visit more, and when she did she would rock Randall and read to him. He'd sit in her lap and laugh as she used different voices to read. She'd tell him about Noah and the ark with all the animals. He'd giggle when she'd make noises for each animal. He'd gaze into her blue eyes captivated by something he saw there. I could always take a nap because peace would settle in the house and I'd drift off into a sweet dream. It's been so long, I don't know if Randall would remember her if he saw her.

I hope Randall behaves tomorrow. I don't really know what he'll do, he's never been left with anyone. I know I keep saying that but it's true and seems so odd. When I left him today he was so excited and when I picked him up he was just chattering the whole way home. I'm his mama and I didn't even know he could talk that much. If I wasn't already bone tired, all his talkin' wouldda done wore me out.

These long days have me tuckered out. On my feet the whole day on the flab line with pork carcasses. We don't get a break and the smell makes me gag. I just want to vomit. The first week I started, I ran out a few times. The foreman yelled at me, told me if I run out or get sick again he'd fire me, so no matter how sick I feel or how bad I want to throw up, I never run out anymore. We pack the pork with salt and put it in barrels to be shipped by rail across the country.

I need to pay Mr. Redding. We got nothing right now, but I trust You, Lord. You brought us this far already. I know You'll see us through.

CHAPTER 18

Olympia, MS
June 1934

A little light-skinned boy darted this way and that with a broom in hand. He swept between each of the barber chairs trying his best to keep it clean, challenging himself to catch the clumps of hair before they touched the floor. Fred, a regular at the shop, called over to Ezekiel. "Zeke, where'd ya find this little whipper snapper? He's pretty fast." Randall looked up and smiled, clearly encouraged by the old timer's comment.

"That little guy?" Ezekiel said, pointing a comb at Randall. "Ah, he just turned up on my doorstep one mornin'." "Well, what's he doin' here everyday? He's so busy runnin' all over the place, he's makin' me tired."

Laughter circled the room. Randall's presence brought a fresh new energy to the shop that was unmistakable. Claude and Joe, Ezekiel's younger brothers, had taken to Randall right quick but some of the regulars were takin' a little more time to adjust. "Awe Fred, don't mind him, he's just workin' off some debt." Claude said before he started working his clippers.

"Claude, you just hush, I can't take all that runnin' around." Fred looked over at Randall. "Come here, boy." Obedient, Randall placed the broom in the corner and went over to the small table where Fred was sitting, stood up straight and put his hand in his pockets before looking at Fred. "Boy, what's your name?"

Wide-eyed and alert, Randall answered, "Hello sir, my name is Randall. What's yours?" Fred seemed a little startled by the boy's boldness. Ezekiel watched the exchange in the mirror as he continued to cut.

Fred rubbed his chin, taking in the boy before him. "Well, I'm Fred. I been here a long time and I never seen you."

"I'm new, sir. Zeke gave me a job. I'm workin' to pay for my hair cut." Fred nodded, studying the boy. He wanted him to say who his people were and where he'd come from, but he hadn't said any of those things, so Fred asked a few more questions. "Well, how old are ya?" "I'm five, sir." Randall said, pulling his hand from his pocket and holding up five fingers. "Well that's fine, real fine." Fred rubbed the stubble on his chin a little more. "Can you play checkers?" "No, sir."

Fred nodded his head toward the front window where a checkerboard and soda pop tops sat. "Go on over there and get that board and the pop tops and I'll teach ya." Randall turned to look at Ezekiel who was still cutting, and waited for approval. "Go ahead, Randall. You can sweep between cuts," Ezekiel said. Randall bustled over to the checkerboard and grabbed it with the can of pop tops, delivering it to the table in front of Fred.

Dumping the bottle tops onto the checkerboard he began to explain how to play. "Now see here, you take these bottle caps," he said, counting out twelve tops for each of them. "Mine are gonna be right side up and yours are gonna be upside down. See, that's how we know whose are whose." Randall bobbed his head up and down as he fingered the pop tops. After setting up the board and showing Randall how the pieces moved, they played a few practice rounds. The little guy's eyes lit with delight as he figured out how to jump and take pieces. After multiple rounds, Randall began to demand to play more and more as his eyes darted across the board memorizing Fred's moves. At the end of each loss, with more enthusiasm than a horse on race day, Randall would say, "Let's play again!" Fred finally got fed up. "Boy, ain't ya got no quit in ya? That's enough for today. I see a whole bunch of hair that needs sweepin'." Randall looked disappointed and begged for one more. Taken by the young lad's charm, Fred agreed. "Alright. One more. But only one." Methodically, as he'd seen Fred do in previous games, Randall moved his pieces, capturing several of Fred's pieces. The barbershop was roaring with laughter. "Fred, you'd better watch out. That little fella is about to beat you."

Fred scowled. "Man, I'm not gonna let no kid beat me." He double jumped and took two of Randall's pieces. Claude laughed. "Maybe today you won't, but real soon. Git him, Randall!"

Randall grinned his toothless grin and nodded. "I will."

Fred won in the next seven moves, but the fire for victory had been lit and little Randall found himself spending his free time playing checkers with anyone who'd give him the time of day. Slowly, he started beating some of the less experienced and those wins fueled his hunger to conquer.

CHAPTER 19

Olympia, MS
June 1935

Ezekiel dusted his hands off and put the lawn mower back in the shed. The fresh cut grass stained the hem of his pants. Randall stood in the middle of the outfield squatting with his hands outstretched as if waiting for a ball to be hit to him. In the past year, the little guy had grown at least an inch and he was smart, he understood the game. He could anticipate and get to where the ball would be and he was focused. Like a hounddog on a scent, Randall was relentless and he didn't quit. Ezekiel watched him as he moved from side to side, his motion was fluid, much more than was normal for a six year old. Ezekiel headed to the outfield where Randall was throwing the ball as far as he could, and chasing after it. He was a non-stop bundle of limitless energy. Ezekiel gave Randall a small bat and showed him how to let the bat rest in his hands and wrap his fingers around the neck, letting the weight of the bat pull it forward. Randall closed his eyes and swung, feeling the easy glide as gravity helped him. The bat was still too heavy for him to swing clean through the strike zone. He attempted to hoist it on his shoulder, the weight of it tipped him forward causing him to stumble, but that didn't deter him. He heaved the bat back up and tried again and again, asking over and over when Ezekiel was going to let him hit. "You gotta be able to swing that thing first, little man," Ezekiel said laughing.

The sun was about four hours from setting, plenty of time to run some energy out of him. His mama hadn't been getting back before dark. If she missed the last bus she had to walk the whole way. Often it was way too late for her to get back and start cookin', much less for her and Randall to walk home. It had been just over a year and the routine of six days a week was really wearing on her. He knew from folks that worked at the meat plant, it was grueling work.

Ezekiel grabbed a bucket of baseballs and positioned Randall at home plate. "Stay right there. I'm going to pitch you some balls. We'll see if you can hit one." Randall heaved the bat up. "I'm gonna get a four bagger Zeke!" "Alright buddy, let's see it." Randall swung the bat and it thudded into the dirt. "Choke up on the bat Randall." The little guy moved his hands up on the bat and heaved it up again. "Bend your knees. Keep your eye on the ball." Randall nodded. "Here it comes." Randall watched it go by. "Well why didn't you swing? That was right over the plate."

"I didn't want that one."

"Okay, here comes another one." Ezekiel tossed the ball real slow, a nice underhand pitch.

"That's not a real pitch. You did it for babies. That's not how Joe does it. I don't think you know how to do it," Randall said matter-of-factly. He set the bat down and walked toward Ezekiel. He grabbed a ball and scooted next to Ezekiel. "Watch," Randall said, "You do it like this." With big wide motions Randall wound up, drew his arm up from behind him and chucked the ball toward home plate. It took a wild bounce before it rolled across the plate. Ezekiel grabbed his belly and laughed. "You gotta throw it like that Zeke." "Alright, little man. No more baby stuff for you." He took a few steps back. "Okay, you want a real pitch, here it comes."

Randall hoisted the bat back up, set his feet, and gave the bat a squeeze. "I'm ready." Ezekiel wound up and pitched the ball. As the ball left his hand Randall pulled the bat from his shoulder and swung. A plink of wood meeting leather sent the ball into the infield. Randall dropped the bat and darted toward first. Ezekiel laughed as the little fella ran the bags and slid into home.

Ezekiel pitched until sunset. "Go collect the balls in this here bucket. It's time to go make some supper." Randall slouched his shoulders. "Awe, do we have to?" Ezekiel rubbed Randall's head. "Hurry up, now." Obedient, Randall ran to pick up the balls.

Ezekiel boosted Randall to his shoulders, and walked home smiling as he listened to Randall tell him how he was going to hit homers and steal bases in the big leagues.

After their walk home, Ezekiel checked on dinner, he stirred the pot of beans and gave them a taste. "Let me try 'em, Zeke." Randall said, pulling a chair up to the stove. "Sure, little man," he said, offering a spoonful of beans. "Whadda ya think?" Randall smacked his lips. "I think a pinch of salt." "You sure are full of yourself today." "What's that mean, Zeke?" "Oh, nothin'," he said, passing the salt bowl to Randall. "Just grab a pinch and sprinkle it in." "Okay, okay. I can do it." Randall grabbed more than a pinch and dropped in a clump. Ezekiel scooped some back out before he let Randall give it a stir, his little face alight. "This is gonna be so good, Zeke!" he said, making two fists and pumping them. "You're right, little man. Chili beans and cornbread. My favorites." "Me, too!"

They made a plate for Jena and set it aside. He always sent something home for her so she didn't have to cook. She needed to keep up her strength, but Ezekiel knew she was wearing down, probably not used to prolonged hard labor, nothing beyond keeping her little garden and working around the yard. She had dark circles under her eyes and despite the meals, she grew thinner. Her arms were long and bony. Her long brown hair was thin and stringy. His biggest concern was that she'd developed a cough.

Still sitting at the table, Randall was shoveling food so fast his cheeks bulged like a chipmunk. He was growing like a weed. He scarfed up breakfast, lunch and dinner. He worked all day, sweeping the barbershop and toting towels to the front for the barbers. He'd become an instant star at the shop and customers enjoyed his youthful chatter. If he'd been shy in his first weeks, he wasn't anymore. The old timers who came by just to chat liked to play him at checkers. When Claude was on a break, he'd let Randall sit in his lap while he read the paper. It wasn't long before Randall was picking out words he recognized. The more he practiced the better he got. He could do simple sums and counted change. He knew all the prices for a cut, shave, and shoe polish. While he flourished, his mama diminished and Ezekiel worried. He prayed and asked the Lord for a solution or some help. Most anything had to be better than what Jena was doing now.

August 3, 1935

Dear Lord,

Help me, please. My arms are weak and my legs feel like lead, I can barely lift them to walk. It seems like my head is spinning all the time. I am afraid I'll collapse. The heat saps my strength. I'm sucking wind trying to catch my breath. Flies follow me for the stench of rotting flesh and pig guts. I need to wash, I need to cook, I need to eat, but I can't. The weight of fatigue drags me down. I want to close my eyes and never wake up. The fog clouding my mind makes my thoughts hazy and unclear. Sometimes I don't know what I'm doing. Help me, Jesus. One more day, then I can sleep.

Please Lord, give me rest.

CHAPTER 20

Olympia, MS
August 4, 1935

Saturday night, after her shift, Jena picked Randall up and they started their walk home. The muggy air was thick and seemed to press in making every movement difficult. Everything seemed to take longer; walking, talking, even breathing. The sun had set and the full yellow moon offered a modest reprieve from the heat that sapped folks spirit. Jena drug her feet while Randall tugged on her hand as he skipped along, wanting her to go faster. “Mama, can we go with Ezekiel tomorrow? He invited us to church. You don’t have to work, Mama. Please?” He tugged at her hand again. With her free hand she rubbed her forehead. “Randall, baby, stop tugging on me, please,” she said feeling woozy. “Mama, we’re gonna go to church and then the baseball game. Can we go? Please, Mama?”

“Randall, stop. I can barely think.” The constant fog that blurred her thoughts, the tops of the trees swirled. Her balance disrupted, she tumbled forward. She squeezed Randall’s hand as she fell forward, pulling him down with her. She hit the dirt with a thud. Her mouth opened and closed like a fish out of water. Randall scrambled to his feet and dusted his pants. When he realized his mama hadn’t gotten up, he grabbed her shoulder. “Mama,” he shouted. She couldn’t answer. “Mama!” he shouted again.

"Get up, Mama," he said, shaking her shoulders. He looked for help, but nobody was on the road at this hour.

"Mama," Randall said with a tremor in his voice. "Mama, are you okay?" he asked, shaking her. A wave of yellow bile came up. "Mama!" Randall shouted. She shook her head and put up a finger. Randall waited. Her body heaved in waves, she opened her mouth as if more were coming, she was thankful that nothing did. She wiped the back of her arm across her face.

Randall started to cry. He wanted to get help, but he didn't know who to get. Ezekiel was home but Randall didn't want to leave his mama alone. He looked around, frantic. "Mama," he said again. Jena rolled over and touched the strawberry-like bruise forming on her cheek.

"Help me up, Randall." Grabbing her forearm, he tried his best to pull his mama up. It took a few minutes before she was on her feet and it took an extra thirty minutes for them to get home. Once they were there, Jena dropped onto the bed and changed out of her work clothes. "Randall, go on and get yourself ready for bed." He obeyed but kept looking over to make sure she was okay. Her skin was pale and red splotches stained her cheeks. Her eyes glazed and her speech wasn't right. The weather was hot, but he knew the fever was coming.

Sitting on a small wooden stool she pulled the curtain to separate the room and give herself a bit of privacy. She bathed with a bucket of water and a soapy washcloth. She squeezed water over her head, the coolness soothed her face. She put on a clean nightgown and together they said their nightly prayers. Jena turned down the oil lamp and the room went dark. Randall could hear her labored breathing. He was scared and wanted to cry out, but he knew Mama wouldn't like that. He drifted off to fitful sleep. He was startled awake when his mama began to cough. Sometimes she couldn't stop, and sometimes there was blood. "Lord, help my mama."

Slipping out of bed he went over and pushed the curtain back gazing at her darkened form. He put his hand on her forehead. It was sweaty and hot. He got the rag from her wash bucket and put it on her head. She moaned and tossed about. He took her fan from the bedside table and began to swing it back and forth trying to make her cool again.

Daylight streamed through the window and Jena woke with an urge to shove off the weight bearing down on her. Instead, she reached down and realized it was Randall, his upper body sprawled across her with his legs dangling onto the floor. She smiled and stroked the waves he had been brushing and training every day. She listened to his rhythmic breathing, deep and strong. He still clutched her fan. While he snored she showered his face with kisses. He stirred, giggled, and feigned sleep for a few more minutes. "Good morning, little man."

"Morning, Mama."

"Thank you for taking care of me last night."

Randall nodded while he laced and unlaced his fingers. Jena knew he did it when he was nervous or scared. "Anything wrong, buddy?"

He shook his head. "No."

"You sure?"

"Well, I get scared when you're sick."

Jena sighed. "Me too, buddy. Me, too."

"Can't you just go to the doctor?"

"No. I don't know any doctors that would see me."

Randall nodded as if he understood. "Well, can't we just pray and Jesus will heal you like the blind man?"

"I think that's a real good idea. Why don't we do it right now and then we'll sing and read our bible, then we can make some breakfast."

"Yeah, Mama! That's a great idea." The invite to church and the baseball game were completely forgotten. He lay in the bed with his mama singing, Blessed Art Thou O'Lord. She read miracles from the book of

Matthew and they prayed for healing. Randall made breakfast. He boiled water and poured in grits. He added a pinch of salt, or maybe a bit more than Mama did, and a spoonful of butter. He added the little cream they had left and stirred furiously so they wouldn't burn. He took them off the burner and set a plate as a cover on the pot and opened a jar of peaches. They ate till their bellies bulged and more than satisfied, Jena fell asleep until long after midday.

When Ezekiel drove up the lane in the late afternoon, Randall was squatting in front of the tomato plants picking bugs and weeds from the garden. "Hey, Randall." "Hey, Zeke!" Randall shouted, running to the car before Ezekiel got out. "How you doing, little man?" "Mama's still in the bed. She needed some extra sleep," Randall said. Ezekiel nodded. "You need me to bring y'all some supper?" As if on cue, a growl rumbled from Randall's belly. "Ummm…I dunno. I don't know if Mama would like it." Ezekiel tried to think of a way to bring some food without his mama being upset. Ezekiel asked about the bucket. "Little man, what's that for?" With great enthusiasm Randall ran over to show Zeke. "See, Zeke," Randall said, taking the lid off. "It's the bugs and weeds from our garden. I'm gonna feed 'em to our chickens. Mama says it helps them make more eggs."

"Yeah, your mama is a pretty smart. That's true. It's a lot of work for you."

"Oh no, Zeke. I like it. I get to pick all the bugs and then they don't get our food and the chickens get some special treats in the pail. They always like it when I come with the pail. You should see 'em Zeke, they go crazy."

"I bet they do," he said rubbing his chin, confident he had an idea that would be satisfactory to Ms. Jena and not offend. "Alright, little man. Well, I'm gonna go get me some lunch but I'll be back. I might bring you a lunch pail." Randall nodded with enthusiasm and giggled. "Like the chickens?"

"Yeah little man, like the chickens. If I bring you a pail with some treats, are you gonna go crazy like the chickens?"

Randall giggled some more and nodded his head. "I'll eat it all up. Just like the chickens."

"Alright then, a bug lunch bucket coming up!"

"Ewe, no! I mean like people food. I don't eat bugs!"

It was Ezekiel's turn to laugh. "Okay, I'll bring you something good."

Randall waved and went back to weed-pulling and bug-hunting.

When Ezekiel returned, Jena was still asleep and it was getting dark and well past supper time. He'd brought a couple sandwiches from Millie's and some fried catfish and greens. There was a few corn cakes, too. He'd stopped by the house and got a tin bucket to put it all in. Ezekiel didn't stay, but gave Randall the lunch pail and told him to go in and check on his mama. She was still asleep and she was sweaty like before. Randall went to draw water. He sat keeping watch and dabbing her face and arms with the washcloth. He thought she'd wake, but she didn't. She just moaned like the night before. After two more wipes Randall's stomach began to growl and he went to the table to eat what Ezekiel had brought. Randall tore into the catfish and gobbled down the corn cakes, almost forgetting to save one for Mama. He washed it all down with some greens and their dark juice. Because he forgot to pray he asked the Lord to forgive him and said a quick prayer. "Thank You, Lord, for that food it was real good. Help me grow big and strong to help my mama. Amen."

CHAPTER 21

Olympia, MS
August 17, 1935

The heat was still blistering, but the days were growing shorter and the leaves knew it was almost time to fall. Trees, dotted with yellow and orange, waved goodbye to the few that were already drifting from their lofty perches anticipating the coming winter. A strong gust rustled through the trees, the ball fields were still lush and green, lining the dusty infield dotted with white sandbags for bases.

The barbershop operated as if Randall had always been a part of it. Unlike Jena, Randall had quickly become a regular fixture around town, but she worked long days. She was up early and back late, she was hardly seen. Ezekiel wondered how she stayed on her feet. She seemed to have lost more weight when she didn't have any to lose. Ezekiel fretted like a father over a daughter. He prayed as he and Randall walked toward the baseball field. They were close enough to hear the crack of a bat and the roar of the crowd. Randall skipped along, tossing his baseball into the air and catching it with both hands.

There'd be a good few hours before dusk. Plenty of time for them to enjoy the game before Jena came back. Ezekiel offered to drop Randall off and wait for her to get home, but she said it wouldn't be proper. He didn't argue. It would look improper for him to be at her place late into the evening no matter what the reason.

The pair turned the corner and Ezekiel saw the peanut man, his small table lined with brown paper sacks filled with warm boiled peanuts. "Hey Randall, you want some boiled peanuts?"

"Hm?" he said, his little nose scrunching up in confusion. "What's that?"

Ezekiel laughed. "Haven't you ever had boiled peanuts?"

Randall stopped tossing his ball and looked at Ezekiel curiously. He shook his head. "No. I don't think so."

"Well, come on. We'll get a couple bags."

With his ball in one hand, he reached for Ezekiel's hand with the other. "Are they good?"

"You bet. You're gonna love 'em."

Ezekiel handed Randall a bag of peanuts. Eager, his hand dipped right into the bag, grabbed a peanut and popped it in his mouth, chewing the hull and all. Ezekiel grinned as a frown crossed Randall's little face, his mouth full of stringy, coarse peanut shells. He looked up at Ezekiel, confusion registering on his little face. Randall knew his mama would have his hide if he wasted food and spit the wad of chewed shells onto the ground. He just couldn't bring himself to swallow the blob in his mouth even as a stream of drool drizzled down the front of his shirt.

"So how you like 'em?"

Randall looked up, catching the hint of a laughter in Zeke's eyes. He shook his head and with a mouthful of goo and a slight whine he answered, "They're nasty."

"Well, go on. Spit 'em out."

Randall hesitated only a second before spitting bits of shell and peanut into the grass, wiping his tongue with the back of his hand.

Ezekiel reached into his own bag and pulled out a peanut showing it to Randall, he put it in his mouth and bit down to crack it. He pulled the shell apart with his fingers and showed Randall the two peanuts resting inside. Zeke took one out and popped it in his mouth leaving the second for Randall. Hesitant, he looked up into Ezekiel's face looking for direction. Ezekiel held his hand out. Slowly the boy reached for the peanut as if it were a snake about to strike. Cautiously, he took it in his tiny fingers and looked at it from different angles before putting it in his mouth. As he began to chew, a smile spread across his face. "It is good," he said as he reached into his own bag to try it for himself. He got the shell split in two and tipped his head back and dumped the meat into his mouth. Within minutes Randall was a pro cracking shells. He got into a rhythm where he'd suck on 'em a second before going after the meat inside. Ezekiel laughed, watching as Randall crammed his fist in the bag over and over.

They continued on down the street toward the field and found seats down the left field line. Half the town was out in the warm afternoon enjoying the games hosting local boys against a barnstorming team that had come through. The real excitement was the Negro leagues were expected to come play soon. They'd host two or three games in a day and the town was already buzzing with excitement. Baseball had the heart of the people. It would be as big of a celebration as the fourth of July!

"Randall, you know what?" "What, Zeke?" "If there were two times you can guarantee people will come together, it's church and baseball." Randall nodded, accepting this bit of wisdom. "Yeah, I like baseball."

They were there only minutes before kids playing along the fence called for Randall to come and play. He looked to Ezekiel for approval. With an approving nod, Randall sprinted off. Ezekiel knew they'd ask Randall questions he wouldn't know how to answer, but better he face it now. Kids could be cruel, but forgiving, too. He could hear them already calling Randall a high yella boy. Not knowing any better, Randall smiled and went right on playing. Ezekiel imagined Randall had never played with kids his own age before. He was awkward, he didn't know the rules for simple games like tag and the other kids took advantage of it. It didn't matter though, he seemed to enjoy being "it" because he was fast and he liked the chase. An amused smile spread across Ezekiel's face. Randall wasn't one to take kindly to defeat. He would learn quick, like he had done at the barbershop playing checkers.

Ezekiel watched the game unfold as he shelled a few more peanuts. Hattie snuck up next to him and gave him a kiss on the cheek. "Hey, Daddy." He reached across her shoulder and gave her a squeeze. "Hey, baby. How was work?" "It was good. Not too busy." He nodded, handing her a bag of peanuts. They cheered in unison as Claude rounded second sliding into third. "Safe!" the umpire shouted.

Finding his way back to Ezekiel, Randall was surprised to see a face he recognized. "Hey!" he said, "I know you." Hattie smiled and squatted down. "Do you remember my name?" "No, but I remember your eyes. And you're not brown, you look white like my mama. You come to our house sometimes."

Hattie nodded. "That's right. You have a good memory. My name's Hattie." Randall stuck out his dirty hand. "I'm Randall." She took his hand and shook it. "What a gentleman! It's good to see you again. I hope we can be good friends."

"I'd like that. Do you know Zeke? He works at the barbershop." Hattie smiled again and stifled a giggle. "Yes, I do know Zeke. You wanna know a secret?" Randall's little head bobbed up and down. She leaned over and whispered in his ear. "He's my dad." Randall's eyes grew wide. "Really?" Hattie nodded. "Yep." "You know what? I don't have a dad," Randall said. The words stung like a quick slap across the face and for a second her face showed it. She blinked twice, recovered quickly and responded, "Well, Randall, everybody has a dad, but sometimes we don't know them." Randall nodded but didn't understand. She tried a different tactic. "Do you know God?"

Randall's eyes lit up. "Yeah, my mom says he's our Heavenly Father."

"Yeah, that's right! So even if you don't know your father here, you always have a heavenly father."

"That's what my mom says too, but sometimes I just want a dad here."

Ezekiel glanced over as Randall confided in Hattie. The boy had a serious contemplative expression.

"I'll tell you what. Do you want to share my dad with me?"

"You mean Zeke?"

"Yeah."

Putting his finger to his lips, Randall considered the offer. "Well, I don't' know. I work at the barbershop. I don't think he can be my dad. He's my boss."

"Well, if you change your mind, the offer is still open. You and I can share and then we'll be like brother and sister."

Randall didn't need much convincing, he bobbed his head up and down. "Okay, yeah. I'd like that. I don't have a dad or brothers or sisters. You guys could be my family!" He paused for a moment. "But can my mama still be the mama?"

Hattie pulled him close to her and squeezed him. "Of course. What else would she be?" A tear snuck down her cheek. Randall asked, "Why are you crying?" Hattie's eyes lit up. "Because I'm happy! I always wanted more family." Randall smeared dirt across her face as he wiped her tear and hugged her back. "I'm glad we're family." "Me, too!"

August 31, 1935

Dear Lord,

Ezekiel has invited us to church lots of times. I told Randall we'd go today. If we go I won't get the rest I deeply desire. Lord, I need Your strength. It's so important to him, he wants to go so bad and I want to make sure he gets to. It's strange that he's never been. As a girl I can't remember a single Sunday I didn't go to church. I raised him his whole life to know You, Lord, but he's never been to church. Seems strange to think on it.

He's blossomed. I haven't been too tired to notice that. He's so chatty about all his adventures. It makes my heart swell with pride knowing he's not a recluse and that he knows most of the folks around town from the barbershop. I don't know what to expect today. The church is on the colored side of town. I'm real nervous, but I'm not sure why.

CHAPTER 22

Olympia, MS
September 1935

Folks kept coming through the doors and filling seats of the little white chapel. Jena sat in the last pew on the edge closest to the door. Randall ran to and fro, greeting all the people he recognized from around town. She preferred it if he'd sit down, but she was too tired to chasten him. Besides, she figured if it wasn't allowed, Ezekiel or Hattie would have told him to sit down. All the children seemed real friendly and visited with friends, the same as Randall, greeting one another before taking their place next to their parents.

Jena noticed everyone was in their Sunday best. Work shoes and dress shoes were polished. Girls had their hair freshly combed in neatly plaited twists or braids. Boys wore collared shirts, starched and pressed crisp. Women's hair was brushed back in a chignon or in simple braids. Today her own hair hung straight down covering half of her face until she pulled a piece back and tucked it behind her ear. Her dress was an old one that hung loosely off of her, but it was her best. Like her granny would always say, "Jesus don't care what you wear as long as you're giving your best."

The service started with a hymn Jena recognized. She closed her eyes and began to sing. The pace was faster than she was used to but she liked it because it had life and energy.

When Reverend Bordeaux concluded the service he prayed over the congregation, "The Lord bless thee, and keep thee: The Lord make his face shine upon thee, and be gracious unto thee: The Lord lift up his countenance upon thee, and give thee peace." The congregation responded in unison, "Amen." The children knew they were set free and bolted from the confines of the pews. There was a stampede of children down the stairs to the yard where buggies held baskets of food. Parents mingled and conversed mostly about farming and news from up North. Jena removed herself and stepped outside. She smiled but didn't speak as people passed. As the groups exiting started to thin, Ezekiel and Hattie appeared with Randall in tow, the Reverend a few short steps behind them. They came over and Reverend Bordeaux stuck out his hand and introduced himself. Jena shook it and was surprised the Reverend's hand wasn't soft like the hands of the clergy she'd met as a child. She didn't think holy men worked doing hard labor and she said so. "Well, Ms. Wilson," Reverend Bordeaux responded unoffended, "Jesus himself was a carpenter with well-worn hands. Everybody wasn't a writer like John and Paul." Jena blushed. "I just never thought of it quite like that," she responded. "Well, you just keep coming and we'll both learn a little something from each other. Like iron sharpening iron."

Jena smiled. "I'd like that."

Randall bubbled with excitement on the ride home, chatting about everything. Ezekiel and Hattie had invited them to Millie's diner for lunch and to the baseball game later, but Jena declined, reminded she needed to wash clothes and get some rest before work tomorrow. Randall crossed his arms and pouted.

"Maybe next time," Ezekiel suggested. "There will be plenty of games. You go on and help your mama."

Jena thanked them. "We had a delightful morning. Thank you for inviting us."

“You’re welcome to join us anytime.”

Randall bounced on the back seat chanting, “Next Sunday. Next Sunday. Next Sunday.”

Jena lightly popped him on the butt. “Stop jumping on that seat. Apologize to Zeke.”

“Sorry, Zeke,” Randall said and sat down.

Jena reached for the door handle and thanked them again. “Come on, Randall.” She waved to Ezekiel and Hattie. “We’ll see you tomorrow.”

Feeling spiritually refreshed, Jena pulled the wash tub off the hook on the wall. She took it outside to the pump and filled it with water and some powdered soap. She set clothes in it to soak while she went back inside to start some lunch. “Randall, what do you want to eat? It’s probably going to be for dinner too, so pick something good.” He pondered the question real hard. “How about some Johnny Cakes and some beans?” Jena looked at the pantry shelves. In years past she’d had canned her own beans and by this time of year the pantry would be full. They were sparse and a bit of her joy was robbed by the fear of winter coming and she knew she wasn’t ready. No green beans, corn, lima beans, squash, or preserves. Empty glass jars looked back at her. There was a chance to get some cabbage put up, but the harvest was coming to an end.

Refusing to let despair take over she offered the prized can of cubed beef at the top of the cupboard. Why don’t you go to the garden and get us a couple potatoes and a couple carrots? I’ll make some stew, but we can eat Johnny Cakes now.” Randall jumped up with a shout, “Yes! Johnny Cakes! Can we have syrup on ‘em?” She rubbed his head. “Don’t you think you’re getting a little carried away?” He frowned at her touch. “Mama, you’re gonna mess up my hair.” She ran her hands through his hair, purposely messing up his waves. “Mama! Don’t! It took me a long time to get those.”

"Well, go on and get them potatoes and carrots and I won't touch your hair."

He ran for the door and looked back at his mama as he pulled his brush from his pocket and smoothed his hair back down. She smiled and laughed before a coughing spell got the best of her. Wheezing, she dropped the skillet. She stepped back and fell onto the bed still trying to catch her breath. Randall burst through the door. "Mama!" he shouted. She put up her hand. "It's okay." He grabbed her around the waist. "Mama, please don't die." She stroked his head. "I won't honey. I won't. I just need some rest." He pulled her shoes off, tucked her feet onto the bed, and pulled a sheet over her. She curled up on her side and her eyes grew heavy. "I'm gonna pray for you, Mama." Randall knelt down next to the bed, bowed his head and asked God to heal his mama.

Millie's diner was usually packed after church. Lots of folks took the day to picnic by the lake, but even in spite of that, Millie's was still the busiest place in town. Ezekiel and Hattie ordered but were waiting on food when Richard, a local farmer, stopped at their table, his face turned up in a scowl. "Zeke, why you bring that white lady to church?"

"Everybody needs Jesus, Richard. Why you mad about it?"

"Zeke, you know that's just gonna bring a whole heap of trouble for ere'body."

Ezekiel looked Richard in the eye. "I know normally having white folks in town is a heap o' trouble, but she ain't got nobody, she don't mess with nobody, and her boy is colored. Where's she supposed to go? You know they don't even let her walk through town on the white side without giving her trouble."

"I don't rightly know and I don't care. That ain't my problem. Her trapsin' around this side of town is my problem and I ain't gonna stand for it and neither is half the other folks around here. Don't nobody like it. It's bad enough you got her boy over at the barbershop."

"Watch it," Ezekiel warned.

"You watch it, Zeke. You and your brothers. You got a son out runnin' around causin' trouble for folks, and now here look at you, bringing a white lady into town. You think you own the place since you got a barbershop and a new fancy radio, but life has a funny way of changin' real quick."

Mabel came over and asked if there was a problem. Richard looked at her mean. "Naw, ain't no problem. Is there, Zeke?"

"Don't make none, won't be none," Zeke answered.

Richard turned to leave, but Ezekiel knew the whole diner heard. He wondered how many of them agreed. They'd gossiped about Jena for years and it was a bit hard to come face to face with the infamy that had been created. Randall was easy to accept because he was a kid and brown. Hattie was fired up. "Daddy, don't you listen to him. He don't know what he's talking about and he's mad all the time anyway." Ezekiel's eyes blazed. "Don't stoke the fire, Hattie." She backed off. She wanted to say more but knew better. Mabel set down two glasses of iced tea. "It's on me. A little something to cool ya off," she said teasing.

"Thank ya, Mabel."

She patted his shoulder. "Anytime."

Turning his glass Ezekiel watched a thick cube of ice swirl in the amber-colored liquid. Hattie watched her dad, and thought smoke might come out of his ears at any moment. Instead he sat there and wondered how many folks felt the same. He was mad and he contemplated why he cared what they thought anyway. The hard thing was that what Richard said was true. Having a white lady in town, at church, in the diner, at ball games was sure to bring trouble. Nobody was ever punished for what happened the night she was attacked, and any man in town that so much as looked at her could be accused, tortured, and killed—even all these years later.

In the past six years, white folks bloodlust for lynchin' hadn't abated. One only had to look at the Scottsboro Boys. After that, white folks bloodlust might only have gotten stronger. Ezekiel was furious that Richard was right. Olympia hadn't had a lot of trouble, but still, it was dangerous to have her in town. And wasn't no argument goin' to change that.

Mabel set their plates down in front of them. "Y'all enjoy," she said, leaving the bill on the table. Ezekiel took a deep breath and exhaled slow. "You want me to say grace, Daddy?" Ezekiel nodded. When Hattie said, "Amen," Ezekiel picked up his fork and knife and began to eat. Between bites Hattie asked a question, but Ezekiel was quiet, his expression grim. "Daddy, what you gonna do?"

Finally he answered. "Nothin'. I ain't gonna do nothin'."

"What's that mean?"

"It don't mean nothin'," Ezekiel answered, feeling helpless as he had when his wife had been the talk of town. It sat in his stomach burning with unquenchable torment.

September 9, 1935

Dear Lord,

That had to be the most exciting church service I've ever been to. Despite my inability to participate, I could feel something electric in the room. And it felt good! You must love that singing Lord, because I know I sure did. The stomping and the clapping went right along with the rhythm of all the shouting and singing right at the top of folks' lungs. It had to be heard all the way in heaven. It reminded me how great You truly are. I've heard some of those songs but never sung like that, with passion and soul, pouring out of the heart. And the singing went on for a good forty minutes or so. My goodness, I think those songs were so filled with Your glory, that singing might have brought miracles and raised the dead. I feel like they've done half brought me back from the dead.

Oh Lord, that was such a blessin'. Thank You for having Ezekiel invite us. It was good to see people and Hattie was there, too. I even saw a few black folks that work at the meat packing plant with me. I don't rightly know 'em, but I see 'em everyday. I think they were surprised to see me, and in a dress at that, not those filthy overalls smeared with hog guts.

Everyone was looking so beautiful with their hats and Sunday best. And the little preacher man, Reverend Bordeaux, looked quite unimposing—at first. How wrong can a person be? That man had the most frightful preaching style I've ever seen. I considered he might be God Himself in all his wrath, telling us to repent from our bad behavior—from our sin. He was quite blunt calling out adultery, theft, coveting, and every sin you can imagine. I repented even though I wasn't sure for what. I figured from that kind of preaching I musta done something.

When I went in I sure was feeling lost and to be real honest I didn't want to go. I think it's been about five or six years since I been in a church. Once I found out I was pregnant and showin' they didn't want me no more. The pastor came over to our house and told my family it was improper for an unmarried pregnant girl to come to church. I think my parents were banned too, because they didn't go anymore either. Or maybe it was too embarrassing. I just don't understand, if I was such a rotten person, I don't know how they ever thought I'd be a better person if I don't go to church, but that was the ruling and the end of my days in Your house. Today, everyone was real friendly, giving me a nod over in my corner of the pew. Only a few ignored me, but I felt okay about that. I was the only white person in the room next to Hattie. Some were surprised, but most were friendly. Maybe they weren't used to me, just like I wasn't used to them.

It felt right good to be in Your house with others that believe in You. And did You see Randall? He didn't miss a beat. You'd think he'd been going to church his whole life. I was proud of him turning the pages of our bible, looking for the verses.

I'd go back, Lord. Just to hear Your word preached was refreshing. Seemed like the reverend had a direct line to your throne and could hear You and speak what You were saying. I hope to be feeling better so I can go again.

CHAPTER 23

Olympia, Mississippi
September 1935

The front door to the barbershop slammed with a thud and a little voice directed at Randall said, "My daddy and I are going to go play catch. You wanna go?" Randall looked up, disbelieving he was the one being invited, he kept sweeping hair until Ray Ray said, "I bet I can beat you around the bases."

Randall scrunched up his face and furrowed his brow. "No, you can't. I'm faster than Cool Papa Bell," a name he'd only heard in the past twenty-four hours when Fred had been bragging about how fast Bell was at stealing bases. The two boys argued until Willie Dixon, Ray Ray's father, interrupted them and asked Ezekiel if they could take Randall with them to play catch after their chores.

"Randall," Ezekiel called out as the two boys started to argue again, "you want to go play catch with Mr. Dixon and Ray Ray?" Randall nodded his head and answered, "Yes, sir." His eyes lit with a fever of excitement that had been growing ever since he touched a baseball.

"Alright, Zeke, I'll be back for him in an hour or so, as soon as I'm done."

"That'll work. He'll have plenty of time to get his chores done here." Willie and Zeke shook hands while the two boys debated over who was the fastest. Mr. Dixon looked down. "Man, you'd think these two were in the league." Laughter rolled through the shop. "Yeah," Fred said, "you two cut out all that arguin' and save it for the field. Maybe y'all can be as fast as Jesse one day."

"Yeah," Claude chimed in, "he broke some records. 'Bout four or five of 'em."

"Naw man, it was like eight," one of the customers said.

"No, some was school records and some was World Records," Joe pitched in, "He broke three World Records and one tie."

"Shoot, who cares, that brother is fast," another customer cut in.

"He's fast and he can jump. The headline in the paper said, Here's the Greatest Leap Ever Made by Civilized Man," Joe said, grabbing a folded paper sitting at his station and waving it for the room to see. "Here it is, right here. Negros making history!"

Fred had to have the last word. "Well, I got the newspaper clipping tacked up on my wall with all them records. You mark my words, he's gonna win some golds in Berlin next year."

Claude said, "That's if those crazy Germans have the Olympics. I hear there's trouble stirring and they don't want Jews or Blacks in the Olympics."

"Guess we'll just have to wait and see," Zeke said.

"Alright fellas, I'll be back." Mr. Dixon waved and the bell dinged as he and Ray Ray left. Claude looked into the mirror and caught Randall looking out the window. "Hey, you better get to work if you want to go to the ball field." Randall let his shoulders sag and asked, "I gotta do everything?" Claude stopped trimming and pointed the scissors at him and said, "Boy, what's wrong with you? A course you do. You want to get paid, don't ya?"

Randall hadn't thought of that. He straightened his shoulders and started to gather the towels. He took them to the wash bucket out back. He filled the metal tub and poured in a scoop of washing powder. He left them to soak while he went back in to sweep and empty trash.

Men around the shop teased him about how fast he was working now. "Look at him, breaking world records here at the shop. I ain't never seen nobody empty trash so fast!" Eli said.

"Go, little man! Don't forget to oil them clippers," another customer teased.

Randall didn't care, normally he might argue back or try to say something funny but today he just wanted to get to the ball field to race Ray Ray around those bases. He just knew he could beat him.

Randall scrubbed the towels on the washboard and sloshed water all over his feet, then he poured fresh water and rinsed out all the soap. He knew better than to leave soap in 'em because Joe caught him once not rinsing the towels and gave him a switchin' and extra chores. Today he made sure not to miss any steps. He cranked the towels through the wringer and hung them on the line. After he hung the wash bucket he raced back inside to see if there was anything else he had to do before Ray Ray came back.

"Zeke, can I go? I got everything done."

"The towels hanging?" Zeke asked as he drew the blade against a customer's stubble.

Joe shouted across the room, "That was kinda fast. You rinse 'em like you're supposed to?"

"Yes, sir. They're rinsed and wringed, and I hung 'em up on the line."

"All the trash emptied?" Zeke asked.

"Yep."

"Your dishes from lunch done?"

"Yep."

"Alright, it's hot out there, get a canteen of water and change into some play clothes so you're ready when Mr. Dixon comes back."

Randall pumped his fist and sprinted for the cupboard in the back where he kept a change of clothes. Zeke bought him black slacks and a white button down shirt like the other barbers wore. He had nice shoes that clicked on the floor like Zeke's. He had a tall cupboard like the grown folks to keep his personals and in there, and he kept hisplay clothes for when Zeke took him to the ball field. He grabbed a ball and a worn leather glove Zeke gave him.

Willie tied his mule to the post and the boys jumped from the bed of the wagon and raced toward the diamond. Willie pulled a bat, a couple of gloves, and a bucket of balls from the back of the wagon and made his way over to the pitcher's mound. The boys were already racing around the bases, kicking up dust, sliding into home. As soon as they passed home plate they'd jump right up and race around again.

Ray Ray was the youngest of Willie's six boys. He'd come much later in life. Even though he was the youngest of six, he was more like an only child since he was born after his mama's time. She thought she'd gone into the change and put on a little weight only to find out about eight months later Ray Ray was on the way. He was smaller than the rest. The midwife said it was because he'd come so late in life, but not to worry, he was healthy and strong.

The boys were full of energy. Willie goaded them on. "Bet ya can't do one more."

He'd spent a lot of time with his older boys playing baseball. His son, Tubby Dixon, was good enough to play in the Negro League. Currently, he played catcher for the Birmingham Black Barons. Ray Ray wanted to be just like his big brother. Willie wasn't so sure he wanted his youngest son to go play in the Negro League. His son Tubby loved to play but the pay was low and some teams were riddled with strife and conflict. It wasn't good for raising families either, since they were on the road all the time. He really didn't want Ray Ray to be a part of that. He was a great athlete, but since he was so smart, Willie wanted him to go to college. All of his boys were doing good. Some married and had families of their own, but none had gone to college and Ray Ray might have a real shot at a good education. He was smart and learning came easy to him.

For these two, everything was a competition. The first time Ray Ray hit six balls while Randall only hit four. The next time Randall hit seven and Ray Ray three. Back and forth they went, trying to best each other. They played until the sun waned. The competition between the boys was intense and Willie laughed at their rivalry.

Just before dusk, Willie pulled the reins of the old mule and he stopped right in front of the barbershop. Ezekiel was sitting in a chair on the sidewalk reading the newspaper. He smiled when he saw Ray Ray and Randall slumped over one another, asleep with their mouths hanging open, Randall still clutching his empty canteen.

Ezekiel picked Randall up off the bed of the wagon and put him over his shoulder. "He behave for ya?" Ezekiel asked. "O' course. They had a great time. He's pretty good swinging that bat. He might be a slugger." Ezekiel laughed and said, "He always wants to hit it out of the park and I tell him he just needs to hit it out of the infield. Thanks for taking him." Willie nodded. "Anytime, we enjoy his company." He tipped his hat and gave the reins a light pop. Ezekiel waved as they rambled off down the street. He carried Randall the rest of the way to his house.

Hattie was already home and had dinner ready. He put a sheet over the couch and laid Randall down. The boy barely stirred as Ezekiel pulled off his dirt caked shoes. Hattie called out from the back. "Daddy? That you?" "It's me. I'm just putting Randall down. He's out." He wiped the dust from the little guys face, his cheeks still rosy from the heat, and watched his little chest rise and fall in a steady rhythm. Hattie crept in to watch her daddy watching Randall. She imagined it had been the same with Jimmie and her when they were small. For a second she wondered what it would be like to have her own kids.

Hattie went back to the kitchen and made two plates. She brought them to the living room so they could eat and watch Randall sleep. Most of the time he was in constant motion, it was practically a miracle to see him still.

After dinner Ezekiel washed up and put a record on the Victrola. He gave it a crank and set the needle on the vinyl. Soft jazz trumpeted into the room. Relaxed, Ezekiel napped in a chair next to Randall.

The long "whooo" of an old owl startled him. Darkness blanketed the street and Ezekiel looked at his wristwatch. It was well past eleven. Where was Jena? Randall was still asleep on the couch and Hattie had gone to bed. Something wasn't right. She'd never been late. Maybe a little early, but never late.

"Hattie," Ezekiel whispered, giving Hattie's shoulder a gentle shake. "I need you to wake up. Jena's not here."

Hattie bolted upright and rubbed her face. "What do you mean? What time is it?"

He reached on her dresser for the car keys. "It's almost midnight. She's not here. She didn't come for Randall. Something is wrong. I'm going to look for her."

Hattie yanked the sheet off and slid her feet into her house shoes. She went into the living room and sat next to Randall who was snoring. She stroked his head. He closed his mouth, groaned, and turned over. She rubbed his back and started to pray. "Lord, You know where Jena is. Please send Your ministering angels. Send her help, Lord." She heard the engine sputter and turn over and her dad pulled out of the drive and headed toward the meat packing plant.

The sun crested in the east before Hattie heard the car pull into the driveway. She rubbed her eyes and pulled her robe tighter. She rushed to the kitchen and put on the percolator for coffee. Daddy and Jena would probably need some caffeine. She'd make some eggs once they got in the house. Hattie was headed toward the front door when she saw her dad close the door behind him. "Where's Jena?" Ezekiel put his finger over his mouth and then pointed at Randall. Hattie's hand flew to her mouth as if to catch careless words from spilling out. She glanced over at Randall to see if he'd heard. He hadn't. He was still sawing logs. Ezekiel pointed toward the kitchen. Hattie nodded and tiptoed in that direction.

In hushed tones Ezekiel explained that he'd gone down every road Jena could have taken on her way home; whether she'd taken the bus or walked, he'd driven each route searching. He'd gone to their place. It was unlocked and untouched. If she'd gone home there wasn't any evidence of it. There was no food out or dirty dishes. The wash tub was hanging on the wall and the beds were made. He'd gone to the meat packing plant, but nobody was there. There was no trace of her and he hadn't come across a single soul on the road.

"Daddy," Hattie whispered, trying not to wake Randall, "what are we going to do?"

Ezekiel didn't answer straight away, he walked toward the percolator and pulled a mug from the cupboard next to the stove. He poured a cup of coffee and answered. "I don't know. I need a minute." He sat down at the table and tapped a finger on his coffee mug while steam crept over the edge. He bowed his head into his hands. His lips moved and inaudible sounds flowed. Hattie knew he was praying.

Randall would be waking soon. Hattie set herself to make biscuits and she fried some fatback with a couple eggs and grits. She needed to keep herself busy so she wouldn't panic. Ezekiel was still praying when she set a plate in front of him.

Smells warmed the house and Randall came in sleepy-eyed, rubbing his face. "Where's Mama?" he asked. Hattie looked at her daddy who didn't seem to hear the question or chose to ignore it. "You want some breakfast?" she answered. "Come on to the table." She reached for him and gave him a squeeze before she directed him to sit. "What's Zeke doing?"

"He's praying."

The answer seemed to satisfy and Randall waited patiently while Hattie fixed him a plate. "Say grace," she said as she placed the food before him. Randall bowed his head and suddenly raised it. "Do I have to pray as long as Zeke?" Hattie gave him a quick pop on the back of the head. "No. He ain't saying grace. He's praying."

"Well, how's they different? I thought saying grace was praying."

"It is, but you just thank the Lord for your food and eat. And then you go get washed up. You're about as dirty as a little piggy."

Randall looked at himself, he was pretty dirty. He was still in his play clothes from the ball field. His mama would never let him come to the table like this. He wondered where she was.

Ezekiel kept the car. Normally, Hattie drove to work and he walked to the barbershop but today he dropped her a block from the hospital and went to look for Jena again. Randall sat in the back seat asking a million questions. Generally, Ezekiel would have answered every single one, or attempted to, anyway. Right now he just wanted Randall to sit down and be quiet. His mind needed silence as it raced through different scenarios. Most of them were heinous or worrisome. This morning Ezekiel retraced his steps from the night before. He drove slower and looked more deeply in ditches and at the base of trees where someone might take shelter.

He circled back to Jena's place and had Randall get some clothes. They left a note in case Jena went there. Standing in the middle of the room while Randall visited the outhouse, Ezekiel rubbed his forehead and prayed, "Help me, Lord. Where is she?" No still small voice spoke, no soft breeze blew. Nothing. Ezekiel was left to his own devices. He decided they'd try her job. Maybe she never left. Not likely, but it was a preferable thought to the others racing through his head.

He pulled up to JB&B Meat Packing and saw a few folks he knew out on a break. He asked if they'd seen Jena. "Naw, not since yesterday," Danny said. The group standing around with him nodded in agreement. "Boss man over there, he might know," he said pointing. "But I don't think she showed up for her shift. He's been hollerin' all morning." Ezekiel nodded and thanked them before turning back to the car. A young black woman in her mid twenties caught up to him and tugged on his sleeve. "Excuse me, sir," she said, her face full of consternation. "I sure hope she's alright. She's always real nice, but they're always yelling at her. She coughs a lot and can't really keep up." The lady looked at the ground as if saying a farewell. "I like her a lot. I'm real sorry. I hope she's okay," she said before she walked away.

A tall heavyset white man with a sandwich in one hand was yelling across the yard. His demeanor identified him as the foreman, but he also wore a fedora which seemed out of place and a long white overcoat with splatters of hog meat. He appeared to be in a perpetual state of motion, keeping all the parts of the plant going with his own personal energy. "Excuse me, sir?"

"What?" the foreman shouted, "We aren't hiring."

"Excuse me, sir, I'm not here for a job. I'm looking for Jena Wilson."

"Well, she ain't here," the man shouted. "Didn't show up for work. When you find her, tell her she's fired!"

"Thank you, sir," Ezekiel said, heading back to the car. He was frustrated that they hadn't found her yet. The foreman was yelling behind him, "I should have fired her months ago. Can't work a lick, she's always tired and slower than a damned mule. Always so red in the face, looked like she was gonna pass out at any minute. Glad to be rid of her. She could barely keep up with all those coughing fits she has."

Ezekiel nodded and kept going. He hadn't realized till that moment how sick she really was. He noticed a little, but now he feared it was something serious.

As soon as he opened the car door and before he sat down, Randall started firing questions one after the other. He was bouncing on the back seat. "Boy! Stop that. You need a switchin'?" Randall looked down. "No, sir." "You know better than to jump on the seat."

The bouncing ceased and the talking ensued. "But Zeke, what about my mama?"

"Boy, slow down. Give me a second to answer."

"Was she there? Did you see her?"

"No and no."

"Where is she?"

"I don't know," Ezekiel answered and sighed.

"Where are we gonna look next?"

Ezekiel took a breath. "I don't know, little man." He looked around the courtyard hoping to see Jena among the people on their lunch break. He cranked the engine unsure of where he was going. He backed out of the parking lot looking at every ditch, rock, tree and low place where a body might be hidden. Nothing. He hit the breaks and slammed his palm on the steering wheel.

"What is it, Zeke?"

"Nothing, little man. I'm just frustrated. Let's go see Bait Man."

Randall's voice got lower, "Okay." Zeke knew he was scared.

Bait Man was down by the creek haulin' in catfish. He had a couple big ones in his basket. "You seen Jena?" Ezekiel asked. Bait Man smiled his toothless grin. "No. I got fish." He held up his basket showing them his catch. "You see her yesterday?" Ezekiel asked. Bait Man shook his head and Randall wiped his face real quick before a tear trickled down. "Want some?" Bait Man asked. "No, thanks. If you see her, you come to the barbershop and let me know." Bait Man nodded and turned back to his fishing. They left and stopped by the little mercantile owned by blacks on the road heading out of town. They hadn't seen her either.

Somebody had to have seen her. Upset, Ezekiel headed back to the barbershop.

Hattie walked the block to work and checked in at the nurses' station. After making her rounds, she checked the patient registry, her eyes scanning for Jena Wilson. Any Wilson or any Jena. Nothing. No one checked in under that name. Not all day yesterday or anytime throughout the night. Not even a Jane Doe to go and look at. When she had time for a break, she'd use the phone and call the barbershop.

The bell jingled and Ezekiel and Randall came through the front door. He grilled Claude and Joe. "Hattie called from the hospital," Joe said. "Well, damn, Joe, what'd she say?" Ezekiel nearly shouted.

"Nothin'. Said nobody checked in under Jena Wilson, no Jen, no Jennifer, no Wilson. Said there wasn't even a Jane Doe yesterday or last night."

Ezekiel rubbed his face. Randall tugged on his shirt. "Zeke, where's my mama?"

Ezekiel looked away. "Joe, can you take him out of here? Take him down to Millie's and get him some lunch."

"Yeah, Zeke. Whatever you need." He set down the broom and dustpan and turned to Randall. "Come on, little man." Randall looked longingly at Zeke. "Go on now. Go with Joe." Randall wanted to object but Ezekiel's voice left no room for objection. "Go on with Joe. I know you're hungry."

Randall frowned but took Joe's outstretched hand and turned toward the door. He started to cry, "I want my mama."

"We all do, little buddy. We all do," Joe said and picked him up. "Don't you worry. Zeke's gonna find her."

Zeke bowed his head and prayed, "Lord, wherever she is, keep her safe." A hush fell over the shop and Claude reached over, put a hand on Zeke's shoulder and joined the prayer.

The wide window pane in the front of the diner had greasy smudges all over it, but Randall didn't care as he stared out at the street. He and Joe sat in his favorite booth. He usually liked to watch all the people going by, but today he looked for his mother even though he knew she never walked through town. The only time she came to town was to pick him up at Zeke's house, which was far from Millie's Diner.

"Hey Randall, you want a sarsaparilla?" Joe asked. He knew Zeke only let Randall have them once in a while, but today Joe didn't care. The kid could have anything he wanted.

Mabel came over to take their orders, but try as she might, she couldn't draw Randall's attention away from the window. Joe ordered for him. "How about a chicken leg and corn on the cob and I'll have pork chops and mashed potatoes."

"You said I could have a sarsaparilla," Randall said without taking his eyes off the street. "You're right. I did say that. I didn't think you were listening." Mabel and Joe exchanged a look. "Well, we'll need a sarsaparilla and a lemonade."

"You got it." Mabel headed to the back, her skirt swishing behind her. Joe watched her as she left. He was soft on her and sometimes they fooled around but today wasn't the day to flirt. He and Randall sat in silence until Mabel returned with drinks and a plate of cookies." "They're on me," she said with a smile.

Randall still didn't peel his eyes away from the window. "What's wrong with him?" she asked in a whisper. "He don't seem like his usual self."

"Mama didn't come back from work last night. We're trying to find her, but no word yet," he answered and took a bite of a cookie. "Hey Randall, these are pretty good. You should try one." He folded his arms across one another and rested his chin on them. "I don't want one." Mabel's heart ached for him. "Y'all haven't seen her here, have ya?" Joe asked hopeful. Randall turned and locked eyes with Mabel. He read the look on her face, but he waited until she shook her head. "No, I'm sorry, sweetie. We haven't seen your mama. She's never even set foot in here." A tear trickled down his cheek and his chest rose higher than usual. Joe could see that Randall was trying to be brave. Joe reminded him of the cookies on the table. Randall snatched one up and crammed it in his mouth. He looked back out the window and Mabel excused herself. The pair sat in silence and stared out the window.

Back at the barbershop Claude voiced the tough questions Ezekiel only thought about. "You think somebody snatched her up?"

"I don't know. I hope not."

"Should we call the sheriff? Tell her parents?"

"I don't know, but her parents haven't cared for her so far. It's been six years. Where've they been?"

The bell jingled and a stranger walked in. "Can I get a cut?"

Ezekiel nodded at Claude. "You go ahead." Claude turned to the newcomer. "Come on, right over here."

The tension in the room broke and Fred and Gerald went back to playing checkers and normal conversation resumed. Claude popped a towel and wrapped it around the young man's neck. He was about twenty-five Claude guessed. "So what's your name, young fella?"

"Why you want to know?"

"No reason. Just being friendly, that's all."

The young man looked into the mirror and glared at the rest of the men in the barbershop. "I just need a cut. I don't need no friends."

Claude patted his shoulder. "Alright, young fella, no need to get riled up. What kind of cut you want?"

"Take a little off the top and sides and can you fix this part right here?" Claude nodded. "Oh, and edge me up."

"You got it," Claude said.

Tension in the room began to rise like a thermometer on a hot day. Fred decided to stoke the fire. "Young man, why are you so rude?" He jumped two checkers and snatched them off the board.

"I'm not rude. I just don't want to talk."

"I see," Fred said. "What do you think about those Kansas City Monarchs? They's playin' real good. Probably going to win another championship."

"I wouldn't know. I don't watch baseball."

"What's wrong with ya? You some kind of criminal? Don't watch baseball."

Gerald laughed. "Yeah, who don't keep up with baseball?"

The young fella snorted. "Well, everybody don't. Contrary to what you country bumpkins down here think, some folks got more important things than wasting half a day watching a stupid baseball game."

"Oh, so you ain't from round these parts." Fred commented. "That must be why you ain't got no manners."

Gerald laughed real good, but Claude said nothing and focused on cutting. Ezekiel heard the fuss and came to sit in his barber chair. He'd heard the conversation from the back and had his own questions. Northern blacks, especially young ones, came down South and stirred up trouble like a tornado tearing up stuff in their path. Ezekiel imagined this was one of those kinds of northern slick talkin' brothers. Zeke suspected the new boy wanted to be quiet because he had plenty to hide. Zeke put his paper up as if he was reading. He cast his own bait. "Y'all hear about that white girl?" The men in the room knew Ezekiel was talking to the young brother even though he had addressed the room. In the mirror Ezekiel saw the young brother's expression and could tell he was interested.

Satchmo's trumpet blared from the radio, Ezekiel walked over and turned it up. Some of the tense energy eased. Ezekiel sat back down and flipped his paper up.

"So what happened to the white girl?" the young brother asked. Ezekiel kept his paper up and waited as if he hadn't heard the question.

"King me," Gerald said.

"Awe, hell," Fred answered back, placing another pop top on Gerald's.

"What happened to the white girl?" the young brother asked again.

"Oh now you want to be friendly," Fred said.

"Awe, why don't you just shut up old man," the young brother said. "You done yet?" he barked at Claude.

"About a minute more. I just gotta clean up your neck." He cut the clippers off and grabbed a blade. Wild and unpredictable, the kid swung his arm and the blade went sliding across the floor. The young brother yanked the towel from his neck. "That's good. How much do I owe you?" "Fifty cents," Claude said, as a dusty black Ford pulled up out front and three strangers got out. The kid paid and bumped into Joe and Randall as they were coming in. "Hey!" Joe shouted, "Watch where you're going." The young brother glared at Joe sizing him up and thought twice about throwing a punch. Three guys were walking toward the front door and shouted at the young brother. "Carl, why you leavin'? We were about to come in and get a cut."

"We ain't staying here. Let's go. You can get your hair cut when we get back to Memphis."

Ezekiel smiled. Soon he'd know why Carl from Memphis and his three friends in a dusty black Ford were in Olympia.

Four days later, there was no news of Jena. The grapevine was silent. Ezekiel began to believe maybe Jena wasn't coming back. Randall had restless nights and Ezekiel had sleepless ones. Hattie had been up pacing and praying. She checked the hospital records daily but found nothing. Ezekiel didn't believe Jena skipped town, but that was the most popular rumor circulating. He tried to shelter Randall from the wagging tongues, but you could never know when somebody might come in and speak without thinking. There were no real leads and no good information. Rumors surrounded the boys that had come through town. Word was they'd come down and had an altercation with some bootleggers which caused a ruckus, but even if that were true, Ezekiel couldn't tie them to Jena.

With his hands dipped in wash water, cleaning up breakfast dishes, Zeke told Randall to go up front, unlock the door, and turn the sign. "Yes, sir," Randall responded, and hopped down from the table, wiped his face on his sleeve and ran to the front. In his absence, Ezekiel prayed again. "Lord, El Roi, the One who sees. You can see Jena right now. You know where she is. Please show us. Good or bad, we need to know. Please lead us to her. In the mighty name of Jesus, amen."

When he finished praying, he could hear Randall chatting up front. He grabbed a towel to dry his hands, turned the corner, and was relieved to see a friendly face. It was Willie and Ray Ray standing near the door.

"Hey, Zeke," Willie said.

"How are you two doing? You're not back for another cut are you? You're still looking fresh from the other day."

"Speaking of the other day, we were wondering if that white lady was Randall's mama and if she was okay?"

Ezekiel folded his arms and leaned back. He wondered if Willie had heard the rumors, but Willie wasn't a fella to be in the mix of trouble. Ezekiel wondered if he knew something. "Well Willie, what did you hear?"

"We haven't heard anything. That's why we came by, to see if she's okay."

"Do you know something, Willie? We haven't seen Randall's mama in near five days."

"Oh Zeke, are you kidding me?"

"No. I'm serious."

Randall looked up. "You seen my mama?"

"Zeke, that same night I took the boys to the ballfield I stopped by my in-laws for dinner. My wife was over there and on our way home we saw a body layin' in the road. It was a white lady with long brown hair and freckles. She wasn't moving and we thought maybe she was dead. She smelled real bad." Ezekiel gave him a stern look. "Anyhow, I figured she might be Randall's mama. We didn't want no trouble Zeke, but didn't want to leave her there either. She was in bad shape." Willie rubbed his chin. "Man, Zeke. I didn't know what to do. You know I didn't want to get caught up in nothing. You know my wife don't need no trouble working for a judge and all."

"Willie!" Zeke shouted. "Just tell me what happened!"

"Oh yeah, yeah. Um…let's see, she didn't look beat up or nothing. She still had her belongings. Looked like she just collapsed. She was dusty, and skinny like a skeleton." Ezekiel cut him off and gave a nod toward Randall who was looking terrified. Willie nodded. "Well, like I said, my wife was with me and we picked her up and put her in the back of the wagon. My wife said we should take her to the white folks hospital because she was wheezing real bad and burning up with fever. Sounded like she was having a real hard time and we couldn't get her to wake up, so we went on and took her over to the hospital."

Zeke rubbed his face. "Willie, that just can't be. Hattie's been checking the registry every day. She said nobody's been checked in named Jena or Wilson. Not even a Jane Doe."

"Well geeze Zeke, I didn't know her name. I only ever met Randall, I don't know his mama. We weren't even positive it was her. You know we didn't want no trouble. She couldda woke up and said we was tryin' to rob her or something. We just dropped her off, we didn't hang around."

Ezekiel turned toward the wall and wiped his mouth. He took a deep breath and tried to control his emotions. "Thank You, Jesus," he said real low under his breath.

"Zeke, I'm really sorry."

Zeke put his hand on Willie's shoulder. "Thank you. Thank you, man. We appreciate what you did. We thought something terrible had happened to her. Some boys from Memphis stopped in and I thought they might have done something to her. I just need to call Hattie."

Ezekiel grabbed Willie and hugged him, clapping him on the back. "Thank you, man. Thank you." He rushed to the back and dialed the hospital. "Please connect me to Hattie Johnson in oncology."

Hattie hung up the phone and raced for the patient registry scanning each name with her finger. She went through each page, not just admissions. Finally she found it. An unnamed female had been updated to Jena Wilson. She was in the infectious disease ward. Hattie's mind raced. Why was she there if she'd come in for a fall? She asked the receptionist why no one called the girl's family. The receptionist responded in a high-pitched nasally voice with a syrupy drawl that was overwhelmingly sincere and sweet. "Ms. Hattie, they didn't list her as a Jane Doe because some of the staff thought they knew her. But, I assure you we did try and call her kin, but she didn't have any identification in her pocketbook and only a paper with a phone number on it and the name Ezekiel. We called the number that night when she came in and even the next morning about ten o'clock. That's when we make most of our calls, but nobody answered."

Hattie sighed. She knew nobody answered through the night because it was a business, not a residence, and her daddy didn't open the shop the next morning because he was out looking for Jena. Hattie's face was contorted in an angry scowl. The girl behind the counter said, "I'm real sorry. We did try the other days but we just never got an answer. I mean, who doesn't answer at six in the morning or after seven in the evening on a weeknight?"

Hattie nodded. It wasn't her fault.

"I do have a piece of good news for you. Somebody must have reached her family because the registry says she's got a visitor right now. You could go and see them to make sure the rest of her family knows."

"What room?"

"205."

"That's where tuberculosis patients are."

The receptionist nodded. "Yes ma'am, that's right." She double checked the room number. "Yep that's what it says, room 205."

"Thanks!" Hattie said over her shoulder as she hurried down the hall to the stairwell.

She couldn't grasp why Jena was in the TB ward if all she had was a fall. She placed her hand on the door and just inside she saw a small woman about the same size as Jena sitting at her bedside holding Jena's hand. Her long hair was gray and pulled back, wrapped neatly in a bun at the nape of her neck. She was solemn. She was either praying or talking softly. Hattie knocked and entered. "Hello." She greeted the woman she was sure was Jena's mother. "I'm a nurse here. I was just coming to check on the patient," Hattie said as she reached for the patient's chart hanging from the end of the bed.

Mrs. Wilson patted Jena's pale hand and offered information. "She hasn't woke yet."

"I just came on shift. How long has she been asleep?" Hattie asked Mrs. Wilson while scanning the chart for information.

"Oh, they say she hasn't woke since they brought her in."

Hattie walked to Jena's side and placed two fingers on her wrist to check her pulse. It was weak and her breathing was shallow despite the fact that she was resting. An IV hung from the bed delivering fluids. She was scraped up.

Mrs. Wilson asked, "You look familiar. Do I know you?"

"No ma'am. I don't think so."

"Your eyes. I remember your eyes."

"I get that a lot ma'am."

"So blue. The nurse that was in the delivery room had eyes like yours. I barely remember much that night but I can't forget those piercing blue eyes. They were like an icy blue flame."

"How is your grandbaby now?"

Mrs. Wilson turned away but kept Jena's hand gently in her own. "I don't know," she said with a long heavy sigh, "I haven't really seen either of them since the day she came home from the hospital and my husband put them both out." Hattie noticed as a tear slipped down Mrs. Wilson's cheek. "It was a boy. It was supposed to be one of the greatest moments of our lives. I couldn't wait to be a grandmother. Our only daughter, we'd planned on giving her a big wedding. My husband even had money set aside to help with a house once she was married. Such a shame."

Hattie put the chart back on the end of the bed. "I'm sorry to hear that ma'am, but it's a blessing you're here now. Maybe you'll get to see him. I bet he's a handsome fella."

Mrs. Wilson dabbed at her eye before another tear fell. "I don't think that will happen. It was quite the scandal."

"Do you want to tell me about it? It might make you feel better."

Mrs. Wilson swallowed hard. "There's not much to tell. It was in all the papers about six or seven years back. My daughter was assaulted and had a baby out of wedlock. When he was born we found out he was negro. My husband made her pick. The baby, or us." There was a long pause. "She picked the baby." Mrs. Wilson tried to stifle a sob. Hattie moved toward Mrs. Wilson and offered her a tissue. "Thank you. I don't know why I'm so emotional."

Hattie smiled. "Six years is a long time to miss your daughter and your grandson."

Mrs. Wilson blew her nose and more tears came. "I just don't understand why she chose a negro over her own family."

Underneath her skin, Hattie's blood boiled and rage bubbled up. Silently she prayed, Help me Jesus, give me the words to say. She closed her eyes and took a deep breath before she answered. "Have you ever considered Jena never saw him as a negro? She only saw him as her son?"

Mrs. Wilson dabbed at her eyes and appeared to be contemplating the question. After a few seconds she looked intently into Hattie's blue eyes and answered, "Well, no. I suspect I never thought of it like that." She took a look at her daughter with a fresh perspective.

"Please excuse me. I have other rounds to make. I will be back later. Do you need anything before I go?"

"No. Thank you."

"May I ask you a question?" Hattie asked.

"Why, of course."

"How did you know your daughter was here?"

"A few days ago we received a phone call and I heard my husband yelling on the phone. He was shouting that he didn't have a daughter anymore. A doctor thought he recognized Jena from her visits six years ago. She's a bit hard to forget. They wanted to check her in under our name but my husband refused and just kept saying it wasn't our daughter. When I came today and confirmed it was her, they updated her name."

"I see," Hattie said.

"I didn't tell my husband, but I just had to come and see if it was her." More tears fell. "I miss her so much."

"And I'm sure she misses you just as much. I lost my mama to cancer. Time is precious. I hope you get to spend more time together."

"Thank you. God bless you."

"And you," Hattie said as she pulled the door closed behind her.

CHAPTER 24

Port of New Orleans
November 1944

His eyes watered and his nose began to run in the salty air. He stood tall as the wind whipped at his face. It was his first time being on a ship, he knew his mama would be proud. The Negro League scouts said he had to play more games. Dally, a ball player he'd met on the road, and become friends with, got him on a semi-pro team in Cuba, The Fuegos, for winter ball. Ezekiel hadn't wanted him to go, but he needed to play year round to get the next level of experience and Cuba was the way to do it. There was talk about having blacks in the majors. He wanted to be one of the first.

His bags were stowed and he didn't quite know what to do with himself. He was a little nervous traveling overseas alone. He thought of all the times Hattie had gone overseas and she went to war zones. He tried to reassure himself that if she could do it, most certainly he could go on a little boat ride to play ball.

Feeling a strange imbalance, never having needed sea legs, he grabbed the railing to steady himself as the boat rocked and dipped. He didn't want to get sea sick like Joe had teased he would. This wasn't anything like rowing their little fishing skiff. He leaned over the rail and watched the bow cut through the water. Riding hours on a bus was much different than this, too. On the bus all you did was watch the land pass by, out here you wished you could spot land. Barnstorming with a team and a manager to organize everything was easier than managing oneself. He'd never had to organize tickets for travel or arrange accommodations. He knew he was supposed to meet someone named Alphonso, who would show him around and have a room, but everything else, he was on his own.

The fellas at the barbershop had made sure he had a few extra dollars and everybody had offered advice, despite none of them having ever been to Cuba. Most of the advice spawned from rumor and tall tales. He hoped the stories about sharks jumping up to snatch passengers on the voyage wasn't true. He thought Joe just made that up because he read Moby Dick. Leaning on the rail, he wondered if he'd made the right decision.

He'd spent the spring and part of the summer traveling across the country and some in Mexico with the Mississippi Blues, a local team. Emotionally he'd been torn; he was living his dream and on the right path to get where he wanted to go, but he hadn't counted the cost. He wondered if it was all worth it. Leaving home was hard.

The bow dipped and a spray of salty water drenched his face. He felt his hands tighten on the rail. The choppy water caused him to slip. He recovered with ease, but his stomach threatened to heave. He looked to the heavens wondering if his mama was thinking of him. She was his biggest supporter and had always encouraged this career move. She said her family would be proud of him and she wanted him to see the world. His mama had given up everything for him. He had to do this, he'd do it for her.

Ezekiel warned him that the road would be hard and that he'd be unsure of his decision, he even said that his mind would play tricks on him. Zeke said lots of good men gave up when the going got hard. Ezekiel made him memorize Joshua 1:6-9 "Have not I commanded thee? Be strong and of good courage; be not afraid, neither be thou dismayed: for the Lord thy God is with thee whithersoever thou goest."

As the wind whipped across his face Randall recited the verse and regained his focus. He reminded himself that the Lord Almighty was with him. He had to finish what he'd started.

September 24, 1935

Dear Lord,

I dreamt of my mother. It was as if I could hear her whispering that she loved and missed me. I was sure I could smell her rose-scented lotion and feel the warmth of her hand resting on mine. When I woke I couldn't believe I'd been unconscious for ten days. The doctor said it was extreme exhaustion, anemia, and a problem with my lungs. They say it's tuberculosis. It's the wasting disease. They gave me some medicine, it's supposed to help me stop coughing and help me to breathe, but even with the medicine it feels like I have a brick on my chest.

I lost my job, but the doctor says I can't work anyway. I don't know what we're going to do. Doctor says I have to stay in the bed for thirty days. I'm going to die of boredom laying down that long.

It's my favorite time of year. The temperatures are cooling and the leaves are changing. It's not too cold and not too hot. The days are getting shorter and winter will be here sooner than I'd like. My coughing fits have slowed, but if I turn to my side and breathe in too deeply, they start right back up again.

Randall couldn't be a better son. He walks to the barbershop in the morning and I'm sure he runs home for lunch because he's out of breath and all sweaty when he gets here. He brings me a day-old newspaper and the daily special from Millie's Diner. I'm sure he pays with the money he makes at Zeke's, bless him. I've never been there, but he keeps saying we have to go when I'm better. I tell him I will, but truth is, I won't. The doctor says I'm contagious. He told me to limit the people I see because they can catch it. Lord, please don't let Randall get this.

The colored folks from my job stopped by and said hello at the door. They brought some vegetables and a piece of salt pork for me and Randall. Hattie comes every day to check on me. She checks my pulse and looks into my eyes, I don't know what she can see in them. Ezekiel comes every few days, but says hello from the door like the others. At the beginning of summer, he and Randall planted some seeds in the garden. It all came up real nice. Ezekiel said we should plant corn and dry it so we can grind it for cornmeal in the winter. I'm sure glad they did. He and Randall cleared a plot big enough for six rows and it's drying, almost ready for sacks. It gives me some peace knowing we'll have food, especially since I lost my job.

Randall saved enough money from the barbershop for us to make rent. They already sent my pay for my last days at JB&B Meat Packing. I'm not sad to never have to go there again, but I worried about the hospital bills because I was in there a long time. Hattie said that an anonymous person paid for my stay and my medication.

One, two, three...the doctor said counting will help me stay calm and breathe easier. Don't panic. Don't panic, breathe easy.

Lord Jesus, if anybody says You aren't good, they're a liar. All You've done for us, I just don't know where we'd be if You hadn't been with us. I could have been left on that old dirt road to die, but some real nice folks took me to the hospital. Hattie and Ezekiel took care of Randall while I was gone. What compels people, Lord?

Something compelled my brother Joseph to come to visit. I could tell by the look on his face he was stunned. I know I look bad, gaunt and hollow. My movements are labored and I'm sure it's difficult to look upon me. I don't remember the last time I saw Joseph. I told him to stay outside so he wouldn't get sick, but he ignored me, and sat with me until Randall came home. He read some of the Psalms to me while I rested. It was good to hear his voice. I closed my eyes and I could see the words come to life. I could see the wide-reaching trees planted by rivers of water and I could see their branches filled with fruit. As he read, I envisioned the Lord as my shield and the lifter of my head. My heart leapt when Joseph read, "I awaked; for the Lord sustained me." I felt energy flow through me and a smile spread across my face. Joseph saw and he paused reading and asked why I was smiling. "Because He has sustained me," I said. I told Joseph about the hospital and how I couldn't wake up but I had dreamt of Mama. He smiled as if he already knew.

Joseph brought Randall a second-hand bike. It was the first time Joseph had seen Randall since the day daddy threw us out. You'd think it would be an awkward meeting, but it wasn't. It was more like, You blessed them and redeemed the time. They spent the latter part of the day out front, Joseph teaching Randall how to ride. He got a few good cranks of the pedals before he turned too sharply and landed in the dirt. I sat on the porch wrapped in a shawl. My heart nearly burst with joy watching them. And only seconds later tears stained my cheeks and my heart longed for my parents. They should enjoy this moment. Randall is their only grandchild. Daddy's been so stubborn, but I still love him. He's missing out on so much and time isn't standing still, it's moving right along. And, Randall is missing out on having a granddaddy. I hope they can meet one day.

Joseph tucked Randall into bed and I cried again when he kissed my baby on the forehead. I didn't want him to go. I think it's hard for him to see us living like this and even harder to see me sick. I try not to talk about it and make things uncomfortable. There are moments I see him looking at me, his eyes pained, his body tense. No matter what, I'm happy he came. I hope he'll come again.

He said Mama and Daddy are doing good, but neither of them ever speak of me which hurts but I'm glad he's honest. It'd hurt more if he said something different and I got my hopes up that they'd have us back. Truth be told, a little ember of that hope always exists, even if it's deep down in my heart.

One day, Lord. Maybe one day we'll be back together as a family. Maybe one day we'll go home.

CHAPTER 25

Olympia, MS
July 1936

Like the rest of the country, Olympia had its share of hardship. Food was scarce and jobs were scarcer. Though the years were lean, they were also some of the best; struggle and hardship brought folks together. Ezekiel heard about it every day at the barbershop where chairs along the wall were always filled, even when the chairs in front of the mirrors weren't. Not too many folks came in for a full groomin' like times past, but business wasn't dead. Instead of weekly visits, folks came in when they could. Kids only came in for a fresh cut once or twice a month, lettin' their hair grow out till it started lookin' nappy.

Zeke didn't mind the slower pace. He and Randall had more time to play ball. They'd spend hours together on the baseball field. He'd pitch Randall a bucket of old, unraveling baseballs until Randall's arms felt like led and he could barely swing the bat. Before they left, Zeke would chase him around the bases as many times as Randall's legs would go. Giggling and laughing he would run hard, as if every turn round the bases were a grand slam. He lifted his arms to the sky with great showmanship as he waved to an imaginary crowd.

The crash of '29 pushed a lot of folks north to Detroit and Chicago to work in the factories, or west to Kansas where they'd heard of settlements and land, for a chance at independence and owning their own farms. Some even ventured as far as California to find work and a new life. A week didn't go by without a car or a wagon headed for greener pastures or bigger cities. Loaded down with folks' life belongings, their kin, and a basket of vittles, people were headed anywhere but the South. There was great fanfare and well wishes as folks pulled away, set on a new adventure and hope of better things. Sharecroppin' barely put food on the table and white landowners struggled to take care of their own, shorting the colored folks who were providing the labor. There were bigger dreams up North and out West.

The barbershop's radio brought some relief and much longed-for entertainment. Folks came by to hear the radio comedies, baseball, and news. In just a few short weeks the Olympics would begin in Berlin and the whole town hoped for Jesse to bring home the gold. Randall wondered if he'd ever be as fast as Jesse and he scanned the daily papers for any scrap of news about him. The black and white pictures in the newspaper made Jesse look light-skinned and Randall felt a kinship with him, even if he didn't know him. He hoped Jesse would win and bring home the gold. He prayed for it every night.

Olympia fared well compared to the rest of the country where unrest dominated. The small town was close-knit and folks pulled together to help each other out. Folks traded more than they spent. Drew had been right with his prediction; the community watched over its own, kept a close eye on outsiders, and made sure folks around town were doing alright. Reverend Bordeaux organized a market once a month at the church, designated for trading. Folks who had a little extra corn traded for some jam or a couple of eggs. The ladies who quilted traded blankets for sacks of wheat and kids who hunted, sometimes had enough to trade doves or raccoons for sweets. Everybody had their vice and most were resourceful enough to get it if it were available to be had.

Bootleggers came through town trying to pick up business, but there weren't many takers and they weren't keen on trading. They were popular at the shanty by the lake, but in town they were out of place and unwanted. They sold booze and hard to get items for cash or nothing. There were no trades. They were admired from a distance and hated up close. Most were mean and surly. Ezekiel hated when they came in but he took real good care of 'em when they did. They paid good, wanted the best, and talked like a loose-lipped snake. He hoped they'd slip up and say something about Jimmie, but they never did.

The barbershop might have made some of the best trades since nobody wanted to pay cash for a haircut. One of Randall's favorites was the hand-carved chess set. Once he figured out how the pieces moved he instantly became the in-house champ. Only problem was, nobody wanted to lose to a kid. He had to beg folks to play him and when they agreed, Randall would offer free tips on how to play.

The shelves in the back room were lined with jars of honey and all sorts of jam. Bags of rice and beans were popular trades, but the biggest of all trades was on a day when Mr. Chester's New Orleans Orchestra came through and all eighteen band members needed a fresh cut for their New Orleans gig scheduled for the following day.

The band members rode in a bus with all their instruments, but the manager drove a 1927 black convertible Model-A Ford with new whitewall tires. The trouble was the handsome black Ford kept overheating, spewing steam everywhere, forcing them to stop every few miles. The band leader and the manager argued incessantly about the little black Ford that caused them to be late to every gig they booked, which, the band leader insisted, caused the band to be on edge and not play well. A trade would save limited cash and, in the words of the band leader, they'd "finally be on time." He wanted it gone. Joe was happy to take it in trade. He cut all day and stayed open late to finish up. Ezekiel and Claude helped but they took regulars before the line of musicians who practiced while they waited.

Wasn't nothing but a week later before Joe had a new radiator and his Model-A was chugging all around town, even to the ball games over in Tupelo just a couple of hours away.

Trades for chickens were always donated to Randall who ended up with more eggs than he and his mama could eat, so he ended up bringing dozens back even after she'd pickled some and sold or traded a few. There was a wide assortment of odds and ends which included tools, fabric, thread, split wood and even a couple of freshly hunted squirrels. Nobody wanted those, but for the little fella that went to the trouble to catch them, Joe took 'em, put them in the back, and gave the boy a real nice cut with a part on the side.

Hattie worked at the hospital five days a week, fortunate that her work was steady. They hadn't seen Jimmie in several years. Ezekiel wondered if he was alive.

Randall took to polishing shoes at the barbershop and made a dollar twenty-five for a patent leather spit shine and twenty-five cents per shoe for a basic shoe shine. For sweeping hair he made two dollars a day and at seven years old he managed to pay the rent, buy groceries, and kept his mother rested and well.

She'd had a follow up appointment and they did all the things the doctor said. She rested, didn't work, and seemed to get better. She still experienced debilitating fatigue and a shallow cough. After an extended rest, she'd taken up doing small things like laundry and sewing. Joseph bought her a sewing machine and she would press the pedal back and forth for an hour or so before fatigue claimed her and she had to rest.

Saving part of his income the way Ezekiel taught him allowed Randall to make small investments to his shoeshine business. He bought good brushes and nylon stockings to get a perfect shine. He could make the most mud-grimed field boots look new. He had a hard brush to remove the crusty clods. Sometimes he had to do a muddy wash and brush the bruised leather until it was dry so that the leather would take the polish. Applying the warm wax to leather was like giving pomade to cracked and dry skin. The leather soaked up the first round as Randall rubbed it in. The second coat gave some color and brought the shoe back to life. With a steady swish-swish, swish-swish of a horse hair brush across the sides and top the job would almost be complete. With a piece of fabric cut from a pair of jeans, he'd use the soft side to finish buffing it out. For a spit shine on dress shoes, he'd use nylon stockings and that's what took the price up. Folks paid to take care of their shoes. A good shine could make shoes look new. Just before the weekend, folks would come in for a fresh cut and shoe shine. On a good Friday, Randall could earn enough for the whole week.

Sundays were reserved for church. Mama insisted he go. She always stayed home to rest. As soon as Revered Bordeaux said, "May God be with you," Randall would dart out the door to the ballfield with Ray Ray. Lightning bugs dotted the night sky before they'd quit and go home. They were either watching games or trying their best to get in one. Randall would come home with dinner, usually from Millie's, and most of the time his mama would still be asleep. She'd wake up for a bit and he'd read the Word to her or tell her about Reverend Bordeaux's message and then she'd fall back asleep till morning.

It was mid-July when Mr. Dixon burst through the front door with Ray Ray in his arms. "Zeke, help me. Please!" Randall was near the front window polishing shoes. His eyes grew wide-eyed as Ezekiel jumped up from his chair where he was reading the paper and rushed to Mr. Dixon. Randall's friend lay limp in his father's arms. Ezekiel rushed them toward the back where they laid him on the table. His arm dangled oddly off the edge. "Where's Hattie?" Willie asked, his voice thick with desperation. "She's at work," Ezekiel said, examining Ray Ray's foot. "Jesus, Jesus, Jesus. Man, this is bad."

Willie rubbed his head and paced the room. "I know."

"Willie, why don't you take him to the hospital?"

Willie was looking at the ground still rubbing his head. "I can't. Ain't got no money."

"Where's Winfrey, the doctor?"

"Out of town. His wife said he's up North, won't be back for a week."

Ray Ray groaned as Ezekiel turned his leg lifting the bloodied bandages. Below the knee, Ray Ray's bones protruded through his skin with a long gash severing his leg from the front almost completely to the back. The only thing holding it together was the big tendon in the back of his leg and a thick chunk of skin. It looked like whatever hit him sliced through both of the leg bones just above the ankle.

"Willie, Hattie ain't no doctor. She can't put this back together. He needs a surgeon."

Willie's eyes were red and watering. "Please, Zeke. I'm begging. Anything. I don't have anywhere else to go."

"Alright. Alright. I'll see if I can get her."

He went to the front, praying under his breath and scribbled a note on a piece of paper. He called Randall over. The room was buzzing with concern. "He gonna be alright, Zeke?" Fred asked. "I dunno, Fred. I sure hope so."

Zeke grabbed Randall by the shoulders and handed him the note. "You remember where Hattie works?" Randall didn't respond, he just stood wide-eyed and frozen. Ezekiel gave him a shake. "Randall!" Ezekiel said, his voice stern, "I need you to go get Hattie. The phone ain't working. I need you to go get her. You understand?" A look of recognition swept across his face and he nodded. Ezekiel placed the note in his hand. "Give this to the person at the desk and tell them it's an emergency!"

He nodded but remained planted. Ezekiel turned him by the shoulders and walked him to the door. "Run, Randall. Fast as you can!" Randall looked up at Zeke. "Go son! Now! Or Ray Ray ain't gonna make it." Fear fueled a flame that raced through his veins allowing Randall to fly, even in his dress shoes and black slacks.

"Joe, go get Reverend Bordeaux!" Ezekiel barked orders while Willie held his son's hand and begged the Lord to save him.

Randall ran like lightning, he could hear the train whistle in the distance. He had to make it before the train. He could see the headlight in the distance and under any other circumstances he wouldn't have risked it, but today was different. The horn blared and the earth rumbled as he raced toward the tracks. He put his head down and closed his eyes as his feet barely touched the ground. His heart thudded wildly and the whoosh of wind blasted his back. When he opened his eyes he realized he'd made it to the white side of town as the train rumbled past.

Breathless, his white shirt drenched with sweat, he looked at the big white building, Hattie was in there somewhere. He did as Ezekiel said and went to the front desk. He shoved the note at the yellow-haired lady in a striped dress. Randall put his hands on his knees sucking air. "Boy, you gotta git outside. No niggers in here," she said. He looked up at her confused. "It's an emergency! What about Hattie?" he asked between huffs. "I don't know but I'll give her this message. You have to get out of here right now." She stood up pointing as if she'd personally throw him out. Randall gave her a queer look wondering why they didn't kick Hattie out too, but he did as he was told and went outside to wait.

Fifteen minutes later, Hattie rushed outside with her bag in her hand. She grabbed his arm racing toward the car dragging him along. He knew she had doctor things in her bag. He'd seen her take it when she went to help folks around town. She was oddly quiet as they raced to the car. She pushed Randall in through the driver's side and cranked the engine to life. She drove faster than Randall had ever seen. He held onto his seat and hoped they'd make it to help his friend.

In the back room, men were gathered around the table and Hattie had to push her way through to get to Ray Ray. Ezekiel saw her and told everyone to back up. "Go on, all y'all back up front." Joe grabbed Randall by the arm. "You too, little buddy. Let's go." Joe sat him next to Fred and Gabriel who all sat in stunned silence. In the back, Hattie washed her hands and looked at Willie. "What happened?" Willie was shaking. "They had one of those reaping machines. I shouldn't have sent him. They said they needed folks that were fast. I thought it would be a good chance to earn a few extra dollars." Willie shook his head. "I don't know what happened. One second he was on his feet working and the next second he wasn't. He didn't even know what happened. Wasn't screaming or nothing, he was just trying to get up but he couldn't. Hattie was listening as she pulled the bloody sheets back. She looked at the mangled leg. It was well beyond her skill set and she refused to amputate a boy's foot. "Willie, I'm sorry. I can't fix this." Willie grabbed her arms, his eyes wild and desperate. "Please, Hattie. Please."

She looked back at Ray Ray's leg. He needed a surgeon, not a nurse. And he'd already lost a lot of blood. Reverend Bordeaux was pacing and praying a steady stream of prayers. A high-pitched voice called to her from the doorway. She didn't turn to look at Randall. She couldn't. "Hattie, you can do it. Please help my friend!" Reverend Bordeaux placed a hand on her shoulder. "Out of the mouth of babes. We believe in you, Hattie. God has anointed you, you're a healer."

She put her hand up to stop him. "I'm not Jesus."

"But we are the body. You're his hands and feet."

The tension was high and Ezekiel didn't like it, he was ready to make a decision for her. He knew Ray Ray's survival was slim and to save his leg he'd need a miracle. It was unimaginable pressure. "Okay," she said, her tone resolved. "But you all are my witnesses, this has a small chance of success. It will only be by the grace of God."

Willie kissed her hands. "Thank you, Hattie. Thank you."

"Daddy, take him out of here," she said, pointing at Willie. "Reverend, you can stay. I'm going to need some help. Daddy, send Uncle Joe or Claude back here, too." Ezekiel nodded and said, "Yeah," and looked over at Randall. "Go on Randall, get Joe and don't you come back here again or you're gonna go pick a switch from that ole hickory out back." Randall slumped his shoulders and drug his feet as he exited the room.

Three hours later Ray Ray lay on the table with fresh bandages and multiple stitches. He'd screamed and thrashed about in pain when she cleaned the wound. She did her best to set the bones back in place and stitch his leg up. She set it with a splint as best she could with strict instructions to rest and not to move his leg. Despite the time, the barbershop was full of folks prayin'. Mrs. Dixon, Ray Ray's mother, paced the length of the mirrors offering her own set of prayers.

When all was said and done and Hattie could do no more, she set a poultice on Ray Ray's leg to help deter infection. She gave detailed instructions and told them what to watch for. She said she'd be by tomorrow to check on him. Willie carried his son to the car and Ezekiel drove them home.

Once the car pulled off down the street Hattie's hands shook and her knees gave way. Randall grabbed her arm and her Uncle Claude caught her before she hit the ground. He scooped her up and placed her in one of the barber chairs. Randall leaned into her blood-smeared uniform and hugged her. "He's gonna be okay, Hattie. You saved him." She cupped his face in her hands and looked deep into his eyes. His face was alight with faith. She closed her eyes and kissed him on the head. "I hope so," she said, wanting to draw from his unwavering faith. She knew all the things that could go wrong. Doubt was a powerful foe and it was pounding on the door of her heart threatening to yank it off the hinges and extinguish every last trace of hope she had. Ray Ray's recovery would be nearly impossible and his survival even less likely. The wound would most likely get infected and spread through his blood. Gangreen stole lives.

Joe had her black bag in one hand and the keys to lock up in the other. "Come on. I'll drive you two home." Claude and Joe helped Hattie into the car and took her home first. Once she was washed up and settled in with a cup of tea, her uncles excused themselves and took Randall home.

A lamp lit the window and they could see Jena peeking out. Randall made a dash from the car and into his mama's arms. "Randall! I was so worried." He wrapped his arms around her middle, his fingers digging into the folds of her skirt. She hugged him back just as fiercely and looked to Joe and Claude for answers. They cut the car off and walked over, their heads hanging low with their hands tucked in their pockets. Joe had smears of blood across his starched white shirt. He was thankful it couldn't really be seen in the dark. Jena struggled to read their faces and she started to imagine the worst.

"Well, gentlemen?"

"Evenin', Jena." Claude said.

"Ya'll gonna tell me what's going on?"

Several seconds passed before anyone spoke. Anxious for answers, Jena started asking questions. "Where's Zeke?"

"Oh, this ain't about Zeke. He's just fine." Joe answered.

"Well, what's all this about? Why are y'all bringing my son home so late and seeming like you're keeping something from me?" Randall's face was still buried in her skirt. "Hattie? Is this about Hattie?"

"No. No, ma'am." Claude answered this time. Impatient, Jena nearly shouted, "Well, what's this all about?" Randall released her skirt. "Mama, it's Ray Ray. His leg got cut off."

Jena gasped and looked hard at Claude and Joe. "Is that right?"

"Well, ugh, yeah, that's not really how it happened," Joe started. Claude helped him out. "You see, Willie came in and we thought Ray Ray was dead the way Willie was holding him and all." Randall spun scowling. "You thought he was dead?"

"Well," Joe said, "naw, Randall. Course not." Joe and Claude weren't helping the situation; in fact it was getting worse.

"How is Ray Ray now?" Jena asked.

Claude answered, "Ezekiel took him and his family home. We're believing for a miracle. Hattie said he ain't likely to make it." Randall burst into tears and shouted, "Yes, he is! Don't you say that!" Joe punched Claude in the arm and hissed, "Now look what you done."

"Awe, shut up, Joe. You ain't doing no better."

Jena swatted Randall on the butt. "That's not how you talk to adults. It don't matter how much you're hurting. Go on and apologize."

Claude shook his head. "That ain't necessary. I shouldn't of said it in front of him."

Randall did as his mama told him and went over, apologized and hugged Claude who picked him up. "I'm sorry, little man. I didn't mean nothin' by it. You know we're all pulling for Ray Ray." Randall nodded. "Why don't you go inside and let us talk to your mama?" Jena echoed the sentiment. "That's a good idea. Go on and get washed up."

After Randall was in the house and the door closed, Claude went on. "Sorry, Jena. I shouldn't have said that in front of Randall, but Ray Ray is going to need a miracle to make it and he probably won't ever walk again." Jena swatted at a mosquito. "How much did Randall see?"

"A lot," Joe answered. "He saw Ray Ray come in, he saw Ray Ray laying on the table, but he didn't see any of what Hattie had to do, but he heard all of it. Poor little Ray Ray was screaming like crazy." Jena crossed her arms, warm tears streaking her cheeks as she stared at the ground. "I'm real sorry for Ray Ray's family. They're real nice folks. Will you please tell them that we'll be praying for them?"" "Course, Jena. We will. Y'all take care tonight. Be safe," Joe said before he and Claude turned and went back to the car. Jena watched as they backed down the driveway and wiped her cheeks before heading inside.

Jena pushed the door open. A soft light from the lantern flickered on Randall's side of the room just beyond the thin curtain. She could see the bent outline of her son on his knees and she could hear his desperate prayers.

CHAPTER 26

Olympia MS
August 4, 1936

Dust churned as Randall drug his feet down the tree-lined road to the Dixon's house. His mom packed a basket and he brought a newspaper to read to Ray Ray. Hattie said he might be able to hear even if he wasn't awake. Randall was thankful for the shade on his long walk. It had been a few weeks since the incident and no good news came about Ray Ray. No visitors were allowed. Hattie wanted Ray Ray to be a bit stronger before he had folks going to see him, including Randall. Today he didn't care what Hattie said. He was going to see his friend. Despite all the prayers folks were prayin', Ray Ray hadn't woken up or gotten any better.

The Dixon's lived in a shotgun tenant house built back off the road. It wasn't on the row like most folks. Their house was in a tenant field all by itself looking lonesome, sitting up on blocks with white wood siding and a front porch that stretched the length of the face of the house. They had some upgrades done by Mr. Dixon and his older sons. The tin roof was noisy when pecans fell, tinking against the metal. It was equally as scary when the wind blew and drug branches across it making a high pitched screech. The red brick fireplace was built in, unlike most folks' small pot-bellied wood stoves. There were three rooms, and the kitchen had a water pump and sink inside. Just like Randall, they had an outhouse and no electricity. Mrs. Dixon had a big wood burning stove with a wide flat surface for cooking. She could make a lot of things because she could fit four pots on there all at once. She was a great cook and she could flip flapjacks on the griddle. She worked five days a week cooking for Judge Carter who lived in a house as big as the courthouse on the white side of town. The tall white columns and wide porch were taller and wider than the front of the courthouse and the house was the envy of the town.

On the colored side of town, Mrs. Dixon was like a celebrity. Working for such an important family in such a grand house gave her a special status. Judge Carter was among the first to have electricity so Mrs. Dixon knew how to work the new-fangled contraptions you could run with electricity.

Behind the Dixon's house were eighty acres that Mr. Dixon and his sons farmed corn, celery, and mellons for the Grangers. Out front, a red maple with its star-like leaves shaded the house and an ancient pecan tree sat near the back of the house. A picnic table sat underneath the pecan tree where they ate dinner most nights. The old weathered tree still produced a twenty-pound sack of nuts faithfully every year and Randall loved when he visited Mrs. Dixon because she was generous with them. She always had a bowl full of shelled pecans which were a welcome treat, especially when she roasted them with a little sugar.

Randall rapped on the front door and entered when he heard the familiar, "Come on in." It was Mr. Dixon. He was reading his bible and sitting on a wicker couch next to Ray Ray who lay lifeless on the bed. Randall knew he wasn't dead because he could see the steady rise and fall of his friends chest under the white sheet draped across him, but his brown skin was an unnatural, pasty color. His leg was propped up like Hattie told them and Randall could see the yellow pus that was seeped through the bandages where he knew the stitches were. He wanted to cry but he held his breath, tensed his body and blinked a couple of times to reign in the tears that wanted to spill over.

Mr. Dixon got up and motioned Randall over to his seat. "Come on over. Have a seat." He patted Randall on the shoulder. "I'm glad you came. Zeke give you the day off?" "Yes, sir. I got most of my chores done early and I asked if I could come over." He thrust the basket of eggs toward Mr. Dixon. "Mama sent these. She said to tell you she's praying for y'all." "Tell your mama we're real thankful for her prayers and these here eggs. We appreciate it." "Yes, sir. I will." Mr. Dixon bowed his head seemingly exhausted, his spirit weary from the past few weeks. "Randall, I'm going to get some work done outside. Can you help me keep an eye on Ray Ray?" Randall nodded. "Yes, sir." "Thank you. He hasn't woke too much since everything happened, but I know he'll be glad you're here." Randall held up the newspaper. "I brought this," Randall said holding up the paper, "I thought he'd want to know Jesse won gold." Mr. Dixon's eyes started blur and he turned away. "He sure will Randall. That's mighty good of ya." Mr. Dixon said and stepped outside.

Randall took the rag that was on the nightstand next to him and dipped it into the basin like he did for his mama when she didn't feel good. He wiped the small beads of sweat that were forming on Ray Ray's head and talked to the Lord. He sat the rag back in the small basin and sat down in Mr. Dixon's chair. He stared at his friend, his mind overwhelmed by Ray Ray's motionless body. He grabbed Ray Ray's hand and expected it to close around his own, but it didn't. He placed Ray Ray's hand back onto the bed and straightened the sheet. Tucked in a knapsack were newspaper articles Randall had saved and brought to read to his friend.

It was a few minutes after Mr. Dixon left that Randall found his voice to read. His voice cracked as he started reading the headline from the morning paper, Owens Whittles 100 Meter Record to 10.2. He read the article to his friend and held up the picture of Jesse crossing the finish line well ahead of the other sprinters, even though Ray Ray wasn't awake. He sat with Ray Ray chatting and reading until dusk when Mrs. Dixon came in from work. She kissed them both on the forehead and thanked Randall for coming. She asked him to stay for dinner, but he excused himself to get home to his mama. He assured Mrs. Dixon that he'd come back to tell Ray Ray when Jesse won the long jump and the 200 meter.

He walked the long road home talking to God, his face tilted toward the sky hoping for a sign as he begged God to save his friend.

The barbershop swelled with excitement in the subsequent days when Jesse Owens surprised the world and brought home four gold medals. The chatter was contagious and the shop was busier than usual. Despite the excitement, Randall worked with his head hanging and his heart heavy. He and Ray Ray had talked about Jesse the whole last year and how they were going to be as fast as him one day. Now, Ray Ray couldn't even walk, much less run.

In the following weeks Randall's gloom hung over the barbershop and no joke or bit of good news could lift his heavy spirit. He tugged at Zeke's smock. "When's he gonna wake up?" "When the good Lord's ready for him to." Randall didn't like that answer, but it was the only one Zeke ever gave. Joe planned a trip trying to get Randall out of his funk. They drove four hours to Hazlehurst, Mississippi to see the New York Black Yankees and the Indianapolis Clowns. It was a grand affair and Joe didn't spare any expense. He bought peanuts and pop, got a motel so they could stay an extra day, but nothing diminished the dreary cloud that hung over Randall. To put his fears at ease, Hattie promised to check in on his mama right after she checked in on Ray Ray. Mabel had traveled with them and struggled to get a smile out of Randall the whole two days. Not even the tip money Claude had given Randall to have a good time with brought a smile. The only glimmer of a happy moment was when he spotted a man selling post cards with Negro League players. There was one with Satchel Paige, a cigar hanging out of his mouth and a baseball bat slung over his shoulder. Another card had the Kansas City Monarchs championship team. There were players from the Homestead Grays and the Detroit Stars. Randall wanted all of them. He looked to Joe. "Please, can I get these for Ray Ray?" "Sure, Randall. You can buy whatever you want. That's what Claude gave ya the money for." Mabel had an idea. "Maybe you can get a couple autographed after the game." Randall cracked a smile. "Now that's a good idea!"

After the game he darted from player to player to get signatures. His hope was aflame knowing Ray Ray would have to wake up for this.

Sunday evening candles burned around the room. Little ones rested in their mama's arms, some nursed while their mama's hummed hymns. Reverend Bordeaux read the requests and led a short prayer with a reading from 1 Thessalonians 5:16-18, "Rejoice evermore. Pray without ceasing. In everything give thanks: for this is the will of God in Christ Jesus concerning you." After a few more hymns, the congregation spent time in individual prayer. Voices could be heard around the room petitioning the Lord for different things. Tonight many prayers went up for Ray Ray. His condition changed daily. Some days he was ravished with fever and other days he moaned in pain. And there were days he simply slept while his body struggled to heal. Jena sat in the back, offering her own prayers. She sat in the last pew with her hands folded, head bowed. Like the mighty Mississippi flowing sure and strong, prayers were delivered to the throne of grace for Ray Ray's parents, his siblings, and for miraculous healing, strength, and determination to rise up in Ray Ray. She also prayed for her son that he be spared losing his friend.

The jingle on the front door summoned Randall from the back. His eyes widened when he saw Hattie. He ran to her and wrapped his arms around her middle. "What are you doing here?" "I'm here for you. I wanted to see if you want to ride with me to see Ray Ray." Randall turned and shouted across the barbershop. "Zeke! Can I go with Hattie?" Zeke looked up from cutting. This was the most vigor he'd seen from the little fella in weeks. "Yeah, but you gotta get your stuff done when you get back." Randall nodded earnestly. "You got it, Zeke!" he said, throwing off his smock and running to the back to change.

She had a poultice for Ray Ray's leg and a bit of comfrey root for the pain. The leg wasn't healing like Hattie hoped. Fevers came and went. It would appear infected and then it seemed to clear up. She was hoping today's visit would be the turning point, since it had been a little over five weeks since the incident. She should see some distinct healing.

Randall sat in the front seat with Hattie's bag in his lap. He was silent while she hummed and the car ambled down the dry, dusty road. They pulled up the long gravel drive and parked near the maple tree that had already started to turn crimson. The front door was open and Mrs. Dixon was waving frantically for them to come. If it hadn't been for Mrs. Dixon's wide grin, Hattie would have turned Randall right back around and sent him to the car for fear Ray Ray turned for the worse.

As their eyes adjusted, Randall could hear before he could see. "Hey Randall," Ray Ray said in a raspy voice that didn't sound anything like his friend. "I'm glad you come to see me." Randall squinted to see if it was really his friend speaking before a wide grin crossed his face. "Hey, Ray Ray. I thought you wasn't never gonna wake up." "Me neither. I just kept dreaming about Jesse winning the Olympics, I saw him cross over that finish line like a million times." Randall nearly smothered his friend with a hug. Hattie tapped him on the shoulder. "Move it buddy. I gotta get in here." Reluctant to let go, Randall eased back watching Ray Ray keenly to insure his eyes weren't playing tricks on him. The wide smile on his friend's face reassured him the moment was real. Poking and prodding Hattie sighed relieved there was no heat in the leg and no dark veins traveling from the wound. Worm-like scars crawled across his leg. They were ugly and deep. Nevertheless, Hattie was pleased. For the first time she felt hope.

Hattie showed Mrs. Dixon how to make the new poultice and how to apply it. The bones in Ray Ray's leg hadn't healed quite right. The severed bones had strengthened but healed off center. The bones weren't perfectly aligned. Hattie ran her fingers down his shriveled calf and wiggled his foot. "Can you move it?" she asked. He shook his head. "Not really." Mrs. Dixon looked on with worry. "But he will, right? He'll be able to move it when it's all healed. Right?"

Hattie set his leg back on the bed. "The great thing is that his wound has healed up real nice. I don't think he's at risk of any more infection. The bone does appear to have set and new bone is forming. But, Mrs. Dixon, as you can see the bones are off a bit and his leg is slightly crooked." Hattie looked into Mrs. Dixon's eyes and didn't shy away from the truth. " It won't be like it was. He won't walk normal and he probably won't ever be able to run. To be honest, he might not be able to use it at all." Mrs. Dixon dabbed her eyes with her apron. "I understand."

"There is good news, Mrs. Dixon. We know how to pray and God is a healer. Look what miracles he's done thus far." Mrs. Dixon's lip quivered as she struggled to smile. Hattie continued on, "The second thing is, we can keep working toward making this better. I'm going to give you some exercises and I want you to do them every day. They will help. Ray Ray's been laying in this bed for over a month and all his muscles have gotten lazy. He's going to have to get up and try to get his strength back." Hattie looked at Ray Ray. "Since you've been injured I've been volunteering in the recovery area of the hospital to see how they help patients get better. I've seen people frustrated and hurting when they're trying to walk again or use their hand after they broke it, but you can do it. You're going to have to believe you can even when you don't want to. It's going to be painful and take a lot of hard work. Are you up for it?" Randall jumped up from where he was sitting and shouted, "Yeah, he is! He can do it!" Hattie gave him a sideward glance. "You can't answer for him, Randall. He's the one that has to do the work." "But I'll help him," Randall said. Ray Ray looked at his friend. "If Randall says we can do it, we can do it."

A look of relief crossed Mrs. Dixon's face. "Well then, it's settled. I'll come by next week with some exercises for you and what you have to do each day and for how long. I'll put it on a calendar and you follow the calendar every day."

Ray Ray saluted and shouted, "Yes, ma'am."

Jena stood in front of the small black stove and scrambled eggs. She'd made a couple of biscuits, and hot tea. Randall came in from doing his morning chores. He was being extra sweet and Jena knew he wanted to talk about something. She wasn't sure what it was but she guessed it had to do with Ray Ray.

She watched from the window as Randall put a cloth on the table outside and dusted the cobwebs from the chairs. Warm rays of sunlight eased their way through the gaps in the tree branches and the whirr of insects was already humming. Jena wiped her hands on her apron and fixed two plates. She put jam on the table and a bowl of fresh churned butter.

They ate leisurely. Maybe it was the early morning heat, but Jena was patient and she'd wait till Randall brought up whatever he wanted to discuss. He'd become a savvy negotiator working at the barbershop. For now, he pushed his eggs around on his plate. Jena took her time buttering her biscuit. After an abundance of scooting food, Randall sucked in a lungful of air, looked his mom in the eye and blurted it all out. "Mama, I want to take off work and go help Ray Ray get better."

Jena bit her biscuit and chewed slowly. Randall fidgeted. "Well, Mama?" he asked.

"Well what?" she asked after she'd taken a sip of tea. "Do you have a plan?"

"Well, Hattie said she'll make us a calendar and we just have to do what it says."

"How are you going do that? Zeke just got you all set up to start school soon. You got chores and work. That's a long way over to the Dixon's."

"Mama, please. I'll get up early, I'll do all my chores and I'll be back at the barbershop by lunch time."

"What about school?"

Randall looked away. "Maybe I could just start next year?"

"Why would I let you do that? You know school is important."

"I can already read and do sums. Claude and Joe teach me. I even know states, too."

Jena took another bite and said nothing. Randall averted his gaze to a ladybug crawling across the tablecloth. He couldn't read the look in his mama's eyes. She leaned back and studied her son. She'd already made her decision, but she didn't want to tell him just yet. Jena admired his tenacity. He was relentless when he put his mind to something and she could tell his mind was set on helping his friend get better. Her only concern was how Randall might react if Ray Ray never walked again. She decided that Randall's heart toward his friend was the most important thing and they could work through whatever else might come.

The months helping Ray Ray was a new kind of work. It was emotionally taxing as well as physically draining. Randall was sure that lifting Ray Ray's legs, pushing them and pulling them, rolling his foot in circles, the leg criss-crossing, and the flutter kicks were all harder on him than his friend. As he walked across the ice-frosted town, his breath creating steam puffs with each exhale, Randall contemplated the day's exercises. They were new and Hattie said they needed to do more of them for longer periods of time. She said they were building Ray Ray's strength.

Being up before the roosters crowed was enough to be deserving of a midday nap. For Randall it was just the first part of his day. There would be no nap. He still had work at the barbershop and had to help mama. He was thankful for the scarf and mittens she had knitted for him as he rubbed his hands together and blew into them.

At the Dixon's house the blazing fire warmed his bones and movement loosened his muscles. Ray Ray whined that it hurt and Randall tried to tune out the cries of his friend. He knew Ray Ray was mad but he didn't care, Hattie said they had to do the new exercises or Ray Ray might never walk again.

After the tedious cranking of legs and wiggling of feet Randall yawned, he didn't want to leave. His eyes fluttered, he wanted to lay down in front of the fire and sleep for a week, but it was time to step back out into the whipping winds and walk to the barbershop. He pulled his scarf around his neck and buttoned his jacket. They wouldn't be enough, his body could already feel the shiver. Mrs. Dixon straightened his wool cap and thanked him. He nodded and looked away. If Ray Ray was mad, he was madder. Just a few steps off the porch he started mumbling, "I don't know why he's mad. He gets to stay in the warm house when I wake up early, walk over here, it's freezing cold, I help do his exercises. Walk back and still gotta work and take care of my mama. What is wrong with him? I'm the one who should be mad."

A steady stream of customers kept Randall on his feet. If it wasn't the weekend, the cold would have kept people home. Randall swept between shining shoes, but he was sluggish. He leaned on the broom and yawned before Claude fussed at him to get some clean towels. "Yes sir," he mumbled before shuffling off to the back.

The barbershop closed late. Randall sighed, the customers just kept coming. Darkness blanketed the city and the wind whipped down the street before they finished up, and the temperature dropped a few more degrees. Joe had pity on him and drove him home. Randall mumbled thank you and noticed icicles hung from the awning; he should knock them down but he didn't. He'd left the stove full of dry oak and plenty of split wood to add if mama needed it. He'd picked up dinner from Millie's because he didn't want to do anything once he got home, he just wanted to crawl in the bed and pull the blankets over his head. He didn't read his bible or pray. He barely said hello to Mama before he undressed and crawled into bed.

Despite the cold weather there were more travelers than usual and all interested in a full groomin', which meant, for Randall, all of them wanted their shoes shined and tip money would be rollin' in. Randall's business was booming as every bit of his energy waned.

Traveling salesmen and thrill seekers headed to New Orleans for warmer weather and fun would stop in. Travel South toward warmer weather brought in all kinds. It was unusual for white folks to be in town, but today a white man sat in his chair with his foot on the polish box reading the newspaper. He was waiting for his friend who was getting a shave. He read the paper as Randall worked the leather dress shoes with his usual rhythm. Most folks chatted with the barbers while they worked, but because he was a kid folks didn't say much of anything to him. He took out the nylon stocking to get a perfect shine. He was startled when the white man addressed him. "Hey kid, you know anybody that needs a camera?" Randall shook his head. "No, sir. Folks around here don't really have use for something like that." Randall kept polishing. "I'm only asking ten bucks. You sure you don't know anybody?"

"No, sir."

"What about you? Don't you like taking pictures?"

"I never have, sir."

"You don't have a picture of yourself?"

"No, sir."

"Well, when you're done here we'll take your picture."

"Sure. That would be real nice."

Once Randall finished polishing the white man's shoes, the man went over to the car and pulled out a box that had rolls of film, a Yoshika 44 with a crank handle, and a canister to develop the film in. "I can give this all to you for ten bucks. I bet you make good money shining shoes."

Ezekiel taught him to never tell people how much he made. They might be trying to rob him, but even if they weren't, it wasn't any of their business. Randall was thinking of his friend and how cool it would be to get him a good camera, but he didn't want the white man to know that. Ever since the accident Ray Ray's family had less money because he couldn't work.

He pulled the stocking back and forth nice and even. He didn't let any interest show on his face. That's what Claude said to do when you were trying to bargain, but even if Randall was trying to bargain he didn't have enough. They needed rent and his mama needed medicine. The man pulled the small box camera out and held it in the palm of his hand. He lifted the top of it and looked inside the box. Randall could see it was a nice one and wondered how it worked. "Look at me," the white man said. Randall looked, a blank expression still on his face. He heard the click of the camera. He didn't know what to do next. The white man cranked the handle on the side. "Come here, I'll show you." They took six more pictures in the shop and finished the roll. The white man took a black bag out of the box and put the film in there and a developing tank. With his hands in the sealed bag, the man opened the film canister without looking and loaded it onto a wire roll, put it in the canister and closed the lid so the light wouldn't get in. When the top was sealed he took the canister out of the bag. He showed Randall how to put the developer in to expose the images on the film and started to shake. "You have to shake it for six minutes." He handed it to Randall to shake. After the time was up they opened the developing tank and looked at the twelve images on the roll. The white man asked for a pair of scissors and cut the film in half. He handed Randall the six shots from the barbershop.

"You sure you don't know anybody that needs a camera?" Randall shook his head, still looking at the negatives with images of him and people around the shop. The white man continued on, "How much is a shoe shine? Two bucks?" Randall nodded even though he really only charged a dollar twenty-five and sometimes he only charged two quarters or whatever folks could pay.

He was mesmerized by the negatives. The man continued on, "If I make the price seven dollars and take off the two dollars I owe you, can you afford five bucks?" Randall looked up at him wide eyed. "Um…no, I only have four fifty." The white man stuck out his hand. "Alright it's a deal." Randall shook hands and pulled four fifty from his pocket. "Thanks, little man," the white man said, placing the camera back in the box along with the canister and developer. "Thank you, sir!" The man clapped him on the back. "Don't use up all the film in one place." "Okay," Randall said, still in a daze when the bell above the door dinged and the man and his friend left.

"Close your mouth," Joe said, "You trying to catch flies?" Randall closed his mouth and held up the camera. Joe was the first to say something. "Wow! Look out now. Check this guy out! Randall's got a camera. What you gonna do with that?"

Randall shrugged his shoulders, still speechless. Ray Ray isn't going to believe this! Randall thought.

The black man drove as they pulled onto the highway with a bag of fried chicken from Millie's Diner, some potato salad and biscuits. "So tell me, John," the driver said to the white man, "Why'd you do that with the camera? We needed that." "I don't know. The Lord told me to sell him the camera for whatever he could afford, so I did." "That's cool. That kid looked like he was in shock seeing his own picture. I hope he can figure out how to use it." The white man took a bite of chicken. "I'm sure he will. God must have big plans for him and that camera."

CHAPTER 27

Olympia, MS
December 11, 1936

Tucked under his blankets, a frown pasted on his face and his arms crossed against his chest, Ray Ray refused to get up. His hair was grown out and looked matted and scraggly. Randall came in and sat on the end of the bed. "Why aren't you up?"

"Why don't you just go home," Ray Ray shot back.

"Why are you being stubborn?"

"I'm not. I just don't want to do any exercising."

Randall stretched out across Ray Ray's lame leg.

"Hey! Get off! That hurts." Ray Ray shouted, giving his friend a hard glare. Randall gave the glare right back. "I got up and came all the way over here. If you want me off your legs, make me get off."

Mrs. Dixon came into the room to see what the commotion was. "Mama!" Ray Ray started to complain. She put her hands up. "I'm not in this," she answered and turned on her heels and returned to the kitchen. She'd learned with her older boys sometimes they just needed to work it out on their own.

"What you gonna do now, crybaby?" Randall taunted. "Your mama isn't coming to save you."

"You shut up, Randall!" Ray Ray shouted and threw the book from the nightstand at him. Randall easily blocked it and laughed. "That all you got?" Ray Ray tried to sit up and push Randall off of his leg. He struggled and fussed and finally kicked off his blankets and started kicking Randall with both legs. "Get off me, stupid!"

Randall yanked him off the bed and onto the cold floor. He landed with a thud. "Randall!" Ray Ray shouted. "Stop!"

"No. You lay in that bed too much. Get up and do your exercises."

"You're not my daddy, Randall!"

"At least you got one," Randall fired back while Ray Ray swung his fists.

"So! You didn't get your leg cut off!"

"Well, you got yours put back on!"

Ray Ray got up on all fours lunging toward Randall and grabbing his legs trying to drag him down. He punched Randall's thigh a couple of times and Randall dropped to his knees. They tussled until Ray Ray got the better of Randall by sitting on top of him and pushing his head onto the ground. "You're gonna pay for pulling me off the bed." Randall threw his own punches and caught Ray Ray in the nose. It made him pause, his eyes stung, blinking to hold back tears. Ray Ray grabbed his nose but it didn't bleed. With a fury he started swinging wildly and got the best of Randall again, sitting on top of him huffing and puffing, indignation flashing in his dark eyes.

Randall was short of breath but had a big grin on his face.

"What are you laughing at?" Ray Ray growled.

"You, dummy."

Ray Ray doubled his fist, threatening to punch Randall again. Randall put his fists up to protect his face, but was laughing and said, "Did you see that?"

"See what?"

"You used your legs. Both of your legs. How do you think you got on top of me?"

Ray Ray looked down at his legs and a flicker of hope lit up his face. "Yeah." Randall said, "You weren't overthinking it. You just did it." Ray Ray started laughing. "Yeah, I did!"

Mrs. Dixon had come in with a plate of warm pecans. "Y'all done fighting?" Ray Ray rolled off of Randall and they answered in unison, "Yes, ma'am."

"Good, because I brought y'all a snack and I don't want you breaking my good plate."

"We won't," Randall reassured her. Both boys scrambled for a handful. As she left the room she offered a warning. "Y'all don't start acting up again. Ya hear?"

"Yes, ma'am," came their reply.

The boys sat on the floor and snacked on pecans and once they'd had their fill Randall retrieved a box he'd brought to share. "You'll never believe this Ray Ray. Guess what's in here?"

Ray Ray leaned forward. "I dunno. A snake?"

"Are you crazy? I don't want your mama to beat me. I wouldn't bring a snake in the house." Ray Ray guessed again. "A knife?"

"Nope."

"Baseballs?"

"Nope."

"Awe, Randall, quit stalling. Just show me."

"You're never gonna believe it," Randall said as he slowly lifted the lid to the box. Ray Ray's eyes grew wide. "Is that what I think it is?" Randall nodded his head, picked up the black box and handed it to RayRay. "Is it real?" Randall frowned. "Of course it's real. What do you think I am? A hack?"

"Does it work?"

"Yeah, of course."

The next few hours were spent going over the directions, examining all the pieces, and taking test photos. Ray Ray hadn't been this excited since his accident. The tension that had been building was released and without words, all was forgiven.

CHAPTER 28

Olympia MS
Spring 1937

Bulbs burst through their dark confines and signs of spring colored the landscape. Randall stood on the train platform and waved until the smoke stack was swallowed by the trees. The Dixon's were going to visit family in Chicago. Most of Ray Ray's older brothers had left Mississippi permanently to chase their dreams up North. One had married and moved to Chicago. He and his wife just had a baby. Another played in the Negro Leagues for the Grays. Mrs. Dixon was excited to get to see her sons, meet her daughter-in-law and hold her new grandbaby.

Ray Ray, outfitted with a wheelchair, armed with his camera and two rolls of film, promised his best buddy that he'd get lots of good shots. Joe had taken the Dixon's to the train station to see them off and Randall tagged along. Now he felt a twinge of jealousy as his friend left for a week-long adventure. One that included family. Ray Ray was an uncle. Randall pondered, since he had no siblings, that he may never be an uncle. He wasn't sure how he felt about it.

Alone, left with nothing to do, Randall went to the soft sandbar by the lake to fish and think. He saw a girl near the wild boysenberry bushes and realized as he grew near that it was Nina, filling a basket with ripe berries. His blood pumped a little faster. She had on a long dark skirt and a white blouse. He'd seen her in the same outfit as she'd passed by the barber shop and waved to him. Her hair was braided with ribbon laced through. He always thought she looked particularly pretty like that. "Hi, Nina." She let out a soft shriek and put her hand to her chest sucking in a breath before realizing who it was. "Randall! You scared me," she said as a smile lit up her face. "I can help you." Randall said.

She held his gaze and nodded. Side by side they worked in silence, his fingers touching hers as he put berries into her basket. She giggled and almost spilled everything. "Hey, now," Randall said, "you better be careful." "I know, my mama would have my hide if I don't come home with enough to make jam." "Well, we better get enough then." With berry-stained fingers, Nina and Randall took a break laying in the tall overgrown grass. "Thanks, Randall. That was a lot faster with your help." "Sure, Nina. Anytime." Randall said feeling shy in her presence.

They watched the clouds pass by and agreed it was probably time to head home as the trees started making long shadows. Randall helped Nina up and walked her home, waving as she turned up her driveway and he kept on down the road to the barbershop. He'd lost his best buddy for the week, but hanging out with Nina made up for it.

Chicago was electric. Motor cars were everywhere, everyone had electricity and indoor plumbing, grocery stores were twice the size of the local mercantile, and nearly anything you'd want, you could get. Flashing lights lit up the night sky and radios had more than a couple channels. Everyday Ray Ray had a new boast about how exciting the city was. Even on the Lord's day folks were out. Kids played ball in the street and folks wore the latest styles. Chicago seemed bigger than life. Listening to the stories and thumbing through the photos, Randall dreamed of the day he could visit the city.

As an early birthday gift Ray Ray's brothers had gotten him trays and paper to develop his negatives. He'd even come back with a set of new fangled crutches to get him out of his wheelchair. The trip seemed wondrous, Randall was surprised they'd come back.

"Hey boy, what's gotten into you?" Claude asked, "Why you so full of piss and vinegar?" Randall didn't know what Claude meant. He offered a frown and a look of complete bewilderment as he strapped the wagon to his bike, loaded his supplies, and peddled down the street. He was ready to get to work. They weren't going to sit in the yard like they normally did. Randall was determined to take Ray Ray to the lake. Hattie said it would be the best kind of therapy for Ray Ray's leg. She said the water would work the muscles and not put pressure on the bones. Mr. Dixon made a hitch for the wagon so that it would attach to the seat post of the bike. With Ray Ray packed up tight, Randall struggled and strained pushing on the pedals to pull the wagon down the bumpy road. Huffing and puffing he steered to the wide sandbar where he and Ezekiel liked to fish.

He unhitched the wagon. "Randall, what are you doing?"

"I'm taking you into the water."

"Randall, that's gonna be cold."

Randall nodded. "Yep."

He pulled the wagon to the edge of the water, pulled the pins holding the side board in place. "Get out." Ray Ray looked at him as if he'd gone mad. Randall started taking off his shoes and his socks. "Come on. We're going in."

"Randall, that water is freezing! We can't go in there. I thought we were going for a ride."

Randall ignored him. "It's real cold, but it ain't freezing. See?" he said, splashing water on his friend.

"Hey! Stop!" Ray Ray shouted, his face turning sour.

Randall laughed. "Come on in. It ain't gonna hurt ya. Bait Man does it all the time."

"Yeah, but he's crazy."

Randall stripped down to his underclothes and waded into the water. Ray Ray was still sitting in the wagon—unmoving.

"Come on or you're going in with your clothes on," Randall warned. Ray Ray crossed his arms, looked sideways at him, and declared, "I ain't doing it."

Randall walked over to the wagon, placed his hands on the underbelly of the wagon and squatted like a wrestler. Ray Ray recognized the look; the glint in his friend's eye held a spark of mischief. Ray Ray started shouting, "Don't you do it! Don't you dare!" But before he knew it, he was splashing in the skin-tingling water. Ray Ray came up hollering, "Randall, when I'm healed I'm gonna whip your ass!"

"Why don't you try it now?" Randall said, putting up his fists. Ray Ray punched water and hurled more threats along with a few small rocks he'd snatched off the sandy bottom.

Grabbing a rope he'd slung across the handlebars, Randall tossed one end to Ray Ray. "Tie this under your armpits."

Ray Ray shouted in frustration, "I can't stand you Randall Wilson!" as he tied the rope. "What now, you idiot."

"I'm going to pull you and you're going to kick your legs like you know how to swim. Hattie said it will work your muscles and it will hurt like hell, but the cold water will make it not hurt as much."

"Randall, you know I can't swim. This is stupid."

"Just shut up and do it."

The pair moved into waist-deep water and Randall convinced Ray Ray to float on his back. "Okay, when I pull, let your legs float behind you and kick hard. Make lots of splashes."

"Hurry up!" Ray Ray said as his teeth began to chatter.

The sky was clear and the sun's rays brought a little bit of warmth but not enough to warm the water or keep them from shivering. A breeze whipped through the tops of the trees and the sun lugged its way across the sky. "Kick harder!" Randall shouted.

"I am, stupid!"

"No you're not, idiot If you were, the water would be getting on me."

"I can't stand you, Randall!" Ray Ray shouted as he kicked like crazy.

` A late lunch was set under the old pecan tree. Mr. Dixon and his sons came running as Randall struggled to make it up the drive. "What happened to y'all?" Mr. Dixon asked, taking the handlebars of the bike. Ray Ray's older brother picked him up and carried him to the picnic table as Randall followed. Mrs. Dixon frowned at them. "What kind of exercises were y'all doing? Pig wrestling? Y'all are filthy. Go on and wash up." The boys groaned but did as they were told. Ray Ray's brothers dropped him in the wheelchair and pushed him to the water pump. "I never want to see water again." Ray Ray moaned after a quick cleaning with icy water from the pump. Randall laughed. "Me

neither." "You just shut up. You're the one that got us into this." "You shut up first. This is gonna work and you're gonna walk and this will all be worth it." Ray Ray scowled at his friend. "Just be quiet. I don't wanna hear no more of your good ideas. Let's just eat. I'm starving." Randall pushed his friend to the table and Mr. Dixon prayed over the food.

With full bellies, the boys fell asleep on the grass in the sunshine while the men smoked tobacco pipes and played dominoes. Half asleep, Randall mumbled, "We're going to do that every day this summer until you can walk." Ray Ray mumbled back, "Then I'm going to walk tomorrow, because I'm not doing that again."

CHAPTER 29

Olympia, MS
May 1937

Nina was bundled in a dark wool jacket when she came into the barbershop. She created quite a stir. Girls didn't really come into the barbershop, in fact they never came into the barbershop, only men. The only exception was moms with boys while their dads were away, and even then all banter stopped. So, when Nina came in, a rare silence enveloped the room. Randall looked up and waved. "Hi, Nina." She didn't reply. She darted over to Randall and thrust a jar of boysenberry jam toward him. "It's from the berries we picked last spring. My mama wanted you to have it but… I was too scared to bring it." Randall took the jar and nodded. All eyes rested on the pair while their awkward silence filled the room. She smiled, turned abruptly and fled. Randall blushed, speechless, feeling only the thudding of his heart against his chest. As soon as the door closed behind her, hoots and howls came from each corner of the room and made Randall frown. "Why do you guys always have to tease me?" he shouted. Ezekiel patted his shoulder as Randall turned and stomped off to the back room. Ezekiel waited a few minutes before he went to check on the boy.

"Randall," Ezekiel said, "Why are you so upset?" Randall shrugged his shoulders. "You like her?" Randall shrugged his shoulders again. "Well, she's a real sweet girl and it'd be normal if you did like her. That's why everybody was funnin' you." Tears of fury welled up in Randall's eyes. "Yeah, but sometimes I hate it when they do that." "I know, but don't you pay them no mind. Do as I tell ya and go chase that girl down and tell her thank you." Randall nodded, wiped his face and snuck out the back.

She hadn't gotten far before Randall caught up with her. His huffing, warm breath made a steam trail in the cold air. "Hey, Nina." "Yeah?" "I wanted to say thanks. Thanks for the jam." She smiled and Randall could feel his cheeks flush. Nina didn't look at him, she looked at the ground, stealing glances. She was a year older than he was and he thought she was real pretty. She looked away and stared at the sky. Randall crammed his hands in his pockets and looked off to a bunch of trees. Nina was the first to break the silence. "So, when are you going to come to school?" Randall shrugged. "Maybe next year. Right now I'm helping Ray Ray." Nina sucked in her breath. "I heard he was injured real bad. We were praying for him at church." Randall nodded. "That's real good. I bet he is real thankful." Nina smiled and Randall liked it. He saw her start to shiver and realized she was cold. "I better go," he said, "I'll see ya around." She kept looking at the ground. "Okay, see you around." They both turned and went their separate ways. Randall felt better and had forgotten all about the teasing at the barbershop. There was a bounce in his step as he walked back down the street.

Muddy roads and ice storms slowed Ray Ray's recovery. While Jena was in favor of her son helping his friend she didn't let him go in inclement weather or on impassable roads. Thunder storms passed through almost daily, making the gravel roads between houses sodden and soggy with deep potholes that made travel with Randall's bike practically impossible.

Pain like a bear trap squeezing one's leg was Ray Ray's daily fight. He tossed and turned, screaming in the night as pain sank its fangs deep in his flesh and bone. Moving caused pain, yet likewise not moving created atrophy and more pain. A good day was torture and a bad day was worse. Ray Ray's mother rubbed his leg muscles with healing balm twice daily and moved his leg the way Hattie showed her, but that didn't fix the gloom that hung over her son and clouded his spirit. Her prayers were more for his countenance than for his leg. She prayed for healing, courage and resolve, but mostly for the joy of the Lord to be Ray Ray's strength. It had been a long while since her youngest son smiled or laughed. Her own despondency left her pillow tear-stained each night and her husband couldn't even speak of the ruination that plagued their household. The starving winter's dreary darkness desired to devour them all.

It was a rare day when Randall argued with his mama. In fact he couldn't remember a day that he'd had to argue with her, but today she was being stubborn. It had been too many days since he'd seen his best buddy and he had to go. There was a break in the weather and streaks of bright light shot through the clouds. Instead of twenty degrees and windy it was calm and warming up to thirty-two. Randall wrapped a scarf around his face and pulled on a wool cap his mama knitted. He made it into town and past Millie's diner before he hit a pothole and flipped off of his bike. He landed hard and pain like a piercing needle shot through his wrist . He wanted to scream but refused to humiliate himself. He shook it trying to rid himself of the stinging. In just a few minutes his wrist was fatter than his forearm; he was sure he sprained it. He picked up his bike and tried to push it, the rim was bent. He kicked his bike and tossed it in the gully. Today, nothing was going to stop him.

A steady plume of smoke wafted from the fireplace at Ray Ray's. The smell of burning wood warmed the frigid air and Randall longed to get inside the house to stop the chill that was constricting his muscles. The hem of his pants drug mud streaks across the porch. Mrs. Dixon was at the door before he knocked. "Hey, Randall. It's good to see you. Ray Ray was hoping you'd come." Ray Ray's face lit up. Randall went straight to the bed and hugged his friend. Mrs. Dixon wasn't blind to the mess Randall was dragging in and across the floor, but today she didn't care. Randall could drag a whole mud puddle in if it meant her baby had a smile on his face.

She excused herself and went to make some lunch. The boys would be hungry soon.

"Ray Ray, why you in the bed? I thought you were going to be up."

Ray Ray sighed and looked away. "Dang Randall, this ain't easy. My leg hurts bad. Some days I just want to quit and never get up."

Randall shrugged. "I get it. My mama gets real sick and she can't do much. Sometimes she gets depressed too but you gotta fight through it." It was quiet for a second. "You wanna do something else? We could play cards."

"Yeah, let's play cards! I bet I can still whip you at cards."

"Oh you might have gotten out of your exercises, but you're not beating me at cards."

"We'll see," Ray Ray said, reaching for the deck on the nightstand.

The boys played hand after hand until Mrs. Dixon came in with lunch. Randall scarfed down his ham and cheese sandwich while Ray Ray picked at his. "You gonna eat that?" Randall asked, reaching for Ray Ray's sandwich. "Yeah," Ray Ray said, popping Randall's hand. "You know you can have another sandwich."

Randall dusted the crumbs from his shirt. "Well, I don't wanna be greedy."

Ray Ray rolled his eyes and challenged Randall to some chess. "I would but I have to get home before it gets dark and it's cold out."

Ray Ray sighed. "You're gonna come back soon, right?"

"As soon as all these storms stop. The roads need to get fixed. Some are washed out and I busted my bike on the way over."

Ray Ray nodded. "Can you fix it?"

"I don't know. I hope so. I bet Zeke will help me."

"I bet he will. Did you know I can kinda tell when the rain is coming. My leg starts to hurt real bad. They say it's the air pressure from the storm, but it feels like my leg has a mind of its own and it just knows and it doesn't like it."

Randall nodded. "That's weird."

"I know."

"Well, I gotta go," He smacked hands with his friend. "I'll see you soon." Ray Ray's countenance changed, his eyes glossed over and he pulled the blankets up as his friend headed toward the door. Another month would pass before he'd see his friend again.

Spring temperatures ignited seeds and flowers bloomed. Adventure called as new life awakened along with Ray Ray's passion for pictures. With his camera slung around his neck, Ray Ray rose, leaned on Randall and hopped all the way to the front door. "I gotta go back. Randall, take me back. I need my crutches." "No, you don't. Come on. Hattie said you can put pressure on it. You gotta try it. You're gonna need two hands for your camera. You can't use crutches forever." Ray Ray froze. Randall grabbed his buddy's arm, pulled it across his shoulder and without thinking started walking toward the stairs that led to the yard. "No, Randall!" They took the first step and to Ray Ray's surprise when his foot went down, his lame leg obeyed and moved in line with his right leg. They took all three steps and were in the yard with Ray Ray's confidence soaring. "Let me go, Randall. I can do it." Randall released him and backed up a few steps. Ray Ray leaned to one side, still favoring the lame leg, but he was standing. Randall smiled wide.

"Randall!" Ray Ray shouted with new zeal, "Go get my bat over there and stand in front of the maple tree. Get ready like you're at bat. I'm gonna take your picture." Randall did as he was asked and posed, ready to hit a grand slam. He heard the click of the shutter and he watched as Ray Ray cranked the handle advancing the film. They went through every frame before heading in to develop it.

In the house, Randall watched Ray Ray work developing the film, shaking it six minutes before rinsing. They took the roll out and admired their handiwork. "We're pretty good at this," Ray Ray said. "Yeah, you're pretty good at this. I bet one day you're gonna be a pro." Ray Ray rubbed his aching leg, but his focus was on the black and whites drying on the table. His new found purpose drove him and the pain that consumed him lost it's power. By the end of the day the throbbing in Ray Ray's leg was unbearable, but he was unwilling to stop. His mom gave him a draught of white willow bark tea which would ease the pain and cause him to sleep. It wasn't until Ray Ray was fast asleep that Randall left and headed for home. He pedaled hard smiling the whole way home. It had been a good day and he knew that soon, his friend would walk again.

Pentecost Sunday, dressed in his Sunday best, Ray Ray took the stairs one at a time waving off all assistance. After he took the last step and stood on the landing he was grinning from ear to ear relishing the whoops and hollers of the congregation. Shouts of "Hallelujah, thank you Jesus," rang out throughout the Chapel. Ray Ray saw his mama in the pew with a handkerchief dabbing at her eyes. Her shoulders shook while her husband held her close. His own eyes were moist and emotion threatened to spill over. Reverend Bordeaux met Ray Ray at the door and clapped Ray Ray on the shoulder. "God is good." Choked with emotion, Ray Ray responded, "All the time."

Step-thump, step-thump was the rhythm as Ray Ray walked down the aisle. He scanned the pews and gazed into the faces of people he knew had bruised their knees petitioning God to heal him. As he passed each row he looked folks in the eye and nodded his thanks, he shook hands, and received hugs. The journey to get here hadn't been easy, in fact it had been long and painful. Amidst the cheers, Ray Ray locked eyes with his friend. A big grin lit up their faces and Ray Ray lifted his fists into the air and the room burst into applause.

May 7, 1937

Dear Lord,

The Hindenburg exploded. There's a picture on the front page of the Examiner. The report says there was a roar and a burst of flames. I can't imagine the horror of seeing people jumping from the luxury airliner. Reports say it was a miracle that anyone survived. I can't imagine the terror they must have felt when the explosion happened. There is a moving picture they say, not just still pictures. What a horrible thing to catch on film. Oh Lord, the world is changing.

Randall and Ray Ray are so fascinated with that camera. The whole country is fascinated with photos and moving pictures. It's like magic being able to capture an image so that we can look at it over and over. Randall has a box of newspaper clippings he keeps under the bed. I just don't want him to have this one. Thirty-four people died. Lord, help us.

CHAPTER 30

Olympia MS
June 1937

Gripping the solid ash bat Ezekiel had custom made, Randall's eyes shone with excitement as he took a hard swing inside the barbershop. A table went crashing to the floor sending clippers flying into the long mirror in front of the chairs, a crack went streaking down the center of it. The room went still and all eyes were on Randall. Joe's mouth hung open. Calude stood with his clippers in his hand. Ezekiel had a frown on his face. The bat clattered to the floor as Randall's eyes grew wide and he realized what he'd done. "Boy!" Joe shouted, "What were you thinking!" Randall looked at the mirror, his voice caught in his throat. "Come on." Ezekiel said. Without a word Randall hung his head and followed him to the back and discovered what the backside of a belt felt like.

Hours later Zeke locked the door and stepped out into the street. Evening temperatures cooled as Ezekiel and Randall walked through town to the ballfield, Randall rubbed his backside. There was no hurry and they stopped to say hello to folks along the way. Ezekiel knew Randall was tired. He still helped his friend with exercises a couple times a week, he worked at the barbershop in the afternoons, and cared for his mama in the evenings. Ezekiel knew people did what they had to, but it was a lot for a youngster and he wanted to make sure Randall had a childhood too, so he was determined to make sure the boy had a chance to unwind.

Once they passed the edge of town, past the celery fields, Randall started to get chatty. "Ezekiel?"

"Yeah."

"Sorry about the mirror."

Ezekiel patted him on the shoulder. "I know it was an accident. You're gonna have to pay the consequences though."

Randall nodded. "I know."

"Joe and Claude are gonna tease ya real good."

Randall laughed. "Yeah they will. Guess I deserve it. Can I ask you something serious?"

"Sure, little man. Shoot."

"Why do ya think my mama coughs all the time?"

"Sometimes folks get sick and have a hard time getting better."

"Sometimes I get scared, because she can't stop."

"Hmmm." He imagined it was quite scary for a little guy to see his mama like that. Not able to breathe, coughing up blood. He recalled his own fear and helplessness watching his wife struggle with the cancer. He remembered begging the Lord to heal her, to ease her pain and suffering.

"You think she'll get better?"

He wasn't sure what the Lord would do. He'd seen it both ways, people miraculously healed and others would go onto glory. "We can ask the Lord to heal her. God's word says he's a healer and we can stand on that."

"Yeah, we can pray for her!"

"Yeah, little man. We'll pray for her."

Randall reached up to hold Ezekiel's hand. They walked in silence the rest of the way. They played until the daylight waned and the mosquitos got bold, Ezekiel said," Time to go, little man."

"Awe, do we have to?"

"Yeah, it's time to go. We can come back tomorrow."

Dragging his feet, Randall collected the baseballs and gloves. "Promise?"

"Yeah, little man. I promise."

"You won't forget, will you, Zeke?"

"No, I won't forget," he said and patted Randall's head.

Randall hugged him. "Thanks, Zeke. I love you."

Zeke picked him up and hugged him back. "I love you too, little man."

June 13, 1937

Dear Lord,

Lord, my handkerchief is filled with blood and the fever's back. I'm scared. I thought the fatigue would go away but it hasn't. Ever since I was in the hospital it feels like I'm being chased by fear that wants to devour me. I can't shake it. The pain shoots through my ribs to my spine with every breath like a thief stealing my strength.

A few days ago, in the heat of the day, I tried to stand, my head started to spin, and my vision went black. I collapsed. I was able to get back in the bed before Randall found me.

He came home and recounted Reverend Bordeaux's message. Maybe he'll be a preacher one day. His re-telling is as if You dropped it right in him Yourself. No matter how tired I am, I delight in hearing him share Your word with me. Lord, he's such a blessing. Irene used to say I saved him. Truth is, I didn't save him. He saved me.

The heat is sweltering. I'm wishing a sweet cool breeze would whisk through the window and bring relief, but the night is still and even the crickets and hoot owls are quiet. Randall brought home some mashed potatoes and I couldn't even draw the spoon to my mouth. Doctor says I have to put on some weight.

This life isn't what I dreamed of at all. Randall needs to go to school. It's past time. Ezekiel said Randall can go to the primary school on the negro side of town. Ezekiel says my boy is smart enough to go to college. I don't know about all that. I never actually thought about what he'd do as a grown man. I've just been focused on making it—surviving. I don't think much about the future.

When I was eight I was still playing with dolls and sitting in my daddy's lap. Randall works at the barbershop, cares for his mama, and brings home most of our income. I only sell a few embroidered pieces. Lord! It's not right! I want my son to have memories like mine, happy, loved, surrounded by family. Year after year I'm surprised their hearts haven't softened. My family is still stubborn and prideful. How can a person hold on to hate for that long, just eating you up like cancer from the inside?

Lord, I'm going to pray till the day I die that they change their minds and let go of their hatred. I pray that Your love would overtake them like a mighty wind blowing away everything that isn't of You. I pray they'd know what kind of grandson You've given them.

Lord, please don't let my daddy's heart be hardened like Pharaoh. Please, Lord. Help him.

CHAPTER 31

Olympia Mississippi
June 22, 1937

The barbershop was packed. It was well past closing, coming close to ten-thirty that night but folks lined the street trying to get in. The broadcast would be on the radio. The Brown Bomber, Joe Lewis, was at Comiskey Park ready to fight James J. Braddock for the Heavyweight Championship. Randall and Ray Ray had the most coveted spots on the floor right in front of the polished Marconi. Joe Louis had been knocking people out and folks were anxious for him to get a shot at a title bout. Only ten short months before, Jesse Owens brought home the gold in Berlin and the expectation of the crowd was high that Joe Louis would bring home a belt.

The roar of the crowd in the stadium could be heard through the radio as the boxers were announced and the energy flowed through the room. Around the shop and into the street folks cheered just as loud when Joe Louis' name was broadcast. The men came to the center of the ring and the referee gave the opening admonitions to the fighters. Randall was in a cloud. He could hear nothing until the referee said, "Come out fighting and may the best man win." The bell dinged and Randall could imagine fighters meeting in the middle of the ring to throw their first blows. The hush extended into the street where people stood unable to hear but waited for information to be passed back from the crowd inside. During the first round, the whole neighborhood could hear Randall's panicked voice when he jumped up and shouted, "Get up, Joe!" The Brown Bomber had been knocked down with an uppercut, which sent everyone into a hushed panic. A sigh of relief was heard when the announcer said Joe had rebounded quickly and was back on his feet. Rounds two and three were tense and you could hear a pin drop as the announcer Clem McCarthy reported each blow and missed swing of the fight. McCarthy described Joe as an economical fighter and a very hard puncher.

The crowd tensed as the eighth round began. It wasn't apparent to the listening audience but Braddock's arms looked like lead, his punches were wide and unclean. A left from Joe missed the body but slammed into Braddock's arm and opened up his face, Joe Louis knocked Braddock to the mat with a right fist to Braddock's chin. The crowd went wild. Randall pressed his ear to the speaker to hear the count. "One, two, three, four, five, six, seven, eight, nine, ten!" Randall jumped up and started shouting with the rest of the crowd. Joe Louis was the new Heavyweight Champion of the World! The street went wild, as did streets across the country. Hope and elation soared. A win for the Brown Bomber was a win for people of color and caused Joe's title belt to be the talk of every newspaper, white and black.

July 5, 1937

Dear Lord,

The pressure on my lungs is like a sack of rocks sitting on my chest, I can barely draw breath. It pains me to have my son see me like this. Can You just take me home, Lord? When the wave of coughing comes his eyes grow wide and I see his lips start to move in prayer. When those moments come and I'm gasping for air, I wonder the same thing, am I going to die? I talked to Hattie and Ezekiel and asked if they would keep Randall when my time comes. My first choice was my brother Joseph, but he said no. I was a stunned and hurt. Since Joseph's been coming around more I thought that maybe things had changed. I went to bed with fresh raw wounds of affliction, but after thinking and praying about it, I understood. Joseph's life would change, Randall's life would change, they'd have to start over. And where would they be able to do that? If Randall stayed here he would keep his friends, he'd still have baseball, and his job with all the people who love him at the barbershop. Regardless of what I want, it would undoubtedly be best for Randall to be here with people that accept and love him.

I've longed for him to have family and I haven't really given credit to the people who have loved us when nobody else would. We have a beautiful family here, with people who truly love us. Forgive me, Lord, I haven't appreciated them. Without them we wouldn't have made it. I feel like You brought them into our lives at just the right moment, each one special, each one important.

CHAPTER 32

Olympia, Mississippi
September 18, 1937

Ms. Washington's third grade class giggled as the high yellow boy with good hair dressed in his Sunday best came into the room and was directed to sit down. Everybody knew he worked over at the barbershop and his mama was white.

The day was overcast and the small playground that sat in the center of the three class buildings was muddy from the downpour the night before. He sat in the second row from the door, the third seat from the front, and fidgeted with his pencil. Ms. Washington was a mean old lady that got results. There were no wiggles or giggles in her class, but as she would say, everybody left able to read, write, and do arithmetic. Ms.Washington slammed a ruler on her desk and the giggles stopped without a word. She walked the rows of the classroom and glared at the students who sat upright, stiff as boards in their seats. She pulled the glasses that sat on the bridge of her nose down so she could see the new boy. "You got mud in my classroom. What do you have to say for yourself?" Randall looked up with wide eyes. "Well?" she said, her tone rising. "Sorry?" He offered as he kept his gaze locked with hers.

She grabbed his ear and tugged. "Get up out of that seat and get this mud up off my floors." He looked around for a dustpan and broom while his head was cocked to the side with Ms. Washington's fingers squeezing his ear. She started walking toward the door, his ear in tow. He glanced in the corner and saw the straw broom and the black metal dustpan on the floor. "Could you let me go? I'll clean it up." The class was beginning to giggle again and Ms. Washington whacked the ruler on the desk, as more giggles erupted. She let go of Randall's ear and turned her attention to the class. A quick hush settled over the room with a few snickers. Randall swished the broom faster than he ever had in the barbershop making sure to get every little clod of dirt he could find and scooted quickly back to his seat slouching low. He was embarrassed but not quite sure why. He spent his days with grown men who teased him relentlessly, but this was something different. Humiliation. He decided he didn't like it.

Ms. Washington moved toward the blackboard and began scratching on it with the chalk. She didn't like that they'd just put the boy in her class without consulting her. He probably should have been put two grades down in the first grade class where he could learn his letters and do sums. He'd never been to school and she'd be surprised if he could make an X for his name.

She spun quickly and pointed at him. "What is the answer Randall Wilson?" He calmly answered. She scratched on the board and turned to him again. He answered before being asked. Once again she marked the board with a more difficult sum and challenged him to answer, all the while expecting him to fail. Effortlessly, he answered correctly. She masked her surprise. She knew the little yellow boy hadn't been to school and she expected him to be dumb as a sack of rocks. She knew he and his mama were poor and lived in the shack over by the railroad. She also knew he worked over at the barbershop with a bunch of lazy scoundrels, the

Johnson brothers, whom she considered uneducated brutes whose only goal in life was to play baseball. She was confident they must have rubbed off on the little half-breed in front of her. She scrubbed the side of her fist across the board and put up another sum. Quickly and competently he got it right. No matter, she thought, she'd catch him when it was reading time. For now, she'd let him hide slouched down in his seat while she taught the lesson.

Only days before, the thought of being around other kids had been exciting, thrilling even, the prospect of going to school for the first time kept Randall awake at night. But now, sitting in the cold classroom he wished he were back in the barbershop sweeping hair where it was warm, wiping the counters, and playing checkers with the old timers. Ezekiel would even let him listen to the radio after Claude made him read the headlines of the newspaper.

Lost in his longing to be free, Randall stared out the window. Last night's storm swept the trees clean. Their orange and crimson leaves blanketed the ground and he wished he'd been tasked with cleaning them from the sidewalk instead of being trapped with Ms. Washington. He couldn't wait to tell Ray Ray how lucky he was to not have to be here. He tried to stay awake as the morning seemed to drag on forever with the most boring lessons on Geography, History and Math. He much preferred Claude's geography lessons using baseball teams. Randall knew all fifty states, their capitals, and Cuba. He knew some Mexican teams and their geography as well. He knew bunches of lakes and rivers because Joe, pullin' ears and tellin' tales, bragged that he'd fished them all and marked them on a big map of the United States that hung on the wall in the back of the barbershop. Randall couldn't remember which ocean was which and Zeke tried to help him by saying the Atlantic was on the east side because the sun rose in the east and A came before P but that was just too much work and what did it matter anyway? Randall bet that if Joe had caught some fish in one of those oceans, then it would be easy to remember which one was which. He knew the marshes were south and the mighty Mississippi let out in the Gulf of Mexico. He hoped she didn't ask where it started because for the life of him he couldn't remember.

He looked forward to the ham and cheese sandwich in his knapsack as his stomach growled, but thought better about going out to play knowing he'd have to sweep mud again. Ms. Washington excused the class for lunch. Despite good sense, the other kids grabbed their lunches, pulled their jackets off of wooden pegs and ran for the outdoors. He saw boots slosh through mud puddles and a few bare feet flex their toes in the squishy brown earth. Randall sat on the bottom step, pulled out his sandwich and took a bite. He sat observing like the old folks did all day in the barbershop. As he watched kids run and play he recalled how he used to think it odd some old men would come into the barbershop and spend their days watching the goings on, but in the moment it seemed normal and what a person should do if they don't have to go to work.

Before he took his second bite Big Freddie Mac, whom Randall had seen before and heard plenty about, walked right up without saying anything and socked him dead in the face. Randall dropped his sandwich and sat dazed before Big Freddie Mac grabbed hold of his shirt and yanked Randall from the steps, tossing him into the mud. The cold wet earth covered his face and soaked through his clothes. He lay on the ground looking up at Freddie. "What was that for?" Randall shouted. "You high yella nigger, think you're better than everybody else! Well I say you ain't."

"Who said I said that?" Randall shot back.

"Didn't nobody have to say it. I just know'd it."

Randall pushed himself up onto his elbows and tried to get up except that Big Freddie Mac was standing right over him. "Well, that's a danged lie," Randall shouted.

"You callin' me a liar?" Big Freddie Mac demanded, balling up his fists.

"Yeah," Randall said before thinking it through and edging himself back to get up on his feet. He'd never fought anybody except Ray Ray but that was his friend, and he'd never called anybody a liar and maybe he didn't have the sense he shouldda to stay quiet, but Big Freddie Mac sure was experienced at these kinds of things and delivered another shot right to Randall's eye shouting, "Don't nobody call me a liar!"

Randall's face stung and his eyes watered, but he could still hear Ms. Washington's heavy steps as she burst through the door and down the steps like a charging bull fussing at Big Freddie. "You get to the principal's office right this instance, Freddie!" He didn't dare glare at her, he just stepped over Randall and headed toward the main office which doubled as the church office. At a safe distance he shouted back, "Don't think I won't do it again, yella boy!"

Mud covered Randall's front and back all the way up to his hair. He wiped his hands on his shirt and fingered the swelling of his face. Ms. Washington was bent over peering at him. His eyes were watering from Big Freddie's fist smashing into his face. Ms. Washington used a whiny voice to tease him, "You gonna cry? You mess up that pretty boy hair of yours?" Randall squinted at her unsure if he was supposed to respond. He shook his head.

She leaned closer and he could smell her breath. He wanted to tease her like Claude would to folks in the barbershop who had bad breath, but he thought better of it. She inspected his face closer. "It's swellin'. It's swellin'," she said over and over. She reached out to touch his cheek and he slapped it away. "Boy!" she shouted, "Did you just hit me?" "Oh no ma'am, it was just a reflex cuz my face is hurtin'. I'm sorry. I didn't mean it." She was still squinting through her glasses and her big bosom was in his face. He didn't know what to do. Ms. Washington was a big lady and he knew she had a switch and wasn't scared to use it. Compared to his mama, Ms. Washington was a monster of a woman. She towered over folks with big man hands and a fierce look on her face. She wasn't dark-skinned, in fact she was almost as light as Randall, and she had her hair pulled back in a tight bun that pulled her eyes from circles to almonds and tugged at her cheeks in the same way. He imagined she was taller than Zeke and Joe, who were both taller than most folks that came into the barbershop. They said Ms. Washington came from the North but Randall had his doubts. He was sure she came from the same place as the demons Reverend Bordeaux was always talking about. She frowned at him some more and finally shouted at him, "Get home and don't come back till ya have some clean clothes on!" She made sure to mention that even the sharecroppers who just came from the field were cleaner than him. He knew that wasn't true but he didn't argue. He wondered if his mama and Ezekiel would be mad he got sent home on his first day.

Ms. Washington said she'd give him a reading assessment tomorrow if he felt well enough to return as she stomped back inside. Before he could get to his feet, she returned and handed him a sheet of sums. "If you know how to do this, finish them at home and bring them back." Her voice was stern and a sliver of terror raced through him, not because he couldn't do them but because there must be some consequence for wrong answers or incomplete work. At a glance Randall knew he'd whip through the sums, but his eye started to throb and swell shut. He just wanted to hurry and get to the barbershop. He imagined the teasing he was going to endure, but anything was better than standing before Ms. Washington's heavy gaze. Claude and Joe were going to be on the ground laughing, not to mention the regulars, but today Randall didn't care as long as he got to leave school.

As he passed the main office, Big Freddy Mack was sitting next to a window and made a fist and thumbed his nose. There were a lot of things

Randall didn't understand about school but the message from Freddy was loud and clear. Deep inside him he knew he couldn't let Freddie get away with that. A primal instinct rose up, something like pride or the acceptance of a challenge. Randall squared his shoulders to be a bit taller and thrust his fist up in the air flipping up his middle finger. He kept it moving and left the school yard toward the street not looking back even when Freddie leaned out the window and hollered, "I'm gonna beat your ass high yella boy!" The threat caused him to shiver, but he wasn't going to give Freddie the satisfaction of seeing his fear. Through the window he heard Principal Miller, who came into the barbershop every week for a groomin' say, "Freddie, sit down and hush."

When the bell dinged over the door of the barbershop Ezekiel tried to guess why Randall wasn't at school. When he saw the shiner and mud from head to toe, he had to ask, "Well boy, what happened to you?" When Claude saw Randall's face he vowed revenge, but Joe just started laughing. Ezekiel waved him over. "Lemmie see that."

Ezekiel poked at Randall's face and kept asking if it hurt. "Yeah, it all hurts," Randall whined. Ezekiel pried to get Randall's eye open. "Can ya see?" "Not out of that one," Randall said, swiping at Ezekiel's hand trying to get him to stop prodding his face. Instead he received a rebuke and a quick smack on the backside. "Boy stop, I need to look at your eye."

Finally Ezekiel stepped back and said, "Your mama is gonna be upset. What happened?" Randall shrugged his shoulders. "I dunno. We were goin' to recess and Big Freddie Mac called me a high yella nigger and punched me in the face."

Joe boomed with laughter. "Well, did you stick it to him? He better look worse than you."

Randall shot Joe a look. "Whatta you mean? I was on the ground. I didn't get in no licks." Joe laughed harder.

Ezekiel sat in his own barber chair and thought for a bit before chiming in, but Claude didn't have any reservations and threw in his two cents. "Well boy, what'd we teach you round here? We teach you to be a sissy?" "No, sir, but," Randall fired back, getting frustrated, "I don't know what I shouldda done. Big Freddie is the same age as me and ten times bigger. I didn't even know he was gonna do that." Randall's temper was rising from embarrassment.

Through his laughter Joe answered, "Well boy, you at least gotta get in a few licks on him or he's gonna kick your little ass every damned day."

"That's enough, Joe," Ezekiel said.

"Awe, come on Zeke. You know it's true. He can't go on like that. Besides, we ain't raisin' no sissy."

"I know, I know. I'll have to have a talk with him. Come on, Randall."

With soft clicking of his shoes Ezekiel headed to the back and Randall followed, unsure what might happen next. Zeke pulled a piece of meat from the cooler and put it on Randall's eye. "Have a seat and press down on that."

"But it hurts."

Ezekiel's voice was stern. "It's gonna hurt worse if you don't do it." He pressed the meat onto Randall's swollen eye.

"Owww!" Randall shouted. "It stinks! And I'm gonna barf." Ezekiel didn't back down and kept the cold meat pressed securely to Randall's face.

"Zeke?"

"Yeah."

"Why's he mad at me? I didn't do nothin' to him."

"Well Randall, it's hard to explain, but you can't let him do you like that again. You're gonna have to fight him."

"But I've never fought anybody."

Ezekiel nodded. "I know, but you're gonna have to learn. I don't want you picking fights but if you have to, you're gonna finish them."

Jena's first response was to pull him out of school until Ezekiel talked her off the ledge. "He's going to have to fight every now and again." Ezekiel assured her, "Sometimes it's tough out there, but I'll show him how to take care of himself." After she shed a few tears she nodded, giving her permission.

CHAPTER 33

Olympia, Mississippi
Fall 1937

Rain poured down and lightning streaked across the sky while Randall and Ray Ray sat on the floor of the barbershop. They had a pile of newspapers strewn across the floor. Ray Ray grimaced and rubbed his leg, the cold brought lingering aches and a deepened limp. Most days he accompanied his father to work, however today, with the rain, he'd be no help. Today, Willie asked Ezekiel if the boy could spend the day at the barbershop with Randall.

Ezekiel didn't mind. Joe and Claude weren't coming in until later, maybe not all. Getting soaked just for a groomin' wasn't on people's priority list. Only the newspaper boy decided to venture in since he had to be out in the downpour anyway. While he sat in the chair he watched the boys in the mirror as they cut pictures out of the paper and moved them around, ranking them in order of which was the most exciting. Without question, the picture of Joe Louis ducking Braddock's punch was number one. The Hindenburg explosion was second, despite Jena's dislike of it. The disappearance of Amelia Earhart was interesting news, but they were grouping the pictures and there were no pictures of her disappearance, only one of her smiling while standing next to a plane.

They put that one at the bottom of the pile. They found one with the president in his wheelchair and tucked it beneath Amelia, but the one of Mrs. Roosevelt doing some shooting practice took a spot toward the top of the pile. "She's a scary lady," Ray Ray said. "Yeah," Randall agreed, "I wouldn't mess with her."

There were pictures of folks in bread lines and ones of the Memorial Day Massacre, news about the Japanese invading China, but none were as fascinating to the boys as an aerial picture of Joe Lewis in Harlem. That black and white picture was their prized clipping. It connected them to life outside Mississippi, to a world where they could dream of bigger things. The Brown Bomber sat on the bench in a locker room, looking up into the camera; it felt like victory.

Randall picked up the newspaper clippings and handed them to Ray Ray for the collection they kept in an old cigar box. "You know, Randall…"

"What?" Randall said as he swept up their mess.

"One day, I'm gonna take pictures like these. I could take pictures of famous people and world events. I could record history."

"Yeah, that would be pretty exciting. You could go all over the world. Like here," he said as he showed Ray Ray the picture of Nanking, China where the Japanese had just invaded.

"I think I'd like that. Now I just have to get good with my camera," he said sighing, "but I don't think that will ever happen."

"You don't know that. It could happen. You gotta work hard and practice like we did with your leg."

Ray Ray smiled. "You're right, Randall. It could happen." He changed the subject. "How do you like school?"

"Awe, why'd you have to bring that up?"

Ezekiel peeked into the mirror to see what Randall was going to say. Ray Ray said, "I heard kids say they like it."

"Well, I hate it. Ms. Washington is the meanest and her class is boring. I already know most of the work but she always tries to get me." Ray Ray folded up a piece of paper and chewed it. "Like how? How does she try to get you?"

"I don't know. Like she tries to get me to do sums fifth graders do and she's always marking me down on my penmanship. She says it's sloppy."

"Is it?" Ray Ray asked.

"I guess. I mean, I ain't no girl. Everybody knows Nina and Sarah are the class pets and have the prettiest penmanship in the whole class."

Ray Ray giggled. "You're mad. You know girls got better handwriting."

Randall folded his arms. "Who cares."

"I heard Big Freddie Mac gives you a hard time every day."

"You sure hear a lot. How you know all this?"

"I got sources."

"And Big Freddie Mac don't do nothing to me since I bloodied his nose."

Ray Ray perked up. "So what happened?"

"One day we were all heading out to lunch and he tried to take my bag but I didn't let him. And when he took a swing at me I ducked like Joe and Zeke taught me. Then I made a tight fist and punched him in the nose. It started bleeding." Randall got animated and stood up, showing Ray Ray each swing. "And then Ms.Washington came out and I got sent home. But Big Freddie Mac didn't get my lunch. No, sir, he sure didn't." Ray Ray laughed and so did the newspaper boy still in Zeke's chair. Randall puffed his chest, clenched his fists, and put 'em up like the Brown Bomber dancing around the room, throwing jabs. His back was to the door when one of the regulars came in and asked him what he was doing. "Nothing," he'd answered, cramming his hands into his pockets like he was real smooth.

"I wish I could go to school."

"No, you don't," Randall said and plopped himself back down. "Your mom already showed you how to read and you can do sums. If you can do all that, you'll hate sitting in that cold classroom. I beg Zeke and my mom all the time to let me quit."

"Why you hate it so much?"

"I dunno. I guess cuz I'm half white."

"What's that got to do with anything?"

Randall shrugged his shoulders. "Ms. Washington's always calling me a half-breed."

"Well, what's it like being half white?"

"I dunno. It's the only way I know how to be."

Ray Ray nodded as if this made perfect sense. "Wanna play checkers?"

Randall nodded. "I'll get it. I'm gonna beat you."

"No, you ain't!" Ray Ray shot back.

Ezekiel finished up with the newspaper boy and sent him on. The only sounds left in the shop were the two boys arguing over who was the best and who was going to win. Ezekiel knew what Ms. Washington's problem was, but he wasn't about to tell Randall. She was mad she was a half-breed, too. Carried a chip on her shoulder and a lot of resentment in her heart which made her downright miserable.

Hattie knocked on the door and barely heard the whisper to come in. Jena was in the bed and the room was unusually dark. It was dusk outside and the soft bits of light weren't penetrating the dusty pane. The overcast skies and light drizzle added to the dank, lifeless feel. "Jena, you want me to light a candle or something?"

Jena coughed until a cluster of red stained her handkerchief. Hattie helped tip her on her side while Jena tried to catch her breath. Hattie poured a glass of water. "There's things you can take for the pain," Hattie said, handing Jena the glass. Jena wiped her mouth and took a sip. "I know, the doctors gave me codeine. I just can't bring myself to take it. The patients I saw on medication seemed nearly dead." She coughed again and tried to gulp air through the fit. "I'm trying to stay as normal as possible for Randall."

"I understand," Hattie said as she tucked the edges of the bed. She struck a match and lit the candles on the nightstand. "Jena, I wanted to talk to you about something."

"Oh Hattie, please don't fuss at me about going back to the hospital. I don't want to." Hattie smiled and patted Jena's hand. "I'm not here to talk about that. I'm here to talk about me. I wanted your opinion on something."

Jena squeezed Hattie's hand. "Well, that was awfully vain of me." Hattie squeezed Jena's hand back and Jena continued, "Of course you can talk to me. What's on your mind?"

"I can't really say this to my daddy or talk with him about it. I'm sure he'll just say no and my uncles will just laugh like the idea is silly." Jena nodded understanding. "There are a few doctors at the hospital talking about taking a team of doctors and nurses to Shanghai to help with medical aid. With all the bombings and the fighting many people are displaced, especially children. One of the doctors knows a British missionary over there that needs help and he wants to go. I think I might want to volunteer."

Jena patted Hattie's hand as she sat on the edge of the bed. "If that is where God is calling you, then you have to go."

"But what about Daddy, Randall,...you?"

"Hattie, don't you worry about us. The Lord will take care of us just like always, but you have to do what He calls you to do."

Randall came busting through the door. "You're back early," Jena said. "Mr. Dixon gave me a ride," he said, holding up a bag of vittles as if that explained everything.

"Hey, Randall," Hattie said as he set the bag on the table and came over to give each of them a hug. Hattie stood to excuse herself. "I better be going. Daddy needs some supper."

"No, he doesn't, Mrs. Dixon brought dinner for everybody. She brought it from the house in town. They had a big party and gave her the leftovers. Ezekiel and everybody already ate." He pointed at the bag on the table. "I brought you some Mama, and Zeke has some for Hattie. There's ham, green beans, pie, and dinner rolls. You could make a little sandwich. That's what Joe did."

"Well, I better go home and get me some." She leaned over and hugged Jena. "I'll see y'all later."

"I'll be praying for ya, Hattie."

"Thanks."

Randall was rummaging for a plate. "Mama, I'm gonna make you some food."

"Okay sweetie, but not too much."

Hattie let go of Jena's hand and stood to go. "I'll see ya later. Maybe I'll come by Sunday and stay with you while the men go to church."

"That will be real nice. We can talk then."

"Night, Randall."

"Night, Hattie," he said, pausing to run over and give her a hug. "See ya later."

"See ya later, little man."

Hattie found the courage to go to Shanghai after she and Jena spent weeks praying and seeking the Lord for direction. Once He answered she was quick to pack despite Ezekiel's objections. She knew he was right, it would be dangerous, but she felt called of the Lord and she had to go. She left bundled in a wool coat and a scarf Jena made. With a suitcase filled with one dress, a pair of stockings and her medical bag, Hattie boarded the train. She left with her father's blessing and a guarantee everyone would be praying for her. Randall and Ezekiel stood on the platform and watched as the caboose disappeared. Randall felt a tear slip down his cheek. "What if she don't come back, Zeke?"

"We can't think like that, little man. We have to believe God is going to watch over her."

"I just want her to come back, Zeke."

"Me too, little man. Me, too."

PART THREE

CHAPTER 34

Olympia, Mississippi
Spring 1940

Soft rain soaked the earth, giving birth to new life. Randall walked down the gravel road toward the ball field to see how overgrown it was. He wanted to see how much work it needed and when they'd be able to get some games goin'. A little black swarm of gnats followed him, he noticed them trailing after his second mouthful. "Leave me alone," he said as he swung his arms wildly above his head to shoo them away. Their dense cloud scattered for a second and then resumed their black billowy form, trailing just above his head. He pressed on past the plantations where sharecroppers were preparing ground and tilling the furrows. He had his own work cut out for him. Ezekiel wanted him to clear the field and make sure it was ready for games. Randall wanted to use a mule to pull a spinning harvester to mow the field, but Zeke and half the barbershop laughed at the idea and told him to "get to pushin' that hand mower!" He'd been looking in the Sears, Roebuck & Co. catalog and saw some mowers with an engine on them and they were a little wider which would make cutting faster because it'd cover more ground, but he'd been unconvincing. The old timers were doubled over with laughter slapping their knees when he'd suggested it. Claude shouted across the room before he started laughing. "Boy, we don't got to spend no money on a gas mower and we don't need to hitch up no mule. We got you!"

"I'm just inventive," Randall argued.

"Boy, you're just being lazy. Now go on and git," Claude said. Joe added, "And make sure it looks good. I don't wanna twist my ankle on no gopher holes out there." Everyone thought Joe and Claude were so funny, but some days Randall wished they'd just be quiet. Now he was the laughing stock and people were going to jaw him all week, calling him "soft hands" and "weak." He picked up a few smooth rocks. He rolled them around as if they were a handful of marbles. Taking one in his left hand, he wound up and threw it. He could see the rock bounce down the road in front of him. Chucking another one a little further he saw a figure walking toward him. He wondered who it was and where they were going. He guessed they probably lived down this road and they were heading to town. In just a few steps he could tell it was a girl with a cream-colored dress. That was all he could make out, but he could tell that she'd slowed down, probably not being able to identify him either.

Randall stuck his hand up into the air and waved showing he was friendly while he kept walking forward. The figure in the distance picked up her pace and moved to the opposite side of the road. Finally, Randall could identify her, it was Nina. He smiled, they were in class together again this year.

"Hey, Nina!" Randall called out, finally happy he'd come this way.

"Hi, Randall."

His heart began to beat a little faster and he pulled up short as she approached. Rolling the few rocks he had in his hand he tried to be smooth and asked, "Hey, Nina, what are you up to?" Shyness pulled her head toward her shoulder and she cast her eyes to the dusty road. "Nothing. Ma sent me to take Mrs. Neilson some fresh bread and some broth. She wasn't feeling good. They think it was all the rain, got her lungs wet. Doctor called it pneumonia."

Randall nodded. "That's too bad, but I'm sure glad to see ya."

Nina smiled and covered her mouth.

"Well," Randall said as he stopped rolling the rocks and dropped them in his pocket. "I gotta go. I'm supposed to mow the ballfield and have it ready for a practice game later, or maybe tomorrow. But anyway, the guys are gonna get ready for the season. They say a few of 'em can make it in the Negro Leagues. Said a scout should be coming soon."

Nina nodded. "I don't watch baseball. It seems silly chasing a small ball around. I don't know why everybody loves it so much."

"What!" Randall shouted, "Whadda you mean by that? There's more to it than that."

Startled, she took a step back. "Sorry, Randall. I didn't mean to make you mad. I better be goin'," she said before moving past him.

He let her pass and watched her walk down the road from which he'd just come. He smacked himself on the head and wondered why he got so mad. His anger slipped away when he saw her stop by the side of the road and pick a few white daisies with a touch of purple in their center. He'd seen them when he picked up his rocks. Chastening himself he thought he probably could have handled that better. He could have easily explained why people loved baseball. It was the competition, it was the feel of the day, it was the smell of the grass, it was the roar of the crowd, and the game. He loved the game. Throughout the day he imagined the weight of the bat and how it felt when it connected with the ball. His fingers would twitch before he made his jump to steal a bag. He loved the feel of the dirt beneath his feet as his cleats dug in and he sprang forward to grab a fly ball. He changed his mind, maybe he couldn't explain it; either you did love it or you didn't. All he knew was that he did, and it consumed him. He thought about baseball all day. He tossed rocks and anything he could find to get better. He wanted to throw farther, run faster, stand in the box and swing, feeling the smack of wood colliding with leather, sending it soaring against a cool blue sky. A sprint across the outfield, the thud of a ball as it hit the worn leather excited him. Racing as fast as his feet would fly barely touching each bag, setting his eyes on home knowing he could beat the throw, was sheer bliss. He fumbled with the rocks in his pocket. Baseball was like an arm or a leg: he needed it, he couldn't separate himself from it.

Cobwebs covered the walls of the storage shed that smelled like mold and housed the lawn mower. In the corner rested a bucket of baseballs, a few gloves, bats and the sandbags used for bases. Randall looked at the mess; he hated spiders. No matter how many holes he plugged at home, they still managed to get in the house. At least a rat was big and he could catch it in a trap. How could you catch a spider in a trap? You couldn't; one day no spider, the next day they'd invaded and set up shop.

He wiped the silky strings that covered the mower and yanked it out into the sunlight. It was in bad shape from all the rain. The blades were rusted and sticking as he gave them a push. He went back in for the oil can and an old rag. He pulled it over to the bleachers and sat down, flipped the lawn mower over, propping it on its handle and began oiling the blades to get them moving.

His chest was bare and he could feel a burn. He sighed. He knew he wouldn't be half done before Zeke and his brothers would be here to hit grounders. He pushed the mower across the infield as if it were a big afro getting cut down to a quarter inch, just like barbering. He wished the big sickle was sharp like the ones the farmhands had, then he could knock down this tall grass and go over it with the mower after. The way things were going now the grass was too tall and the blades kept getting stuck. This was going to take all day.

It was warm and he wished he'd brought some water with him. There wasn't a pump at the ball field. He wiped the sweat from his forehead and wanted to quit. If it weren't for Joe and Claude teasing him, he might have, but he'd never hear the end of it if he did.

He finished the infield. Tuckered out he laid down on the fresh cut grass and stared at the clouds that looked like big puffs of cotton spilled across the sky. He tossed a ball holding it like Zeke taught him so it'd go straight up and come right back to him. He tossed the ball up over and over watching the red stitches spin into a blur and then come back into focus right before the ball returned to his hand. He could close his eyes and toss it over and over by feel. He got up and grabbed a bat knocking the ball further than he thought he could. After he did it, he realized his mistake. The ball landed in the thick of the outfield where he was going to have to hunt through the overgrown grass to retrieve it.

Just as Zeke and his brothers showed up, Randall finished clearing centerfield. "Boy, what's taken you so long?" Claude hollered. "Why ain't you got this done? You done been here all danged day! Looks like Africa over there with some lions and hyenas hiding in the grass." Joe laughed and slapped his knee like it was the funniest thing he'd ever heard.

Without answering, Randall let the mower drop and ran over to Zeke. "Did ya'll bring me any supper?"

"Now why do you think he brought you anything?" Claude teased picking at him. Joe grabbed Randall's neck and rubbed his head till Randall wiggled away. "O'course he brought you something. Even though ya don't deserve it. You didn't even finish. Spoilt. That's what you are," Joe said, throwing a few jabs in Randall's direction. Randall put up his fists protecting his head and threw a couple of jabs back. He'd learned a lot since his first fight with Big Freddie Mac and now he had a few moves of his own.

Ezekiel handed Randall a canteen with some water and a bag he recognized from Millie's. Eager, he dipped his hand into the bag and pulled out a sandwich wrapped in wax paper. It was meatloaf on buttered bread. Randall crammed it in his mouth and took a bite too big to chew. "Slow down, boy," Claude chided, "Stop eatin' like you a slave." Joe laughed again and whacked Randall on the back.

Quiet, Ezekiel just watched while Randall scarfed down the sandwich reaching into the bag for something more. He pulled out an apple devouring it just like the sandwich. There was still a little something at the bottom of the bag. Randall smiled, he bet Millie sent cookies. He pulled them out and offered one to Zeke. "Thanks, little man," he said, taking one.

Zeke was tired but Randall hadn't noticed. "Thanks for dinner," Randall said with his mouth full. "You're welcome," Zeke said, clapping Randall on the shoulder. "The field looks good. I'll take over and finish." Randall gulped some water and shook his head. "Naw, it's okay. I'll finish. It just took me a long time to get the mower goin'cuz the blades were stuck. I had to oil 'em." Ezekiel grabbed one of Randall's hands to examine it. Covered in dirt Ezekiel saw soft oval translucent spots forming on Randall's palms. "You're gonna have blisters. I'm gonna finish and you can pitch to Claude and Joe. They're gonna want to hit all night and I'm too tired to pitch for 'em. Can you do it?"

"Oh, yeah. You know it!" Randall beamed.

Ezekiel went over to the shed and rummaged around a bit. When he came back out he had a sickle and a wet stone. As a boy, clearing wheat, Ezekiel had become acquainted with the highly effective tool and in the right hands he knew it'd be faster than the mower. After sharpening the blade he went to the tall grass and smooth as silk he twisted back and forth dropping chunks of grass in his wake. Within an hour the field was cleared and he easily pushed the mower across the patchy grass leaving alternating smooth lines across the outfield.

It wasn't until stars lit up the night and Randall's arm felt like rubber that they called it quits. Randall's arm had finally refused to obey despite Claude's yelling for him to throw it harder and faster. They'd kept cracking balls long after sundown. The full moon offered good light and they'd stayed late, but Randall's reactions were slowing and Joe nearly hit a line drive right into Randall's stomach. He turned and the ball hit his side, dropping him to the ground. Claude and Joe were the first ones to the mound. "Awe, Randall. Why didn't you catch it?" Joe said. They pulled up his shirt and saw a round red welt forming. "You can tell you're half white with that ugly thing," Joe teased. "You gonna be okay baby boy?"

"I'm not a baby!" Randall retorted. "I ain't even crying."

Joe clapped Randall on the shoulder. "Well, if you ain't hurt, go and get them balls from the outfield." Randall slouched his shoulders but obediently headed for the bucket to collect all the balls.

"Dang, Joe, you hit him with a line drive and then make him go pick up all the balls?" Claude asked.

"Yeah, like he said, he ain't no baby. He's gonna get worse than that. He'd better learn it early. Ain't that right, Zeke?"

Ezekiel pondered the question for a minute before answering. "If he makes it young, he's gotta be ready for a grown man's game." Ezekiel folded one arm across his chest and rubbed his head with the other. Randall was looking like he could really play. He was fast, not just for his age, but he could beat adults and he could hit the strike zone with pretty good heat. He couldn't swing fast enough to hit if Joe was pitching but with a slower pitch Randall could knock the ball into the outfield. No doubt the boy had a chance. He could almost steal a base in a grown man's game and he could beat any kid his own age. If he kept working at it, he could play in the Negro Leagues. Ezekiel was sure of that. He just hoped everything worked out with his mama.

The ride home was quiet. It'd been a long day and Ezekiel had received some bad news about Jimmie. He was doing time up North for bootlegging and had asked for some money to help him get a lawyer. Against his own better judgment, Ezekiel wired the money. That had taken its toll and now Ezekiel needed to talk to Randall about his mama. It was a conversation he didn't want to have, but one he had to have.

Randall pulled the door handle and started to step out of the car. "Randall," Zeke said, despite wanting to let him run to the house."I need to talk to you."

"Hey, Zeke, I'm sorry I didn't get the field done. Please don't be mad. I won't let it happen again."

"I'm not mad," he said, touching Randall's head. "I'm not mad at all. I need to talk to you about your mama."

"What about?" Randall looked over curious.

"You know she's been sick for a long time."

Randall nodded. "Ever since I can remember."

"Well, you ain't supposed to be sick that long. She got the TB, consumption, the wasting disease they call it."

Randall looked confused. "Whatcha mean, Zeke?"

"The doctor done checked on her today and your mama is real sick. He gave her some medicine, but she's in a bad way.."

Confusion etched his face. "I don't understand." As long as he could remember she'd been sick.

Ezekiel patted his shoulder. "I know, son. I don't really understand it either. Just know this; it's a miracle your mama is still livin'. Most folks don't make it this long. Thank the Lord and we're gonna make a plan tomorrow. There's a tent revival comin'. They say the man comin' is a healer. Maybe we can take your mama."

Randall didn't have any idea what Ezekiel was talking about; he just wanted to get inside and check on his mama. "Okay, Zeke."

"Alright, you go on now. Try not to tire your mama out. Let her rest."

"I will," Randall said, closing the door to the car. "I'll see you tomorrow."

"Alright, little man. See ya tomorrow."

CHAPTER 35

Olympia, Mississippi
August 1946

It had only been a year since the war ended, and the impact was still reverberating around the world. Countries were recovering from the bloodshed and economies were trying to bounce back. Parades lined streets in every city across America, flags waved in celebration, handkerchiefs dabbed tear-stained cheeks. Soldiers were still trying to find normal after returning home and families were adjusting to loss.

The bell over the door dinged and a broad-shouldered man came in wearing a white linen button up, a pair of khaki pants, brown leather dress shoes, and a brimmed hat with a swanky ribbon round about the middle of it. His hat was tipped downward and hid his face. "Randall? That you?" Ezekiel said walking over. Tipping his hat up revealed a familiar face with a big grin. He was taller than when he left and about two shades darker. Playing ball all day in the sun had given him a deep rich color, and his incoming stubble suggested he was older than seventeen. He stood tall in the doorway, his shoulders back, his head high. Ezekiel liked the maturity radiating off him, his heart swelled looking at the man before him. Randall met Ezekiel with a tight embrace. "I've missed you, Randall." "I missed you, too." "I'm glad you're home." "Me, too." They clapped one another on the back. Ezekiel leaned back still holding the boy's shoulders and gave him a good once over. "You look good." Randall grinned wide and rubbed the front of his shirt. "Thanks. I wanted to look sharp for you guys."

On his way to the barbershop Randall noticed Olympia hadn't changed, and the barbershop even less. Perched on the bench along the back wall Fred fanned himself with a newspaper. "Randall, what have ya been doin' out on the road? All the girls chasing ya?" Randall blushed. "Naw, not too much." Girls did chase him and in the big cities they were more forward than he knew what to do with. They cat called to him on the field. When he played on first base he could hear them calling. "Hey pretty boy. Hey, look over here with them cat eyes." He tried not to glance over because it only fanned a fire and they'd keep it up. Sometimes after the game they'd crowd around and want to touch his "good hair". He hadn't known what to do with all the extra female attention but he wasn't about to admit that here at the barbershop. He'd never hear the end of it.

He sat in Ezekiel's chair and let him edge him up.

"So what do you do out there on the road? You meet anybody famous?" Joe asked. Randall's face lit up. "Yeah, of course. Sometimes we play three games a day. We stay busy and we get to meet all kinds of famous folks. Everybody loves baseball. All kinds of folks come to our games." "Shut your mouth!" Fred shouted, surprised. "Who'd ya meet?"

"You know Jazz singers, artists, musicians. I got to meet Josh Gibson, the best slugger in the league! I gotta chase down all them balls he hits and more than half are over the fence."

Fred nodded. "Yeah, I read in the paper that ole Josh kicks balls out of the park and introduces them to the moon with one mighty swing!"

"That true?" Joe asked.

"Just about. When Josh smacks that ball you can hear it screamin' all the way to the moon."

The room erupted in laughter. Joe said, "I guess you're not getting that one no matter how fast ya are." Randall wore a grin that covered his face and a glint lit up his eye. "In the winter league he hit it right over the 500 foot mark in center field. Nobody moved, we just watched it go."

"Naw Randall stop funnin' us. You serious?" Joe asked.

"There's some tall tales out there but trust me, Josh can hit like nobody's business." Randall laughed and added. "But if he hits one anywhere on the field, it's mine."

Ezekiel chimed in. "That's some mighty big talk. You just go on out there and back it up!"

"Yeah Randall, go on and make us proud!" Claude added.

Changing subjects Randall asked, "What's been goin' on here?"

"Just the same ole stuff," Claude replied. "Joe's gonna propose to Mabel one day. Hattie went overseas again. Europe this time. We get her letters but she's all over the place; France, Germany, she even went to England. She says there's a lot going on over there. Trying to settle everything down after the war and all. Folks are coming back. A lot are messed up."

Randall nodded. "I saw some pictures in the paper and I've been reading a bit."

"Speaking of pictures, you ever hear from Ray Ray? Check these out." Claude walked over to some framed photos on the wall. "He sends us these every now and again. We cut his pictures from the paper, too." Claude handed Randall a stack of newspaper clippings all with Ray Ray's name at the bottom.

"He's doing pretty good." Joe added.

A twinge of hurt tugged at Randall's heart. He hadn't realized how much he missed his friend. He recalled a shutter click at home plate once and he'd spun back expecting to see his friend back there, but instead the ball sped past him and the umpire shouted, "Str-r-ri-ke three! You're outta here." The photographer got the shot he needed and Randall's face was on the cover of the paper with a look of surprise and a headline that read, Wilson Stunned as Smokey Burns One Past Him.

The article made him look like a baby trying to play with the big boys. He was mad. He'd hit on Smokey plenty of times and scored on him at home with a steal. What was that reporter talking about? Randall grimaced at the memory.

"What else they got in them big cities? Do the white folks ever come to the games?" Claude asked. Randall laughed. "Yeah, white folks come to the games. A lot actually. If the Indianapolis Clowns are playing, those white folks will pack out the stadium. Nobody wants to miss out on the baseball circus."

"Yeah?" Joe said, "Remember when we went when you was little? I was gonna take Mabel to go see 'em when they played the Brooklyn Stars. It was a triple header, but it was gonna take four hours to get there."

"I remember. You shoulda went. They're even funnier now. They're worth the drive. Especially if King Tut is playing. He'll split your sides. He sits at second base in a rocking chair smokin' a cigar."

"Randall, you're pullin' my leg."

"Naw Joe, I'm serious. He has a giant glove and he does all kinds of ball tricks."

Joe folded his arms and rubbed his chin contemplating what he might have missed. "Yeah, well, I'll see him the next time."

Randall made his voice deep and mimicked the radio commercial. "You don't wanna miss them again. They're the Greatest Show in baseball history."

"Awe Randall, they can't be that good," Joe said.

"They're even better. Shoot, I don't even pay attention when I play against 'em. I'm too busy watching their antics."

"Naw, you don't say," Claude said.

"Yeah, one time I was stealing third but Tut hid the ball in his glove and tagged me out as I dropped down and slid into the bag. I was sure he'd thrown to second. When he tagged me out and held up the ball he said, 'Go sit down young blood. You fast, but not fast enough today.' Maaan, I felt so dumb."

"You should feel dumb, falling for that old trick. Shoot." Joe said.

The room roared with laughter again. Randall kept telling stories of life on the road. The ups, the downs and everything in between. He told 'em how they had weeks of not taking showers, sleeping in fields, not knowing when you were gonna eat and all the other mundane things you don't know and don't wanna know if you're not there. He shared the pre-game acts like jugglers and acrobats. And how the ballfield was always electric and fun, even in the small towns with a dirt field and no stands. Folks came out with their families and their little ones. Promoters on the radio would shout, "Entertainment and fun, thrills galore." In black towns the games were the biggest thing to happen all year.

Although Randall didn't have a family like the ones he saw in the stands, he enjoyed seeing them and looked forward to one day having his own little ones to tote around and play with. A few other players would have their kids at games or practice and Randall always enjoyed taking time to goof off with them. Sometimes he glanced into the stands wishing he would see his own family even though he knew he wouldn't. Nobody was traveling that far up North or across to Cuba for a game.

His teammates were much older than he was and he tried to live clean like Ezekiel taught him. He wasn't old enough to drink or smoke, but nobody would have stopped him if he tried. He just didn't have a taste for it. The road grated like falling into a patch of stinging nettle. It got under your skin and made you itch until your skin was raw and puss leaked out. Playing ball was the beauty of it, the rest was a red prickly rash.

He wrote Nina letters and he hoped she thought about him as much as he thought about her. He told her about the big orchestras in Cuba and the fast-paced dances; he could never quite get the hang of the fancy footwork. The big cities up North had their clubs and music and big lights and fast life, too, and at first it was all exciting, but later he just longed for home. He'd call the barbershop and talk to Zeke which usually made the longing for home even stronger, but he loved baseball and couldn't bring himself to leave it behind.

Outside the picture show, Randall removed his coat and wrapped it around Nina's shoulders. "You wanna get a slice of pie at Millies?" Randall asked. Nina looked at the ground and twisted a piece of her hair. "No, thank you. I gotta get back home."

"Okay." He turned toward where they'd parked. He wanted to slip his hand in hers, instead he crammed his hands in his pockets. Nina silently slipped her arm through his and his heart beat a little faster. She looked up at him. "When do you leave next, Randall?" He shuffled his feet to delay their walk to the car. "I leave at the end of September. I'm not sure exactly what day yet. I still have to get my ticket." Nina sucked in her breath. "It must all be so exciting!"

"Sometimes it is. It's alright."

"Are you ever scared?"

"Naw, most folks on the road are real nice. Black towns the folks are down right hospitable and let you stay in their barns, in their churches, and even at their houses. They have barbecues and music, it's like a big party. The poorest towns got the most hospitality. They can't pay much to come see us play, but they sure make up for it."

"I heard y'all can't go to all white towns and that there's no coloreds allowed."

"Yeah, we do come across that every now and again, but out West we don't find too much trouble. Mexico is great, just about everybody is treated the same and well…you know how it is out here in the South. The manager usually knows what spots to avoid."

She nodded and leaned in closer, her voice got lower. "I get scared for ya sometimes."

He pulled her close and surprised himself when he kissed her on the forehead. "Don't worry about me Nina. I'll be alright." She smiled and squeezed his arm. "I'll keep praying for ya." "Yeah, don't stop praying for me."

Randall stopped the car in front of her house. He leaned over to place a kiss on her lips. She turned slightly and he ended up giving her a peck on her cheek. "I'll write you," he whispered as she exited the car. She tilted her head and smiled, her hand rested where he'd placed the kiss. For a second he considered giving up baseball for her. Her smell intoxicated him and the gaze of her brown eyes mesmerized him. His body stirred with longing. Her mama waited at the door. He waved and pulled away. He wondered what it would be like to be with her the rest of his life.

April 25, 1940

Dear Lord,

I'm wasting away. I'm skin and bones. The doctors make a big fuss about rest, but I know it's because they don't have nothin' else to offer me. I feel guilty being sick for so long. Ezekiel reminds me that I don't control it but I can't help but be frustrated.

Hattie's back, but she's different. I try and have conversations that aren't about my sickness, I don't want folks to think that's all I can talk about is myself and how I'm dyin' right before their eyes. I read the papers and stories so that I have something to talk about, but Hattie would rather talk about me than what she saw in Shanghai. She says I couldn't even imagine the death and destruction. She says she can't sleep. She says it was the grace of the Lord that brought her home in one piece. She didn't even go back to work at the hospital when she came back. She's just been home, praying and seeking the Lord. Her pretty blue eyes look haunted and even wild sometimes. She says the nightmares keep her up at night.

For my body there's a tiny bit of improvement. I can get up and sit in a chair for an hour. Randall puts the rocker on the porch for me. I do the deep breathing exercises and let my skin soak up the sun. Articles in the paper say folks go to sanatoriums to do just that, go outside and sit in fresh air. Well, I can do that right here and watch the hens as they work the yard scratching and pecking. Just a few days ago a fox got two of them. I sure was sad to lose them. One was our best laying hen. We still collect enough for me and Randall, but if that fox comes and takes any more we'll be in a bit of trouble. Randall puts the hens up early, but I think that sly ole fox is just waiting for an opportunity.

Most days, I can be laying flat just like I'm supposed to and the squeezing in my chest will start and a fit will overtake me. I try to not talk above a whisper but it doesn't stop the tightness or the overwhelming pain. I'm afraid Lord, but I know You are with me.

My x-ray showed something bad and the doctor said I need a specialist. I know we don't have money for that. The doctor said a lot of scary things, but most important is that Randall needs to stay away from me. I feel like a leper. They want to collapse my right lung. They say the left lung is doing good, but they want to collapse the right. I'd have to go away until I'm fit to take up a semi-normal life. I kept asking how long that would take and the doctor kept saying, "however long it takes."

What in the world does that mean?

It's a lot of money and Randall would be alone. They say I might be able to get a contribution toward the cost from the county fund. That would be helpful. There's got to be another way. There just has to.

Lord, please help me. I don't want to leave my baby.

CHAPTER 36

Olympia, Mississippi
June 20, 1940

It was Friday night and the whole town walked toward Granger field where they'd set up a tent large enough to hold hundreds. Traveling preachers were becoming more and more common and folks were drawn to the big tents. The signs outside boasted of revival and one said, Come and Expect a Miracle – super natural explosion. As Randall carried his mama to the tent he hoped the sign was all they hoped it would be. The service went long and his mama coughed nearly the whole time. Her handkerchief was soaked red. He was fed up and ready to leave seconds before the preacher pointed and shouted at them to bring her forward. Randall was angry. They'd sat through hours of singing and preaching without helping his mama and now they wanted to make a spectacle of her. Ezekiel nudged him. "Go on, Randall. This is what we came for." He lifted his mama and carried her up front. The preacher turned to the crowd. "I wanna know how many of you know this woman." A few hands went up. Others weren't sure what the preacher was getting at and didn't raise their hands but Ezekiel knew almost everybody in the room at least knew of her. With each step Randall felt his anger rise. The preacher turned to him, "Set her down." "Sir, she can't stand." "Boy, put her down!" the preacher shouted, "The Lord is in control." With great reservation and a complete lack of faith Randall set his mother on her feet. Before he could help her get her balance the preacher grabbed her hand and started hollering, "In the name of Jesus Christ of Nazareth, sickness, you come out!" Randall reached for his mother as the preacher swung her around like a rag doll. "I command you by the authority in Christ. Come out now!"

Jena began to cough and spit up more blood. Randall's fury blossomed and before he could snatch his mother back two men had his arms pinned behind him. His mama was on all fours shaking and coughing, while the preacher shouted, "Rise!" The coughing ceased and Jena rose to her feet. She took a deep breath and shouted at the top of her lungs, screaming like a banshee. "Hallelujah!" Tears flowed down her cheeks and more hallelujahs rang out around the room as a frenzy of hope poured over the room. It was common knowledge, nearly everybody knew Jena was dyin' and could scarcely walk or talk, but right now she was upfront dancing and shouting hallelujah.

Folks didn't have to be asked, as soon as they saw that, they just started lining up. Jena moved off to the side and raised her hands to the heavens as she shouted with all her might, "Thank You, Lord! Thank You, Jesus!" The men who were holding Randall released him and went to help others. Randall fell to his knees, his mouth hanging wide open, his eyes wide. He couldn't believe it. He'd never seen his mama dancing.

December 8, 1941

Dear Lord,

The world is upside down. The Japanese have attacked Pearl Harbor. It seems unreal. The world is at war. Folks are sayin' this is the greatest war of all time. There's never been nothing like it. When have so many countries been fighting one another all at the same time? I've been reading your word and Reverend Bordeaux says we need to pray. Help me, Lord. I don't know what to pray.

It's been over a year since I got healed. I spent the year trying to catch up on living and there's so much I've missed. I've been sewing a bit. I made some shirts for the fellas at the barbershop. They came out real nice and I felt real good doing something productive. I took in some work and have a little income. My foot can push the pedal on my sewing machine without me growing weary, which feels like a miracle all by itself. The hardest thing about being sick was feeling completely useless.

I take walks and I've gotten stronger. I'm not so tired anymore. I can do things I couldn't do before. I can sweep and lift a skillet to cook. I spent the summer on my knees, in the sun picking weeds and tending our garden. We have some of our garden put up from the summer. Pickles and sauerkraut are in crocks and there's plenty of canned tomatoes, green beans, corn, carrots and peas. We had a good harvest. We dried some corn to mill. We'll have enough for grits, cornbread, and corn cakes all winter.

I feel happy to finally have dinner ready when Randall comes home instead of him having to bring food or cook when he gets here. Being so needy for every little thing wears on your spirit. I'm grateful for everyone that helped us, we wouldn't have made it without help. Thank you Jesus! You are so good to us.

CHAPTER 37

Olympia, Mississippi
June 1942

Jena sat on the wood bench and beamed as the crowd stood to cheer for her son. A thread of electricity ran through the crowd. He was the only boy on the field; scrawny and skinny next to grown men playing a team from a neighboring county. On his first at bat, Randall bunted a fastball which sent it bouncing. Sheer speed had gotten him on first. He was edging toward second. The ball left the pitcher's hand and quick as lightnin' he was off for second. The catcher was on his feet, the ball was on its way. Jena closed her eyes. When she heard the joyous roar of the crowd she peeked and saw the umpire with outstretched arms and her son standing on second dusting off his uniform. She'd altered it and stitched on his name earlier that day. Ezekiel had come by to see if she'd let Randall play. They were going to be short a few players. She never imagined he'd have half the crowd cheering, "Wil-son, Wil-son, Wil-son!"

Alongside the dugout, Ray Ray had two cameras slung around his neck and walked with a limp snapping photos. At home Jena heard Randall brag about how fast he was, and she thought that's all it was, boyish bragging. It wasn't until he was in the outfield running for a deep hit ball that she realized how fast he actually was. "He'll never get it," she heard the crowd murmur as they watched the ball sail further and further out. Jena thought it looked impossible, too. Folks were out of their seats watching as Randall tumbled head over heels in the outfield. He lay in the grass for a mere second before his arm shot up in the air holding the last out of the inning. The hometown crowd exploded in cheers. He'd stopped the winning run.

The bench cleared. Players sprinted into the outfield where Joe scooped Randall up onto his shoulders. Folks from the stands joined the hullabaloo on the field while Jena's heart raced, a mama's pride flowing through her veins. She stayed in the stands and clapped and shouted with the crowd, barely holding back tears of joy. They were talking about her boy.

"Keep an eye on that kid. He's something special," one person said.

Jena was shaking, she covered her mouth with her hands and grinned. She couldn't believe it, people were proud of her boy. Nobody cared he was mulatto. They accepted him. She looked up and watched as people clamored around him, still hoisted up on Joe's shoulders dancing around the field. A worry that had hidden itself in the recesses of her heart was removed. A peace she didn't know she longed for settled where the worry had been. She took a deep breath and exhaled. The Lord had made a way where she thought there'd never be a way.

Two weeks later Randall came home with two black and white photos of himself. One with his arm held toward the sky holding the winning out, and the second sitting up on Joe's shoulders, victory etched in his face as the crowd surrounded him. He fingered the photo over and over. "Mama look," Randall kept saying. "I've seen the picture, Randall. And I was there, remember?" "Yeah, but I just can't believe it. I really can't. I made the winning out."

Jena hugged her boy tight. "You sure did."

Randall put his pictures on the nightstand and flopped on his bed. "Mama, you think I could play in the pros?"

"I think with the good Lord's help you can do anything He puts in your heart to do."

"Folks say I can. They say if I keep going like this, I could do it easy."

"Well, I'm sure it's not that easy or everybody could do it. You're definitely blessed with some special abilities. I'm sure you'll have to work hard at it. But you're still young."

Randall crossed his arms over his chest and huffed. "If you don't believe in me, there are other people that do."

"Son," Jena rebuked her son. "I believe in you. I know you're blessed and you're fast, but that doesn't mean you don't have to work hard."

Randall sighed and dropped his shoulders. "I know. That's what Ezekiel says, too."

"Well, a wise man listens to good counsel. Are you wise?"

"Yeah, I'm wise and one day I'll be famous and your family will see me and they'll be sad they never came to see us." The comment startled her. She didn't think that Randall ever thought of her family. They never discussed them. He never asked and she never offered. She changed the subject. "What do you want for supper?"

CHAPTER 38

Olympia, Mississippi
Spring 1943

Thunderclouds billowed in the darkening sky. Ray Ray commented on them. "A storm is coming." Randall said nothing. He frowned, gripped the hammer in his fist and smashed the pecan resting on the front porch. He smashed another and another before Ray Ray hollered, "Hey! Cut that out. We're supposed to be shelling these so Mama can sell them, not so you can make smashed pecans."

Randall didn't look up or stop until Ray Ray swung his cane at him. "Man, I said stop! My mama needs these whole." Randall looked up fury blazing in his eyes. He dropped the hammer and without saying anything he got up and walked down the long drive to where his bike was propped up against a tree. Ray Ray stood and grabbed his cane attempting to give chase until Randall hopped on his bike and took off down the drive toward home. Ray Ray's dad met him on the lane and placed a hand on his son's shoulder. "Give him some time son. This is going to be hard on him."

Randall gripped the handle bars with all his strength and pedaled hard. He rode as fast as he could until the storm clouds dumped their load soaking his body and stinging his face. He didn't know where he was going but he didn't want to go home and explain things to his mom. He didn't want to go to the barber shop where Claude would say something like; well that's the way of things. Then Joe would add something in like; ain't nobody said life was fair, so quit all that cryin'. Randall could already feel his anger rise at the thought of their comments. He knew what they were gonna say would be true, but he just didn't want to hear it. Ezekiel would understand but he'd wait till later to talk about it.

There was a bus pick up close by the edge of town. He decided to stop. The roads were getting muddy and he kept getting stuck. He pulled under the awning and threw his bike down. He sat on the bench and punched the wood with his fist. He couldn't believe what he'd heard from Ray Ray. After everything they'd been through, everything they'd worked toward. It just couldn't be true.

He sat watching the rain until the storm passed. His mama was going to be worried, but he didn't care. He didn't care about anything.

It was only a week later that Alvin, Ray Ray's oldest brother, was there ready to take the family's belongings, Mrs. Dixon, and Ray Ray to Chicago. Mr. Dixon and the other two boys would follow by train.

Despite Ezekiel's best advice, Randall refused to see them off. In fact he hadn't seen Ray Ray since the thunderstorm and according to him he was never going to see his friend again. Ezekiel kept telling him it wasn't Ray Ray's fault, lots of people were going North and it wasn't worth being mad over. Ezekiel reminded Randall how there'd be more opportunities for his friend in a bigger city. Nonetheless, a stubborn streak prevailed, and when Ray Ray and his dad came to the barbershop to say goodbye, Randall was nowhere to be found.

CHAPTER 39

Olympia, Mississippi
May 28, 1944

The arms of the great oak spread fifteen feet across offering a repreve under its huge canopy of shade, Randall leaned against the broad trunk and let his mind wander. Flies chased one another in the swelter of the day, while bees worked diligently stopping at each dandelion and wild flower, pollinating and collecting as they buzzed along. Randall plucked at a blade of grass and fingered it. He could hear giggling and laughing as children splashed one another, refreshing themselves down at the lake. The early summer wasn't torridly hot, but a warm zephyr carried the woodsy scent of slow-smoked meat across the field. Older folks fellowshipped in the shade of the cluster of oak trees where tables were draped with pressed cloth and heavy laden with food.

A bead of sweat rolled down Randall's back. He thought of Nina in her yellow and white polka dot dress and her brown legs peeking from beneath the hem. Ezekiel had teased him about his first crush and warned him that girls were trouble, but he'd also laughed and patted Randall on the shoulder reassuringly. When he was younger they'd had a talk about the birds and the bees and about how all the feelings he was going to have were perfectly normal, but today didn't seem normal as he tugged at the long whiskers gathering on his chin. He missed his friend whom he refused to talk about. Previous years they'd be laughing and playing in the lake, chasing girls with horny toads, and eating barbecue. This year, the memories mixed with budding emotions for Nina collided in him. He didn't know how to feel or what to do.

He thought about Ezekiel reading a bunch of bible scriptures about women with honeyed lips and sweet words that would trap him and lead him down a path like an ox to a slaughter. He sighed, he didn't know what they meant and he was too embarrassed to ask. He really didn't know what it all meant other than Ezekiel's warning, Don't fool with girls unless you're ready to get married. Randall decided he wasn't ready for that, but Nina sure was pretty and he liked it when she smiled at him.

Randall watched a butterfly land nearby and let its wings slow to a steady rhythm, ready and waiting for its moment to take flight. He felt that way, ready to take flight, but unlike the butterfly he didn't know how. Grabbing a rock Randall chucked it into the tall grass, scattering a group of grasshoppers. He was resting, but restless. His mind drifted like a boat with no anchor, aimless from thought to thought. He thought about baseball, the power he felt with the bat tilted slightly behind him, waiting for the right moment to swing and make contact. He could see the ball soaring into the outfield and maybe over the fence. He felt his muscles tense as he imagined the race toward first, rounding the bag on his way toward second.

The grown men were playing dominoes on picnic tables next to the black barrel smokers where they could keep an eye on the heat, adding a piece of wood to the smoker box every now and again. He wanted to stuff himself with all the food that would be here and not think about anything else. Even now his stomach growled. The meat would be tender, he imagined the pork falling apart as he dipped it in Sam's vinegary sauce.

The pit master was Sam the butcher. He started the smoker the day before. He'd get the fire started and tended it until he had the embers at a steady orange glow. For the summer picnic he stayed up all night and smoked a whole hog. At the Thanksgiving get-together, where he had the same dedication and routine, he'd be out all night in the cold smoking turkeys for dinner at the church. Nobody missed either. Ms. Sally would bring potato salad, something his mama never made. Henry, who owned the auto shop, would bring a kettle full of beans sweetened with maple syrup, and Mavis would have enough collards with ham hock to feed an army. Millie's restaurant would be closed today since nobody would be there and she brought most of the pies and desserts.

Everybody brought something; big watermelons were just getting ripe for pickin', along with squash, green beans, and fresh sliced tomatoes. Randall's favorite was cucumbers and onion in vinegar. He'd eat half of Mrs. Sally's crock. Sweet tea would sit in the sun slowly steeping while kids ran around the picnic tables playing tag.

Boys caught toads in the mud by the lake and chased girls with the big slimy creatures until screams of terror aggravated the adults and Mrs. Jones shouted, "Ya'll cut that out! Leave them girls alone. I don't want to hear no more of that screamin', or I'll give you something to scream about!" Mrs. Jones could pull a switch out of thin air and she'd pop anybody—anywhere. Nobody crossed Mrs. Jones, not even her husband.

He threw another rock as Hattie came up and took a seat next to him. "What's going on with you?" she asked. Randall looked in the opposite direction to avoid the gaze of her piercing blue eyes. He remained quiet as if she hadn't spoken. Hattie bumped him playfully with her shoulder. "I know something is bothering you." Randall shook his head and kept his eyes averted. She leaned over and whispered, "Then I'll just sit here until you confess."

Randall felt a lump form in his throat. Danged Hattie, he thought, she always knew when something was wrong. He knew she'd pick away until she got it out of him. He hated that she always got information out of him. He could run bases like lightning, dive to catch a deep hit ball, and hit grand slams, but he couldn't run from Hattie. "I know you miss him. Even though you don't ever say his name." She'd planted the seed and now she'd wait till he cracked.

Today he was going to change his streak, he had come over here to be alone and she wasn't gettin' nothin' out of him. He was determined. He wasn't talking. They hunkered under the cover of the old oak tree while Hattie hummed hymns casually singing a few bars now and then. "I'll fly away old glory, oh I'll fly away." Her sweet voice soothed his restlessness. They both swatted at flies and he threw a few more rocks. She stopped singing and shot up in haste. "You hear that?" He didn't, he had been focused on her singing and trying to forget about Ray Ray. "What is it?" he asked before he heard it; screeching, wild, uncontrolled cries. "They're drownin'! Somebody help us!" Hattie and Randall jumped up and raced toward the lake.

As they approached, Randall could see at least five people flailing in desperation, their mouths wide open, gulping water. A crowd stood on the banks of the lake. Women were screaming and men were wading out into the water. Randall knew what the problem was, he fished here all the time. There was a nice shallow for about twenty feet out where kids could play and wade, still touching the bottom, but then there was a steep drop off and he'd slipped off it more than once. He remembered being caught by surprise trying to reel in a fish when just one step too far had taken him over the edge. He'd been so mad, he lost the fish, his fishing pole, and got a good soaking. The water over there was quick and strong. He'd struggled a time or two getting out of it. Whoever slipped in would likely get pulled under.

Ripping off his shirt and tossing his shoes as he ran, Randall headed for the water. Hattie screamed, "Randall, don't!"

He hollered back, "They can't swim!" She already knew that. She saw drowning victims at the hospital frequently and they usually came in twos, the victim and their rescuer.

She sprinted for the tables where she hoped to find a rope. She passed her dad who was heading toward the water. She bellowed into the mass hysteria, "I need a rope!" No one was listening. Folks were deaf and blind to her plea as they ran toward the children. She turned in circles, frantic to find a rope. "Help me, Lord." She turned one more time and her eyes fell on one holding down a tent flap. She ran over and yanked it from its eyelets and ran back to the water. Randall had already pulled two small kids from the water and she could see him swimming toward another. Their little bodies lay prone in the mud while their mothers shook them like rag dolls hoping they'd wake up. Ezekiel grabbed Hattie and turned her toward him, "Honey, give me this and you go help the kids." She nodded and he took the rope dangling from her hand. She didn't say anything but was spurred to action. Kneeling next to the first little boy she checked his pulse–nothing. She darted over to the dainty girl who couldn't have been more than five. A weak but a steady pulse flowed through her little wrist, but she wasn't breathing. Hattie used both her palms and applied pressure to the girl's chest to expel the water. The mother of the girl screamed profanities and beat on Hattie's back with her fists until the father snatched her back and held her while Hattie worked.

Women standing on the shore shouted to the men standing in the water. "Save my baby! Save my baby!" Hattie ignored everything to focus on the little girl in front of her. She gave two firm quick thrusts on the chest before the little girl convulsed and began coughing up water. Hattie turned the little girl on her side and gave her back a few good whacks. Breaking free from her husband the mother snatched her daughter from

Hattie's hands wrapping the little girl in both arms she rocked back and forth in the mud crying out, "Jesus, Jesus, my baby, my baby." Hattie took a breath and looked up. Randall had handed off three more people to the men standing in the shallows. They ran them to the shore and she went to check on them. With a few quick thrusts two were coughing up water. She went to check on the third. As Hattie passed by the mother of the first boy, the lady grabbed Hattie by the arm and begged her to bring her boy back. Hattie knew he'd been gone too long. The mother begged and begged until Hattie went to tend the boy. She thrust on his chest trying to expel the water and get his pulse back. She shook her head. "Ma'am, I'm sorry. He's gone." She looked up into the eyes of the desperate mother and recognized the look of disbelief. She'd seen it on the fourth floor of the hospital when she let people know their loved one was gone. "I'm sorry," she said, getting up out of the mud to help others. Loud wails gushed anew filled with fathomless anguish. Cries that had been hopeful were now mournful and deep.

Scanning the lake Hattie spotted Randall, he was swimming toward a grown man twice his size who'd slipped under the water. It was Mr. Thorm, a farmer, the man people called if they needed help lifting something. He was a hefty man with strength to match. Mr. Thorm's gigantic hands splashed frantically just above the surface of the water searching for something to grasp. Hattie watched as they locked on a target. He had hold of Randall's neck. Hattie ran headlong into the water until Ezekiel grabbed her by the waist. "You know better. You can't swim."

She watched wide eyed as the two struggled in the water. Mr. Thorm was marked by terror, his eyes wild and his limbs out of control, he tried to climb onto Randall's head as he gasped for air. They went under again. Randall's chances looked slim.

Frozen, staring wide-eyed, mouths gaping, folks watched in horror as they anticipated the two men's deaths. Hattie saw an opportunity.

"Daddy! The rope!" They tossed it out as far as they could,trying to get Randall's attention."Randall! Randall!" Hattie shouted.

Struggling with the giant in the murky water, Randall changed his strategy. He thought to dive deeper in hopes Mr. Thorm would let go. It couldn't hurt, Randall thought. He'd never be strong enough to loosen Mr.Thorm's grip. Desperate, Randall used his hands and a quick kick to thrust himself downward. The deeper depth was colder and an undertow stirred beneath his feet. His lungs squeezed, he was desperate for air, but he couldn't surface until Mr. Thorm released him. A few seconds that felt like eternity passed and finally Randall felt the big man's hands loosen. Mr. Thorm struggled toward the surface. He bobbed up once caught his breath and continued to struggle.

From the mud-churned shallows where Ezekiel and Hattie stood, they watched as Mr. Thorm popped back up with no sign of Randall. Hattie pulled at her hair and began to scream, "Randall! Randall!" Her voice rose to a high pitch.

Ezekiel, with the rope still in his hands, felt a slight tug just like a fish nibbling on a line. Ezekiel pulled, creating some tension. He watched as the line jerked. He adjusted his grip, leaned back and heaved. The weight in his hands was reassuring as hand over hand he drew the line and Randall surfaced. Ezekiel sighed with relief when he saw Randall wave a hand to stop. Randall was treading water now, the rope still firm within his grasp. He took a few strokes and began swimming back out to the middle of the lake, circling wide he drug the rope around Mr. Thorm so that the big man could grab onto it. Randall shouted to him, "Grab the rope." Mr. Thorm's movements had slowed and he wasn't thrashing about. It seemed as though he'd go under again. "Mr. Thorm, tuck it under your arms." Close to exhaustion, it didn't seem as if Mr. Thorm could hear or understand. Randall signaled for Ezekiel to pull, hoping the rope would catch Mr. Thorm like a lasso even if he didn't grab hold.

The men still standing in the water moved to the rope and heaved along with Ezekiel and Hattie. The rope caught Mr. Thorm under one arm and tightened across his chest towing him in like a fish with no fight left. He was on his side, his head dragging under with each pull. Hattie hoped he wasn't taking in water.

Seeing Mr. Thorm was secure, Randall went for another. There was no movement, but maybe there was hope, the body was face up. As Randall drew near he saw the yellow and white polka dot dress. No, no, no, was all he could think. He hesitated to reach out and touch her fingers, they were cold and lifeless. Her lips were blue and her eyes closed. He drew her near and whispered her name, "Nina." He thought he heard a soft exhale. "Please Lord, spare her," he said as he pulled her close to his chest. He turned onto his back and began to tow her toward the shore. He thought he saw her draw a breath but he couldn't be sure. It could have been the water playing tricks on him. "Nina, hold on. We're almost there."

Hattie waited near the edge of the drop off and grabbed Nina as soon as Randall was close. She checked Nina's pulse. "Good job, Randall. She looks cold but I think she'll be okay. Help me get her over there," Hattie said pointing to a sunny spot on the shore.

They rested her body on the bank. Randall didn't want to leave. He brushed the back of his hand across her cheek. "Wake up, Nina. Come on."

"Go Randall," Hattie said, "I'll take care of her."

He looked at the lake, his body was shaking and he didn't want to go. The last three bodies were face down and not moving.

Fishermen in a rowboat about a half mile out towed Mrs. Sweeny's thick body back to land. She'd been the first adult to run in after the children. When the fishermen reached her body they described her as an angel with her white summer dress fanned out around her like a water lily.

In her big bosom she cradled a three year old who appeared unharmed. Despite her untimely death she looked at peace when they'd brought her in. The lake was still and eerily quiet, not a soul had hope that the few left in the water were alive.

A crowd surrounded Nina who lay in the mud, her head resting on her mother's lap while Hattie rubbed her limbs, trying to get her circulation going. They'd covered her with towels and blankets. Randall drug himself from the water having recovered the last bodies. He stood in the crowd shivering, watching. He was relieved to hear Nina's ragged breathing and soft coughs. He moved away and took a seat on a felled tree. Ezekiel followed and sat next to Randall placing a hand on his shoulder. The shudders came in waves and progressed into uncontrollable shaking sobs. Ezekiel put an arm around Randall's shoulders. "I couldn't save them," Randall cried, "I couldn't save them." Ezekiel didn't have any words of wisdom or comfort. His heart broke along with Randall's and the pain was unreal. They'd lost so many. With a lump in his throat Ezekiel could only hum, Come, Lord Jesus.

The sun burned bright, but darkness settled on the lake as some kneeled and others rocked cold, wet children in their arms. There were no words.

No more than a week later, eight caskets lined the walls of the church. The hardest to look at were the tiny caskets of the children. Every pew in the church was filled while many stood in the back, out the door, and on the steps leading up to the church. All the windows were open so that people could stand beneath them and hear the eulogies. Randall and Ezekiel were pallbearers for Mrs. Swanson. She was hailed a hero, none of the children in the water were hers, yet she'd gone in to save them all the same. Randall was touted a hero, he covered his ears cringing at the suggestion. Guilt consumed him. He couldn't save them all.

His mother was present, the only white woman in the room. Mr. Thorm thanked her for teaching her son how to swim and he apologized multiple times for his panic and almost drowning her son. Nina's mom stopped and thanked her as well. Some even asked her to teach their kids to swim. All these years no one paid her much mind, but today, after the great misfortune, she had become a needful piece of the town.

War was raging in Europe and the Pacific. News came daily delivering blow by blow updates that pummeled the heart and spirit of America. More and more notices of those killed in action. Folks rallied together to accomplish the mission at home, but the war had everyone on edge. Rumors of invasion and bombing of big cities circulated. Folks built shelters and prepared for air raids as much as they could. Most trudged along like a mule hitched to a heavy load. Praying under the burden of depression and woes, folks scarcely had a hope that the war would ever come to an end.

June 5, 1944

Dear Jena and Randall,

I hope that this letter finds you both well. As you know, I completed my training and have been stationed with troops in the Atlantic. I cannot express how much I enjoyed our last visit and treasure the time spent together. Your love and faith in me have carried me through my many moments of doubt. I have the utmost confidence that the Lord hears your prayers and they are a great help. There is a tremendous amount of tension here as we anxiously await orders. It is unnerving not knowing what is happening. I do know we will be heading across the channel to France, however our invasion has been long-delayed and the call to go may come at any minute.

Each man here has his head bent over paper with his hand pouring out his heart to family back home in the event they don't return. In all sincerity, I believe this will be my last. I may be wrong, but I feel fairly certain. If I could explain more clearly, today is like watching the violence of a tornado spin and twirl its way right to your doorstep. You can hear the roar like a train coming for you, and you are unable to move from its path. You know you'll be lucky to survive. The upcoming days are bringing destruction like we've never seen in our lifetime, but I believe the victory will outweigh the losses. Fear is thick and we are like young boys wishing we could cling to our mothers' skirts. I think that is about as cowardly as a man can be, but truth be told, that's how I feel as I pen this note. I wish to be in the comfort of youth and the safety of home, but rest easy, I will be brave when my moment comes.

The Allied forces are pushing into Europe. Despite my cowardice I give myself willingly to the fight. I hope our sacrifice creates change, not just here but in America as well. My secret prayer is that we might be able to see that life is short and there is no time to hate one another. In that light, I have sent Mother and Father a letter with the hope that their hearts will change toward you. I am hopeful in that endeavor. I have put my affairs in order and am sending you the remainder of my savings. It is a small amount but should enable you and Randall to buy a house and a car.

Before I give my life for my country I have one last grievance I must make right. I am disturbed in my person and wish to ask each of you for your forgiveness. Sister, I wish I would have possessed your boldness and courage the day you gave birth and each day forward. I wish I had stood more closely by your side. I hope that you can forgive me. You were right. You did the right thing.

Randall, despite the difficulty in which you have been raised you have become a man I am proud of and with great honor, call you family. I only wish I could have had a son as unparalleled as you. I know you will continue to take care of your mother, and make the most of life. There are a great many things I wish I'd done differently. I wish I'd taken you to ball games and out for ice cream. You've become a great ball player and I know one day, you'll play in the bigs. I've missed so much. You're an incredible young man. Please forgive me.

To you both, I love you.

With great love and affection,

Sargent Joseph Wilson,

Beloved brother and uncle

CHAPTER 40

Olympia, Mississippi
Independence Day

July 4, 1944

The main street was draped in red, white, and blue in celebration of Independence Day and this year the parade would be in honor of those who lost their lives in the most recent conflict in Europe. D-day had claimed two of Olympia's sons. Their coffins were draped with the flag and rested on the back of freshly-painted white wooden wagons hitched to massive Clydesdales.

Jena reread her letter. Deep down inside, she'd known the last time he came to the house wearing his uniform that it would be the last time she would see him. She'd held him a little longer than usual and kissed his cheek before he left. That day, he'd given them a wad of cash that would catch up their rent and pay a couple months extra. It would last for a bit if they were frugal.

The day her brother had come by there was a boldness about him. His training had changed him. The uncertainty of youth was gone. He had arrived in the shadows of morning when they were still out weeding the garden and stayed well past dusk. He brought personal gifts for

Randall. Wrapped in brown paper were new clothes and a few of Randall's favorite snacks. The thing that tugged at Jena's heart was tucked into a wood crate covered in one of Joseph's old flannel shirts. Randall uncovered the surprise to find Joseph's freshly oiled glove, his baseball bat, his baseball cards, along with a baseball jersey with Wilson and the number ten stitched on the back. Randall was quick to try on the jersey and glove punching his fist in the well-seasoned leather.

Joseph's letter had come as no surprise. She'd known they were saying goodbye for the last time. The day after they received Joseph's letter, Randall came in with the Olympia Eagle and there on the front page were service photos next to the names of those slain on the beaches of Normandy. She'd known before she saw, but she finally allowed herself to feel the loss. Her heart ached and a river of sadness as mighty as the Mississippi overtook her, tears ran wild and unrestrained. She'd cried enough to send herself into coughing fits and gasping for air, she saw the red speckles. Her body ached, the fever came, and she slept.

Standing in the shade of a long-hanging willow, Jena, Randall, Ezekiel, and Hattie watched the parade a good distance from the road, opposite of where the families of the slain stood. The procession started after the bugle finished it's woeful wail of Taps and the crowd sang along, finishing strong with the comforting line, "All is well, safely rest, God is nigh." Drum sticks were quick to follow as they snapped on the snare drum with rapid precision, signaling the marching band to begin their stroll down main street just ahead of the clacking hoof steps and flag-draped coffins. Jena and Hattie fanned themselves with small fans trying to fend off the stifling heat and the relentless swarm of gnats that liked to get in your eyes and ears at every chance.

In a place of honor, she saw them. They were standing on the courthouse steps with the family of Robert Barnett, the other young man to be honored that day. Like a hawk watching prey, Jena watched them as the body of their only son passed. Her daddy, dressed in his best black Sunday suit, was well composed and dignified as his eyes followed the procession with his son passing down the street. Jena could barely see her mother's face for the black hat and short black veil. Her mother continuously dabbed at her eyes. Her mother's shoulders shook and Jena knew she was trying hard to not let her grief come gushing out like a flood in front of the whole town.

The procession had taken a turn at the next block and was finally out of sight, people started moving toward their cars. Jena grabbed Randall's hand and pulled him in the direction of her parents. Maybe Joseph's dream would be realized. Maybe, through this tragedy, good could come. Maybe they would welcome her and their grandson home.

Her mother caught a glimpse of her first and shook her head, as if in warning, but Jena pressed on. "Daddy!" She coughed her breath short. "Daddy!"

Mr. Wilson turned with a look of murderous fury. "Don't you ever call me that!" he shouted pointing a finger in her face. Quicker than anyone expected Randall was between his grandfather and his mother with a fire of warning in his eyes. She spoke from behind her son. "Daddy, how long are you going to be mad?" Mr. Wilson turned to leave. "Daddy!" she shouted again. "We're your flesh and blood. How can you be so hateful?"

He spun back around, his eyes like an autumn blaze, fiery and red, filled with violence and indignation, his fists were clenched. Randall took a step forward to defend his mother. Crimson-faced and full of rage Mr. Wilson swung a fist. Speed and youth enabled Randall to effortlessly move from within reach. A crowd began to gather and Jena could hear their talk, it was like the day at the grocery all over again.

Mr. Wilson shouted at the two of them, "Neither you nor this nigger boy are any kin to me and don't you ever speak to me or your mother again. I have no children. And don't you dare show your faces at Joseph's funeral or I'll kill you both myself. I shouldda done that years ago."

Unable to believe the words she'd just heard, Jena gaped at her father. He should have killed us? She ran the words over and over in her head. No tears came and her mouth felt like it was full of dry scratchy cotton. Time stood still even though the clock in the town square was ringing the half hour. The malice on the faces of people stunned her. "Come on Mama, let's go." Randall began to pull his mama away from the scene. "No Randall, he can't mean it." She turned to her mother whose pale skin looked nearly translucent in her black dress. Jena said nothing but reached toward her and her mother reached back. Before their fingers touched Mr.Wilson slapped his wife's hand away.

"Jena, you made me the laughing stock of this town, hell, the whole state of Mississippi keeping that little nigger baby and I ain't having no more of it. You two better git! Right now!" he shouted, waving his hand. "Leave or you're gonna make me do something real ugly." He grabbed his wife intending to leave.

Like an explosion, sudden and unexpected boldness flooded through Jena as she raised her voice. "You lie!" she shouted at her father. "In front of all these people, you lie! I am your daughter and this here is your grandson. I've lived like you taught me! I've lived with love and honor. I played the hand I was dealt and it wasn't pretty, but I would do it all again." She pushed past Randall and stood square with her father. "You could have made them see! You could have made the whole town see, my boy is something to be proud of!" With a loud thud Mr. Wilson backhanded his daughter and knocked her to the ground. Randall lunged toward his grandfather but not before a giant white man with a red beard snatched him up, pinning his arms behind him. A deep stern voice gave him an abrupt warning, "Get your mama up and get her outta here. Quick." In one swift motion the red bearded man released Randall, scooped Jena up and handed her to Randall. He created a gap in the crowd that had enveloped them so they could escape.

The tone of the crowd was picking up. People shouted lewd comments. Randall hustled his mama toward the willow. "You okay?" he asked her. "Yeah," she answered as she dabbed at her swelling cheek. From the distance she watched the crowd as it closed in around her father. She wanted to say more, but now, there was nothing more that could be said. Randall glanced back scanning the crowd for the giant white man. If he ever had the chance he wanted to thank him, but he was nowhere to be seen.

They hustled toward the willow where Randall knew Ezekiel and Hattie were waiting. Jena looked back at faces of people she'd known as a girl, they began to spit at her and gossip and shout obscenities. She was able to hear bits and snatches. "Yep, that's the girl." "Embarrassing nigger lover." "She should have stayed home instead of making a scene." "Her poor brother must be rolling in his grave. A war hero, disgraced." Jena wanted to go back and scratch their faces off. They didn't know anything. The only disgraceful thing was her daddy saying she wasn't his daughter and Randall wasn't his grandson. Lies.

Ezekiel hustled to open the door and Hattie got in on the other side to lay Jena down. Pulling a fan from her pocketbook she pumped her wrist back and forth trying to bring some normal color back to Jena's face. The swelling in her cheek was turning bluish green and her face was red as a boiled crab.

Randall got in the front seat of the old Ford. Ezekiel reached over and placed his hand on the boy's shoulder. "You okay?"

Randall nodded.

"Let's go to the diner. We'll get you something to eat."

"Thanks Zeke, but I just want to get my mama home."

Ezekiel patted his shoulder. "Sure son. Let's get y'all home. Hattie and I will bring something by." Randall nodded again as Ezekiel put the car in gear and headed down the old country road.

Jena passed out. Her breathing became labored and her face hot to the touch. Randall carried his mother into the house with Hattie close on his heels. He laid her on the bed and Hattie pulled Jena's shoes off. "Don't worry Randall, she's gonna be okay. All that was just too emotionally overwhelming. Her brother, her dad." Randall nodded again. "I know. I just can't help worrying." Hattie loosened the collar on Jena's dress and pulled the sheet up. Hattie tried again to reassure Randall. "She just needs rest. You make sure she takes sips of water. Dip the rag in some water and wipe her down. We'll go get some food."

Jena stirred but didn't wake, she was mumbling something no one could quite make out. Randall placed a cool wet cloth on her forehead. Everyone was silent when Ezekiel went over and placed a hand on Jena's forehead and started to pray.

As Hattie passed over the threshold to leave, Randall stopped her. "Hattie, wait. What's wrong with me that they hate me so much?" She came back inside and placed a hand on his cheek. "Honey, they don't hate you. They don't even know you."

"But Hattie, you didn't even see the hate in his eyes. He wanted to kill me. He said that he shouldda killed me a long time ago."

"I've seen that kind of hate before and I can't explain it. I don't think they can either. If you asked 'em and they were calm, I bet they couldn't answer. Maybe they get so mad because they don't know why either."

Zeke chimed in. "Well, the main thing is we don't let that settle in our hearts. We can be mad for a minute, but by sundown we gotta find a way to forgive. The Lord will help you, Randall."

"I know," Randall said, hanging his head. "It's just that I never done nothin' to them."

Hattie reached out to hug him and he melted into her arms. They stood there for a minute before Ezekiel cut in. "Alright, come on Hattie. Let's give him a minute and go get them some supper." Randall released Hattie and watched them go. He sat back in his chair while his mama wrestled in her exhaustion. He'd never seen her like today. Never seen her so bold, so full of fire. Normally she was mousy and quiet, real gentle. He'd never seen her so...unafraid. Now, however, she seemed restless, caught in a nightmare, tossing to and fro, tangling herself in her sheet. He went to get water from the pump and attempted to give her a drink. He propped her up and she sipped, but didn't wake. He set the glass down on the nightstand and sat back in his chair where he could keep an eye on her.

In just a few short hours his life felt upside down. Today, he'd come face to face with grandparents he'd never met and he struggled with his granddad's words. He'd never known such hatred. Maybe he'd been called some bad names, or had a couple of upset customers fuss at him, but pure hatred, he couldn't understand it. He grieved the loss of his uncle, his mama's only brother, the only white man he'd ever known that loved him.

He opened his bible and searched for nothing specific. His eyes roamed the pages but it was his heart that spoke. "Peace I leave with you, my peace I give unto you; not as the world giveth, give I unto you. Let not your heart be troubled, neither let it be afraid." He knew they were Jesus' words. He said them a few times over and over. Peace came like cool water on a burning hot day, and soon he was asleep.

Ezekiel and Hattie rode over to Millie's Diner and ordered all of Randall's favorites; fried chicken, mashed potatoes, macaroni salad, greens and for dessert a whole pecan pie. Mabel recognized the order. "This for Randall?"

"Yeah." Ezekiel answered, rubbing his face.

"I heard there was quite a scene downtown today. Randall and Jena okay?"

Ezekiel nodded. "Yeah, it was messy, but they'll be alright."

The waitress turned to Hattie. "Well, would you give him these from me? He's such a great kid. I'm sorry to hear about all that." She handed Hattie a brown paper sack with a dozen butter cookies and a jar of milk. "Food'll be up in a minute." She patted Hattie's hand and went to the back to check on their order. Ezekiel sighed.

"What's wrong?" Hattie asked.

"Well, he's never asked. Never harbored any animosity. Never felt unloved. He's wondered about them, but there wasn't a lick of ill will. No root of bitterness in his heart. But after today, well...how could he not?"

Hattie looked away. She knew how hard it was to stop the anger from building up in your heart. She'd had plenty of her own struggles. She understood the constant choice to reject anger and bitterness. Even at a distance Hattie could feel the rejection, the air charged with malevolence surging through the crowd, swinging its unrelenting stinging whip, tearing at flesh and spirit.

"Hattie, I don't think he ever imagined that today would be like that. I think he just expected to honor his uncle."

"You're right. I don't suspect he did."

Mabel brought the food out in brown paper bags. The grease from the chicken was already seeping through. "Give Randall and his mama my condolences. I put a few deviled eggs in there too. They're Ms. Jena's favorite."

"Thanks Mabel. I know she'll appreciate it.

August 15, 1944

Dear Lord,

Today is an important day. We're on our way to Kentucky. Randall and Hattie are hopeful that this sanitorium will be able to help me. I don't think it will, but I'm willing to try. I'm sure Hattie pulled some strings to get me in. We got on the road early, well before sunrise. I'm down to my lowest weight, maybe ever and when I see my reflection I hardly recognize myself.

The sickness is back. I think all the emotional trauma the past few months opened a door to let it sneak back in. At first I thought I was just tired. But then the fever came and I started losing weight, couldn't get my appetite. It's stronger this time. Or maybe I'm just weaker. I don't rightly know, but coughing up blood confirmed it before the x-rays.

Tears splotch my paper. Lord, I don't have it in me to fight anymore. I hardly have the will to live. Randall's nearly grown and I know I'm holding him back. He has so many opportunities, but he won't leave if I'm sick. He's got so much ahead of him and I have conceded, my folks are never going to welcome us. I know that now. Not Joseph's death, not a lynchin', not a world war, not nothing on this earth is going to move my Daddy's stubborn heart. I don't know what drains me more, this disease or my folks. Their hard-heartedness drains my soul. I'd give Mama a pass except she turned away like she didn't know me. I don't know which hurt worse, Daddy's mean words or Mama's actions. She could have wrote to me. She knew Joseph came to see us.

Jostling down this bumpy road makes writing in my diary scribbly, but I must remove the anchor that's holding us in the past. I can't hardly draw air and my head just spins. Trying to push the pen across the paper is a monumental task, but my life's joy, the highlight of it all, is my boy. He makes me proud. He's accomplished in ways I never dreamed. He's a good man and well respected. He's honest and kind. Folks around town know him and love him. I know that the favor on his life is Your doing.

You've brought us through a lot. There's lots of joy to be remembered. I loved when he would snuggle up in my lap and we would read about Noah and Moses by the light of an oil lamp, next to the warmth of our little wood stove. Sometimes we'd read Jesus' words and we'd marvel at his miracles rocking back and forth on those noisy wood planks that squeaked and creaked as if amen-ing each word. I loved those moments. Such blessed memories, Lord.

We worked our meager garden, Randall's chubby hands tugging on the carrot tops till he wiggled the root loose. He'd tip over grinning just as proud as can be with a dirt-crusted carrot as his prize. Even when the country fell on hard times, You always provided. Lord, I'm so thankful we always had more than enough. You never left us, Lord.

They say the sanatorium is real nice. Doctors want me to stay a year. Some folks never get in, they just die at home, a burden to their families, never really having a chance to get well. I was well, but now I'm not, maybe I lost my faith, or maybe it's my time. Only you know, Lord.

Kentucky is about eight hours away. A long ride, but Hattie packed a nice picnic of fried chicken and some green beans. Ezekiel sent ham and egg sandwiches wrapped in foil for breakfast, I already nibbled at one. Did I already say that? I can't remember. My eyes are heavy. My thoughts are foggy, but when I look to You everything seems clear. Despite all that has happened in my life, I'm not ashamed of my decisions. I hope my parents can one day say the same. I forgive 'em, Lord. I really do. I love 'em.

CHAPTER 41

Olympia, Mississippi
August 17, 1944

The black Ford ambled up the drive just as the cool of evening started to settle in and the mosquitos started to come out. Randall set the brake and took a deep breath. He'd dropped Hattie off and come home. His mama didn't want to stay in Kentucky and he couldn't leave her. Hattie said it was the best thing for her, that his mama would live longer but he wasn't so sure. He was convinced she'd give up as she saw the car drive down the winding road, cross the railroad, and disappear into the distance. Even if she did survive their separation, what kind of life would it be? She had cried, and every bit of strength and reason left him.

They'd driven eight long hours, stopping frequently. They'd stayed the night at a local hotel and their approach to Waverly Hills Tuberculosis Sanatorium the next morning was impressive. Its architecture was gothic and it looked like a castle on top of a wooded hill right off of Dixie Highway. Winding their way up the road, chills ran down Jena's spine. The road leveled off and as they pulled up in front of the five pillars, blackened clouds rolled in. It was wearisome to get out of the car and enter the four-story brick and stone building she envisioned as a tomb. She'd held her tongue, even when she saw twenty metal beds lined up in a row facing the windows they'd be looking out all day long, not moving except to breathe.

Once they finished the tour, the director left them to sit in the gardens with a gargoyle's vicious stare glaring at them while they talked. "I can't stay here, Randall." She shook her head as the tears fell onto her lap. "I'm so sorry, son. I know you paid a good bit of money that we can't get back. I just can't stay. It feels like I'll never come home. I'll die here all alone." Randall and Hattie said nothing, but Hattie had moved next to his mother and draped another blanket around her. He tried to convince her that this was the best way, but she said she'd rather be back in Mississippi and die at home with the people she loved.

Sitting on the bench with his elbows on his knees and his chin resting in his hands, against Hattie's best medical advice, Randall agreed to take his Mama home. In the end, Hattie's heart spoke louder than her medical wisdom and she too caved and agreed to take Jena home. They helped Jena back to the car. They'd stayed the night at a hotel and headed back early.

As Randall helped his mama back to the car, he had no regrets, he was glad they'd come, even though she wasn't impressed by the basket weaving or the typing she would get to do when she recovered. To be honest, he didn't have any peace there either and he didn't want to leave her, but he'd chalked his feelings up to being selfish. He was quiet on the ride back. Like Zeke taught him, he knew there was a consequence to every decision or indecision. Ezekiel was going to ask why. There was no good medical or scientific answer, but his heart felt right and he could live with that. It would be hard watching his mama struggle, but he couldn't leave her to die alone.

Exhausted from the trip, she slept. Bundled in her blankets, he carried her into their shack, the place they'd called home all these years. She sighed, content like a small child being tucked into bed. She was home. Only days later, she went to be with the Lord.

The white-washed wooden screen door made a soft thumping sound as Randall knocked and sent it bouncing against it's frame. A tiny woman resembling his mother walked around the corner and toward the front door wiping her hands on her apron. She glanced up and in a drawl so sweet it sounded like a song she said, "May I help you?" He remembered her from the funeral, in the town square, where they had honored his uncle Joseph on Independence Day. Her face had been covered, but he could make her out.

She came closer and pushed the screen open. "Yes?" Words wouldn't form in his mouth while the sharp emotions warred within him stabbing at his heart. This was his grandmother, his mother's mother and this time he was looking her square in the face. She kept wiping her hands. It looked like she'd been mixing sticky dough. She asked again, "May I help you?" He thought she would recognize him.

The words he imagined saying disappeared like smoke in the wind and he couldn't get them back. Only two words remained. "She's gone."

She stopped wiping her hands, hurt registered in her eyes. "Jena?" Randall nodded. She reached out to touch his face. "You look like her," his grandmother said. He pulled back and eased himself off the porch. She said nothing else and made no move to follow. Safely in the yard Randall turned and ran. He looked back only once. She had stepped out onto the porch and watched him go. He thought he saw her wipe her eyes.

CHAPTER 42

Olympia, Mississippi
October 23, 1944

Winter wasn't fully upon them, but the ice storm suggested otherwise. Randall was anxious to leave, he wanted to focus on his game, but the storm had delayed his trip to Cuba. He hadn't expected to lose his uncle and his mom in the same year, but the country was at war and they'd all been caught unaware when her sickness came back with a vengeance.

After his mama passed and they'd laid her to rest, Randall moved in with Hattie and Ezekiel. The night was unusually dark and cold. The windows rattled as the wind outside whipped, tossing loose leaves and branches against the house. He curled up under his quilted blanket and the block afghan his mother made. His wool socks were thin and stinging shards stabbed at his feet. The whipping winds froze icicles sideways from tree branches and power lines. The fireplace couldn't keep up with the plunging temperatures and the electric heater was no help. Dark as pitch, Randall crawled out of bed to bulk up the fireplace. With no light to guide him, he felt his way down the hallway and to the back porch where he hefted a thick unsplit log. He wanted it to burn long and slow to keep the house warm for several hours. Maybe the warmth would finally penetrate the house and Ezekiel and Hattie could sleep in a bit. Nobody would be going anywhere, the whole town was shut down. He set the log next to the fireplace, grabbed the iron poker and stoked the ashes. He'd always loved watching the fire catch and grow, he added some slim pine branches that would be aflame in minutes. They would ignite the thick hard wood and fight off the stinging chill. After adding a few more pieces of split pine a soft crackling and flickering glow lit the room mesmerizing Randall with their dancing orange and red waves. He placed the thick oak log in their embrace. He prodded the embers, flames inched their way up around the sides of the log consuming the dry bark crackling and popping as they went. He nudged the ashes a bit more making sure the log was at a good blaze.

He wiggled his toes until the stinging iciness melted away and held his hands toward the warm glow. He thought of going back to bed but it might be hours before the heat filled the house. He went to get his blankets to sleep on the couch. As he came back down the hallway toward the living room the front door burst open. A blast of frigid air whipped through the house. A silhouetted figure stood in the doorway. Randall dropped the blankets and ran toward the intruder tackling him back onto the front porch.

The ruckus woke Hattie and Ezekiel. "What's going on out there?" Ezekiel hollered and rushed to the front of the house. Ezekiel could make out Randall and another man exchanging blows. The intruder was heavier and stronger than Randall and after wrestling around he got the best of Randall hammering him with blow after blow. Randall protected his head. Randall's disadvantage was Ezekiel's opportunity. With the fire poker in hand he slammed the intruder's side with a loud thud. The intruder gasped and collapsed onto his side. He rolled back and forth groaning and cursing.

Hattie, breathless until now, rushed to Randall who lay still but conscious. Ezekiel pulled the snow-crusted icy hat and scarf from the intruder. "It can't be," he whispered.

"Daddy! Randall's bleeding."

"Can you get him inside?"

"Yeah, maybe." She tugged on Randall and tried to heave his body up. He was too heavy. "Come on, Randall. I need your help. You're gonna freeze. We gotta get you inside."

Once she had him on his bed she piled blankets on him as his body started to shake. She couldn't tell if it was from the below zero temperature or from shock or both. He had a gash above his eye. Hattie grabbed clean cotton shirts from the dresser next to her to staunch the flow. "Stay awake, Randall," she said, her voice full of fear. She took one hand off his head and grabbed his wrist, searching for a pulse. It was low and slow. "Look at me, Randall." She peered into his eyes but it was too dark to see anything. His head lulled to the side. She wanted to check his pupils. "Daddy!"

"Hold on, Hattie." Ezekiel had pulled the frozen wet clothes off of the man lying on the couch and covered him with a blanket. The man's breathing was labored and painful. Ezekiel knew one or more ribs were broken. Thankfully none were protruding. "Stay here, I'll be right back," Ezekiel said in an I-mean-business tone. The man only groaned in response. Ezekiel was confident he couldn't do more damage in his condition.

Ezekiel went to the room where Hattie had lit a candle. "Daddy, we need to get him warm and stop the bleeding. He probably has a concussion," Hattie said. After pulling the t-shirt away, Ezekiel watched as blood pooled and ran down Randall's face. Hattie poked at the gash. "It needs at least fifteen stitches. It's not just long, it's deep. That's his skull right there," she said, poking at a spot over Randall's left brow.

"Well, can you fix him up?" Ezekiel asked knowing the hospital was out of the question with the weather.

Hattie sighed. "Of course, but not with this candle as the only light." Ezekiel reapplied pressure. She sat on the edge of the bed. "Do we have any oil lamps or more candles?"

"We got a couple oil lamps. I don't know about any candles."

"They'll have to do."

Ezekiel lifted the glass and lit the kerosene lantern. It was dim. He lit the other two and the room had enough light to work. The wind howled while the house creaked in protest. "Hattie, let me go put another log on the fire, I'll grab your bag so you can stitch him up."

"Okay." She peeked underneath the bandage. "Yeah, I think this is slowing."

In the living room, snores came from the figure on the couch with a slight whimper with each breath. The log Randall had placed was putting off good heat. Ezekiel put his hands up to warm them. He heard the man behind him rasp, "Daddy." But he couldn't bring himself to turn around and look at his son.

Coffee percolated, bacon sizzled, a place was set before an empty chair. Jimmie came in looking sheepish. Hattie gave him a stiff glare as she cut off the stove, placed food at the table, and took a seat. He had slept a full twenty-four hours and movement in the room stopped as he placed his hands on the back of the chair to steady himself. He looked at the damage he'd done to Randall's face. The boy had a long gash and haphazard stitches. A swollen black eye and a goose egg on his forehead. For the first time he could remember he sincerely felt bad for his actions. "I'm sorry, Randall. I apologize." Randall nodded and looked at Ezekiel before speaking. Ezekiel gave him a nod and Randall spoke, "I forgive you."

"I know I don't deserve it."

The room was tense. "You sure don't," Hattie shouted at her brother.

Ezekiel reached across the table and placed a hand over his daughter's. "Hattie," he said gently. "Don't, Daddy. Don't try and calm me down!" She pushed her chair back and moved toward her brother. She stuck a finger in his face and started yelling. "You've been gone for years! We didn't know if you were alive or dead. We didn't know what to think. Then you just show up here and start fighting people who live here. Daddy should have thrown you right back out in the cold and let you freeze to death. Why'd you come back anyway?"

Jimmie looked at the floor. "I didn't have anywhere else to go. Y'all's my family."

Hattie's temper blew. "But you wouldn't know it the way you treat us! What's it been? Ten, fifteen years?"

"You're right, Hattie. You're right," Jimmie said, backing away from his sister. "I'll just go."

"Go on and sit down," Ezekiel said.

Jimmie obeyed and sat. Hattie paced the floor taking a deep breath trying to calm herself. "Jimmie, you're my son. I love you. But you can't come stay here and turn everybody's lives upside down."

"I know," Jimmie said with a hard edge to his voice.

"Well, do you have a plan? Where have you been? What have you been up to? I mean doggone Jimmie, you've been gone so long you're practically a stranger."

Jimmie put his elbows on the table and hung his head in his hands. His temples throbbed, his body ached, he longed for a drink. He wanted to clear the air, they deserved that much. "As I'm sure y'all know, I was getting into some trouble. I fell in with bad folks and I ended up doing a little time up North."

Ezekiel rubbed his head wondering if he wanted to hear anymore.

Jimmie went on, "I had an opportunity to serve my country by going overseas. I went to France. I dug graves and buried bodies. I drank a lot, still do. I didn't get in as much trouble, but still got in some while I was over there. French folks were real nice to us Americans. They didn't care if you were black or white, just as long as you were there to help 'em. That part was real nice. The bad thing is, my dreams are filled with those dead bodies blown to bits and filled with bullet holes, and I drink to wash them away."

Hattie closed her eyes. She had seen them too, but in the hospitals, clinging to life. She folded her arms across her chest and prayed silently. Ezekiel wasn't buying it, at least not all of it. He folded his arms looking skeptical. "Now Jimmie, you were drinking long before you went overseas. And you got in plenty of trouble before that."

"You're right. I started out drinking for fun and good times. I got in trouble because I was mad and wanted revenge."

"What's different now? What do you want? Us to feel sorry for ya? Lots of folks seen bad things and ain't fallin' down drunk all the time fighting folks."

Jimmie slammed his fist on the table. "Whadda you want from me? I'm trying to tell you and clear the air."

Ezekiel's voice rose slightly. "Don't you slam your fist at me. I'll throw your ass out to freeze right now."

Jimmie put his hands up. "Okay, sorry. I'm just trying to tell you what happened."

"Okay, tell us." Ezekiel was fed up. He'd heard it all before. They'd have sympathy on Jimmie, let him come home, hope he'd changed and he'd throw everybody's life into chaos.

Jimmie continued on. "I'd drink so much just to make it from day to day, there are a lot of things I don't remember, but I'll never forget the smell." Hattie could relate, even him just mentioning it could conjure up the smell of rotting flesh. She rubbed her arms as if it were on her. Jimmie continued, "Sometimes I think I can still smell death on me. No amount of bathing or scrubbing could get the smell of dead bodies off of you. I remember the high pitched whistling of a bomb as it whirled overhead just before an explosion." Jimmie hung his head and rubbed his face. His hand shook as he longed for a cigarette and a drink. After a few seconds he went on. "There were bad things. People died, but they were the lucky ones. It's the ones who survived that live in hell. Women had it bad, sometimes groups of men would have at them. Those are the sounds that torment me at night. I can see them in my nightmares." Jimmie paused again. The room was silent. Waiting. He glanced at Randall and then looked away. "I can always hear the screams of the women and the girls." He rubbed his face again, the urge grew, he wanted a strong drink. "They reminded me of Randall's mama."

Ezekiel's eyes went wide and Hattie's mouth dropped open. Randall was confused. "What do you know about my mama?"

Hattie's face had gone red and she clenched her fist. Ezekiel's voice was stern, "What do you mean, Jimmie?"

He shook his head. "It wasn't me. I was just the look out."

Fury bloomed like gasoline on a fire. Hattie jumped up out of her chair and swung on her brother shrieking as her blows came one right after the other. "How could you! How could you after what happened to our mama!" He didn't swing back, nor did he answer, he only put his arms up to protect his head. She connected with several blows before Ezekiel was able to grab her. Randall sat stunned, unsure of what just happened. What did Jimmie mean he was just the look out?

The dam broke and Randall was caught in the middle of the flood waters, but he didn't know how. Hattie stormed out of the room. Randall felt out of sorts, he knew something big had happened but he couldn't piece it together. It had to do with his mama, but he didn't know how.

Ezekiel wasn't talking, he excused himself and went to his room. Jimmie went outside to smoke and Randall didn't know what to do. After everyone left the room, Randall sat and stared at plates of food wondering what had happened and what Jimmie meant.

Power had been restored, and roads were being cleared of trees knocked over in the storm. There was a lot of damage to the town and now that the sun peeked through the clouds folks were coming out to assess the damage. Ezekiel didn't say much in the next few weeks. He didn't go to work and a few days he didn't get up out of the bed. Randall tried to rouse him, but Ezekiel told him to go to the barbershop with Joe and Claude. He did as he was told and when the grown men saw him they couldn't believe his face. "Boy, what the hell happened to you?" Randall only said one word. "Jimmie." They just shook their heads. Claude rapped Randall on the shoulder. "Don't you worry about him. He won't come over here while we're here." They both shook their heads. "I'm gonna beat his ass when I see him. Why'd he do that to you?" Joe asked. Randall shrugged. "He was drunk." Claude poked at Randall's face. "Dang, you ain't gonna be pretty no more. This here's kinda ugly, but you'll survive. At least Hattie was there to stitch you up." Claude left him alone and turned toward the mess around them. "Come on, let's get this place cleaned up." The front window was busted and debris was scattered around the room. There was water damage and some of the flooring would have to be repaired. Randall started to sweep and Joe left to get glass. When he came back and they were placing the new pane, Randall asked them what Jimmie meant when he said he was just the look out. Claude shook his head. They both told him he had to talk to Zeke about it, but Zeke wasn't talking. Randall figured he was going to have to take it up with Jimmie.

The screen door slammed and Randall came in. He'd gone to Ezekiel's room to talk to him, but he was asleep. In the kitchen, Jimmie was frying catfish he'd caught earlier in the day. "You want some?" Jimmie offered. Randall was unsure how to respond. "Sure." "Alright, go and get washed up. I'll have dinner ready in a minute."

The flow of the house was out of order, Randall didn't know what to do, so he did as he was told and he went to wash up. When he returned there were two plates at the table and Jimmie was pouring cold milk into glasses. The food looked good. His stomach growled. "Go on and eat," Jimmie said. Randall hesitated. "We normally wait till everyone's at the table and we say grace."

"Yeah, it figures. Dad would make everybody wait to say grace."

"You don't say grace?"

"I don't even like God. What's he done for me?" Jimmie asked, setting the milk down and taking a seat.

"Well, we both could have died the other night when you burst in here."

Jimmie took a bite of fish and talked with his mouth full. "Yeah, but there have been plenty of other times I could have died and didn't. That ain't nothin' special." Jimmie went to take another bite before Randall stopped him. "Can you wait for a second? I'll say grace."

Stunned, Jimmie set his fork down. "Okay. Well go on then. And hurry up."

Randall bowed his head and closed his eyes. "Thank you Lord for your provision. We ask you to bless this food in Jesus' name, amen." Randall lifted his head up and picked up his fork. Jimmie used his fingers, took another mouthful of catfish and questioned Randall. "Why did you thank God for this food? I caught this fish and the rest of this stuff was here at the house, my daddy probably bought it. God didn't provide this for you."

"Thank you for cooking the food Jimmie, but I beg to differ. Everything we have is from the Lord."

"How can you, of all people, say that? Are you from the Lord? Where's your daddy, Randall?"

Randall squinted his eyes, he knew he was being baited, but he had to know where this was going. "I don't know who my daddy is."

"Of course you don't. Don't know how you got here either. Do ya?"

Randall shook his head.

"Did you think your mama was in love? Do you think you're like most folks?"

Randall didn't know what to say. He didn't know the answers to any of these questions. He didn't know why he never knew his daddy and it never occurred to him to ask. He never thought about how he was mixed; he just knew he was.

Jimmie kept on. "Your mama was violated by several men. They grabbed her from behind. She screamed at first but they covered her mouth and hit her so hard we thought she might be dead."

"What do you mean 'we'?" Randall asked, his temper flaring.

Jimmie ignored the question and took a bite of his potatoes. "They've been lyin' to you Randall. All these years, just lyin'."

Randall lowered his voice and glared at Jimmie. "Well, why don't you tell me then. Who's my daddy? Since you know everything, tell me the truth!"

Jimmie kept eating.

"You know what?" Randall said, "You're the liar. You don't know what you're talking about and you're a coward. You were the look out? You should have violated her too, at least you'd have a real reason to be guilty and need to drink all the time. You know why you don't like God?"

"Why?"

"Because you know he's going to judge you and you're scared."

Jimmie laughed out loud. "You think you're smart, hunh kid?"

"Don't call me kid. My name is Randall."

Jimmie put up his hands. "Okay, Randall. Why don't you just eat your food?"

"Naw, you brought all of this up. What else do you want to say?"

Jimmie shook his head. "Nothin'."

Randall wasn't backing down. "You think I'm less because of what happened to my mama?"

"I didn't say that."

"No, but you're acting like it. You grew up with two parents and a great sister. What's your excuse? What happened to you?"

Jimmie got mad and pushed himself away from the table. "You don't know me, no matter how long you've lived here or been around my family."

"Back at ya. You don't know me either."

Jimmie rubbed his face. He wanted a drink. He wanted this kid to shut up. He shouldn't have said anything. "Just shut up. I'm going out. Clean these dishes up when you're done." Jimmie left letting the door slam behind him. He flicked his lighter and lit a cigarette. He took a long drag and held it. There was a bar just a few miles down the road. What was he thinking coming home? This was stupid. He shouldn't have come. He walked down the road, ordered a pint, and kept drinking until he couldn't think.

A week later, water dripped from the rooftop as temperatures warmed and the midday sun melted ice. Randall was outside cleaning up debris from the storm and trying to fix the railing on the porch he and Jimmie broke in their tussle. He was still sore and bruised up. He was supposed to have already left for Cuba to play winter ball and waiting to get his stitches out was going to prolong that trip even more. Ezekiel watched him from the window and shook his head, Randall lost his uncle, got in an altercation with his granddad, lost his mama, and now had Jimmie bust him up. This wasn't turning out to be a good year for Randall. Ezekiel wondered how the little man hadn't had a breakdown. He rubbed his head and chastened himself, Randall wasn't little any more. He was grown, a good six-foot-two inches and an easy one-hundred fifty pounds, wiry and all muscle. He'd always been smart with a good head on his shoulders. He was tender hearted and thoughtful. Randall didn't deserve the trouble Jimmie would bring. It was time to get Jimmie out of the house, he was trouble waiting to happen. Hattie knew it. She left to stay with a friend. She was still upset with her brother and infuriated he was at the house. Ezekiel knew it too, but even after all these years he had a hard time dealing with his son. He figured it was guilt that caused him to make bad decisions where Jimmie was concerned. He felt bad Jimmie had lost his mama and that he hadn't been able to stop the attack. Despite all his prayers, Jimmie probably wasn't ever going to change and he couldn't let that poison Randall's future. While Randall worked outside in the cold, Jimmie was hung over, asleep.

In the next few weeks, Ezekiel didn't say much. The barbershop reopened, but he didn't go to work and there were a few days he didn't get out of bed. An overwhelming sorrow had come over him and he couldn't shake it. Maybe the lack of daylight or the cold weather made him want to hibernate, or more truthfully he wanted to ignore the fact that his son was back and Randall was leaving. He knew once Hattie pulled the stitches, it was time for Randall to go. The time was right. They'd prepared for this moment, but it was hard nonetheless. Ezekiel knew the seasons were changing and as much as he wanted Randall to stay, he knew the boy had to go chase his own dreams.

The screen door slammed behind him with a blast of icy air whipping through the house as Randall came in. He set the paper bag he'd brought back from Millie's on the coffee table and dropped another log on the fire to dull the sting of cold that hung in the air. Blankets were disheveled on the couch, he folded them before he grabbed the food and went to the kitchen. The house didn't feel right. He wanted to have dinner and talk to Zeke nice and comfortable like they used to, but things weren't like they used to be. They were upside down.

Randall made some good money. Ezekiel's regulars had let the young whipper-snapper cut their hair and give them a shave. He felt out of sorts being at the barbershop without Zeke. Randall pushed the older man's door open a bit and whispered into the room. Zeke didn't rouse. Randall walked over and touched Zeke's forehead for fever, there was none, in fact he was a bit clammy. Randall sighed, relieved Zeke's fatigue wasn't like his mama's, coming and going with the cough and fever, but he still worried because he'd never seen Zeke like this. He pulled the blanket up over Zeke's broad shoulder. He hung his head and prayed. When he could say no more, he left the room to wash up for dinner.

Randall changed his clothes before heading to the kitchen. There was a lot on his mind. He needed to get his ticket to Havana, he was already late, but he couldn't leave with the discord that consumed the house. He asked the Lord for help and tried to shake off the loathsome feeling.

He found Jimmie in the kitchen, sitting at the table smoking. His head hung in his hands while the cigarette dangled from his lips. "You should put that out. Zeke don't like smoking in the house."

"Don't tell me what my Daddy does and doesn't like. You ain't the boss 'round here."

"You're right, but you could respect the one who is."

Jimmie lifted his head and glared at Randall. "Unless you have some alcohol, shut the hell up. I need a drink." He took a long drag on his cigarette and flicked the ashes onto the table.

Randall looked disgusted. "You're so disrespectful."

"Whadda you know?"

"It doesn't take a genius to know you hate yourself. That you're like poison and that you make everybody around you miserable."

Jimmie jumped up from the table and got in Randall's face. "You want a scar on the other side?" he said, poking his finger in Randall's face. Jimmie expected the boy to tremble–he didn't. There was only a calm air of authority. He pushed Jimmie out of his way, walked to the table, and set the bag of food down. "You want some dinner? I got enough for everybody."

"Yeah, gimmie some."

Randall started pulling food out of the bag. "We got chicken, fried potatoes, some greens, and biscuits." Jimmie was so angry he tried to smack the food out of Randall's hand, but the boy's hands were quicker. Randall got plates and set three places at the table placing the silverware on a napkin. Jimmie was looking for a fight. He wanted one. He yearned for the boy to lose his cool and start swinging. Then he'd really give him a good ass-whipping. "What are you doing all that for? This ain't no fancy dinner."

Randall didn't even look up as he placed the glasses and said, "You know, you don't have to act like that."

"What do you know?" Jimmie shouted, taking another long drag and blowing it in Randall's face. Randall fanned the smoke from his face and continued to set the table, getting milk from the cooler. Jimmie paced the room like a wild animal trapped, calculating his next move. Randall sat. "Would you like to join me?" Jimmie didn't answer but took a seat. Randall bowed his head and blessed the food. He started putting food on his own plate and handed each item to Jimmie, who tore into the chicken before fixing the rest of his plate. He ate like he was starving, cramming cornbread into his mouth and taking gulps of milk while spilling crumbs on the table and floor.

Randall shook his head. "Nobody's going to take your food. You can eat like a regular person."

"Don't you worry about me," Jimmie snapped back. He waved a chicken leg and asked, "What happened at the barbershop today?"

"Not too much, it was weird without Zeke there."

"I bet those two lazy-ass uncles of mine had some shit to say about me."

"Why don't you forgive yourself and ask God to forgive you?"

"I don't have anything to be forgiven for."

"Well then why can't you let go of all that hate?"

"Because I don't want to."

"It's eating you up."

"What do you know, you're just a kid."

Randall buttered his biscuit and poured some honey on it. "I know you don't have to live like this, in torment all the time, mad at folks for no good reason. Shoot, you're even mad at the people that love you."

Jimmie stabbed his fork into the table. "You don't know shit little boy."

"I know you're human. I know you got problems like everybody else. I know that no matter how tough you try and act you don't want to carry around a bunch of crap that drags you down and makes you drink. I'll pray with you if you want."

"I already done that. It doesn't work."

"If you ask God to forgive you, He will. You have to forgive yourself, you know."

Jimmie glared at Randall who calmly wiped his face and put his plate in the sink. "I'm gonna go check on your dad. If you want you can go with me to the barbershop tomorrow. It'd probably be good to get out of the house."

Jimmie lit another cigarette. "I'll think about it."

Weeks went by before Randall got his ticket to Havana. He'd packed his bag and it sat next to his bedroom door waiting patiently to depart. The handle of his bat hung out of his bag and fueled the fever that was burning him up to play. He was ready. Guys on the teams he'd traveled with assured him Cuba was like Mexico where everything wasn't based on color. Nobody would care if he wasn't all white or all black. They'd only want to know if he could play, and he could. He hesitated leaving. Ezekiel hadn't been himself, but he'd gone back to work. Jimmie had his moments. He'd calmed down to a point of being bearable, until he wasn't. But Randall knew staying wasn't going to change that.

Hattie left a note, she was going back overseas where she was the most needed. It came as a surprise to everyone. She'd come by the barbershop with her bag in hand, said terse goodbyes and left for the train station. Ezekiel took it like a shot to the gut, his hair seemed grayer, his hands less steady.

Jimmie came to the barbershop with them and swept and cleaned towels. He did most of Randall's old jobs while Randall cut hair and shaved faces. Randall was just days away from leaving. He had to be at the port in New Orleans on Saturday. He and Jimmie sat in the back room of the barbershop eating lunch. "You gonna keep it together and help Ezekiel?" Randall asked.

Jimmie shrugged. "Why are you worried about it? You're leaving."

"Because if you're not, I won't leave."

"What's between me and my dad is between us. You don't need to worry yourself about it."

Randall sighed, knowing he wasn't going to get a real answer out of Jimmie. "What's that for?" Jimmie asked.

Getting up Randall glared at him. "You know everything isn't about you. Sometimes it's about other people. Maybe you should think about the things people did do for you instead of the things they didn't do. Focus on the great family you have instead of their shortcomings. You know, you don't live up to all their expectations either. You let them down. You say God didn't do anything for you, well, are you living for Him? You talk a lot of trash Jimmie, but you do the same things you complain about everybody else doing."

Jimmie's voice rose. "You better watch it little boy."

"You don't scare me." Randall said, grabbing his smock and turning his back to Jimmie, who glared at him wanting to inflict pain. "Hattie told me you wanted to be a preacher. That your mama read the Word to you every day so that you would be able to preach sermons before you were old enough to read. What happened to that?" Jimmie's anger seethed. Randall could feel it consuming the room. He let Jimmie steep in it and went back up front. Jimmie stormed out the back to get a drink.

CHAPTER 43

Olympia, Mississippi
May 1945

The barbershop buzzed, business was good. Travel picked up as the war was coming to a close. Hearts were still troubled but more and more allied victories eased the tension. "Hey Fred, what's that headline say?" Claude asked as he sharpened his razor.

Fred popped the paper and started reading. "Nazis yield to Allied Powers at Eisenhower's Headquarters. Says here it was an unconditional surrender."

Joe shouted, "Whoop! Whoop! Now that's what I'm talking about! Go U.S.A.!" Men hugged and high-fived one another. Elation filled the room. Ezekiel got bottles of pop from the cooler in the back and passed them out to celebrate. "To winning the war!" Everyone clinked glasses and drank. "Wow," Joe said, "We've been at war five years." Fred burst the festive bubble. "Well, technically we're still at war in the Pacific."

"Yeah, well I hope they surrender too," Joe said.

Jimmie added to the conversation. "The generals in the Pacific say the Japanese will never surrender. They say the Japanese would rather commit harakiri before they surrender."

"What is that?" Claude asked.

"When they kill themselves," Joe answered.

"Yeah, like they nose dived into those ships in Pearl Harbor," Jimmie said.

"How do you know so much?" Claude asked, taking another sip of his pop.

"I heard about it when I was over in Europe. They talked about the war and what was going on all the time. Never talked about nothing else."

Fred kept reading. "Says here one-hundred-seventy thousand Americans are dead or missing in Europe."

"That's a shame, so many gone." Ezekiel said. He lifted his glass. "In memory of those who gave their lives." Everyone lifted their drinks. Ezekiel patted his son's shoulder. "And were thankful for the ones who made it back."

Jimmie nodded. "Thanks, Dad."

Ezekiel clapped his son on the shoulder. "Yeah son, I'm glad you're home."

"Speaking of coming home, when is Randall due back?" Joe asked.

"Called a few days ago. Says he should be back sometime this week to start Spring Training. I think he's just dropping through here and then on his way up North," Ezekiel said.

"Who he play for? The Grays?" Claude asked.

"Yeah, I think that's what he said. Up in Pennsylvania or something." Joe answered. "Look at Randall making it happen."

Ezekiel sat in his chair and popped a newspaper in front of him. He scanned the headlines for any news that might give him insight to what was going on where Hattie was. She had written and said she was helping in France. She was talking about staying, said she'd met a doctor and they were talking about marriage. He couldn't quite believe it. He didn't really want to believe it. But change came, kids grew up, and it was right for them to go off and be on their own. He just wished it didn't have to be so far away.

September 2, 1945

Dear Randall,

The Japanese surrendered. Can you believe it? The war is finally over. Not just overseas, but in me, too. I've been clean for over a year. Not a drop of the spirits have passed these lips. I thought knowing that might make you rest easy.

The year has brought lots of changes. You were the catalyst for many of those changes. I have to admit you said some things I didn't want to hear and had long forgotten. The first was when you said, "You don't have to act like that." Your words reminded me of my mama telling me that we always have a choice.

The second one, that had an even bigger impact, was also about my mama. You reminded me about wanting to be a preacher. That's all I ever wanted to be, and she did everything she could to help me get there. She and I spent so many hours together reading and studying God's word. We would laugh and there was joy that filled everything she touched. My fondest memories of her are of her reading the Word to me.

The night she was brought home bruised and bloody she was changed and I couldn't understand. The joy had disappeared. She cried sometimes, and she had nightmares that woke us all up at night. Then when Hattie came she didn't look like us. Mama loved her and started to smile again, but I was confused and angry. I really didn't know what to do and over the years when I saw Hattie I could only see that night mama had come home beat up and bloody. Day by day, little by little my anger grew. My heart changed. My dad tried to help me, he's always tried to help me, but I couldn't see it and truthfully, I didn't want help. I wanted to be mad. In my mind I had every right to be angry. I chose to fortify myself with anger.

When the cancer came and mama was in pain, I hated Him even more. I couldn't stand to see her like that. I would run outside and cry beneath the old oak tree. I'd beg him to spare her. How could He? She loved Him so much.

When she was sick, she was tired and everything was hard for her. She'd ask me to read His Word to her, but I wouldn't. I flat-out refused. I wanted her to be angry with Him too, but she wasn't. She would use her last breath to praise Him.

I would lay my head on her chest and listen to her heartbeat. She'd stroke my head and remind me how she and my dad had dedicated me to the Lord and tell me how special I was. She'd remind me that I gave my life to the Lord and that there was a great calling on my life. When I was little, I knew I wanted to be just like Jesus' disciples. I wanted people to know about Him and help them know His love. How could I get so far off?

My anger was misguided. I did a lot of wrong things, but I'm hoping to set some things right. I want to apologize for my role in what happened to your mama. I wish what happened to her had never happened, but I thank God for you. You are how God turned that horrible thing to good, for His good purpose.

My mama taught me that, if I prayed in faith believing, Jesus would save me. She said his blood already paid for me. I prayed that as a boy in my mama's lap and shortly after you left I prayed it again. I asked Him to forgive me, to take me back. I'm working through some things, consequences to my actions, but Randall, He is so good, He did take me back and my joy is full.

I talked to Reverend Bordeaux and we've been working some things out. I quit drinking. I started going to church. And get this...I'm going to seminary to be a preacher. Yep, that's right. Me, a preacher. If God can use a murderer like Saul he can use me. I'm really learning the power of his love and I can see that love in my dad. I was so full of hate I could never see it before. You were right, I wasted so much time.

Please forgive me Randall, for everything. Your mama, our fight, all the dumb stuff. (And I know there's a lot of dumb stuff that I did.) I start school in just a few weeks. The fellas at the barbershop took up an offering for me and collected enough for me to go to school. Isn't that a miracle? God is so good and I'm realizing, he loves us so much. I'm still working through being upset about what happened to my mama, and what we did to your mama. I still ask God, why did it happen? I don't have an answer. As I gaze upon you and Hattie, two of the most beautiful souls that I know, I know God was not without a plan. In birthing you and raising you, our mamas served their King! Their love conquered so much hate.

I would like to stay in touch. I'd like to be friends. You mean more to me than you'll ever know. You helped me find my way back and for that I'll be eternally grateful.

With the deepest appreciation,

Jimmie Wilson

CHAPTER 44

Havana, Cuba
Winter league 1946

Randall clenched his fist, whoever was following him knew his name, but that didn't mean much, folks could find out your name easily enough. The American hollered again, "Randall, you don't recognize me? Boy, I remember you. I'd know you anywhere." Randall turned and paused. He squinted trying to make out the figure in the shadows.

Was it really? Could it be? Excitement raced through his veins. The figure walked toward him, step-dip, step-dip. It could only be. "Ray Ray?" There was no doubt. "Ray Ray!" Randall shouted and bounded toward his friend clasping him in a tight embrace. "What are you doing here?" Randall asked.

"Awe you know, I'm just here to cover the winter games."

"You still got that limp?"

"You still slow?"

"I got a little faster." Randall rubbed his stubble. "Man, I can't believe it's you. It sure is good to see you."

Ray Ray took a step back and gave his old friend a once over. "Look at you! All grown up. You're looking good."

"You, too. Ezekiel showed me your pictures at the barbershop. You're really out there making a name for yourself. I didn't even recognize you. Your voice is all deep and stuff."

"Well, you're not doing so shabby for yourself either. I hear you're playin' tomorrow."

"Yeah, for the Championship. You gonna be there?"

"Oh you know it. I take pictures all over the world just like we dreamed. I'm pretty good, too."

"I saw some of those photos with celebrities in Chicago and New York. You meet everybody; movie stars, jazz players, ball players, who don't you meet? Looks like you're having a good ole time!"

Ray Ray looked away, he swallowed hard. "None as good as the ones we had in Mississippi."

The jovial banter took a quick turn and Randall looked away. He shook his head. "Man, I'm sorry."

Ray Ray clapped his friend on the shoulder. "I'm not mad at you. I just missed you."

"I missed you, too. Mississippi wasn't the same after you left."

"I knew I'd see you again. I was just waiting for the day."

Randall laughed. "It's here Brother! It's here!"

"I don't want to mess up this moment, but you better get to bed. You gotta win that game tomorrow. Let's catch up after. I'll buy you a beer."

Randall nodded as the church bell clanged twice. "Awe man, I can't believe it's so late." "I'll see you tomorrow at the game. I'll be behind home plate." Ray Ray said as he hugged his friend.

"I'll be shaggin' balls and stealin' bases."

"Just like old times."

Randall clapped hands with his friend. "Just like old times."

Palm trees waved listlessly around the field while the crowd thundered in expectation as the bat connected with the first pitch of the game and sent it soaring. The right fielder made a clean catch. The crowd groaned. The broadcast went out across the island and nearly everybody was tuned in. The Championship was the biggest event of the season and the whole island was focused on the men on the field. Transistor radios dialed into the game. Announcers broadcast in Spanish with a second broadcast transmitting in English. Ray Ray switched on his transistor radio and tuned into the English version. "We are seeing some heat today and I'm not talking about the temperature! Did y'all see that! Whoa, that heat burned the thread off the leather!"

Second man on deck was Randall, he stood at the plate waiting on his first pitch, the announcer added commentary. "Now this youngster is one to watch, he first came down here as a light-skinned sixteen year old who came out of nowhere like a tornado on a sky-blue day tearing up teams, frustrating pitchers, and helping his team on a win streak. Last year he and the Fuegos took home the title, let's see if they can do it again." Randall took a swing, the ball took a bounce down the first base line and he was on base. The next two batters struck out.

The bases were empty in the bottom of the third inning. "Ladies and gentlemen, so far this is a humdrum game, but we got Randall Wilson up to bat. Let's hope he can do better than his last at bat. Keep your eyes on this kid. Don't blink, he's fast. He's gonna be a big name in a few years. Maybe he can spice it up by stealing first like he stole all those bases the other night." The crowd rippled with amusement. Randall let the first one pass over the plate. "Stee-rike one!" the umpire shouted. Randall tapped the bat against his shoe and looked at the pitcher with a slight glint in his eye. He already knew where the gap was and where he was going to drop the ball. The left fielder was looking at a hot girl in the stands. The second pitch was wild. "Ball!" Randall watched the pitcher wind up. It was gonna be fast and right over the plate. Randall twirled the bat over his shoulder and eyed his spot. It wouldn't take much to get it where he wanted. "It's a hit!" The announcer shouted as Randall was rounding first. The outfielder didn't know what was coming as Randall took second standing. The crowd roared. Three heavy hitters came behind him. The first two struck out and the third sent a grounder through the infield. Randall rounded third and headed for home. They'd missed the out at first, but they weren't going to let him score. The catcher stood in front of the plate ready for the ball and for Randall. The timing was close, they reached the plate at the same time. Randall dipped his shoulder and hit the catcher in the chest. He went flying back, practically landing on and covering the plate. The ball bounced from his glove and rolled toward the umpire. The catcher scrambled for the ball as Randall smacked home plate with his hand. The crowd went wild.

Four more innings flew by with three up, three down. The Tigers tied the score in the top of the eighth. There were two runs in scoring position before the Fuegos put them down. Randall easily fielded the pop fly to center to end the inning. Fans kept the stands full, anxiously awaiting some excitement. Big Juan was up and he'd struck out every time at bat. He was a heavy, deep hitter and due for a hit. The pitcher nodded to the catcher, a curveball flew past, just out of the strike zone. "Ball!" the umpire shouted. Big Juan leveled out his bat and tightened his grip. The pitcher gave a nod and wound up, Big Juan swung hard. "Striiike!" Big Juan cursed at the umpire in Spanish. The next pitch came. With a thwack, the ball went sailing into the outfield, it took a bounce and Big Juan was on base.

The next hitter hit a line drive to second and they caught Big Juan in a double play. A pop fly ended the inning. Top of the ninth the teams were tied one to one. Tension was high. The crowd was tense. The Tigers had a runner on base when heavy hitter Henry Hawthorn hit one out of the park and they were up three to one. Edwin, the Fuego's pitcher, took the next batter down, one, two, three.

The inning was uneventful for the Fuegos. R. Brown, the Tigers' pitcher, saw to that. The first batter struck out. Johnny got on base, but a double play on the next at bat dashed their hopes of taking home a trophy. The Fuegos lost three to one.

Despite their loss the night was festive. The city was alive with celebration. It was the end of the season and most folks would be returning to the States. It was a great night to celebrate.

"Dos Cervezas." Ray Ray ordered beers. He took a seat next to Randall at a bright yellow table and handed him a beer. "Man, you got me a couple good pictures with that steal at home." Randall took a sip. "I would rather have been sitting up on somebody's shoulders, but it is what it is." The pair clinked bottles. "So tell me Randall, what have you been up to all these years?" Randall shook his head. "Man, it feels like a lifetime. I don't even know where to start." They ordered sandwiches. "What have you been up to?" Ray Ray shrugged. "After we left, I went into one of my little funks again. I didn't want to get out of the bed and the winters in Chicago are no joke. Way colder than Mississippi. Y'all only get an ice storm once in a while, they git them every week in the winter. The wind is so sharp it will peel the skin off your face." Randall laughed. "You're pullin' my leg." "I ain't. I'm dead serious. I used to hate that wind." "So how did you break out of it?" Randall asked.

The waitress brought their plates. Randall prayed and took a bite. "I'm going to miss the food here." "Don't worry, you can come back next winter." They polished off their food and Ray Ray dusted off his hands. "I liked Chicago, but I missed Mississippi."

"How so?"

Ray Ray leaned back and threaded his fingers together. "There's lots of cool things up North. It's exciting all the time, it feels like folks never sleep. There's people everywhere and even a guy like me can go to school. There's late night parties, and you can buy almost anything you want. I can get all my photo supplies. I even have my own darkroom at the house. Indoor plumbing..." They both laughed.

Randall said, "Yeah, no more freezing your buns off in the winter."

"I remember those days," Ray Ray said, seeming forlorn.

"Well, why do you sound so sad? It sounds amazing. I've been through there to play ball. It seemed like the happening place to be."

"On the surface it is, but the folks there are disconnected. There's no Revered Bordeaux, no Hattie to come fix you up, no folks that will pray for ya when there's no hope, and there weren't any friends like you."

Randall looked out the window while Ray Ray continued. "I didn't have any friends. My lame leg wasn't a sign of victory like it had been in Mississippi, it was something that made me weird and different." Randall didn't know what to say. He couldn't believe his best friend hadn't made new friends or that people had given him a hard time. If he'd been there they would have fought them together. "Like Reverend Bordeaux would say, God's got a plan. I spent a lot of time alone and I got good at my pictures. I could go to events and take pictures and sell them to newspapers. I did pretty good. I still do pretty good."

"Damned good, I'd say. I saw your pictures in newspapers way out in California."

"Really? I've never been that far west. I want to get out there. I hear it's great."

"Yeah, it was cool. You know, I bought those papers just because of your pictures."

"I like that," Ray Ray grinned. "But enough about me. Tell me about home. How's your mama? Ezekiel? The Barbershop? And how the heck did you get that big gash over your eye? You look like Frankenstein's monster." Randall fingered his gash. "Yeah, I got this from Jimmie."

"He came back?"

"A few years ago, we had a bad storm. I was awake and putting a log on the fire when he busted the door in. I tackled him, we got into it, and he got the best of me. Ezekiel came and cracked his ribs with the fire poker like he was swinging for the fences." Ray Ray laughed.

"He was drunk, didn't know who I was, and he started swinging like a madman. Hattie stitched me up, but it wasn't real good because the power was out and she couldn't see good. So now I got this beauty right here."

"Damn, that's crazy. How's your mom?"

Randall sucked in a breath. "She passed in '44. My uncle died, she got in a big argument with her dad, and then the sickness came back. She didn't last long after that."

"Man, I'm real sorry."

Randall shrugged his shoulders. "It's life." He took a long swig of beer.

"How about Hattie? The barbershop?"

"They're all good. Hattie went overseas again. I don't think she's back yet. To my surprise, since I've been on the road, Jimmie writes to me pretty often and we chat when I call home. He's a preacher now. He's married and has a baby."

A look of genuine surprise took over Ray Ray's face. "You have to be kidding me."

"Nope, I ain't kidding. He's the real deal, too. No drinkin' or acting crazy. He's a different guy."

"I never would have guessed that, not in a million years."

"It's been good to watch him change. Be who God wanted him to be."

"Amen to that! What about everybody else at the barbershop?"

"The Barbershop is stuck in time, with the exception of your pictures on the wall, it's nearly exactly the same. Same radio we listened to the Joe Louis fight on. Same clock ticking away the hours. Same cracked mirror." Ray Ray leaned back and stretched. "Man, I gotta make it back. Those were good times." "Zeke and the fellas are all still there. They'd love to see you. The town has gotten smaller. Lots of people moved after the war."

"Yeah, I'm always on the move, too. Nothing really holding me down in any one place. I follow the money."

Randall chuckled. "I'm following baseball. I got voted into the All-Star game at Pax Field. You gonna be there?"

"Oh you know it. My whole family will be there."

"Alright, you better be. I heard scouts are coming to recruit some guys for the majors."

"Is that right?"

"That's the rumor. They say Satch and Josh will go first."

"Don't worry, Randall. You got youth and speed on 'em. You'll make it!"

They clinked bottles and decided to go have some fun. The night was young and lively, they made their way to a club with dancing and stayed till the roosters started to crow.

CHAPTER 45

Comiskey Park, Chicago
All-Star Game 1947

Randall stood in right field tossing the ball back and forth with the center fielder. He bounced on his feet and felt the firm ground under the thick patch of grass. He liked the well-kept field compared to the dirt fields he sometimes played on. The midday sun warmed his back and the hum of the crowd was in his ear. This is what he loved. He tossed the ball back feeling the weight of it leave his fingers. He'd spent the past few years playing everywhere he could. The Grays, having seen him play in Cuba with the Fuegos, offered him a spot and he'd performed better than they could have imagined. That's how he'd been selected to play in the All-Star game. The best players from the Negro Leagues were here. Rumor was scouts from the majors were here too, and they were getting ready to integrate the Majors with negro players. Jackie had already signed.

He turned to the infield and tossed with the second baseman. Randall watched the stands fill with men in straw hats and bright colored bands. Sunday suits and women in their best dresses and wide brimmed hats shading them from the sun. Kids ran up and down the stadium stairs while toddlers remain tucked firmly in their parents' grip. The energy was electric.

Ezekiel, Claude, and Joe would be in the crowd. He'd sent tickets for them to come. He hadn't made it home to see them after getting back. They promised to be here and even without a promise he knew they would come.

The stands were packed. Scouts had been in Cuba recruiting him the past few months preparing the details. The past two years he'd played solid ball in the Negro Leagues with good stats and a strong game. He'd grown taller and stronger, worked with some of the best, and he was still fast as ever and getting faster.

Today he wore his uncle's number ten with Wilson on the back of his jersey. He adjusted his sleeve and threw another ball. A slow bead of sweat trickled down his forehead, he wiped it away, thankful to be back in the States. While he was away he'd learned to speak Spanish but it was good to hear his native tongue and be able to converse without thinking and translating each word. He took the opportunity to stretch and pulled his arm across his chest, loosening muscles. He twisted at the waist and bent down to touch his toes. His body was warm, he felt good, today was going to be a good day.

Fifteen minutes before game time. He went over to the dugout. Just as he ducked under the awning he heard her familiar voice. "Randall," she shouted. He popped his head up and looked into the stands. Her blond hair was loose and blowing in the breeze, her wide smile and bold energy stuck out in the crowd. He moved toward the stands and took the stairs two by two. He snatched her up and squeezed tight. "Hattie! I've missed you!" Behind her stood Ezekiel, Claude, Joe and Mabel. He grabbed each one with the same fierce embrace. Hattie tugged at his arm. "Randall, I have someone I want you to meet." She waved to a white man holding a baby. "Randall, this is my husband Jacques." Randall looked surprised and smiled wide, guessing, "And this is your beautiful baby girl?" Hattie blushed, "Yeah. We met in France when I was there during the war." "WILSON!" Randall heard the coach shouting, "Get over here."

"I gotta go. I'll see you guys after - we'll catch up!"

He waved as he went back down to the dugout and as he turned his head he saw Jimmie who gave him a wink and a nod. He was in a suit and he looked good, clean, healthy, strong, and happy. A woman stood next to him with a toddler on her hip and her hand entwined in his. Randall smiled at the peace he saw and ducked into the dugout.

The team lined up for the Negro National Anthem; he watched the flag blow in the wind with his cap in hand over his heart. Pride swelled up, his family stood behind him, he felt like his mother and uncle stood with him. He watched the stars and stripes fly with a feeling he couldn't quite describe. The flag furled out in the breeze as they sang, "Lift every voice and sing till earth and heaven ring. Ring with the harmonies of Liberty...."

The song finished and a single tear trickled down his cheek. It was the beginning of the end. His pride swelled. He heard the click and shudder of the camera again. He'd come like he said he would.

The anthem ended, the crowd roared, the opposition took the field. The umpire shouted, "Now, let's play ball!"

Randall was on deck, he'd be first at bat; his job was to get on base, steal second and on an infield double, take home. As he approached home plate and placed a foot in the batter's box he looked to the umpire and right behind him in the first row was Ray Ray with a wide brimmed hat, stylish sunglasses, and a camera pointed right at him. Randall smiled, he heard the camera click and turned back to face the pitcher. He stepped into the box and swung the bat nice and easy. The umpire shouted, "Play ball!"

Randall let the first ball pass. "Strike!" the umpire shouted. Randall adjusted his grip and glanced across the field looking for a gap. The next pitch was outside. "Ball!" the umpire shouted. Randall dug his feet into the soft dirt; this was it, clean and fast. Randall's intent was to drop the ball in mid left field right before the outfielder; instead he bunted. The crowd roared as the umpire at first shouted, "Safe!" He could hear the chant, "Wil-son, Wil-son, Wil-son!"

Foot securely on the bag he stood up, dusted himself off and waved his cap in the direction he knew Ezekiel and the family were seated. He could hear Hattie's whooping shout and knew Ezekiel would be clapping and telling him to focus. The next batter, Johnny, was a solid hitter and Randall edged his way toward second. The pitcher turned and threw to first. Randall dove back to the bag. The next two pitches were wide and outside. Randall eased off the bag, the pitcher looked but didn't throw. Johnny swung and missed. "Strike!" The next pitch Johnny connected but it was easy to see it was wide and headed for the stands. Randall paced, waiting for his moment. Another ball, full count. His fingers twitched, he was itichin' to go, he was ready. "Come on. Come on. Gimmie something," he said under his breath. Another ball thudded in the catcher's mitt and Johnny took first, Randall moved to second.

Two men on. No outs. Things were looking good until the next batter struck out, and then the catcher, Eddie, hit a line drive to the shortstop and nobody moved. Ezekiel sat in the stands whispering into his granddaughter's ear, "Watch this, Uncle Randall's gonna take third on the next pitch." Sure as shootin', as the pitcher wound up, quick as lightning' Randall made his jump. When the catcher got the ball and sent it sailing to third it was too late. Randall was already dusting off his pants. "If you blinked you missed it," Ezekiel said and laughed. Randall was hungry for more. The right fielder, Oscar, came to the plate. Randall teased the pitcher easing off third toward home. The pitcher paused and looked over his shoulder as if daring Randall to go. For several seconds they stared at one another, daring the other to move. The pitcher drew his attention back to the batter and the third base coach spoke to Randall, "Take it if you got it." Randall tipped his hat and rubbed his hands on his pants. The pitcher turned and checked him, Randall slid easily back to third. Oscar swung his bat loosely in the batter's box; Randall knew the sign, they understood one another. They'd played together in Cuba.

Pitchers hated to pitch to Oscar; he could hit nearly anything. The first pitch Oscar swung for the fence. "Foul ball!" the umpire shouted. The second pitch was the same. The count was 2-0. The pitcher leaned back feeling confident. Randall made a quick jump to draw his attention, the pitcher threw to third. Before the third baseman knew what happened Randall was halfway home, Oscar moved out of Randall's way. They watched in slow motion as the catcher screamed for the ball, his glove open and ready. Randall dove for home. The camera clicked and wound as fast as it could. The catcher had the ball but it was too late, the ump shouted, "Safe!" The crowd went wild. The pitcher's face was beet red. He and the catcher were screaming at the umpire that Randall was out. "You didn't even touch him!" the ump shouted back. The argument went unheard while the crowd drowned them out chanting, "Wil-son! Wil-son! Wil-son!"

"Get back to the mound and play ball," the umpire ordered. Oscar stepped back in the batter's box and hit the next pitch into left field where the left fielder snagged it.

The next six innings were scoreless and folks stood for the seventh inning stretch while vendors shouted, "Peanuts! Cracker jacks! Hotdogs!" The stands were alive with movement and Randall went to swing the bat and warm up, he'd lead off the inning. From the corner of his eye he saw an older man in a long black coat moving down the stands, his hands were in his pockets. The man came down onto the field and shouted, "Wilson!" Randall turned to face him, and just behind the man Randall could see Ezekiel rushing down the stairs toward them. He swung the bat again and realized too late, the man pulled a gun from his pocket and fired six shots. Randall stood as if unphased. The man continued to move toward him. It seemed as if time had stopped. Ringing echoed in his ears from the shots fired, everything else was silent.

Randall touched the front of his uniform where crimson began to stain his shirt from two small holes. The crowd looked on as Randall dropped to his knees. Ezekiel and Jimmie raced toward the field. Randall found it hard to breathe, his arms went slack and the bat dropped from his hand. He glanced around the crowd. He could see Hattie, her hand was covering her mouth and her eyes were wide. Ray Ray began to fight his way toward Randall. His limp barely hindered him as he pushed people out of his way.

The man in the long black coat was still moving toward him, the gun still in his hand pointed at Randall, his finger clicking the chamber round and round. His eyes were wild and Randall recognized them. They were the same ones he'd seen years ago on the fourth of July, the day they'd gone to honor his uncle. He touched the sticky fluid saturating his shirt and heard his grandfather say, "I should have taken care of you years ago. You're not going to humiliate and embarrass me by wearing my name in the Majors."

Before Randall's grandfather reached him, Jimmie bowled him over. And even still the old man thrashed wildly struggling to get his hands on Randall who had collapsed. Ezekiel placed his hands over the holes trying to stop the bleeding. "Hang on. Hang on Randall. Help is coming."

Mr. Wilson clawed his way closer while Jimmie tried to hold him. Randall smiled at Ezekiel and Ray Ray and patted them, but his words weren't for them. He turned toward Jimmie struggling with his grandfather. Other players had come to pin Mr. Wilson to the ground. He was huffing and puffing, his face in the dirt, muddied with blood. "Granddad," Randall said struggling to catch a breath and get the words out. Everyone went still. Even Mr. Wilson stopped struggling. Randall reached his hand toward his granddad and touched his face and said, "I love you, Granddad." Mr. Wilson's eyes went wide and Ezekiel thought his own heart would burst. "I wish I could have known you." Mr. Wilson started thrashing about screaming, "You don't talk to me like that! Shut your damn mouth!"

Ezekiel rested Randall's head in his lap and prayed. Ray Ray squeezed his hand and under his breath said, "No, no, no."

Whispers could be heard circulating, "That's his granddad?"

Randall struggled for air. He looked at his granddad one last time. "I forgive you, Granddad." Mr. Wilson went limp. He was drug away from the scene as Hattie pushed through the crowd shouting, "I'm a nurse! Let me through." Jacques was close behind her. "I'm a doctor," he said as players tried to stop him. Hattie threw herself on the ground next to Randall. She was shaking her head and her mouth was moving but no words were coming. Jacques reached for Randall's wrist. His pulse was faint and his eyes glossed over. A hint of a smile tugged at his cheeks. He looked peaceful. Ezekiel looked up to Jacques hoping there was something that could be done. Jacques shook his head and Hattie's voice came out in a shreking wail. Randall squeezed Ray Ray's hand one last time.

CHAPTER 46

Olympia, Mississippi
1955

Ezekiel wiped his cheek. Steven pretended not to notice. He brought a box with a lid and sat it in front of Steven. "Ray Ray, he still works in Chicago, these are his photos. If you need more pictures of Randall, he'd have them."

Steven opened the box filled with hundreds of pictures of Randall. He thumbed through them pulling a few out. There were even pictures he recognized from games in Cuba. "What happened to his grandfather?" Steven asked as he thumbed through the photos.

"He was found dead in his recliner. Heart attack they say."

"He didn't go to jail for what he did?"

"No, not that I know of."

"I can't believe it."

"Well, go look it up. It was in all the papers. He was arrested at the game, booked at the jail house and somehow ended up back home in Mississippi free as a jaybird."

"That can't be."

"Hattie fought it for a few years. He had been bonded out and fled the state, then nobody would extradite him to stand trial."

Steven covered his face and shook his head. "That just isn't right."

Ezekiel didn't respond.

The pendulum ticked away the time. It was a few minutes before either of them spoke again. "He's buried next to his mama and my wife in the old cemetery by the church."

Steven nodded. "I'll stop by there on my way out."

Both men stood and Ezekiel reached out to shake hands. He grabbed Steven's shoulder. "When you write that book, just remember; a man who forgives frees his own soul and brings peace, but a man who harbors hatred destroys himself and contends with strife."

Steven nodded. "I'll do him justice, sir."

www.ingramcontent.com/pod-product-compliance
Lightning Source LLC
LaVergne TN
LVHW100514110826
845146LV00002B/635